*Julia London captivated readers and critics
alike with her acclaimed* Rogues of Regent Street
trilogy. Now the author Romantic Times *calls
"a rising star" returns with the passionate story
of a man and a woman pursued by secrets,
shadowed by scandal, and surprised by love. . . .*

The Secret Lover

EIGHT YEARS AFTER fleeing England in the
wake of a terrible scandal, Sophie Dane is no longer the
trusting debutante betrayed by love. Now, as companion to a worldly French widow, she returns to London,
where her arrival instantly sets tongues wagging . . . and
attracts the roving eye of aristocrat Trevor Hamilton.
But it is his mysterious brother, Caleb, in whom Sophie
senses a kindred soul—and who captivates her as no other
man has before. Reared on the Continent, Caleb has
come home to his ailing father—only to be shunned by
society as a fortune-hunting imposter. Sophie alone seems
to believe in him. But an unexpected series of events sets
them both in flight once more. As scandal pursues them
to a remote ancestral estate, a man and a woman haunted
by the past will defy every convention on earth for a future in each other's arms. . . .

The Secret Lover

Julia London

A Dell Book

Published by
Dell Publishing
a division of
Random House, Inc.
1540 Broadway
New York, New York 10036

ISBN: 0-7394-2488-2

PRINTED IN THE UNITED STATES OF AMERICA

for Liza

Deep in my soul that tender secret dwells,
Lonely and lost to light for evermore,
Save when to thine my heart responsive swells,
Then trembles into silence as before.

THE CORSAIR,
canto 1, stanza 14, "Medora's Song"
Lord Byron

Prologue

SOPHIE COULD SCARCELY hear what Stella was saying; her heart was pounding so loudly in her ears and filling her throat that it was difficult to even breathe. It was bitterly cold, so cold that every bruise on her body seemed to throb with eager vengeance. But it was precisely that throbbing pain which forced her to put one foot in front of the other, to keep moving down the walkway, *calmly*, despite an inner voice warning her to turn back.

Turn 'round, turn 'round, turn 'round! It's not too late! He'll not know you attempted to escape if you turn 'round now!

"Ooh, milady! That'd be his lordship Allenwhite just ahead! What are we to do?" Stella whispered frantically.

Sophie lifted her gaze, saw the portly gentleman walking briskly toward them. Instinctively, she lifted her chin, wincing at the pain in her jaw where she had been struck just that morning. "We shall say good day and keep walking," she said low, ignoring her maid's fearful grip of her fingers.

"Lady Stanwood, how do you do?" the man asked, pausing to tip his hat.

"I am very well my lord, thank you." Stella's grip tightened painfully. "You'll forgive my manners for hurrying past, sir, but I am quite overdue for an appointment with my modiste, and I confess, I'm rather chilled to the bone."

Allenwhite seemed almost relieved, gave her a curt nod. "Yes, indeed, a nasty day to be abroad. I'll not keep you, my lady."

"Good day, my lord." She continued walking, pulling Stella along, her step quickening in time to her pounding heart. She would not allow herself to look back, would allow herself nothing but to stare straight ahead. *They were almost there.* It was too fantastic to believe, but they were almost there. *Almost free.*

They rounded the corner onto Bond Street, felt a respite from the wind. *Where was Claudia?* Sophie's heart plummeted into the pool of her fear—Claudia was not there. She had promised to meet them at the corner of Audley and Bond streets! Had something happened to her? *Julian! Julian had discovered their plan and stopped Claudia from coming!* The panic spread thick in Sophie's throat. No. *No!* She could not come so close and be denied! It was so unfair! *God!*

Frantic, she glanced furtively over her shoulder—Lord Allenwhite had continued on, his head down, oblivious to her and Stella. How long would it be before someone asked him if he had seen her? Sophie fumbled anxiously with her cloak, pushing it open so she could stare at the small watch pinned to her breast. Five minutes past two o'clock. Claudia was five minutes late.

She was not coming.

"By the saints, what could have become of Lady Kettering? Ooh, there's something amiss, I feel it in me bones!" Stella squeaked, gripping Sophie's arm tighter still.

Unable to assure Stella they would indeed succeed, Sophie swallowed and stared at the deserted corner of Audley and Bond Street. The words simply would not come, smothered by the weight of her heart, now lodged in her throat along with the fear and the biting disappointment . . . and an insane sense of relief.

It is over.

Her little fantasy of escape was over. It was foolish to have thought she might have succeeded. There was nothing left but to turn around now, hurry home before William discovered what she had almost . . . *No!* She would not allow herself to think what he might do. She would simply hurry home *now,* before she was forced to imagine it.

She would find another way out of this nightmare, surely.

Or perhaps she would live with the consequence of her foolishness all the rest of her days.

Tears suddenly blinded her, and Sophie looked again at her watch. Seven minutes past. *Claudia was not coming.*

She should have known it was impossible. She should have realized there would be no escape from the private hell she had created for herself. Sophie blinked, felt the tears freeze on her lashes. Huddled beside her, Stella was frightened unto death. Sophie opened her mouth to tell her they would go back now, end this silly escapade, but a hack careened around the corner of Bond Street onto Audley before she could speak. Her heart swelled; Stella turned, too, just as Claudia flung open the door ahead of the coachman and leapt to the ground. She glanced quickly up the street and then down, her gaze landing on Sophie and Stella several yards away. She began walking purposefully toward them.

Sophie's heart filled to almost bursting.

Freedom!

For the first time in several months, she could taste the sweetness of freedom mix with the acidity of fear.

Chapter One

1844
LILLEHALLEN
THE HILLS ABOVE CHRISTIANIA, NORWAY

IT HAD BEEN eight years since she had fled England and had forced the memory of that life from her mind like a bad dream. *Eight years.*

Sophie shook her head, continued slicing carrots. It was impossible to conceive of going back. Impossible. She glanced at Arnaud Bastian again, disbelieving. "You must be mistaken," she said simply.

"I mistake nothing, *ma chérie,*" the insufferable Frenchman crooned as he sidled even closer to the rough, knife-marked table on which Sophie was working. "My heart, it is but tiny pieces when you return to England." He reached for a slice of carrot, snatching it just ahead of Sophie's knife.

"You've obviously drunk too much wine again, Arnaud."

"*Non,* no wine. Vodka." He reached again, but this time Sophie stopped him with a solid *whack* of her knife against the tabletop just a fraction of an inch from his fingers.

Arnaud jerked his hand back, stared at her with a look of horror. "*Ow!* You are cruel to wound me so!"

"Honestly, *monsieur,* you should consider a theatrical

career," she said, and raised her knife again when he attempted to pilfer a mushroom.

His hand wavered uncertainly. *"Non?"*

"Non."

Arnaud sighed. *"C'est la vie,"* he said cheerfully. "What is this you prepare?"

"Fish stew. All right, Monsieur Bastian, truthfully if you please, did Honorine say she would sail for England?"

Arnaud clucked, adjusted his rumpled, expensive waistcoat just so, and smoothed the curl of what had been, hours earlier, a meticulously styled coif. *"Oui,"* he sniffed in belated response to Sophie's question, and paused to study the contents of her kettle. "I think this is so. *Je ne rappel pas.*"

Of course he would not recall. That would require ability beyond the capacity of what Sophie believed was a pea-sized brain. She put the carrots and mushrooms into the kettle, swatted Arnaud's hand from her bum. "Then perhaps it was just another of your attempts to seduce me."

Arnaud gasped, his hand fluttered to the neckcloth at his throat. *"Mademoiselle!* Do you accuse me of *lying?"* he demanded indignantly.

"I do indeed."

"Ieee, how could I lie, *ma chérie?* My eyes, my ears, my mouth, all of them, filled with dreams of sweet Sofia!"

Filled with dreams of sweet rolls was more like it. Since Arnaud had discovered her ability to cook— something that was valued almost as highly as royal lineage among the French expatriates living in Norway— he had sought her out daily, sometimes begging marriage, sometimes simply demanding salmon in crème sauce. Today his poetic wailing earned him nothing more than an exasperated snort as she put the lid on the kettle.

It certainly wasn't the first time Sophie had been the

recipient of such false ardor from one of Honorine's discarded lovers. Really, it seemed that a man's self-esteem was awfully large and fragile, and when Honorine refused to succumb to a man's unwanted attentions, they all seemed compelled to look to the nearest female on whom they might test their charm and assure themselves it was still intact. More often than not, that female was her, seeing as how they were practically on the edge of the world here.

She turned away from the kettle to see Arnaud sniffing about the bread she had baked earlier. "*Monsieur,* be so good as to keep your hands in your pockets, *s'il vous plaît,*" she warned him. Arnaud frowned and walked petulantly to the window. He stood pouting and staring out beyond the old walls of Lillehallen as she finished putting the cooking implements away.

"Why do you keep yourself here, away from everyone?" he asked after a few moments, still staring absently out the window. "Look at them now skating. Why do you not join them?"

Because she *had* joined them last evening, had even enjoyed herself until the early hours of the morning. But as she had never developed the stamina a full night of revelry required—particularly if said revelry was to stretch into the following morning—she had at last retired, exhausted.

That, and she didn't know how to skate.

"*Ach,* what foolishness," Arnaud said, seeming to read her mind. "Come now, let us attend this skating. This sun, it will make a smile on your face." He very gallantly offered his arm.

Sophie eyed it warily.

Arnaud chuckled. "*Mademoiselle!* I am a gentleman!"

That was highly debatable, but the stew was under way, and what little remained Hulda would see to when she returned from the Christiania market. Besides, Sophie would delight in hearing the jest from Honorine's lips at the same moment as Arnaud. This silliness, this *insanity* of sailing to England was just that, a jest, said simply to annoy Arnaud, because the man quite feared being left alone in Norway for reasons that were entirely unclear to Sophie.

The weak sun could not take the chill from the air, and Sophie was already freezing when she arrived on the banks of the pond a dozen steps ahead of Arnaud's wandering hands. Honorine, bundled in a bright red-and-purple cloak, her long, silver-streaked hair unbound, skated awkwardly, her arms held out, whirling furiously when she felt her balance slipping. Fabrice, her sometimes butler, skated expertly, his arms clasped behind his back as he twirled effortlessly around her. Roland, Honorine's mysterious vintner-without-a-vineyard, skated well, too, but was more interested at the moment in racing furiously across the pond than attempting the same finesse as Fabrice. The rest of the party skated sedately, as if out on a Sunday stroll of sorts, smiling and waving at Sophie as they glided past.

She watched them for a moment, noticed that the ice looked rather thin in some spots.

"Sofia! Aha, you will join us again!" called one of Honorine's more frequent guests.

"*Oui, Monsieur Fabre,* for the moment."

Monsieur Fabre laughed before an unexpected hiccup surprised him and sent him reeling backward.

"Sofia, *bien-aimée,* come and sit beside me!" urged Madame Riveau, who was, unquestionably, the largest human Sophie had ever seen. She sat on the banks with her hat cocked at an awkward angle, her fur coat a mountain around her. As she leaned over to pat the blanket beside her, she very nearly rolled onto her side like an egg. "Come!" she called brightly.

Not on Sophie's life—Madame Riveau had the uncommon capacity to talk until each star fell from the sky without so much as taking a breath—in French *and*

English. "Thank you, Madame Riveau, but I must speak with Honorine. Monsieur Bastian would sit beside you and keep your company," she said, suppressing a smile at Arnaud's grumbling. But he fell dutifully in a heap next to Madame Riveau and reached for her wine bottle as the woman snuggled close to him.

Sophie returned her attention to the skaters. "Honorine!" she called.

Honorine, moving more confidently now, glided in the general direction of Sophie, but at the last moment, merely waved and went round again.

Obstinate woman. "Honorine! Come round, would you?"

This time Honorine simply laughed.

With a sigh of exasperation, Sophie put her hands on her hips. *"Hon-o-rine!"*

"Mon dieu! Que désirez-vous?"

"I would like a word, if you please!"

Honorine grumbled something loudly beneath her breath, but started forcefully toward the bank with one good push, hurtling forward, her arms held straight out.

Thankfully, she somehow managed to stop herself before mowing Sophie down. But standing in one place on skates was something she clearly had not mastered; her feet moved backward and forward, and she shot her arms out for balance as necessary. "A word, a word! Then speak, will you?" she demanded as Fabrice sailed by, skating backward.

"Arnaud said you intend to sail for England soon."

Honorine cocked her head to one side. "Does he?" She shook her head, made a clucking sound as she shifted her gaze to where he was now lying peacefully, his head propped between Madame Riveau's enormous breasts. *"Imbécile."*

An unexpected wave of relief swept over Sophie; she laughed a little too anxiously. "Honestly, I can scarcely believe what outrageous things the man will say to gain attention."

"*Oui,* it is too much."

"I am so foolish to listen to him!"

"It is *he* who is foolish. I did not say *soon.*"

That brought Sophie up short. "I beg your pardon? What exactly does *that* mean?"

Fabrice sailed by again, only with Roland this time and so close that Honorine moved suddenly, whirling her arms to keep her balance. "This means for England we sail in the late spring. This is not *soon, oui?* Arnaud, he embellishes too much."

Sophie gaped at Honorine. It was impossible. Inconceivable! Yet Honorine simply stood there, looking for all the world like she had announced only that they might stroll to market. In the last seven years, she had *never* expressed a desire for England! Rome, Madrid, Stockholm, yes! But England? She could not possibly expect Sophie to return to England!

Honorine smiled.

Sophie forced herself to take a breath. A very *deep* breath.

All right, all right, perhaps Honorine didn't expect her to travel to England with her; of course she didn't. She obviously meant to leave Sophie behind, at Château la Claire, her sister's home. *Yes, yes, of course!* She intended to go for a holiday of sorts while Sophie remained with Eugenie!

"Close your mouth, Sofia—a bird should make his nest there."

"You might have at least mentioned your intent to take a holiday," she said irritably.

"I tell you now, *chérie.* It is *magnifique, non*? Many years, they come, they go since I have seen my London."

My London?

"And it is very cold here."

"All right. I understand. I shall go to Eugenie, of course," Sophie said. "How long do you intend to be away?"

Honorine laughed, whirled her arms again. "Foolish

girl! I do not leave you to Louis Renault! You come to London too!"

Oh God. Oh God oh God.

"London!" spat Roland as he sailed past, arm-and-arm with Fabrice. "A dirty city!"

"*J'adore* London," Honorine curtly informed him over her shoulder.

Disbelief almost choked Sophie. Honorine had not been to London in more than fifteen years; she had told Sophie this herself when she had engaged her as a companion seven years ago. "But . . . but you scarcely *remember* London!" she insisted.

Honorine shrugged, shot one arm wide and down again. "I wish to see it again."

Sophie did not like this sudden change of plans—she *liked* it here in the hills overlooking Christiania! Norway was perfect for her—far away, obscure—"I *cannot* go to England, least of all *London,* Honorine!" she exclaimed as Fabrice and Roland twirled behind Honorine and glided away.

"*Ach,*" Honorine said with a dismissive flick of her wrist.

"I *cannot!*"

"*Pourquoi?*" Honorine demanded, as if she hadn't the vaguest idea why, watching as Fabrice executed a perfect twist in the air, landing gracefully on one leg. "*Ooh, très bien!*" she called out to him.

"Because," Sophie said low, ignoring Fabrice and staring pointedly at Honorine. The woman knew her entire history, knew of the whole sordid scandal that had taken her from England in the first place. How could she suggest Sophie return?

Honorine shrugged. "Because? This is all you say?"

"Because? Because of the *scandal!*" Sophie whispered hotly, wanting very much at that moment to put her hands around Honorine's neck and squeeze tightly.

"Only that?" Honorine snorted at the same moment Monsieur LaForge suddenly went down behind her, one leg through the ice.

"Only *that?*" Sophie fairly shrieked.

Honorine bent once to touch her toes, then with arms akimbo, glided backward, oblivious as her guests rushed to where Monsieur LaForge was half submerged in the pond's icy waters. "But the smell of *le printemps* is in this air, *non?* I do not want this Norway. It is too cold!"

"The smell of spring is most certainly *not* in the air!" Sophie snapped, folding her arms across her middle, only vaguely aware that Fabrice, Roland, and Monsieur Fabre were using a tree limb to leverage Monsieur LaForge from his icy trap. "And what of Monsieur Kor—"

"*Phht,*" Honorine spat with disgust, and threw up her hand as she turned away from Sophie toward the commotion. "How lovely is London now, I remember very well," she continued, idly watching the rescue of Monsieur LaForge, who had now managed to get both his legs into the hole and was clinging to the limb for dear life. "We shall wear our new *chapeaux,* will we not?"

"No, *we* will not."

"We shall of course! You must, *Sofia,* for we cannot here find a man for you."

Sophie would kill her. "I don't *want* a man, Honorine."

"What is this? Of course you do, all *les femmes* want this! It is as God made us. We live better and longer with many lovemakings, and besides, you cannot allow this past to rule you always, *chérie.*"

As if she had any choice. As if she hadn't practically been banished from England for what she had done. But that was beside the point. "My brother will not allow it," she insisted as they dragged Monsieur LaForge across the ice.

"Nonsense. He has given his permission," Honorine

said, turning carefully to see the rescue. "Ah, poor Monsieur LaForge! This water it is very cold!" she said, and skated off before Sophie could find her tongue to speak, leaving her to stand speechless on the banks of the pond in horrified silence, unwilling, unable to accept this news. It could not be true. *It could not be true!*

All right—she closed her eyes, pressed her fingers to her temples—she was panicking for naught. Even on the very *remote* possibility Honorine had somehow conjured up the discipline to actually *write* Julian, was Sophie to have no say in it? Lord God, how did they think she would ever face her old friends? How would she look at members of the *haut ton* knowing they all knew every sordid little detail of her past? She could not bear it. She could not bear to see the censure in their expressions again. She had lived through her own personal hell in London, and there was nothing in this world that could make her go back.

She watched as Honorine grabbed onto Roland and peered into the hole Monsieur LaForge had created.

She did not want to leave here. She loved the relative obscurity of this place, the fact that they were—all of them, really—a little band of outcasts from society, trapped by their own private scandals at the top of the world. It made them alike, made them less eager to judge one another. They *belonged* together here. She did not want to leave and she most certainly did not want to go to England.

How ridiculous! Of *course* she wasn't going back! After eight years, she was not going back! All this preposterous talk was probably something as simple as Honorine misinterpreting some correspondence from Eugenie.

A thought struck her; Sophie blinked, smiled in relief. Yes, of course! That was the problem here—a simple

misunderstanding. There could be no other explanation.

Her sense of direction tentatively restored, she picked
up her skirts and marched from the gathering, ignoring
Arnaud's call to come back and skate.

Chapter Two

Three Months Later
Château la Claire, Normandy, France

Not only would Julian give his permission for her to return home, he had already done so, just as Honorine had claimed. In fact, he had personally come to France just to see them home—another little surprise that had Sophie almost apoplectic.

It was bad enough to have to leave Norway and the ancient corridors of the old Lillehallen estate where they had lived; it was the one place she had enjoyed above all others in her seven years with Honorine. Arnaud had wailed like a child with only Madame Riveau to comfort him the morning she and Honorine, along with Fabrice and Roland—who accompanied them everywhere—had climbed into the traveling chaise that would take them to a ship bound for the coast of Belgium. Sophie felt like wailing, too. She felt the chaos of her emotion boiling beneath the surface—it seemed that in going back, she was returning to the fires that surrounded the damned.

When they had at last set sail, Sophie had stood bundled in fur watching the rugged coastline of Norway grow smaller and smaller until she could no longer see it through her tears.

But even leaving the relative sanctuary of the walls of

Lillehallen was not as great a trauma as the realization Honorine had actually *written* Julian. Not only that, he had agreed to her ridiculous scheme and had hied himself across the Channel so that they could all skip merrily back to London. It was as if the whole world had gone suddenly and completely mad. Had they all forgotten what had happened eight years ago? Did they think she could just waltz into the drawing rooms of the *haut ton* without a care?

Sophie became completely unhinged at the prospect after Eugenie calmly explained it all to her during a game of croquet one day.

"You've all quite lost your minds," she said flatly to Eugenie, and placing her foot on Eugenie's blue ball, nestled against her bright red one, whacked the thing across the lawn.

"We've given the matter much thought," Eugenie responded calmly.

"It's impossible—"

"Claudia was very persuasive." Eugenie sipped her wine, then exchanged the glass for a mallet the footman held out to her. "I think she is right, really," she continued. "It *has* been eight years since . . . well, since . . ." She paused to hit her blue ball smoothly through the next two wickets.

Not that there was really any need to repeat what everyone knew. It had been eight years since Sophie had fled the man with whom she had eloped, then sought a parliamentary divorce and caused the worst of all Mayfair scandals.

"Really, darling, you cannot avoid it forever; none of us can. This is an opportune time. It's just before the Season begins—there won't be so many people about— and really, the prospects for engagements *are* rather limited, what with Madame Fortier and all."

With Madame Fortier and all, her prospects of engagements would be broadened beyond the family's wildest imaginations! Speaking of whom . . . Sophie glanced up at the sound of very heated French being spoken, to where Honorine and Louis Renault, Eugenie's husband, argued over the croquet game. As she watched, Honorine whacked her ball so hard that it flew into the hedgerow. Louis's grumbling could be heard across the entire river valley as he stomped off to retrieve it while Honorine casually studied a cuticle.

"Your turn, dear," Eugenie reminded her. "She does seem quite devoted to you," she added, looking at Honorine. "I am sure she will keep a watchful eye."

Eugenie had no idea what she was saying. Sophie aimed her mallet and swung with a little too much gusto. The red ball made it through one wicket, but was thwarted by Eugenie's ball before making the next.

"Ooh, what fun!" Eugenie laughed, and moved languidly to her ball, which she once again tapped through the wickets.

What a ridiculous game! Sophie sighed irritably. "Genie, please listen to me. I don't *want* to go to London. I am perfectly happy in France."

"Of *course* you want to go to London!" Eugenie said, as if that were the most patently ridiculous thing she had ever heard in all her life. "You are *English*. You can hardly gallivant across the world all your life, can you? There is no better way for you to return home. If you were to reside with Julian and Claudia, or even Ann, it would be remarked. But with Madame Fortier, why, your presence may not be generally remarked a'tall! Of course you will go! You can't hide yourself away from your homeland or your family forever, Sophie. You could not ask for a better circumstance, not really, not after your misstep."

Her misstep.

The *ton* did not forget. Yet her family had nonetheless convinced themselves it was safe for her to return, just as long as she did not think to enter society in any "remarkable" way. Even worse, not one of them had thought to inquire as to *her* desires.

Ah, but that had been the way of her life, had it not? The youngest and plainest of them all, the one who needed constant governing. Well, she was a grown woman now, one who had traveled the world over as Honorine Fortier's companion, and her family would do well to stop treating her like a child. And Sophie might very well have taken issue with Eugenie on that important point, right then and there in the middle of that insufferable game of croquet, but for one small problem—she had not the vaguest idea *what* she desired.

She swung her mallet; the ball scudded across the grass before splashing loudly into the fishpond.

How she despised this insipid game.

"Perhaps if you didn't try so hard. You always try too hard," Eugenie offered, and politely exchanged her mallet for her wineglass as Sophie stalked off to retrieve her ball. Another string of colorful French prompted her to look over her shoulder just as Eugenie handed her wine to the footman and picked up her skirts. "Louis, darling, not with the mallet, if you please," she called, and glided to where Louis was threatening to smash the croquet wickets as Honorine stood by, watching his tantrum with a look of pure tedium.

It was the perfect opportunity for escape.

Sophie continued walking right past her ball and the fishpond, headed in no particular direction except away from all those who claimed to know what was best for her. Her mind was consumed with the indecision and confusion that had come over her the moment Honorine had mentioned London.

She desperately wanted to see England again, but she just as desperately dreaded the prospect. It hadn't been so long that she couldn't recall, rather vividly, thank you, how people had looked at her those last few weeks in London, morbid curiosity and censure so plainly evident in their expressions. The *ton* fed like wolves on scandals such as hers, devouring it until there was nothing left but a few details to pick over. How well the scandal had held up to the test of time? Did they truly remember? Could she go to London and risk bringing dishonor to her family once again?

But she missed her home! In spite of her attempts to convince herself otherwise over the years, deep down she yearned for her home like a child for an absent mother. There were days she longed to walk on English soil, to smell the salt air of the sea, to see the tall, stately trees surrounding Kettering House, the splendor of St. James Square, the endless green lawns of Hyde Park.

There was so *much* she missed! Simple things, really, such as speaking her native tongue, or the roses that bloomed beneath the sitting room window at Kettering House, or the way her Aunt Violet snored when she napped after luncheon. And Tinley, the family butler, who had died last fall after more than forty years in their service. She had never even bid him farewell.

So much she missed, yet so much she feared, she thought morosely as she reached the old fountain on the east lawn, that she did not know quite what to do with herself.

Sophie paused, looked behind her. Louis and Honorine were still arguing. As she watched them, she was suddenly struck with the monumental realization that she had *never* really known what to do with herself. For eight and twenty years now, it seemed as if she had been searching for her place in this world, and instead of growing stronger, she was less certain of who she was or where she belonged each passing year. Sir William, the scandal, her exile . . . all of it had created the chaos deep within her, until she no longer knew *who* Sophie Dane was. Or wanted to be.

Certainly nothing pointed to that more painfully than her infatuation with William Stanwood.

How long ago that seemed now.

She had been searching then, too. She had never really fit in with the *ton,* and Sir William had paid her kind attention at a point in time it was clear she would have no true suitors. Her infatuation had been instant, her relief that someone had noticed her overpowering. She had been naively blind to his motives, blind to her own wealth, which he had so blatantly coveted. Blind to it all—she, Sophie Elise Dane, the youngest sister of the powerful and influential Earl of Kettering, had eloped with the bastard, had run away when he beat her, and then had sought the unmentionable, positively shameful, parliamentary divorce.

Oh yes, the most scandalous of scandals, a slap to the face of the *ton* and everything it stood for. She had eloped with a known blackguard, had endured his beatings, had risked the consequences of her escape, then had allowed her brother to drag her name through the high-profile mud of the *ton* in pursuit of a parliamentary divorce. It was the only way in which she could be completely free of Stanwood and protect what little of her inheritance he had not squandered.

The whole, sordid scandal had cost her family standing and had made her a pariah among the English aristocracy.

She had been sent to France, effectively banished from the *ton's* sight. She could still remember the awful coach ride along the rutted path to Château la Claire, the axle groaning beneath the weight of all her worldly belongings. The weight of her life. It was unspoken but nonetheless understood between her and her family that she would not return to England and her disgrace, but would remain in France, where she hoped the scandal would not taint her.

With a restless sigh, Sophie trailed her fingers along the edge of the fountain pool, her mind returning to a time in her life that she had managed to bury in the dark recesses of her heart. But now a shiver crept up her spine as the memories edged into light.

She turned her face upward, to the sun, and let its delicious warmth seep into her skin.

Those first wretched days of her arrival were thankfully

a blur now. She could recall little more than her inces-
sant crying, the inability to eat anything, and the fitful,
recurring dreams in which William threatened her and
chased her until she lay breathless in her bed.

In those first weeks she had wanted to escape forever
the enormity of what she had done, to sleep for all eternity so that she might forget his betrayal and the sickening feeling each time he raised his fist against her. She had
wanted to die, a thousand times over she had wanted to
die for being duped so egregiously and having caused her
family such grief and irreparable notoriety.

But Eugenie had been frightened by her lethargy, and
after weeks of watching her drift from one nightmare to
another, she had finally dragged her from her bed, ad-
monishing her to raise herself up and learn from her mistakes, not drown in her despair of them. Eugenie had
pushed Sophie to Dieppe, had forced her to find a charitable cause on which to focus her thoughts and actions.
Anything was better than the misery she was putting
them both through.

It was no accident that Eugenie had pushed her to
work with the ladies of the *Eglise St. Jacques,* who twice
weekly carried food and medicine to Dieppe's poor. She
had resisted at first, but in the course of those calls, Sophie
met women and children who suffered from poverty and
despair far greater than anything she had ever endured.
Gradually, she began to understand that these women
and children could not escape the poverty or the surroundings poverty bound them to, and that it was only
by virtue of her aristocratic birth that she had managed
to escape her despair.

By the following spring, Sophie was collecting used
clothing and sundries for the poor.

That was when she met Honorine.

Oh, she remembered her first encounter with Honorine,
all right. It wasn't something a body could easily forget.

She smiled, recalling the day that she had been shown
into the drawing room of one benefactress in Dieppe.

The woman's guest stood as Sophie entered, wearing a gown of bright orange and yellow and the most outrageous hat Sophie had ever seen. It was covered with feathers and lace and was a most atrocious shade of blue. Startled beyond her senses, Sophie was nonetheless instantly struck by Honorine's good looks and even more so by her winsome smile.

Honorine had listened politely as her friend explained who Sophie was, but she had seemed almost bored with the woman's charitable proclivities. Sophie had left with a pair of faded silk slippers, curiously amused by Madame Fortier.

Over the next several days, she forgot about Honorine, but one bright morning as she and the sisters of *Eglise St. Jacques* prepared their daily packages, Honorine swept into the small narthex carrying a hatbox in each hand. Behind her were two men—who Sophie later learned were the ever-present Roland and Fabrice—each carrying several precariously balanced hatboxes. She had brought, she explained half in English, half in French, bonnets from her Parisian milliner for the women Sophie served. Her smile impossibly broad, Honorine had eagerly removed the lid from one hatbox . . . and withdrew another god-awful bonnet in an appalling shade of purple, adorned with yellow silk flowers under the brim and edged along the bottom with what looked to be pink hydrangeas. *Pink hydrangeas.* The men removed the lids of all the hatboxes, displaying bonnets that were identical, with the exception of the many wild combinations of atrocious colors.

It was Madame Fortier's intent, Sophie understood, to offer the bonnets to Dieppe's poor women.

She had tried to explain that the poor were hardly in a position to wear such colorful bonnets.

"Pourquoi?" Honorine had insisted.

"Well, because they aren't!" Sophie had responded, flustered.

Honorine shrugged and fidgeted with a long green

ribbon dangling from a yellow bonnet. "*Les femmes,* they all want for fine bonnets!" she said. "They will want them, of course they will want them!"

Oui, the women of Dieppe *did* want them.

Much to Sophie's great surprise, women from all walks pounced on the bonnets with glee, and soon it was not an uncommon sight to see bonnets of mind-boggling hues bobbing along the crowded streets of Dieppe.

Honorine kept coming to the church. She and Sophie forged a fast friendship that summer, so strong that by the end of that summer, Honorine had convinced Sophie that she would make her a wonderful companion.

Not that it was particularly hard to convince her—after what she had been through in England, the talk of travel and adventure in exotic places had excited her. The moment Honorine saw that Sophie was seriously considering her offer, she took the liberty of speaking to Louis Renault.

Naturally, Louis was reluctant—he knew Madame Fortier by reputation, and her odd appearance did not exactly inspire his confidence. But Eugenie thought the idea a splendid one and exactly what Sophie needed. Moreover, she was amused by Honorine's uncommon manner and impressed with her impeccable credentials, a fact that she pointed out with great verve to Louis. Honorine's husband had been a member of one of the oldest and most revered French families, one of the few names among the aristocracy to have escaped the carnage of the last century. Monsieur Fortier had been quite a lot older than Honorine, had lived an austere life, his wife a dutiful shadow of himself. But when he died, Honorine had emerged like a butterfly, colorful and free. It was a well-known fact that Honorine Fortier now did as she pleased, society be damned.

And that pleased Eugenie enormously.

It frightened Louis tremendously.

He had, at first, valiantly resisted the suggestion that Sophie trot off to lands unknown with a woman who thought nothing of wearing bright pink, puce, and red in the morning. But as he had never been able to deny Eugenie a blasted thing, he was soon convincing Julian that companion to Madame Honorine Fortier was indeed a worthy occupation.

With Julian's eventual consent—another surprise, seeing as how her brother had always been so bloody strict and protective of her—Honorine did not waste a moment, and very soon thereafter, whisked Sophie off to Italy in search of olive oil, which she maintained would keep her skin looking as smooth and firm as a girl of twenty years.

In Venice, Honorine set up an elaborate house, but it wasn't long before Sophie understood that while Honorine provided the house, her true method of survival was to live off the kindness of gentlemen. Which left Sophie, Fabrice, and Roland in search of the basic necessities of life.

Sophie quickly took up cooking as her primary hobby.

Fabrice and Roland eagerly served as her guinea pigs, enthusiastically trying her many dishes, embellishing their praise when they thought something delicious, but making no effort to soften the blow when they disliked the food. By some miracle, Sophie actually developed quite a knack for cooking, and before too long, she was routinely preparing dishes that had both Frenchmen swooning.

In the midst of her learning to prepare sumptuous dishes, a fawning gentleman from Portugal captured Honorine's fancy, and one morning, over poached eggs and fresh tomatoes, she announced they were to Lisbon. There was no time to protest or offer an opinion of any sort, as they left the very next afternoon. Their belongings trailed a few days behind them.

In Lisbon, they had scarcely settled into a household when Honorine lost interest in Marcelo in favor of the very dashing Ernesto, the Spanish diplomat. Within a matter of weeks, they had up and left for Spain and Ernesto. When Ernesto turned out to be quite married, it was on to Vienna, then Rome, then Brussels, and from there to the remote city of Stockholm, where Honorine was determined to rest in the city where the sun never set. But Alrik, a Swedish prince with a passion for French-women, saw to it that she did not rest at all.

It took Balder, a Norwegian aristocrat in the Swedish court to rid Honorine of the pesky Alrik. So captivated by her Nordic prince was she that Honorine next whisked her entourage to Christiania, Norway.

Even now, on the banks of the placid river that ran below Château la Claire, it was exhausting just *thinking* of it all. With a small shake of her head, Sophie contin-ued walking through the daisy-dotted grass that covered the riverbanks.

In spite of the helter-skelter way of her life, Sophie had learned a lot from Honorine in the last seven years. Not that she couldn't be terribly exasperating at times, and her penchant for indoor picnics and evening dances was enough to put a person in Bedlam. That, and her in-cessant remarks about Sophie's love life—or lack of one. "These pantaloons!" she had exclaimed one day as she rummaged through the clean clothes a maid had brought to Sophie's rooms. "They are very old! Ah, but this mat-ters very little, as no one shall see them, *non*?"

Or her penchant for tapping Sophie just above her left breast. "*Le coeur,* it will dry to a peanut with no *l'amour!*"

Yes, well, Sophie had long ago resigned herself to her fate, and she really didn't need Honorine reminding her how empty she was.

But in spite of that, Sophie adored Honorine im-mensely for her unconquerable attitude toward life. She admired the fact that Honorine was a woman of inde-pendent means who marched to the beat of her own drummer. The woman simply did not care a whit for what French society thought of her, much less the inhab-itants of the world at large, and least of all, her whimpering son, Pierre, who was among her greatest critics. As she often recited to Pierre, she had but one life to live, and she would be damned if she wouldn't live it very well indeed.

No one could dispute that she didn't do just that.

And while Honorine was busy living these last seven years, Sophie had quietly tapped down the chaos in her. There was a silent but tenacious desperation growing in her, a need for something she could not name. But she pushed that desperation down, stomped out the little fires that blossomed with long walks, cooking, and when she could, charitable endeavors.

Charity was one thing she was determined to continue, as it was the only way she knew to repay the kindness of the women at the Upper Moreland Street house in London. That was where Claudia had taken her the day she had fled William; to a secret house full of women in need of refuge, just like her. Those women had seen the worst life had to offer, yet they had showed her strength, had given her the courage she needed to continue her flight to France. Sophie would never forget them.

But certainly she never thought she would *see* that little house again—wasn't certain she even *wanted* to see that house again. It was all so confusing! She felt quite literally torn in half between a longing so deep and a fear so impossibly wide. How would she ever face so many demons?

Nevertheless, Sophie found herself sailing for England in the late spring, with Julian, Honorine, and naturally, Fabrice and Roland, who sported identical beaver hats.

They landed on England's eastern shore at dawn, where they were met by two traveling chaises brought down from Kettering House. They drove through a heavy fog for most of the morning, but by early afternoon, the

fog had begun to lift, leaving the countryside wet and
fresh beneath a slate-gray sky and drizzling rain that accompanied them all the way to London.

The sights and sounds of that bustling city assaulted
their collective senses, particularly after the serene life-
style they had enjoyed in Norway.

It all felt very foreign to Sophie—she had forgotten
this London. She had forgotten the unbearably con-
gested streets where carts, horses, and carriages all vied
for space in the thoroughfare. She had forgotten the din
of dozens of drivers shouting at one another, and the
pungent smell of horse manure mixed with smoke.

It seemed to take them hours to push through the crush
and press of humanity in the narrow lanes to the old
Fortier house on Bedford Square.

As usual, Honorine was unabashed by the journey.
"Lovely!" she cried as she bounced out of the coach and
looked around the old courtyard. "Sofia, we shall have a
dog!" she announced, and marched up the steps to the
massive town home that had once been her husband's
foreign residence.

Sophie exchanged a weary look with Julian. "She is
fond of animals."

"Let us hope she is not quite as fond of animals as she
is of ale. I was beginning to think we'd be forced to seek
permanent quarters at the public house in Bruhaven.
Well, all right then, darling," he said, brightening noticeably, "I shall leave you to get settled. Your sister Ann is
quite excited to have you home and will undoubtedly
call at the day's first light. I imagine Claudia will be
close behind her. We'll supper at Kettering House on the
morrow if it pleases you and Madame Fortier."

Out of ancient habit, Sophie nodded obediently to
Julian's suggestion. When he had seen to it that her
things had been unloaded from his coach, he bid her a
good evening with a warm hug and a promise to see her
on the morrow.

"Bonne nuit!" Honorine called after him from the door of her home, and hurried down the steps as the coach rolled out of the courtyard. "Come, Sofia, you must see!" she exclaimed delightedly, and grabbing Sophie's hand, dragged her inside for a tour of the house.

It was clear that the house had been a home of some grandeur at one point in time. Paintings and portraits lined the corridor walls. Elaborate papier-mâché friezes adorned the ceilings of the dining hall and ballroom; thick tapestries from a bygone era hung in the sitting rooms.

But much of the furniture had been covered with muslin sheets and there was a choking layer of dust throughout the house. Honorine clucked and muttered to herself as they moved through each room. When they agreed they had done as much as they could for one evening, they pulled the muslin sheets from the beds in the bedroom suites and said good night.

Sophie lay down on the bed in the suite of rooms that would be hers and immediately sank into the down, unconscious of the moment she fell into a deep, exhausted sleep. It seemed only moments had passed before her sleep was rudely interrupted by a clattering and banging below, as if someone had dumped the entire contents of a trunk onto the tiled foyer. Sophie bolted upright, struggling in the fog of a deep sleep to remember where she was. The room was dark—the shutters had not been opened. Then it slowly came to her—this was the house on Bedford Square.

This was London.

With a groan, she pushed out of bed and padded across to the first window, struggling with the latch before managing to shove the heavy shutters aside.

Bright daylight streamed into the room, blinding her. Blinking and sneezing all at once, she stepped back and looked around her. In the dusty light, the room was magnificent, painted in soft blue and gold. The canopy bed was draped in blue china silk; the settee and daybed were covered in matching fabric. Sophie opened the second set of shutters and leaned against the thick panes of glass. Below were manicured gardens, edged on one end by a crowded cluster of dwellings. This was indeed a beautiful home, sitting peacefully and serene in the midst of the chaos of London.

It reminded her of Kettering House on St. James Square and a faint glimmer of pain flitted across her chest.

The banging started again. With a groan of exasperation, Sophie turned from the window to rummage in her things for a dressing gown, stubbing her toe in the process.

Chapter Three

SHE FOUND HONORINE in the sunroom, wearing a pink, black, and orange silk caftan, her hair piled directly on top of her head. She whirled when Sophie entered, thrust the halves of a broken porcelain pot into her hands, which Sophie barely caught. "Do you see?" she exclaimed, and whirled around again, staring down at the mess of broken pottery. "*Mon dieu!* So much work there is to be done, Sofia!" She sighed, arched her back in a stretch, then tossed a smile over her shoulder. "Eat. Eat now, then we take our rags and our buckets and *voilà, Maison de Fortier* will sparkle like stars again, *non*?"

Well, *non*.

As the house had been inhabited only sporadically in the last fifteen years, the dust and decay was thick. Honorine, Sophie, and Fabrice and Roland of course, began the cleaning in rooms gone unused for fifteen years. The intensity of the cleaning was matched only by the intensity of the bickering between Fabrice and Roland. They were an odd pair, those two, seemingly inseparable yet constantly arguing. The one time Sophie had tried to make Honorine explain them, she had smiled enigmatically. "Old friends" was all she would say.

As usual, their bickering was far more trying to Sophie's nerves than Honorine's, who ignored them as she hummed and flitted from one room to the next. By noon, the temperamental Frenchmen were so at odds over something so incomprehensible that Sophie banished them to different floors and opposite ends of the house.

And she retreated, alone, to the filthiest of all rooms. The kitchen.

Sophie wrinkled her nose, and with thumb and finger, lifted an upended cup. The rancid smell made her eyes water. This would not do, not do at all, but as there was nothing to be done for it, she took a large gulp of air and plunged into the mess that was the kitchen.

Her relief from the nasty task came with the exuberant arrival of her sister Ann.

Ann hugged her tightly, oblivious to the stench. "What are you doing in here?" she asked, incredulous, then pulled Sophie away and into the main salon, where her son, Vincent—who was seven years old and the spitting image of his father, Victor—and Sophie's aging Aunt Violet were waiting. Claudia—Julian's wife and Sophie's savior those many years ago—was not far behind with her two young daughters, Beth and Bridget. The children were delightful little terrors, upsetting the Frenchmen, who, having been in Honorine's employ for several years and therefore wholly unaccustomed to youth, cringed at the mere sight of the rambunctious little darlings.

But Sophie was absolutely delighted in the play of her nieces and nephew, found their every utterance adorable, and was thrilled when Claudia announced she was expecting her third child in the autumn.

She quietly pushed down the secret desire for children that had burned so long within her.

Claudia's pregnancy was proving to be a difficult one, however, so it was Ann who called almost every day. Four years her junior, Sophie had always looked up to

Ann. They resembled each other somewhat, Sophie thought—both had the long legs, a trait of the Dane family, and dark hair and eyes. But Ann's eyes were beautifully shaped, and her hair thick with a healthy sheen. Standing next to her, Sophie had always felt drab and pale. That had not changed in eight years; Ann was still a beauty.

What *had* changed was Ann's apparent determination to take Sophie under her wing. "Things will be different this time, you will see," she confided one morning, then looked thoughtfully at Sophie's dark blue gown. "You don't intend to wear that dark thing all day, do you?"

And so went the reacquaintance with her family.

While Sophie was occupied with her reunion, Honorine was in search of a decent meal—something that was always a very important issue for her. Finding nothing edible in the house, she ventured out alone that day, leaving Roland and Fabrice behind in something of a snit over their accommodations—Roland was disturbed with the way the morning light protruded into his room, and Fabrice found the green walls in his room quite objectionable. Honorine was not of a mind to hear any of it, and marched out of *Maison de Fortier* in what she considered one of her best ensembles—a blue-and-white striped skirt over stiff petticoats, an orange bodice with sage-green trim, and a bright yellow shawl.

She marched across Bedford Square, smiling and nodding at those who turned to gape at her, across a crowded thoroughfare, and into another, larger park. There, she continued marching along, wondering exactly where one found a plate of *fromage et jambon* in this town. But the longer she walked, the farther away from civilization she seemed to be going. With a great sigh of exasperation and her belly growling its discontent,

Honorine paused at a crosswalk, shaded her eyes with her hand, and scoured the land around her. Greenery and more greenery. Muttering with exasperation, Honorine punched her fists to her hips and glared up one direction of the walkway, then in the opposite direction. Aha . . . not thirty feet away was a man sitting on a wrought iron bench.

She began marching in his direction.

He looked up as she approached, and she could scarcely help noticing that he was indeed a handsome man with a kind smile and dancing eyes. As she neared him, he casually took in the length of her, smiling his appreciation.

Honorine smiled her appreciation, too. *"Bonjour!"*

His polite nod belied his wolfish smile.

"Please, you will help me, *non*?" she asked sweetly.

"M-my pleasure, if I c-can."

A stutterer. Her son, Pierre, stuttered, too, the poor darling. She moved closer to the man, still smiling. "I am come new to this town," she informed him.

His smile brightened. "N-no wonder y-you are so ch-charming," he said. "V-very bright and f-festive." With his head, he indicated her ensemble.

"Ooh, how *kind*," Honorine gushed with pleasure, and plopped herself down on the bench next to him.

"N-new, are y-you? I d-do n-not think I have seen you in the p-park b-before today."

"Oh no, I come here only on *this* day," she clarified. "We arrive to London yesterday. From France. And now, my belly, it is very empty!" she exclaimed. "There is no food!"

"N-no f-food?" he asked, his eyes shining with amusement, and Honorine was struck again with the notion that he was indeed a very handsome man. "Why of c-course we have f-food. We c-cannot have such a ch-charming guest go hungry."

Before Honorine could agree, something behind her

caught the gentleman's eye, and he lifted his chin, seemed to acknowledge someone. Honorine looked around; a man was approaching them, pushing a wheeled chair. That surprised her; she glanced at the gentleman again, noticing for the first time that he was sitting with a lap rug covering his legs. She looked at the wheeled chair as the man stopped it in front of them, then at the gentleman's lap, and lifted a curious gaze to him.

Still smiling, he offered her his bent hand. "M-my n-name is Will."

"Will," Honorine repeated, then beaming with pleasure, took his bent hand in hers.

Sophie did not venture out of Honorine's massive house for three full days. But then the lack of food and qualified servants—a distinctly separate category from Fabrice and Roland—began to annoy Honorine. She complained they hadn't enough help. "*La ménagère,* this is all I wish," she whined over a soufflé Sophie had made one evening. "And a chambermaid. You will bring *la femme de chambre, oui?*"

And perhaps a groom and a scullery maid and a laundress, too. The list went on and on, and by the next morning, Sophie was charged with finding suitable help. She supposed she ought to be enormously thankful that at least *this* time she could conduct her search in English. Yet the thought of venturing beyond the iron gates was unnerving—as the days in London slowly unfurled, Sophie discovered, much to her vexation, that she had developed a whole new set of irrational fears.

The greatest among them was the fear of discovery.

Rationally, she knew that the chance of someone recognizing her on the street or dredging up the old scandal was somewhat unlikely. But her emotions silenced her logic and she feared someone who might have known her then would indeed see her somewhere public and recognize her now. She was so unnerved by the prospect that when a young man had delivered provisions, she was quite certain he had looked at her curiously, as if he knew something about her. Her heart had started to pound; her palms had perspired as she slowly counted out the coins for him . . . until she realized he could not possibly have known her then. Given his youth and his social class, it was highly unlikely that their paths would have ever crossed.

Feeling suitably ridiculous, she had told herself that such fears were not only irrational, they bordered on lunacy. Yet she could not quite shake the fear of being discovered, knowing that sooner or later she would surely make an acquaintance and her past would be unearthed and rise swiftly on the wing of the *ton's* gossip.

She did not want to go out.

Honorine was adamant.

So out she went.

Fortunately, she quickly realized she was seeing London from an entirely new perspective than eight years ago and was able to relax a bit. Then, she had traveled about London in a coach as a Kettering, her destination the most prominent houses, the most elegant balls, the finest modistes and milliners. Now, she was simply Sophie Dane, traveling by foot and in search of the best markets.

That cast London in a whole new light.

The first thing she discovered was that Covent Garden was quite entertaining, what with all the hawkers and shoppers. For years she had believed what her Aunt Violet told her—full of riffraff, unsuitable for a young lady. The best bargains were to be had on High Street, where she found a pair of blue-green slippers for the price of a song. Rarely did her new responsibilities take her to places of old; only once did she pass one of the secret places at which she and William would meet during those weeks Julian had forbade her to see him. An unexpected shiver coursed her spine, but it was quickly gone.

Yes, *this* London suited her. She enjoyed her anonymity, enjoyed buying her own food and chatting amicably with shopkeepers. She liked the smells of the market, the vivid colors of the flowers in the baskets of the young girls who sold them, the sounds of the many hawkers vying for coin, and the bustling activity among the shops on High Street.

And so did the tranquillity of Regent's Park particularly appeal to her. In the afternoons, Sophie took long walks alone there, mildly surprised that she never saw anyone she knew. Despite the dozens milling about, she was alone in that park. Honorine had likewise discovered Regent's Park, too, and found it very much to *her* liking. This was due, naturally, to the fact that she had met a man there about whom she prattled on in the evenings, her words drifting in one of Sophie's ears and out the other. Nevertheless, she was exceedingly thankful that Honorine's daily visits to the park kept her suitably occupied.

Sophie was suitably occupied, too, and would have been quite content to remain that way, except that Ann had other ideas.

Her sister meant well, but she was adamant Sophie should slowly reenter society—not in any *remarkable* way, of course—and had taken that monumental task as her own cross to bear. It surprised her, but Sophie could feel herself falling into the old way of life—an older sibling dictating the course of her life, her following dutifully along. She felt it most keenly when Ann became convinced she should accompany her to Lady Worthington's garden tea. Sophie was less than enthusiastic about this—she had managed to avoid the trappings of the *ton* so far and did not relish a foray into their salons. But Ann was relentless in her arguments about why *this* tea was the thing, and finally worn down, Sophie agreed to attend.

It was a decision she regretted almost instantly. In

addition to Ann telling her what to do and how to present herself—"Do *not* draw attention!"—it was hardly a small affair, but a garden event with ladies covering every conceivable inch of the grounds. Three of society's old grande dames, ensconced in giant wicker chairs on the back terrace, peered at Sophie as if they expected her to suddenly sprout another head as Ann introduced her. One of them instantly asked after Madame Fortier, which prompted several questions about her supposed idiosyncrasies. The talk of the flamboyant, eccentric Honorine was undoubtedly making the rounds of the most elite drawing rooms; it was clear she was a source of great curiosity to these ladies, a fact that made Sophie feel exceedingly uncomfortable.

Fortunately, they moved on to more current gossip.

Sophie sat politely and quietly next to Ann, trying very hard not to squirm like a child as she listened to the grande dames.

"You know, don't you, that Miss Farnhill is to wed Mr. Braxton in the autumn. He has twenty thousand a year," one confided to the little group.

"That is indeed the best she could hope for," sniffed another.

"I hear Miss Amelia Cornwall has caught the eye of young Lord Ditherby!"

"It's a perfect match, is it not, what with his fifty thousand a year and the title."

Sophie bit her tongue, looked away. It had been so long since she had concerned herself with such things that the very subject seemed almost asinine now.

When one mentioned Mr. Whitehall's unfortunate penchant for whiskey, she could tolerate no more. Anxious to be gone from the prying women, Sophie slipped away from the terrace under the guise of viewing the gardens. Ann smiled broadly, approving of her decision to venture on.

Sophie walked down the gravel path in something of a fog, trying to regain her composure. Was this what she had missed all these years? Could they not spare a kind word? Worse, what must they be saying about *her* now? So caught up in her thoughts was she that she hardly noticed the two women strolling arm in arm toward her. She glanced up; one of them looked vaguely familiar. The woman, in turn, stared intently at Sophie. Hoping to high heaven they could not see the sting of self-consciousness in her cheeks, Sophie nodded politely as she passed.

"Excuse me, madam?" the woman said.

Oh God. Sophie gripped the seam of her skirts tightly, forced herself to pause and smile. "Yes?"

"I beg your pardon, but don't you recognize me?"

No. No . . . but perhaps? Sophie cocked her head to one side and looked closely at the woman. *Melinda. Melinda Birdwell.*

The woman smiled. "Why, Della, I do believe Lady Stanwood has forgotten me! Oh, I beg your pardon—" She laughed, exchanged a glance with her friend. "I'm afraid I'm not sure of the proper address."

The earth seemed to shift beneath Sophie's feet. "Ah . . . S-Sophie," she stammered, trying desperately to find herself. "You . . . you have always known me as Sophie, Melinda. How do you do?"

"Oh, *very* well, thank you," Melinda said, and looked at her friend. "I was acquainted with Sophie many years ago . . . we made our debuts in the same Season."

They had been acquainted, all right—Melinda had terrorized her that year. Of all the people she should meet, Melinda had to be the most disastrous.

Her critical eye quickly assessed Sophie's gown and hair. "I had not heard you were in England again. I thought I understood you were living abroad?"

Sophie's throat felt parched, the smile on her lips tremulous. "Actually, I've come home for a time."

"Ooh," exclaimed Melinda, "how very nice for your family." She grasped the arm of the woman accompanying her, took two steps back. "Well then. Welcome home," she said, and turned quickly with her friend. The two of them, holding tight to one another, hurried down the path, Melinda looking back over her shoulder for one last glimpse of Sophie before whispering into her friend's ear.

As she watched them scurry away, Sophie could feel herself sinking into the same black hole of humiliation that had all but drowned her the last time she was in London. It was all coming back in a rush of dull pain. Melinda Birdwell had never been a friend; in fact, in the Season of Sophie's debut, she had delighted in stealing her first promised dance and humiliating her. It had been easy to do—she was full of false charm, and Sophie had been . . . well, she had been Sophie, for Chrissakes!

Here it was, exactly what she had feared—oh, but she could just imagine how Melinda would regale her family over supper this evening! *"You will never believe who I chanced to see! You remember poor Sophie Dane, do you not?"*

Oh yes, they'd *all* remember, and at that moment, Sophie vowed to avoid the *ton* at all costs. She would not endure such humiliation again. She would not be their laughingstock. Her heart was too full of the old painful memories to add any new.

She survived the remainder of the afternoon by staying close to Ann's side, avoiding conversation and most of all, avoiding Melinda Birdwell. That was not the easiest thing to do—in the first place, Melinda had gained two stones or more in eight years and was a commanding figure, to say the least. And in the second place, Sophie had the terrible feeling that Melinda was pointing her out to others.

It was, all in all, a horrible affair.

When her sister called over the next several days, Sophie made it a point to be absent under the pretense of staffing Honorine's house. At least the endeavor kept her fully occupied—the Season was beginning in earnest, and there wasn't any good help left to speak of. Their situation was looking increasingly grim, so grim, that Sophie silently rejoiced when Fabrice announced that a woman had called inquiring about the position of housekeeper and cook.

But she was not exactly heartened by the sight of her first applicant—bent with age, she had a foreboding beak nose and a generally unpleasant demeanor.

"I been sent to do yer cleanin' and cooking," she flatly informed Sophie, and thrust a list of references at her. Sophie glanced at them, noticed two names she vaguely recognized. "The name is Lucie Cowplain."

"A pleasure to make your acquaintance, Mrs. Cowplain," Sophie said politely.

"Not *Mrs*. Cowplain. *Lucie* Cowplain," the woman said abruptly.

"Ah . . . I see. Where have you served before, Lucie?"

The woman pressed her lips so tightly together that they all but disappeared. *"Not Lucie.* Lucie Cowplain. Seems rather simple to me, mu'um."

Now *that* was a different response than Sophie was accustomed to and she hardly knew what to make of it. "Oh," she said, nervously rubbing her palms on her gown. "Ah . . . where might you have served before, Lucie Cowplain?" she asked carefully, cringing a bit when the woman's lips disappeared again.

"Ye got the paper right in yer hand, ye do," she said, motioning impatiently to the references Sophie held.

"Umm, yes, so I do indeed." *Heavens, was this the best the placement agency could do?* She glanced blindly at the list of references as she tried to think of how to politely send the woman on her way. "Let me see . . . you served Lady Kirkland. I would suppose she'd entertain quite frequently."

Lucie Cowplain's eyes hardened into tiny rocks of coal. "Will ye want me for yer employ or not?" she asked.

"I . . . I—"

"Have it yer way, then. But there ain't too many willin' to work for ye and the Frog," she said, and shoving her battered bonnet onto her head, pivoted tightly on her heel, prepared to quit the study.

Stunned by what she had said and awed that someone could be so impossibly rude, Sophie could only gape as the woman began her uneven march to the door. But as Lucie Cowplain reached for the brass handle, it occurred to Sophie that Honorine was never in the company of such an unbending woman and would not have the vaguest notion how to bear her.

Something about that made Sophie smile. "Lucie Cowplain, please!"

Lucie Cowplain paused; her shoulders stiffened as she turned slowly to glare at Sophie.

"I should very much like it if you would consider our offer of engagement."

Lucie Cowplain's frown deepened. "Do ye indeed? Then ye'll kindly show me to yer kitchen."

Having no desire to be the one to deny her, Sophie gestured lamely in the general direction of the kitchen, and Lucie Cowplain marched crookedly in that general direction, mumbling to herself.

This, Sophie thought as she followed the woman's slanted walk toward the kitchen, would be *most* entertaining.

She was not to be disappointed. In spite of all outward appearances to the contrary, Lucie Cowplain turned out to be a fine housekeeper and an even better cook, producing an array of dishes with sauces as delicate as any Sophie had learned in France. Though she thought it rather odd that someone as hard and bitter as that old woman could make such delectable food, Sophie was eager to learn from her, and Lucie Cowplain was, surprisingly, eager to teach.

Fabrice and Roland, however, were not particularly pleased with Sophie's choice, at least in the beginning. From the moment Lucie Cowplain hobbled into their midst with a tray of tea and biscuits, they were taken aback by her.

It didn't help matters at all that Lucie Cowplain practically laughed at them as she set the tray down. "Now then, what'ave we here?" she asked, peering at the two of them seated side by side on the divan. "Blimey, I ain't seen a bonnier pair of lassies in me life," she remarked, then cackled at her own jest.

Fabrice gasped with astonishment and came quickly to his feet, one hand on his hip, the other waggling a finger at Lucie Cowplain. "You do not speak to *me* thus!" he insisted.

Lucie Cowplain merely laughed and waved an old hand at him. "There now, don't be getting yer knickers into such a knot, laddie. Have a spot of tea and see if that won't cure yer vapors," she said, and still chuckling, hobbled out of the room as a stunned Fabrice and Roland gaped at her departing back. They spent the rest of the day and that week avoiding her.

Honorine, however, seemed oblivious to the juxtaposition of the woman's personality and culinary skills, much less her severe countenance, and made the mistake of trying to engage her in conversation. Lucie Cowplain did not respond to Honorine's endless chatter, but merely glowered at her, until the evening she apparently reached her limits. "Madame Fortier," she said in a gruff voice, "ye'll pay me to work, not to speak. If ye want me in yer employ, I'll thank ye kindly to leave yer prattling to the likes of her," she said, waving bent fingers at Sophie, "or find yourself another. I ain't hired on to be yer nursemaid, no I ain't."

That clearly took Honorine by surprise. For once she was speechless, her mouth open and wide blue eyes blinking. Lucie Cowplain shifted from one hip to the other, regarding her calmly, waiting for Honorine to decide. After a moment, Honorine said softly, *"Oui, madame."*

Satisfied, Lucie Cowplain nodded her ancient head and wobbled like a crab from the dining room.

Honorine turned to Sophie, tears brimming in her eyes. "So cruel is this woman!" she whispered, and quit the dining room almost as dramatically as Lucie Cowplain.

For Sophie, Lucie Cowplain's arrival signaled a slow-down to the rhythm of her life. Worried that Ann would see her idleness as new opportunity to take her round to the drawing rooms, she was suddenly desperate for an occupation. In similar circumstance in other cities of the world, she had turned to charity work. In London, however, that seemed a rather daunting prospect, as there were more charitable organizations than one could count, and many women of the *ton* involved in all of them.

There *was* one charity that interested her above all others—the house to which Claudia had taken her when she escaped Stanwood. But Sophie could not quite bring herself to mention the house on Upper Moreland Street, much less find it. Those jarring memories were always on the fringes of her consciousness, and she wasn't very sure she wanted to resurrect them.

So she spent her time wandering Regent's Park each day, usually carrying a small picnic made up of the delectable treats she was learning to make from Lucie Cowplain. Having discovered a small pond she thought particularly pretty, she took her picnic there each day, along with a book. But more times than not, she spent her afternoon gazing across the small pond, to where a house was being constructed, fascinated by the building of it. Well, actually . . . she was far more interested in the men who built it than the structure itself.

Men had become something of an enigma to her; strange creatures that made her skin flush with just a look, or tingle with a careless touch. Her dreams of them, *oh Lord* . . . they were decadent, sensual, and so very close to satisfying as to drive her mad. *Close,* they were, but not quite. Tormenting was more like it.

One man in particular had caught her eye—she gathered he was a foreman of sorts, as he always appeared on horseback, in a gentleman's suit of clothes. He would gracefully leap down, and arms akimbo, stalk about surveying the work done that morning. At that point, he would inevitably shed his coat and waistcoat, roll up the sleeves of his lawn shirt, and wade into the middle of the work, directing the others.

She would watch him for what seemed like hours. The man had wavy, sandy blond hair that brushed the top of his collar, impossibly wide shoulders, and narrow hips conveniently outlined for her viewing pleasure by the fabric of his tight trousers. He was truly a magnificent sight to behold from all angles, and Sophie did indeed behold him, locking his image away in the corner of her mind. He was delectable, a work of art. Watching him move about, hammering things, carrying large timbers . . . could she help it that she imagined him completely naked? It *had* been eight years since she had been so much as kissed by a man, unless one counted Arnaud, which she certainly did not. She was a woman, for heaven's sake, a living, breathing woman, and she could hardly help the churn of desire in her when this man would appear. Desire? Bloody hell, it was a slow burn. She had not felt a burn like that since . . .

All right, then, it was a fact that after she had escaped William, she had spent several years trying to rid her mind and body of the memory of him, and had convinced herself, completely and irrevocably, that she would never desire the touch of a man again. *Never.*

A prime example, apparently, of why one should never vow *never,* as she had been flat wrong.

It had returned, unexpected, two years ago.

She could still remember the moment. It had been in the markets of Stockholm; a gentleman with hair as white as her petticoats had walked up to the butcher and requested a flank of beef. He had stood beside Sophie, his arm lightly brushing hers, and she had felt herself begin to melt, starting somewhere deep inside and quickly spreading throughout her body. He was gone before she could breathe again, but she could not shake the surge of desire he had sparked in her.

It had happened again and again after that, and with increasing frequency, each incident seemingly more intense than the last, until she began to fear there was something quite seriously wrong with her. She longed to speak to someone about her condition of wantonness, but she could not bring herself to admit that, much to her horror, when she saw an attractive man, her gaze was immediately drawn to the square of his jaw, the breadth of his shoulders, the trim of his waist, and . . . *and to the bulge between his legs.*

The man across the pond certainly was not lacking in that regard.

So Sophie watched him, pretending to read, feeling the heat creep into her skin as her gaze feasted on him, imagining him in various activities. Lewd activities. Activities that crept into her dreams at night. And she was watching him move about one day—well, watching *it,* actually—when she suddenly realized he was *looking* at her. Looking right at her looking at him. It unnerved her so badly, her book flew halfway across the park. She didn't return for two days.

But she could not stay away, and she finally crept back to the pond like a sinner returned to God, taking care to arrange herself just so in a way that she wouldn't appear to be looking. She thought herself quite clever.

So it was the worst sort of panic that swept through her early one bright afternoon when the foreman on horseback actually appeared on *her* side of the pond. She was reading, having lost interest in the building since *he* was not there and absently looked up at the sound of an approaching horseman.

She almost toppled right off her wrought iron bench,

and in the struggle to keep that from happening, knocked her picnic basket to the ground. She quickly bent to retrieve it, cringing when she realized the horseman had stopped.

Slowly, she sat up, clutching the basket so tightly that the food all but oozed out the wicker sides.

"Good day," he said, tipping his hat.

Mother of God, he was gorgeous! Dumbfounded, Sophie nodded.

He smiled, flashing brilliantly white teeth, matched only by the brilliance of his pale green eyes. "Lovely day for walkabout."

Walkabout? Sophie blinked. *What was this? What did he want? Was her face as red as Honorine's Christmas cape?*

His smile faded a bit and he shifted uneasily in his saddle. "I beg your pardon if I have imposed. It's just that I have noticed you sitting here on several occasions, and I wondered if perhaps you might know the occupants of the house at the end of the lane just there," he said, motioning behind him.

Sophie didn't actually see the house he indicated, as she had, unfortunately, caught sight of his thigh—the heat quickly spread to her chest, constricted her breathing.

"Madam?"

She jerked her gaze up to his. "Ah . . . ah, the house? *That* house? Ah, no. No," she stammered.

He smiled again, absently rubbed his hand on that sculpted thigh. "There is a particularly sturdy gutter on the perimeter of that house. I thought to inquire as to where it was made." He looked at her again with his high, well-defined cheekbones, and his square, clean-shaven jaw. She meant to speak, she truly did, but she had apparently swallowed her fat tongue.

"Ah well, then. I beg your pardon for the intrusion."

Like an imbecile, she nodded.

He tipped his hat, started to turn away, but hesitated,

looking down at her. *Why? Why was he looking at her like that?* Sophie's eyes grew wide.

"Excuse me," he said politely, "but I think you are about to snap the handle of your basket."

Sophie looked down—she was holding the basket so tightly it was a wonder the lid had not exploded from it. She immediately let go, dropping the thing as if it were a red-hot coal.

"Well then. Good day," he said, and he was gone, galloping around the pond to the site of construction.

Sophie stared at the place he had vacated. Lord, oh *Lord,* he was more handsome than she could possibly have imagined, exceedingly masculine—

And she had made a *complete* cake of herself!

She abruptly stood up, and in something of a panic, grabbed up her basket and book, the basket once again clasped tightly to her chest. Before she realized it, she was walking toward Gloucester Gate. When she reached the crowded thoroughfare, she felt a pall of confusion come over her. Where did she go? What corner of the earth could she find where the humiliation would not swallow her whole? She had sat there like a fool, unable to speak, staring at him as if she had never seen a man before! *Augh!*

"To Marleybone! All bound for Marleybone!"

She jerked around; a hackney driver motioned to the cab of his coach. " 'Ere you are, miss. Up to Marleybone, if you're of a mind."

Yes. To Marleybone. Yes, yes, yes. Sophie nodded eagerly, fished in her reticule for two crowns, and handed them up to the driver before hoisting herself into the coach and squeezing onto a bench next to a gentleman who was in desperate want of a bath. When the coach lurched forward, she gripped her things tightly in her lap and wondered where in heaven's name she thought she was going now. Anywhere but Regent's Park, where the eyes of a stranger had melted her into a warm mess of muck.

. . .

Two hours later, Sophie stood in front of a small townhouse with green shutters. She couldn't be entirely sure, but she thought it was the townhouse she was looking for. She peered up at the windows, dredging her memory for any sign that it was the right one.

It looked to be the same one, but honestly, she had come to it under a cloak of darkness and snow. And deadly fear. She had left much the same way, in the company of Julian, too frightened of the journey ahead to look to the right or the left. And it wasn't as if she had ever ventured from the house in the two weeks she had stayed here—it was, after all, in a part of London that was unfamiliar to her.

And there had been the ugly, telltale bruise on her jaw.

Sophie sighed, glanced up the road to where Upper Moreland intersected Essex Road. What did it matter, really? It had been eight years ago and she was a long way from those days—they were nothing more than a forgotten, hazy memory, an occasional bad dream. And now, she was a long way from *Maison de Fortier*. She ought to go back before they began to worry about her. This was silly—even if it *were* the same house, there was no one left here now who had been there then. Except perhaps Mrs. Conner—

"Miss? Is there something you'd be wanting?"

Startled, Sophie whirled around. A woman had appeared on the steps of the house with the green shutters and smiled warmly at Sophie as she swept the top step.

"Ah . . . no. No, thank you, I was really only . . . ah, I was merely—"

"You look as if you could use a spot of tea, luv."

Tea. How delicious that sounded. She hadn't eaten a bite since early morning, having forgotten her little picnic the moment she had seen the startling green eyes of the foreman. She was famished, she realized; still, one could hardly impose on a stranger. "I . . . I beg your pardon, madam. I should not have been lurking about, but I thought perhaps . . . that perhaps it was the same house a good friend once occupied."

"Does it indeed?" Still smiling, the woman moved down and swept the next step. "Perhaps it is. What was your friend's name?"

A jolt of self-consciousness seized her; Sophie unthinkingly twisted the gold bracelet around her wrist. "Umm . . . her name? Her name was ah, Mrs. Conner. Doreen Conner. But I've probably the wrong house," she added quickly.

The woman paused in her sweeping, stacked both hands atop her broom. "You've the right house," she said gently. "But Mrs. Conner is no longer with us."

"Oh." Sophie twisted her bracelet again and glanced nervously toward Essex Road. She should simply have asked Claudia where Mrs. Conner had gone, but it was so hard to mention those days aloud, especially to her family. She still felt the shame she had brought them all.

"She died this winter just past."

Died? That announcement shocked her—Doreen Conner had seemed so . . . *invincible!* "She died?" she echoed weakly.

The woman smiled sympathetically, as if she somehow could not believe it, either. "She lay ill for a very long time before the fever took her."

It was impossible to imagine Mrs. Conner—who had stood exactly where the woman was standing now that bitterly cold day—could be ill. The woman had been an absolute beacon of strength, a rock in the maelstrom in which Sophie had found herself—

"How 'bout that tea, then, luv?"

Blinking through the fog of her memory, Sophie glanced up. The woman was still smiling so warmly that she could almost feel it shining through her. "My name is

Sophie. Sophie Dane. I am . . ." She faltered. *Who was she?*

"Nancy. Nancy Harvey," the woman responded, and held out her hand to Sophie, just as Doreen Conner had done that night eight years ago.

Chapter Four

WHEN SOPHIE RETURNED to *Maison de Fortier* that afternoon, she found Roland in the foyer, staring up at the immense chandelier that hung from the crown dome above. He continued to stare at it while he informed Sophie she was wanted in the orangery.

"Why?" she asked, peering up at the chandelier, too, curious as to what he was seeing.

"This, I do not know," he responded, and with a heavy sigh, he shook his head and wandered off in the opposite direction of the orangery, muttering to himself.

Sophie had not endured seven years of Honorine et al. without learning it was not always prudent to question what they were doing. She proceeded down the long corridor, out onto the lawn, and across to the old and empty orangery, which Honorine had, of late, determined should be converted into a studio. Except that she didn't paint, a thought that occurred to her sometime later.

As she walked across the lawn, Sophie could see Honorine through one of the floor-to-ceiling windows dressed in a red-and-yellow patterned skirt—*where did one find such combinations of color in one cloth?* She could hear more than one voice; oddly, it sounded as if a child were with Honorine.

Preposterous.

Sophie stepped up on the small porch leading into the orangery, heard Honorine say, "A ballroom. Can you see?" just as a boy darted by the open door. "I remove these furnitures, *non*? And put in their place pretty plants. *Oui,* pretty plants for the corners. It is good, this ballroom, *non*?"

The sound of a deep male voice startled Sophie; as she stepped inside, Honorine instantly broke into a wreath of smiles.

Sophie felt the floor opening beneath her.

Standing next to Honorine, smiling charmingly, was Mr. Trevor Hamilton—the man who, in her last Season, had been the most eligible and sought-after bachelor among the *ton*. Seeing his trim figure now, Sophie was struck with the distinct memory of being ignored by him the summer of her demise. He had not acknowledged her existence in any way, not even after Julian had made the proper introductions. That distasteful memory was eclipsed only by a panic so immediate that her knees began to tremble. *What was he doing here?*

"Ah, Sofia! You see Monsieur Hamilton. He is the son of Monsieur Will."

Will. The name of the man Honorine had met at Regent's Park. *Will Hamilton. Lord Hamilton, Viscount. That* was whom Honorine chattered about so incessantly? Frozen by her shocked disbelief, Sophie gaped at Honorine.

Honorine smiled cheerfully. "Monsieur Hamilton, he has a son, too! *Mon petit Ian.*" To Mr. Hamilton, she said, "My Sofia! Pretty, *non*?"

Mr. Hamilton bowed. "A pleasure to make your acquaintance, madam." He straightened; one brow floated upward, and Sophie instantly dipped an awkward curtsey.

"M-Mr. Hamilton."

"Madam . . . ?" he asked politely.

What? Sophie blinked. It took a moment for her to understand . . . she had been so appalled to find him here that it had not occurred to her, not even for a moment, that he might not recognize her. Surely he recognized her! How could he not know who she was?

"Ah, *mon amie*," Honorine offered, "*Madame Sofia Dane*. She belongs to the Kettering!"

Mr. Hamilton's brow fell; he stared at her in such obvious astonishment that Sophie wished to die, right there on the orangery floor. She wasn't sure which was more humiliating—to be remembered for her horrible scandal, or not remembered at all! The urge to flee was overwhelming, but there was nowhere to turn, no place in this empty orangery to hide.

"Lady Sophie?" he asked, incredulous. "Forgive me, but you are . . . you seem quite . . . well. Quite well, indeed."

Quite well? *Quite well?*

"You've been abroad, then?"

She could not speak. She was so perplexed that she had absolutely no idea what to say—

"*Oui*, abroad. Sofia, she is my . . . how do you say . . . *compagne*," Honorine explained.

Mr. Hamilton looked at Honorine in surprise, then at Sophie. "Indeed, your companion?"

That was followed by a moment of awkward silence in which Sophie still could not find her voice. Honorine's glare wasn't helping any, either . . . "Yes," she finally managed to croak, "I've been abroad several years now. With Madame Fortier. Traveling. And . . . *ahem*. And, ah . . . traveling."

"Ah, I see."

She rather imagined he did.

"What a tremendous opportunity for you. Perhaps you might regale me one day with tales of your travel. Perhaps over tea," he said, gesturing for Ian to come to him.

Over tea? Well, all right, then, she simply had to be

dreaming because Mr. Hamilton would not invite her to tea—

"*Oui, oui,* we join you and Madame Hamilton—"

"I'm afraid there is no Mrs. Hamilton," he said.

"Oh, *non?*" Honorine clucked, peering down at Ian as he inched by, looking intently at her colorful clothing and loose hair.

"I am a widower."

"Oooh, *je regrette infiniment,*" Honorine managed in spite of the delighted twinkle in her eye.

"Thank you kindly. Well, then," he said, flashing a smile at Sophie as he took Ian's hand in his, "I shall leave you ladies to your plans for a ballroom."

"Oh, but you must come soon again!" Honorine said, hurrying after Mr. Hamilton as he turned toward the door.

"Thank you. Good day to you, Madame Fortier." He looked pointedly at Sophie and added, "I look forward to that tea." With a low bow, he pulled Ian out the door.

"*Au revoir!*" Honorine called after them, and stood, smiling broadly, until the sound of the Hamiltons' steps on the gravel walk faded. Then she whirled around to Sophie and threw up her hands, exclaiming heatedly in French that Sophie was absolutely hopeless.

"This man, he is very *pleased* with you, Sofia!" she spoke at last in greatly exasperated English, "and you there, standing with no tongue! Do you not *see?*"

"Oh, I see all right, and I know *exactly* what he must be thinking now!"

"He thinks you are very pretty."

"Don't be ridiculous!" she retorted sharply. Her head was reeling, spinning—she moved forward, purposely ignoring Honorine as she marched from the orangery.

"It is not I who am ridiculous, Sofia!" Honorine snapped right back, and was quickly on her heels. "This fear you have, it is . . . *mon Dieu!* How do you say in English? *Injustifié!*"

"And exactly *what* brought Mr. Hamilton to the orangery?" Sophie demanded, stopping and turning so abruptly that Honorine almost collided with her.

"The boy! Never mind of this! Do you see Monsieur Hamilton, how he smiles for you?"

With a snort of exasperation, Sophie whirled about and picked up her pace, unwilling to listen to Honorine as she began, for the thousandth time, the litany of attributes Sophie possessed, concluding that if only she would smile, hold her head up, look a man in the eye . . . Blast it, but it was enough to drive a woman to drink!

Which is exactly what she did, marching into the grand salon and helping herself to a spot of port to calm her nerves, putting aside, for the time being, that she could hardly swallow the stuff. But then again, it had been a rather extraordinary day for Sophie Dane—two men, two *complete* disasters, and one of them being Trevor Hamilton, of all people. *Trevor Hamilton!* In the summer of thirty-six there wasn't a single debutante who didn't hope to dance a waltz with him, didn't dream of making a match with him! Of all the people for her to happen upon now, of all the persons in the world, it had to be *him*. What a bloody disaster!

Unfortunately, Honorine would not let her forget it, and was obviously intent on driving her quite mad, as she continued well into the evening, ranting about Mr. Hamilton, Sophie's lack of male companionship in general, and her obvious need to . . . *ahem* . . . tend to *all* her needs. By the middle of the next morning, Sophie was imagining all the inventive ways she might strangle her. To make matters worse, Honorine went to Regent's Park on a lark and accosted the little moppet son of Hamilton's, along with his governess, after a walkabout with the boy's grandpapa. Somehow, Honorine had managed to convince reasonable adults that the boy should call at *Maison de Fortier*. Lord Hamilton was, apparently, quite smitten with Honorine.

And Honorine decided, much to Sophie's annoyance,

to teach young Ian to dance. She coerced Roland—who happened to be a passable violinist and, having no other apparent occupation in London, was available—into playing. Young Ian proved to be an eager and capable little dancer, in spite of his governess's attempts to tell him that one did not dance *precisely* that way in England.

Fortunately for his governess, Miss Hipplewhite, Honorine soon grew bored of dancing with a seven-year-old boy, and sprawled on a settee, regaled Ian with outrageously creative stories of her life. Ian lay on his stomach on the Oriental rug, his chin propped on his fists, his eyes wide with awe at some of the more colorful tales presented him.

Miss Hipplewhite sat on the edge of her chair, her mouth agape in horror.

Sophie could hardly keep from rolling her eyes or muttering her disbelief of the more inventive tales, particularly the one that had Honorine rescuing a child from some sort of Norwegian pirate-viking. Sophie's demeanor, however, did not sit well with her employer. When Honorine suggested, in proper and distinct French, that she might perhaps find another activity more to her liking than drumming her fingers on the arm of her chair and muttering under her breath, Sophie could not agree more.

She set out for her daily walk and found herself in Regent's Park.

Inevitably, she came to the pond she visited every day, in spite of having already made a monumental fool of herself there. She paused at the wrought iron bench where she usually sat and looked across to where the men were normally working, but was surprised to see that there were no activities at the house today—it was silent. That was just as well, really; she was not very keen to see the foreman after the awful display of her conversational skills yesterday.

But still . . . she was rather disappointed.

She sat on the bench, stared at the water, and wished she had thought to bring a book. A carriage rumbled by in the distance; Sophie adjusted her bonnet, folded her hands primly on her lap.

After a few minutes of that, she stood up, walked to the edge of the pond and around the banks, deeper into the flora than she had gone before, trying to see past the dark surface to gauge the depth of it. But the lily pads were too thick and the water murky. The sound of a frog captured her attention, sitting on a lily pad beneath the overhang of a willow tree, his chest puffed proudly. For some strange reason, he reminded Sophie of all the gentlemen of the *ton*.

She glanced down at her feet, spied several pebbles.

He didn't think she had come today. He had ridden around the park twice now, had given up hope that she would appear. He was on his way out of the park when he saw the flash of pink bonnet around one side of the pond.

She *had* come, this woman whose solitary existence had so intrigued him.

He had watched her watching him, had wondered who she was and why she came every day with her basket and her book. He had even fantasized that he knew why—there was something about her that reminded him of himself. She was a loner, not really fitting into the world around her, preferring her own company to that of society. And when he had seen her yesterday, up close, her chocolate-brown eyes and pristine skin had enchanted him. The woman was pretty in an unconventional way. But anxious. Extremely anxious. And that just made him wonder all the more.

He dismounted, tethered his horse, and strolled to the wrought iron bench where she usually sat. A flash of pink again, and he saw her, squatting down, looking in the grass for something. When she stood, she adjusted her bonnet backward and slightly off to one side, apparently aiming at something. He looked to the pond, saw the frog, and smiled to himself.

Suddenly, she jerked her arm back and threw the stone with such enthusiasm that she very nearly wrenched her arm from her shoulder. The stone sailed wide of the frog and landed with a splash great enough to make the creature inch nervously about on his lily pad.

The second pebble, thrown delicately as a little girl would, was far too short. She muttered under her breath as the frog inched closer to the edge of his pad, shook her arm a bit to loosen it, then assumed a firmer position with her feet planted widely apart.

Lord. "You've got it all wrong, I'm afraid," he called out to her.

At the sound of his voice, the woman nearly toppled over backward as she whirled around and clasped her hand to her breast, stone and all.

Bloody hell, then—she was even prettier than he had thought. Her brown eyes, wide with surprise, were so dark that they almost looked black; her pursed lips, plump and red, stood in stark contrast to the creamy paleness of her face. He had startled her badly; her chest was heaving up and down in a tantalizing shade of green brocade.

He idly slapped his riding crop against his thigh. "As a veteran of frog-tapping, I can say with some authority that you've got to get your weight behind it. May I demonstrate?"

"I . . . ah, I don't really . . . I mean that I'm not usually in the habit of throwing stones," she said, and instantly closed her eyes, pivoting away from him toward the pond in a self-conscious manner he found utterly charming.

He walked down and stood beside her. "I beg your pardon, but that is rather obvious, madam. You've no idea how to go about it."

Her cheeks flushed, she glanced at him from the corner of her eye. "I . . . I was getting the feel for it."

He chuckled, squatted down, and picked up a few stones. "It appeared as if you were getting the feel for launching the stone all the way to Scotland. If I were so intent on unseating that frog, I would take a stance to improve my aim. Put one foot back thus," he said, planting one foot back and the other forward.

Now she leveled a completely baffled gaze at him, as if he were speaking a foreign language.

"Won't you try it?"

For a moment, he thought she would tell him to leave her be, but she slowly put one foot behind her, the other forward, without once taking her eyes from him.

He couldn't help himself; he chuckled again at her charming discomfiture. "Ah, there you are. All right then, when you throw, shift your weight forward onto your forefoot." He threw his stone, which landed just shy of the lily pad to force the frog away from the edge. "You see? Now you have a go."

She regarded him skeptically, then just as skeptically regarded the frog, and mimicking his movement, threw her stone. It landed almost exactly where his had, but the splash sent the frog leaping off the pad and into the water.

They both stared at the empty lily pad for a moment.

"There you go—can't have them all, you know," he said with a nonchalant shrug. "Perhaps you should consider croquet."

A quiet smile spread across her lips. "Ah yes, *croquet,*" she said softly. "I am particularly skilled at *that* sport."

"Then perhaps you might teach me," he said as he reclaimed his riding crop. "I've only played the game once and found it rather tedious."

She smiled fully then, but said nothing.

He tapped his crop against his leg, cleared his throat. "If I may be so bold . . . having now shared this moment of rock throwing, might I inquire after your name?"

The request instantly doused her smile. Coloring slightly, she looked off to the left. "Ah . . . well . . ."

Embarrassed regret swept through him and he cringed inwardly; he certainly should have known better. He glanced up the embankment to where his horse was tethered, suddenly anxious to be on his way—women of the aristocracy did not consort with men like him—

"Sophie. Sophie Dane," she said softly.

Sophie. The name sounded sweet on her breath. "Miss Dane, a pleasure to make your acquaintance. I am Mr. Caleb Hamilton, at your service."

The quick but unmistakable look of bewilderment on her pretty face unnerved him. He was accustomed to the reaction to his name, naturally, particularly in this part of London. But to think that she knew the lies said about him was very bothersome, more so than it had ever been before.

"A pleasure, sir," she said politely, and nervously adjusted the cuffs of her walking gown.

"Well then. I suppose I've done all the good I can do here for today," he said with a smile, and took a tentative step backward. "I shall leave you to your walkabout then, Miss Dane. I thank you for sharing a bit of it with me."

She nodded, watched him as he took another step backward. But he hesitated, alarmingly uncertain what to do with himself. This was highly unusual for him, this awkwardness and indecision—he was hardly inexperienced with pretty women, but this was oddly, disturbingly, different. There was obviously nothing left to say—he could hardly confess to having watched her surreptitiously from across the pond these last few days. So he did what any gentleman would do and lifted his hand to tip his hat. With a final look at her pretty brown eyes, he turned away.

"Mr. Hamilton?"

His heart leapt; he looked over his shoulder. "Yes, Miss Dane?"

"W-what are you building, if I may ask?"

Irrationally pleased she had asked, he could not help the smile he knew was impossibly broad. "A house. My house."

"Oh."

She said nothing more, and Caleb told himself he should continue on. But his feet would not move—they apparently were not willing to say good-bye just yet. She was too intriguing, this Sophie Dane, seemingly so unlike the women he typically consorted with. Her countenance, her demeanor, was so unlike that of society women. That, and she simply had too many enticing curves for a man to just walk away.

She was still looking at him with a sweet expression of curiosity.

"If you come for your walk tomorrow, I would very much enjoy the privilege of showing my house to you."

With a beguiling smile, she glanced down at her hem. "Perhaps," she murmured.

Now *that* was the best thing Caleb had heard in several days, and in fact, her tentative response thrilled him like a child. As absurd as it was, he *wanted* to show this woman his house. He wanted her to see what he was capable of building, the house he would one day call a home, would one day fill, God willing, with children and happiness and love.

Shyly, she peeked at him through her lashes; Caleb grinned, gave her a jaunty wave with his riding crop. "I shall come round here on the morrow to see if you are so inclined. Good day, Miss Dane."

"Good day, Mr. Hamilton."

He turned, walked up the hill without looking back, feeling more buoyant by the moment. He sensed something wholly unique about Sophie Dane. There was something about her that made him feel hopeful in a strange sort of way.

And he needed to hope.

. . .

He was, of course, far more handsome than she had thought, impossibly rugged and strong and . . . the bulge between his legs . . . Sophie practically floated back to *Maison de Fortier* and through the rest of the afternoon, closeting herself in the small library off the west corridor.

Seated in an overstuffed chair, she brought the book she was supposedly reading up to bury her face in it for the thousandth time since her encounter with Mr. Caleb Hamilton. She felt hot, red hot, burning from the inside out with her racy and hopeful thoughts, exactly the way she had felt when she had first seen him standing above her on the embankment of the pond. Her own behavior had astounded her—she had never been so bold as she was today, calling him back as she did. The very thought of it made her blush furiously, and she could think of little else but him, his image seemingly affixed permanently to her mind's eye.

So enrapt in the memory of him was she that she scarcely heard Fabrice when he wandered into the study.

He cleared his throat impatiently; Sophie slowly lowered her book.

"Monsieur Trevor Hamilton," he said, and Sophie all but sent the book flying across the carpet as Trevor Hamilton strolled in behind Fabrice.

"He said I should follow," he said apologetically, to which Fabrice shrugged and paused to adjust his neckcloth just so, then promptly strolled out of the room, his duty complete.

"I . . . I . . . Won't you come in?" Sophie stammered nervously as she tried to artfully kick her book beneath the ottoman.

"Thank you." He moved to the hearth, watching her, pausing there with his hands clasped behind his back, a smile playing on his lips.

What was he doing here again? Several things fluttered through her mind—none of which she found terribly appealing. All right, there had to be a perfectly reasonable explanation, and if she would take a breath and stop acting so addlepated, he might very well tell her! Sophie clumsily gained her feet, preparing herself . . . *Because of your reputation, I'd prefer my son not be seen in your house—*

"Lady Sophie, won't you sit? You look a bit flushed."

Oh, she was flushed, all right. Her heart was battering so wildly against her chest she was surprised it didn't leap from her bodice and land squarely on the carpet between them.

"I . . . Yes. Yes, thank you." *She should be the one asking him to sit!* She moved abruptly to a chair at the hearth, hardly able to think what to do. She sat—fell, really—and weakly motioned to the leather wingback chair directly across from her. "Please, Mr. Hamilton." *Tea.* Yes, she should ring for tea!

"Thank you," he said, and took his seat at the precise moment she stood to ring for tea. He quickly came to his feet again, but not before Sophie had flung herself into the chair again. He crouched, halfway between standing and sitting, eyeing her warily. "Are you quite certain?"

"I thought to ring for tea," she said, feeling the rush of blood to her cheeks. *She could not do this.* No one was more incompetent at this sort of thing than she; she always had been. "Please, sit," she urged him.

He cautiously took his seat. "Thank you for receiving me without notice, Lady Sophie. I won't keep you."

"Oh, think nothing of it." She clasped her hands in her lap, noticed her knuckles were white with the exertion of it. *Get on with it, then. Say it, say it, say—*

"I'm not usually so impulsive, but I confess, I have thought a lot about that tea we agreed to, and I've come to the conclusion that perhaps something a bit more enduring is in order. After all, Madame Fortier has said that you traveled extensively and to locales that are not often on the grand tour, so to speak."

This was certainly *not* what she expected to hear— *what* tea? She had never agreed to any tea! Just what did Honorine think she was doing!?

"I was hoping that you would agree to be my guest at supper, Wednesday next," he continued. When she did not immediately answer, he cocked his head to one side and patiently awaited her answer.

"Supper?" Was it her imagination, or had she shouted the word?

"If it pleases you."

"I . . . well, I—"

"My father would like it very much."

His *father*? All right, no man of his stature in the *ton* would want to associate with a woman who had eloped and then divorced her husband! This was some sort of trickery—

"Unless, of course, you are previously engaged, in which case I would be happy to offer the supper at a time when it might be more convenient for you to attend."

Sophie swallowed, unable to move.

"Are you previously engaged, then?"

"No. No, I am not previously engaged . . ." What was she *saying*? She could not sup at the home of Mr. Hamilton!

"Splendid! Then shall we say eight o'clock?"

"Mr. Hamilton, I—"

"Naturally, the invitation extends to Madame Fortier."

"That is very kind, but I hope you—"

"I am very pleased you will come. Well then, I shan't keep you from your book a moment longer. Thank you, Lady Sophie. I look forward to our evening with great anticipation." He stood, shoved his hands into his pocket, and was already walking to the door before her mind could comprehend that she had, somehow, accepted his invitation. Her mind was spinning now, thinking furiously how to call him back when he paused at the door and turned toward her, smiling.

"I had in mind a rather intimate gathering. Not more than a dozen, I assure you." Sophie gripped the arms of the chair to keep from slipping out of it in sheer mortification.

The suggestion of meeting a room full of the *haut ton* was enough to make her ill—astounded, petrified, and completely discomfited, she frantically sought to put an end to this ridiculous situation. "Mr. Hamilton, I truly appreciate your offer, but I—"

"It is my pleasure. Thank you again, Lady Sophie. Until Wednesday next," he said cheerfully, and walked out of the room.

Chapter Five

H ONORINE WAS NO help at all.

The woman was ecstatic when Sophie told her about Trevor Hamilton's call, observing first that Sophie would need to quickly replace all her undergarments, which Honorine considered too plain—"the frilly little things, the men, they enjoy them"—then secondly that her little peanut of a heart might at last fill up with *amour*.

And she topped it all off by proclaiming that the supper party was a grand opportunity for Will Hamilton to continue to court *her*.

When Sophie offered her own, less enthusiastic opinion about the supper, Honorine waxed romantically about her Will, then promptly quit the room, humming an old French love ballad to drown out any protest from Sophie.

It was enough to make a person positively deranged.

Frankly, Sophie had never seen Honorine quite so enamored of a man before. She could only attribute it to being several weeks in London now without dozens of fawning males. That, and the viscount Hamilton was undoubtedly paying her quite a number of grand compliments. Honorine adored compliments.

Claudia and Ann were no help, either—blast it if both of them didn't readily agree with Honorine over luncheon the next day that Hamilton's invitation was *exactly* the thing for Sophie.

"It seems perfect. At least it will be a very *small* affair," Claudia reasoned. "You'll not be exposed to the *ton,* not really."

Oh no, they mustn't show their tarnished spinster-sister to the upper echelons of society.

"Hamilton has just come from the country. He's been there all this time with his father since Elspeth died. It's so tragic, is it not?" sighed Ann.

"Frankly, I can't imagine why he'd come to London now. I suppose for the sake of the boy he must think of reentering society, at least in some small way," Claudia added, and she and Ann nodded in perfect unison.

"How very unpleasant that man has presented himself as Lord Hamilton's son," Claudia added, frowning.

"Pardon?" asked Honorine, perking up.

"It's shocking, really," Ann said, inching forward, eager to tell. "There have been rumors floating about for years now that the viscount had illegitimate issue. A French-woman, they say," she said, nodding authoritatively. "Of course no one had ever *seen* this child, but suddenly a man has appeared, claiming to be the son of Lord Hamilton!"

Sophie felt a faint lurch of her belly.

"It's despicable," Claudia muttered. "How can people be so vile?"

"Victor says he is one of those who claims to be involved in the railroad," Ann sniffed disdainfully, and she and Claudia both shook their heads, as if there were something inherently evil about that.

"What is wrong with the railroad?" Sophie asked innocently, and received twin looks of exasperation.

"Because, darling," said Claudia, "they build this railroad through the countryside and divide up lands that have been owned by some families for centuries. It mars

the landscape and makes a horrible noise. It will never succeed; you may trust me on that. I suspect this chap has lost every last farthing on the railroad and has come up with this despicable scheme to extort money from Lord Hamilton."

"This man, what is the name of this man?" Honorine asked, ignoring the talk of railroads.

Sophie caught a breath in her throat as she waited for Ann's answer.

"His name? Hamilton, of course. Caleb Hamilton," Ann said as she speared a strawberry on her fork.

Caleb? *Her* Caleb? She looked at Ann, hoping that perhaps she had not heard correctly. There could be hundreds of Hamiltons, couldn't there be? *"Who?"* she asked.

"Caleb Hamilton," Ann responded, looking at her curiously.

As the blood drained from her face, Sophie quickly looked down at her plate. *Oh God, not the foreman, her beautiful secret foreman!*

"He's quite the man about town, if you catch my meaning," Ann added, and plopped the strawberry into her mouth.

"Oh my yes," Claudia agreed with a roll of her eyes. "I have heard that he does indeed appreciate the company of a woman or two."

"Or three or four," Ann added. "Victor has it on good authority that he is a frequent caller to Madame Farantino's," she said, exchanging a look of disdain with Claudia. "I do feel rather sorry for Mr. Trevor Hamilton. His troubles have been so great, and now this."

Sophie sat, frozen with disappointment. She should have known it was too good to be true. She should have understood that a man with the fine looks of Caleb Hamilton could only be toying with her. "Why doesn't Lord Hamilton simply say whether or not he is his son?" she asked petulantly.

"Lord Hamilton has been ill," Claudia informed her. "Trevor has been seeing to his care. First Elspeth, now his father."

"He is very pleased with Sofia," Honorine offered nonchalantly from her daybed on the far end of the room. "This, it is very plain. He wants this supper for Sofia."

Both Claudia's and Ann's forks froze midway to their mouths and their heads swiveled in perfect unison toward Honorine at that pronouncement. *"Really?"* Ann gushed, and flashed a beaming smile to Sophie. "Trevor Hamilton, Sophie!" she whispered excitedly. "Do you think that perhaps—"

"No!" Sophie exclaimed, feeling suddenly unwell. "Honestly, Ann! You mustn't think for a moment that—"

"Le monsieur, he finds Sofia pretty to him," Honorine blithely continued.

"Well of course she is!" Claudia said, perhaps a little too emphatically, and put her fork down to better stare at her sister-in-law. "Dear me, I had not really thought of it, but he comes here to make his personal request of you . . . oh *Sophie*! This could be just the—"

"Ooh, this is *marvelous*!" Ann eagerly interjected, coming quickly to the same conclusion as Claudia. "How I've worried for you! Oh my, we must find you something suitable to wear!"

"By my word, you cannot give credence to anything Honorine says, I—"

"My modiste showed me four gowns not two days ago, all canceled orders. Sophie is so trim, I should think any alterations would be minimal!" Claudia exclaimed.

"What of her hair?" Ann demanded in response. "We must do something with her hair! It is too fine for ringlets—I know, we shall put it up with velvet ribbons!"

"Here now, one moment, if you please," Sophie tried desperately, holding both hands up. "I've no need of gowns and ribbons and—"

"Your gowns, *chérie,* they are too *ordinaires,*" Honorine opined with a yawn.

Sophie shot her a fierce look of exasperation. "How very kind of you to say so, Honorine. Nonetheless—"

"She is right, darling. You really should add a touch of color to your wardrobe," said Ann.

Oh, wasn't *this* just bloody grand! Now she was receiving a critique of her wardrobe, too—well, God help them all if they listened to Honorine's advice on *that* front. And what did it matter, anyway? She was not going to that supper party. *Not.* There was nothing they could say to convince her she should subject herself to the scrutiny of the *ton*.

"As I have no intention of attending this supper party, I cannot imagine what difference the color of my clothing could possibly make."

That declaration was met with small, simultaneous gasps from Claudia and Ann.

"Not *going*?" With a snort of incredulity, Claudia exchanged a look with Ann. "Of *course* you are going! You cannot decline Mr. Hamilton's invitation!"

"Yes I can. I'll think of something! An ague, perhaps—"

"An *ague*! What a ruckus you will cause if you turn down his invitation! How unseemly it would be to reject his gracious hospitality after . . . Everyone will talk!" said Ann, her voice rising. "*Trevor Hamilton,* Sophie!" she said, jabbing the tip of her finger against the tabletop as if Sophie had not realized *who* had invited her. "Have you lost your foolish mind?"

"I have not lost my mind! I am not going."

"*Yes,*" countered Ann and Claudia at almost exactly the same moment and in almost exactly the same cross tone of voice.

And across the room, a very self-satisfied Honorine merely chuckled as she sampled one of Lucie Cowplain's delectable crème puffs.

· · ·

Ann and Claudia meant what they said, apparently, judging by the modistes and milliners that arrived, en masse, that afternoon. Sophie escaped that, as well as the argument that had begun between them over a particular pair of slippers, by asking Ann's driver to deliver her to Upper Moreland Street.

As the carriage rolled past Regent's Park, a well of disappointment bubbled up in her. She had found Caleb Hamilton so very appealing, more appealing than any man she had met in the last dozen years. He had seemed kind, far too kind, to be the man she had heard about yesterday. Part of her refused to believe the rumor.

Nancy was delighted to have her return and proudly showed her about the house, sharing what she knew about the current residents and reluctantly relating the troubles she was having with the bookkeeping. "Never had a mind for numbers," she admitted dolefully. Sophie offered to look them over, and with only a cursory review, could see that Nancy was struggling with the upkeep for the house.

"I don't understand," she remarked as she looked through the ledger. "I had understood Lady Kettering sought donations for the upkeep."

"Aye, that she does," Nancy readily agreed. "But the Whitney-Dane school takes a good amount of her time, and nowadays, most of the donations come in the form of hard goods, not coin." She laughed, shaking her head. "Honestly, we've more gowns than would clothe an entire village!"

"What do you mean?"

"Some of them are used. But most are much too fine for the gels here. They've no need of a ball gown, not with their lot in life."

"Ball gown?" Sophie asked, confused.

Nancy nodded. "Come on then, have a look."

She took Sophie to a small room on the third floor that was almost bursting at the seams with gowns, hats, slippers, and reticules, all made of the finest fabrics. Some of the garments were finer than anything Sophie had seen in any corner of the world. She wondered aloud why ladies of the *ton* would part with such fine clothing, to which Nancy chuckled.

"I rather imagine they can't fasten a single button any longer." She laughed, picked up a pink silk gown. "Some of them come to us actually torn at the seams."

Enthralled by the sheer number of gowns, Sophie picked up a pale yellow walking dress and held it up to her. It looked an almost perfect fit and was much more becoming than the gray one she was wearing. *Gray.* Why on earth had she commissioned such a drab gown?

She glanced at Nancy from the corner of her eye; Nancy smiled knowingly. "Well then, go on with you. Try it if you'd like—so have we all."

As Sophie discarded her clothing and donned the yellow gown—oh, it was lovely, truly lovely—an idea came to her. The women of Upper Moreland Street might not have practical use for these gowns, but she would wager there was a class of women in London who would. While only members of the Quality could afford garments as fine as these, there was a whole class of moderately wealthy families in London who aspired to the ranks of the Quality. She had seen a dress shop or two on High Street and absently wondered if perhaps she and Nancy might sell the gowns to those proprietors, who in turn could sell them, secondhand, to their clientele. Or perhaps hire a bit of space at Covent Garden for the purpose. Whatever the gowns might earn could be put in the coffers for the upkeep of the house.

When Sophie finally bid Nancy a good afternoon—wearing the yellow walking dress—the idea had firmly taken root.

She walked to the corner of Essex Street, intent on finding a hack to return her to Bedford Square, but the image of Caleb Hamilton danced in her mind's eye, just as it had all day. She tried to shake it off; it was ridiculous to pursue this little fantasy. Of course she had no intention of taking him up on his offer to see the house he was building, not now, not after what she had heard. It was impossible to think to meet him again, even if she did imagine him pacing impatiently at the pond, waiting for her . . . But had she not heard from her sister's own mouth the man's reputation with ladies, not to mention the possibility that he was a bona fide scoundrel? Had she not demeaned her family name once before consorting in a similar manner?

It was a preposterous, disastrous notion.

She shifted her weight to one hip, tapped her foot impatiently.

After all, Caleb Hamilton was most certainly an imposter of some sort—everyone said so.

The hack appeared around the bend in the road, and Sophie raised her arm to catch the driver's attention.

And he could very well be a diabolic fiend.

The hack coasted to a stop alongside her. "Where to, mu'um?" the driver asked.

He was undoubtedly a scoundrel of the first order, Sophie thought, and dug in her reticule for a crown. "Regent's Park, please!" she said as she handed him the coin, and promptly marveled at how those words could spring from her lips without any conscious thought at all. But there they were, hanging between her and the driver. Too late to take them back now, wasn't it? With a defiant shrug, Sophie climbed into the hack.

The men were working on the house across the pond, but there was no sign of Mr. Hamilton. Of course not. He had only been toying with her, so what did she care if he was working or not? Sophie sat stiffly on her wrought iron bench, her reticule on her lap. She looked down at the watch pinned to her breast for what must have been the hundredth time only to discover that a mere quarter of an hour had passed since she had reached the pond.

Then again, perhaps something had detained him—he had said he would come round. Just because a man was a known swindler didn't mean he wouldn't keep his word, did it? Perhaps he had forgotten. Perhaps he never meant to come at all, had merely invited her to see his house for want of something better to say. After all, *she* had brought it up. Surely he didn't mean—

"Aha! I hoped you would come!"

His voice instantly sent a wave of delight through her. Sophie turned so quickly that her bonnet slipped, but she hardly realized it, because Caleb Hamilton had snatched the very breath from her lungs.

Oh, but he was magnificent. He was wearing a navy riding coat, tight buckskin trousers, and an irrepressible smile, and Sophie could scarcely take her eyes from him. *All* of him.

The sudden and abrupt image of a woman on each of his arms popped into her mind's eye. *Scoundrel,* she reminded herself in an attempt to cool the heat that was beginning to build, and straightened her bonnet.

"A jolly good day, Miss Dane. How pleased I am that you could come."

"G-good day, Mr. Hamilton," she replied tightly, and swallowed hard. *Oh really, do try not to act the ninny for once, will you?*

"You've not been here long, have you? I was detained longer than customary."

"Ah, no. No, I only just arrived."

"Splendid," he said, and cheerfully plopped himself down beside her on the bench.

Sophie shifted an inch away from him.

"Might I say you look quite fetching, Miss Dane. What a lovely color is your gown—its suits you very well."

That caught her off guard—no one ever complimented her clothing. And the fact that she had practically filched it from a poorhouse only made her that much more self-conscious. She was already sitting so rigidly that the small of her back was beginning to ache. "Thank you, sir."

"I give you my word I'll not take your reticule if you'd like to set it aside."

She looked at him curiously.

He nodded to her lap. "You seem to be holding on to it for dear life."

Sophie immediately set the thing aside, but then did not know what to do with her hands. After a moment of awkwardness, she folded them primly in her lap.

"Miss Dane, if you would rather I leave you—"

"No!" *Marvelous. Why don't you go ahead and fling yourself at his feet, then?* Sophie forced a laugh, and the amused sparkle in his green eyes set off another sweet wave of pure longing through her.

Bloody hell. Her attempts at feigning disinterest were ridiculously inept. If anything, what she had heard about him had only made her that much more curious. He just did not seem the sort to stoop to swindle.

She sighed. "You must forgive me, Mr. Hamilton. I am not in the habit of meeting people I've only just met—in the park I mean—and I find that I am rather . . . well, there isn't a word for it really, but I *would* like to see your house, as it seems to be a very fine house, and I am rather fascinated with it, so I thought, there is really little harm, is there? No, don't answer . . . I am just . . . oh my, I think I am rambling on a bit . . ."

Mr. Hamilton placed his hand on top of the two she held in a death grip and squeezed kindly. "I do believe I understand, Miss Dane. Perhaps if we go on about the business of seeing it, we'll both feel a bit more at ease, do you think?"

"Oh *yes,* I think," she said and sighed with relief, unnoticing of his smile of amusement.

He stood up, gallantly offered his arm. They walked slowly, in silence, to the main path that led around the pond and to the construction site. Sophie was acutely aware of his body next to hers—he was at least a full head taller, perhaps as much as an inch or two over six feet. His legs were quite long and muscular, and his hands looked as if they could hold the world in their rough palms.

These things she noticed from the corner of her eye, in the midst of a heat whorling inside her. She desperately thought of something to say, she hoped something clever and witty, and realizing that she had no such thing to say, blurted, "Might I ask your occupation, Mr. Hamilton?"

She instantly regretted her choice.

"I am in the business of building railroads. Have you seen one?"

What she knew of railroads and the controversy around them could be summarized in a single word: *Nothing.* "Ah, no . . . but I saw a locomotive once." At least she thought it was a locomotive.

"Indeed?" he asked, brightening noticeably. "And where might that have been? Leeds?"

"Brussels."

"Brussels, truly? How interesting. What did you think of it?"

"What did I think of it?"

"The locomotive," he said, and paused in his walking to hear her answer.

What did she think of it? It was big, it was black. "It was b— . . . There appears to be an awful lot of dissatisfaction with the railroad, doesn't there?" she asked, wincing inwardly at the boldness of her question.

He blinked. Then he laughed. "Indeed there does, Miss Dane. And what do you make of it all?"

Well here she was then, the proverbial fish out of water. Did she *have* an opinion? "I . . . I really don't

know enough to have formed an opinion, Mr. Hamilton.
I have heard complaint that it will mar the countryside."

He nodded thoughtfully.

"But then again, I suppose it must be quite an efficient form of travel."

"Yes, it is," he said eagerly. "The speed with which
people and goods can be moved could mean a whole new
era for the nation's commerce. And travel. As one who
travels, surely you can appreciate the convenience."

She pondered that, nodding slowly.

"Do you travel often?" he asked, motioning them to
proceed ahead.

"I do, actually. I am the companion of a Frenchwoman, and it is her pleasure to travel quite frequently."

"Ah, splendid! What places have you seen, then?"

"Italy. And Portugal, then Spain. Italy again, then on
to Vienna, Stockholm—"

"Good Lord, Miss Dane," he exclaimed with a laugh.
"I thought that perhaps you had been all the way to
Paris, but Stockholm? Vienna? Fascinating! What is the
most interesting of them, do you think?"

How he did it, she couldn't fathom, but Sophie fell
into an easy discussion of her time abroad, and as it happened, he had been to many of the same locations. It
amazed her how easily the conversation flowed between
them. He seemed genuinely interested in what she was
saying, at least as much as she was interested in him. He
never took his eyes from her, smiled genuinely, and by
the time they reached the site of his house, they were
laughing with one another about the peculiarities of the
Spaniards, as if they had been friends for weeks instead
of minutes.

Mr. Hamilton was eager to show her the house he was
building. He walked her around through the rough wood
frames, painting the different rooms of his house with his
hands, pointing out where he intended to put different
amenities. His enthusiasm was contagious—Sophie could

actually *see* his house as he talked, could envision the splendor of it. It would obviously be a grand home, and it was just as obvious that Mr. Hamilton was very proud of the house as well as the fact that he was building it with his own hands.

When they had at last finished the tour, they took a leisurely stroll around the other side of the pond to the wrought iron bench where they had first met. After Sophie assured him she was quite capable of reaching home on her own—he was adamant in his desire to see her there—he finally relented, took her hand in his, and smiled as he leaned over it and kissed the back of her hand. A fire instantly scorched her arm.

"Thank you, Miss Dane, for a perfectly lovely afternoon. I have not enjoyed myself so completely in some time."

Lovely hardly began to describe how Sophie felt at the moment, and she cast him what she knew was a perfectly silly smile.

"I suppose it rather bold of me, but would I be so fortunate as to have the pleasure of your company again?" he asked, letting go her hand. "On the morrow, perhaps?"

She shouldn't, she really shouldn't—one afternoon with a scoundrel was quite enough, wasn't it? She could not be thinking to continue this, no matter how much she had enjoyed herself—it was disastrous. Not to mention pointless. And imbecilic, if not downright dangerous. "I would like that very much, sir," she said, smiling like an idiot.

"Marvelous! I look forward to our meeting then, Miss Dane. Very much so." He stood for a moment, looking at her, seeming to take in the features of her face before he lifted his hand to the brim of his hat. "Good day then," he said, and stepped away.

"Good day, Mr. Hamilton."

She waited until he had disappeared around the bend in the path, watching the powerful stride of his muscular legs as he walked. When she could no longer see him, Sophie practically skipped in the opposite direction.

It had been a splendid day, an absolutely glorious one, and while a small voice inside her head told her it was foolishness to pursue this any further, she could hardly wait for night to fall and morning to come so she could return to the park.

Which is precisely what she did the next afternoon, having heard enough of Honorine ramble on about Will and Ian, and having received a note from Ann that her modiste would have the gown delivered by Tuesday afternoon, in the unlikely event last minute alterations were needed. *Which* gown Ann had selected was unknown to her, and she might have protested loudly—but as it stood, she could only think about the handsome Mr. Caleb Hamilton and their scheduled meeting.

She arrived at the usual time, wearing a plain brown gown that was so dull she had sought one of Honorine's many scarves to brighten it up. In her basket, she had packed a delicious *pâtè de foie gras* she had learned to make in Paris, a wheat *brot* she had learned in Stockholm, and a selection of Italian olives Honorine had carried for the last four years and would never realize were missing. She fairly flew to the park, not allowing herself even a moment to think of her folly. His company made her feel giddy and light; it was as if she were walking about in a happy dream. She was not Sophie Dane, she was a woman with desires and hopes who knew what she wanted—and that most decidedly was *not* Sophie.

Much to her great delight . . . and truthfully, her great relief . . . Mr. Hamilton arrived at his usual time, proclaimed her radiant, and took an immediate interest in her basket. Sophie explained she had made the contents; he looked quite surprised by that, but was eager to sample everything. They selected a spot under a weeping willow tree, where Mr. Hamilton spread his coat for her to sit. Mr. Hamilton ate every last bite of everything she offered him, then proclaimed her the cleverest of all women for having learned such culinary talents.

After they finished the meal, he propped himself against the weeping willow and spoke easily of how he had come to invest in the rail system with what he had inherited from his mother's estate. He said he was in London to visit his father, whom he had not seen in more than one year. He did not offer anything further, for which Sophie was very glad. She did not want to let on that she knew anything about him, not yet, and least of all, that he was purportedly an imposter. She would cross that bridge when she came to it.

In turn, he asked her about herself, and she spoke more than she had in ages, telling him more about her travels, artfully skipping many details before her life with Honorine. And while Caleb recognized her family name, he did not appear to know of her scandal, for which Sophie was ecstatically thankful.

They parted company more wistfully than before, with a promise to meet again. And meet they did, every day that week. Sophie told no one of her meetings in the park, and the irony was not lost on her that she was, once again, sneaking behind her family's back to meet a man. Yet she did not dare breathe a word, lest they attempt to stop her from coming to the park. She needed this, needed the secret sweetness of it, the sunlight he was forcing into her life. Honestly, she did not care where this growing infatuation took her—she was, quite simply, living for the beauty of the moment.

She so enjoyed Caleb's companionship. For the first time in years—her lifetime, really—she felt truly at ease. They laughed easily with one another, and sometimes it seemed there was so much that they had in common, she felt as if she had known him all her life. They liked the same literature, the same music composers. They both preferred country living to life in London, both professed a profound dislike of singing at supper parties.

She believed he was someone to whom she might say anything without fear of retribution, a man who valued friendship as much as she, but privacy, too. He possessed many attributes she wished *she* had, and all the characteristics of a man she thought she would never know.

Moreover, with each day that passed, Sophie felt herself becoming more and more physically attracted to him. He made her blood rush hot when he smiled, made her skin turn to fire when he casually touched her. She could not remember being so physically affected in all her life, but this man, he seemed to seep through her skin and consume her imagination. She dreamed of lovemaking, would watch his big hands and imagine them on her body, watch him laugh and imagine his mouth on her . . . *all* of her. She stole glimpses of his hips, his legs, would wonder whimsically how lovely it might be to feel him deep inside her, moving in time to the rhythm of life.

Sophie was not the only one experiencing such a profound connection. Caleb felt it, too, stronger than he had ever felt anything in his life. He asked one day, as they strolled through the gardens of Regent's Park, if they might address each other by their given names, to which she readily agreed. He discovered she had a wonderful sense of humor, and together they laughed about everything and nothing. Each time she left him, she took a little bit more of him with her, and left him marveling at what he believed was a heartfelt bond between them.

In truth, he had never had a relationship like this with a woman—or a man, for that matter. His life as the bastard child of a wealthy viscount had left him with few acquaintances that were not repelled by his status; even fewer who were not ashamed to call him friend. As a result, he had spent a lonely youth and a rather solitary existence for a grown man, answering his physical needs at brothels, maintaining nothing more than superficial ties, and always moving about, particularly now, what with his interest in the burgeoning railroad.

But Sophie was very different. She was guileless, artless, and seemed to be genuinely interested in him.

They spent a lot of time at his house, inspecting the construction as it was completed. She asked him several questions and seemed genuinely engrossed in the various methods of construction he was employing, listening carefully as he explained them. She also offered her opinion on the more aesthetic aspects when he asked, and much to his delight, Caleb discovered they had similar tastes in such things as furnishings and wall dressings. It was Sophie who suggested a window in the morning room, remarking that the rising sun always made her feel quite rejuvenated. And, she had added, blushing slightly, a window on the east wall had the added benefit of allowing him to see the pond where they had first met. That was enough to make him seriously consider the improvement.

One afternoon, they wandered idly through the ballroom that was nearing completion. The only thing that remained was the frieze moldings and painting. Caleb watched Sophie as she strolled into the middle of the room, and with hands clasped behind her back, she gazed up at the ceiling where a workman had begun to lay a papier-mâché frieze of grapevines. As she stood in the center of the room, he imagined her in the completed ballroom, wearing a gown fit for a queen, smiling that genuinely sweet smile as guests swirled about her in time to the music of a waltz. The image was so real, he could almost hear the music, and impulsively, he crossed the room and grabbed her hand.

"What?" she asked, laughing.

"Dance?"

"Dance?" She laughed again as he began to hum a waltz. "All right then," she said with a smile, "make me sway, sir, if you can."

He twirled her from one end of the room to the other, artfully avoiding ladders and buckets. The fit of her in his arms was perfect, the feel of her divine. And as he looked down, she gazed up at him with eyes that seemed like endless pools, reflecting his own hot passion back to him. It was a raging thing now, a desperation to touch her, to taste her lips. Caleb slowed the waltz, coming to a standstill in the middle of the room, unable to take his eyes from her. There was something about this woman that had slipped under his skin and had lodged there, could not be shaken loose. His hand drifted up her ribcage, to the side of her breast; she drew a small, uneven breath. His gaze dropped to her lips, ripe and full, and before he could stop himself, he bent his head to brush those lips with his own.

Her body seemed to rise up to meet him and melt into his embrace all at once. He felt her hand go round his neck, felt her breast press against his chest and hand. He tightened his hold on her, molded her plump lips with his mouth and teeth, savoring the sweet taste of her with his tongue. Sophie pressed against him and sighed, opening her mouth beneath his, inviting him into her warmth. He boldly swept into her mouth; her breath shot down his body like lightning, inflaming every fiber, burning every place they touched. He felt himself go hard, impulsively dropped his hand to her hips and pressed her against the rigid length of his cock. *God, he wanted her.* Wanted her *there,* on the muslin cloth that protected the floor. Wanted her so badly that his body ached with it, ached like he had not since he was a boy.

Ached so much that he finally forced himself to lift his head. He gazed down at her, amazed that her dark eyes seemed, impossibly, even deeper. Her lips were slightly swollen from the passionate kiss they had just shared, enticing him further. With a sigh, he brought his hands to the sides of her face, kissed her forehead, then caressed the length of her arms with his hands. Oh yes, he wanted her, as badly as he had ever wanted a woman . . . but he had no *right* to want her. Not like this. He would not charm his way into her petticoats as he was accustomed to doing. She deserved so much more than that.

So much better than he.

She seemed to read his mind. "I should go," she whispered, and he nodded. She smiled, lifted her hand, and pressed it against his cheek. "Caleb," she murmured, as if testing his name on her lips. She came up on her toes, softly kissed the corner of his mouth, then glided down again, stepping away from his embrace.

"Good-bye," she said, moving unsteadily toward the door, turned halfway around so she could see him as she left.

Words escaped him; he said nothing, just watched her disappear through the door, then leaned heavily against a ladder, unnerved by that kiss and the raw sensations it had dredged up in him. Raw *need*. Bloody hell, he had long ago made a pact with himself, had sworn he would never fall in love—what point was there in it? He had no name to offer a woman, especially a woman as pure and gracious as Sophie. *What in bloody hell was he doing, then?*

He turned away from the door, stared at the blank wall before him. He had come here with a purpose, and that was *not* to go chasing after some blue blood. He was not of her class—she was too far above him to ever make this real, and he would do himself a world of good if he focused on his reason for being in London at all.

Caleb shook his head, tried to dissipate the fog in which she had left him, but it was no use. He forced himself to make his way to the morning room, where he found a hammer and some tenpenny nails. He picked up a piece of molding and began to hammer the feel of her body from his mind.

The following day was Wednesday, the day of the dreaded Hamilton supper party, from which Sophie had not been able to extract herself.

On Wednesday, Caleb did not come to the pond.

Sophie sat for two hours on the wrought iron bench, watching the men across the pond as they worked on Caleb's house and checking the small watch pinned to her breast almost constantly. Each minute that passed without sight of Caleb was longer than the last. At first she told herself that he was merely late. Soon, she was reminding herself that he had not said with all certainty he *would* come today. *But he came every day.*

Surely he would come today, especially after the kiss they had shared.

When it was apparent that he was not coming, Sophie mentally reviewed a list of reasons why he had not come—he had been unavoidably detained, he was ill. He had fallen from his horse and died. She tried very hard to ignore a little voice that sounded remarkably like Ann, a voice which told her that he could very well be an imposter, a scoundrel, a blackguard with little regard for her feelings. She had fantasized the connection between them, had attributed feelings and meaning to his word and kiss that were not there. It certainly would not be the first time, would it?

Yet even though she could not ignore the voice, she still could not believe it. The Caleb Hamilton she knew did not have it in him to be so callously deceiving. And as she gathered up her things and took one last look at the house across the pond, she very firmly reminded herself that she had no right to expect him to come. She had no right to expect anything of him at all.

No right, perhaps, but she thought of him every waking moment, impatient with the thoughts that cluttered

her mind that were *not* about him. He was never gone
from her thoughts, even for a moment, and she had absolutely no idea how she would endure the Hamilton
supper party tonight, especially now, especially since he
had not come.

Chapter Six

A T PRECISELY TWO minutes past nine o'clock, Trevor Hamilton leaned against the corridor wall and watched as Lady Sophie Dane entered the foyer of his father's home and handed her bonnet to the footman. She smoothed her hands down the front of her gown—a rather sedate shade of blue, he thought—and then nervously clasped them together as she quickly took in her surroundings.

Beside her, the Frenchwoman was chattering away as if the footman were her host. She was, in Trevor's opinion, an insufferable woman. As she had called on his father almost every day this week, he had chance to hear firsthand the foolishness with which she filled Ian's head—not to mention the viscount. She was the type of woman who should be reined in, who could learn a bit of respect for those on whom she imposed.

She could learn to be more like Lady Sophie.

Ah, Lady Sophie. It was interesting to see her after all these years, he thought, as she calmly took the bonnet the Frenchwoman thrust at her and handed it to the footman. Her subdued, demure demeanor appealed to him. Truthfully, he could scarcely remember the scared little rabbit that had caused such a delicious scandal all those years ago—she had been almost as unnoticeable as the umbrella stand by which she now stood. Amazing that, with a few years, she had become so disimpassioned, the epitome of quiet grace. Yes, *this* Lady Sophie appealed to him a great deal. In fact, she was the first woman to have interested him since Elspeth had died two years ago. Quiet, unassuming. Obedient. Rich.

Trevor sauntered forward.

Sophie glanced up as he approached, noticed the way in which he looked at her and felt her cheeks color instantly. As Hamilton reached them, he paused, said a curt hello to Honorine, then turned fully to Sophie. She very reluctantly offered her hand. He took it too eagerly.

"Thank you for coming."

"Oh," she said with a nervous little laugh that she despised, "how kind of you to invite us. Madame Fortier and I . . . we are very grateful of your hospitality."

"Very nice!" chirped Honorine. "And your *papa* . . . Where is he?"

His smile seemed almost forced as he shifted his gaze to Honorine. "Father is in the green salon."

Honorine's face lit in a wreath of smiles. "Ah! I shall wish him *bonsoir,*" she announced, and started off down the corridor as if she owned the house, leaving Sophie quite alone with Hamilton.

She smiled sheepishly as he placed her hand in the crook of his arm. "I look forward to introducing you around. You may recognize a face or two."

"How lovely," she muttered. *Bloody marvelous,* she thought. As they moved down the corridor, her stomach turned to knots; she felt conspicuously foolish and out of place. Even her gown seemed all wrong—it was a peculiar shade of blue and rather plain, save the overly colorful embroidery along the hem. She would have preferred something a little less matronly, but as usual, her choices had been made for her. This was an all too familiar sense of discomfort—she felt trussed up like a Christmas goose,

as if she were once again on parade before a dozen potential suitors. The only difference between tonight and
nights just like it eight years past was the attention
Hamilton was paying her. Was she imagining things, or
had his lips lingered too long on her hand? Was he truly
looking at her in a way that seemed to burn a hole right
through her? She had seen men look at Honorine that
way—but *never* her.

She stole a glimpse of her escort from the corner of
her eye. With his hand protectively covering hers, a little
smile on his lips, he actually looked quite pleased to be
with her. And as if to prove it, he suddenly paused just
outside the door Honorine had swept into, motioned the
footman to shut it, and turned to face her fully, stepping
so close that she could see the intricate folds of his cra-
vat. "I am very pleased you have come, Lady Sophie," he
said, his breath warm on her lips, "*Very* pleased. You are
different now, I think. Grown up, mature. I am sure you
must understand how a man may desire a woman like
you."

Sophie instantly recoiled backward, bumping into the
wall behind her. Hamilton smiled at her discomposure
and straightened, nodding at the footman who manned
the door. Her head was spinning; she hardly noticed the
footman push the double walnut doors open and step
aside. The implication behind Hamilton's words was inconceivable to her; all of her instincts told her to beware—

But all that was lost the moment she caught sight of
the more than two dozen heads swiveling as one in her
direction. Her knees betrayed her immediately as he led
her across the threshold and into that sea of faces. Some,
she recognized, others blurred with faded memories that
struggled to revive themselves in her mind. As Hamilton
escorted her deeper into the room, some of them leaned
into their companions, whispering.

She knew it instantly—her scandal was not forgotten,
not for a bloody moment. Her face felt hot; Sophie won-

dered if she might possibly even faint as Hamilton introduced her to Lord and Lady Pritchet.

As he led her on to the next guest, she surreptitiously tried to find Honorine in the crowd. *Where was Honorine?* Her stomach was churning furiously now as Hamilton pulled her deeper into the pit of vipers—*"You recall Lady Sophie Dane? She's been abroad."*—the knowing smiles, the expressions of condescension were suffocating, but there was no escape, only more guests. Sophie was acutely aware that they all whispered their casual slander about her, eyeing her critically, no doubt trying to detect a crack in the facade, perhaps even hoping she might entertain them by crumbling beneath the weight of her shame before their very eyes.

By the time they reached the back of the room, Sophie was numb.

"I'd like to introduce you to my father, if you please," Hamilton said.

Mute, she nodded. At least she would have the pleasure of meeting the object of Honorine's unabashed love.

Hamilton turned toward a small alcove. A footman moved away; Sophie caught sight of Honorine's colorful skirts and felt a sense of relief. But as she moved around Hamilton, her smile faded in her confusion.

Lord Hamilton was seated in a chair with wheels designed for the infirm. One hand was curled unnaturally around a pen in what looked like a death grip; the other was covered with a lap rug, which also concealed his legs, leaving only one foot to protrude at an awkward angle.

And he was smiling up at Honorine.

"Sofia! You will try this champagne, *non?*" Honorine trilled upon seeing Sophie, and snatched two flutes from the tray of a passing footman, as if nothing were amiss, as if she fell in love with frail men every day. They had said Lord Hamilton was *ill*, not incapacitated!

Sophie took the flute as Hamilton leaned down to his

father, very nearly drinking the whole thing in an effort to hide her shock. She looked to Honorine for some explanation, but the woman was lost in Lord Hamilton.

"Lady Sophie, you remember my father, do you not?"

Sophie dragged her gaze from Honorine to Lord Hamilton; he had shifted in his mobile chair and was looking up at her. "Of course!" she said brightly, and was suddenly struck with the indecision of what to do with her hand. *Dear God, did she offer her hand?*

Lord Hamilton answered that dilemma by extending a wobbling hand to her. She instantly shoved her flute at Honorine and took the man's hand in hers. "IT IS A PLEASURE TO SEE YOU AGAIN, MY LORD."

"There is no need for this shouting," Honorine said matter-of-factly.

"L-Lady S-Sophie," he stuttered. "A p-pleasure to see you."

"Thank you," she murmured self-consciously as he withdrew his hand from hers.

"How f-fortunate you are t-to accompany M-Madame F-Fortier."

"Yes, indeed."

Honorine beamed like a Yuletide candle. "Monsieur Hamilton," she sighed like a girl, *"merveilleux!"*

All right, the woman had finally gone round the bend and lost her foolish French mind. Hamilton was undoubtedly thinking the very same thing, for Sophie could feel the tension emanating from his body as he presented his back to Honorine. "My father is actually much improved since suffering the seizure," he said, almost apologetically as Honorine leaned down to whisper something in the viscount's ear.

"I had no idea," Sophie responded, still flustered. "When did it happen?"

"Several weeks past. Actually, it seems rather long ago now." He smiled thinly, looked at the mantel clock. "Ah, it is almost the supper hour, Lady Sophie. If you will excuse me, I would see to it that everything has been arranged." He bowed politely and stepped away.

Honorine tugged at the sleeve of her gown. "You see? This supper, it is pleasant," she said cheerfully.

Pleasant? She thought this was *pleasant*? Sophie dragged her gaze from the crowded room to stare at Honorine in utter disbelief. Flashing a quick smile at Lord Hamilton, she grabbed Honorine's arm and pulled her aside. "Have you lost your mind?" she whispered hotly. "This is the man to whom, just yesterday, you declared your undying devotion?"

Taken aback, Honorine blinked. *"Oui,"* she said simply, and saints above, the woman actually *blushed*.

"Do you think that you might have at least *mentioned* his infirmity? God, Honorine, what are you thinking?"

That remark only served to get Honorine's back up. One hand went to her hip; she frowned darkly, and Sophie was suddenly and keenly aware that everyone in the room seemed to be watching them. "You speak as if he is nothing!" she snapped. "This . . . this *infirmité*, as you call it, it has only his body!"

"And madness has yours," Sophie muttered under her breath, glancing covertly around them.

Oh, wonderful, here approached more good tidings.

Lady Pritchet was making her way toward them, her daughter Charlotte in tow. Sophie remembered Charlotte as someone who had suffered the fate she most assuredly would have met had she not eloped. As no one of suitable caliber was interested in making Charlotte a wife, she had, finally, in her twenty-sixth year, been taken off the shelf and married to a Scottish baron. When Sophie made her debut, it was well known that Charlotte was the man's wife in name only; he apparently kept to Scotland and his mistress, and Charlotte to her mother.

As they approached, Sophie quickly discarded the argument over Lord Hamilton and murmured to Honorine a cautionary *"en garde."*

Lady Pritchet came to an abrupt halt in front of them and eyed Honorine openly and critically. One thing was certain—the woman's bitter countenance had not changed even a whit in all these years.

Shifting her pinched gaze to Sophie, Lady Pritchet practically sneered. "Lady Sophie," she said, as she took in her gown. "You've been abroad."

"Yes I have, Lady Pritchet, in the company of Madame Fortier."

"Bonsoir," sang Honorine.

"Bonsoir," responded Charlotte with a smile.

"Perhaps you had opportunity to take in the sights of Rome? I found the Colosseum to be quite grand," Lady Pritchet remarked, now eyeing Honorine.

"We were actually longer in Venice," Sophie clarified.

"Venice?" asked a woman behind them.

Honestly, could this night possibly become any more monstrous? Apparently so—Miss Melinda Birdwell had seen fit to join them.

"Truly?" drawled Melinda, arching one sculpted brow over the other. "I've heard Venice is quite decadent."

"Ooh, oui, oui," Honorine readily agreed with a little laugh and a wink for Melinda. *"Beaucoup décadent."*

A tiny mewl of surprise escaped Charlotte; Lady Pritchet's sneer deepened. But Melinda merely smiled. "We so look forward to hearing tales of your *décadent* adventure over supper."

All right, then, there it was—this *would* be the longest night of Sophie's life.

In the end, however, she couldn't be entirely certain what was the worst part of the whole affair. The awful supper in which everyone around her attempted to ask— under the guise of polite conversation, of course—about her ignoble past? *Have you by chance seen Sir William? Oh, I suppose he is still in Spain?* Or Honorine's peculiar and unabashed adoration of Lord Hamilton? Or perhaps Hamilton's seeming fixation with *her*?

In between her attempts to fend off the many intrusive

questions put to her, Sophie caught herself exchanging several looks with Trevor Hamilton. His smile, she noticed, was rather infectious, and she began to feel a little self-conscious of it. Impossible though it was, the man was actually flirting with her! How terribly ironic that was—eight years ago, Sophie would have delivered her entire fortune for just one favorable glance from Hamilton.

Now, it made her feel strange—his attentions were too curious, too uncharacteristic for someone who had once been one of the *ton's* most eligible bachelors. And it didn't help, naturally, that she could not push the image of Caleb from her mind's eye. *Why hadn't he come today?* She could imagine him here, much more comfortable than she, sharing a secret jest with her over some of the things being said, conversing with the others.

But it was Honorine's peculiar and unabashed esteem of Lord Hamilton that fascinated Sophie the most. Even though she could clearly see now that her initial assessment of his ability had been too harsh, he was still hardly the sort of man to whom Honorine was typically drawn.

Not only was Honorine drawn to him, she was making a scene.

She doted on him over supper, monopolized his attention. It was painfully obvious that no one seated around the table could take his eyes from her. Sophie desperately wanted to stand from her seat, walk the length of the table to where Honorine sat cheerfully babbling with Lord Worthington and Lord Hamilton, lean over her shoulder, and inform her that she was behaving like an imbecile. Unfortunately, she could hardly do such a thing without making the scene worse.

The minutes stretched into hours.

After supper, when the ladies had at last retired to the drawing room while the men had their port, Sophie attempted to put Honorine off to one side where it would be inconvenient for her to engage in conversation with anyone. She might very well have succeeded had not the very affable Mrs. Churchton begun a discourse on the secrets of the Hamilton family, beginning with what sounded like a very unhappy marriage between Lord and Lady Hamilton, and ending with her conjecture that the rumors of an illegitimate son were true.

Sophie's heart clutched at the mention of Caleb; Melinda pounced on Mrs. Churchton's remark with gusto.

"Do tell, Mrs. Churchton!" she exclaimed, smiling conspiratorially at those around her. "I've often heard it said there was a bastard son, but I never thought it true!"

"Oh, it is quite true," Mrs. Churchton sniffed with much authority. "Lord Hamilton spent several years abroad. They say the mother is French."

Everyone turned to Mrs. Churchton; Sophie, too, inched to the edge of her seat.

"It's been thirty years or more, but when Lady Hamilton was with child, Lord Hamilton took to the Continent, where he remained until little Trevor was three years or so. Only then did he return, though I daresay they never reconciled, not really. Lady Hamilton died a very lonely woman, I assure you."

"But has anyone ever *seen* this illegitimate son?" Melinda pressed. "Could he possibly be the same man who has recently appeared in town claiming to be the illegitimate son?"

"I wouldn't know," Mrs. Churchton responded as she casually plumped the ringlets above her ears. "There are those who claim Lord Hamilton traveled to France twice yearly to see his bastard son. And there are others who insist that he was actually at home in the country during those periods. I daresay no one can say for certain who this man is, and it hardly matters any longer, does it? The poor viscount can't remember much a'tall, and physically, he is hardly more than an empty shell—"

"Do not speak this of him!" snapped Honorine, who had been uncharacteristically quiet up until that point.

Sophie clamped a warning hand down on Honorine's

wrist but she shook it off, startling Sophie with her abruptness and the fire suddenly blazing in her eyes. "This man, he hears your speech, he *sees* how you look to him! He is not dead; he lives and he breathes!"

That heated pronouncement was met with deadly quiet. But the silence hardly quelled Honorine's temper— if anything, it made her angrier. "Look at you!" she continued hotly. "How you sit in his home, eat his food, drink his wine, and still, you say such hateful things! *Mon Dieu!*"

"I beg your pardon, Madame Fortier," Mrs. Churchton said hoarsely. "I certainly did not intend to offend your sensibilities so greatly!"

"Of course not," said Melinda, turning smoothly in her seat to face Honorine with all superiority. "But you do not know Lord Hamilton, Madame Fortier. We have been acquainted with him for many years and we do not deceive ourselves. May the Lord have mercy on him, but he is a mere shadow of the man he once was."

"You are wrong," Honorine said low.

Sophie knew that voice, came instantly to her feet, and stepped in front of Honorine before she erupted. "It is indeed a tragedy," she said quickly, "but surely nothing on which we should dwell at the moment. Lady Sanderhill, I recall with great fondness your skill on the pianoforte. Would you be so kind to reacquaint us all with your talent?"

That woman blushed prettily, fussed a little with her collar as she stood. "I should be delighted," she said, and moved to the pianoforte, oblivious to the murderous look Melinda cast Honorine.

But both women had resumed their seats by the time the men rejoined them, and to all outward appearances seemed enraptured by the song Lady Sanderhill played. When Lord Sanderhill stood to join his wife in a duet, Sophie slipped to the far side of the room, away from the ever-watchful eyes of Melinda Birdwell.

Hamilton followed her.

He stood behind her, quietly leaning over her shoulder as the singers began, his spicy scent filling her nostrils.

"Lady Sophie, I should very much like to show you my father's gardens one day," he whispered. "He spent years building them and they are among the finest in all of London."

Caleb's likeness slipped into her mind, and a little shiver ran down Sophie's spine. *Where was he? Why hadn't he come?* "Perhaps one day," she whispered.

"I shall consider that a promise."

She couldn't help herself—Sophie glanced at him over her shoulder. His gaze boldly dipped to the low neckline of her gown, and Sophie felt the shiver again, only stronger than before, and shifted away from his pointed gaze. That gaze . . . she had experienced that gaze before. William Stanwood had looked at her like that, a sort of wolfish look. A thought that perhaps he was more like Stanwood than she knew flitted across her mind—and perhaps, like Stanwood, his interest was really in her bank account, not her breasts.

"Until then," he said, and she watched him move away, his hands clasped nonchalantly behind his back.

But Sophie quickly forgot her vague suspicion and thought of Caleb, wished Hamilton *were* Caleb, and her heart suddenly felt as if it weighed one hundred stone.

As the Sanderhills droned on with their cheerful little duet, she took a window seat, staring into the dark night that engulfed Bedford Square, her heart and mind full of Caleb.

In the middle of Bedford Square, Caleb flicked a cheroot to the path, ground it out with the heel of his boot as he idly watched Hamilton's guests through the enormous windows of the salon. From where he stood, he could see most of their activity and smiled to himself, imagining the agony of sitting through the duet that was being sung. There was a time he might have been jealous of the fine living to which Trevor was accustomed, but at the moment, he only wanted to know about his father.

He shifted his gaze once again to the window seat where Sophie sat staring so wistfully out over the square. He had not recognized her when she first appeared and had peered so forlornly out the window. But she had looked familiar, and he had risen from the bench on which he had passed the evening, walked slowly to the edge of the square to have a better look.

The recognition had unnerved him in a strange sort of way. Even though he knew she lived nearby, he had not realized, had not even thought that Sophie might be acquainted with his father, and certainly not his brother. The very idea made him oddly angry. He did not *want* her to know them, did not want her involved with them in any way. She was the treasure he had found in the park, the woman who had intrigued him above all others, and he did not want her anywhere near Trevor Hamilton.

Even more than that, his curiosity about her was now overwhelming. *Who was this woman, Sophie Dane?*

He had missed her today, more than he would have thought possible after such a short acquaintance, and certainly more than was reasonable in light of his recent attempts to force her from his mind. But he could still taste her, feel her in his arms. Could still feel the uncommonly strong desire to be touching her. Unfortunately, other issues had arisen that he could not avoid—Trevor's unexpected trip to the country park, to a racing meet, to be exact.

Caleb didn't know exactly what he thought he might discover in following Trevor—some clue as to his father's true condition, he supposed—but he had been overwhelmingly compelled when he had seen him leaving Bedford Square this morning, looking furtively about, as if he were trying to hide. Whatever Caleb had suspected, it had not been horse racing—honestly, he had thought it more sinister than that, given that Trevor had publicly and privately worked so hard to keep him from seeing his father.

But it had been nothing more than a gentleman's foray into a bit of sport, and Caleb would have sent word to Sophie somehow had he known, but by the time he realized how far they would go, it was too late.

He extracted another cheroot from his coat pocket and lit it. Drawing the smoke into his lungs, he glanced up at the bay window again, wished he could see her smile, that guileless, heartwarming smile. Wished even more fervently that he might kiss those unsmiling lips again.

And soon.

Chapter Seven

Sophie had not even finished her toilette the next day before Ann sailed in and plopped herself down on an overstuffed armchair. "Sophie, *Sophie*," she said with a smile. "I've heard already how Hamilton could not take his eyes from you last evening—you must tell me everything!"

The speed of rumor and innuendo among the *ton* had always amazed Sophie, but this was absurd. She snorted disdainfully and resumed the brushing of her long brown hair. "It was *scandalous*! There were not one dozen guests as he had assured me, but *two* dozen."

"Very amusing. Come on, then, tell me all!"

"All right." Sophie put down her brush. "If you must know, what transpired was a perfectly awful evening. Everyone looked at me as if I had been convicted of high treason. Melinda Birdwell did her best to unhinge me, and Honorine is absolutely besotted with Lord Hamilton! Need I go on?"

Ann sighed, drummed her fingers impatiently on the arm of the chair. "No one looked at you in any such way, Sophie. Your imagination is far too industrious."

Oh, righto, there it was—she had merely *imagined* everything.

"And Melinda Birdwell is hardly worth your consideration. That woman has the poise of a whale."

That, she could hardly argue.

"As for Madame Fortier"—Ann sighed heavily—"what can one do? But never mind all that!" she said, brightening again. "What of Hamilton?"

Sophie shook her head in bewilderment. "I don't pretend to understand it, but he *does* seem rather infatuated with me."

Ann's instant squeal of glee made Sophie groan; she abruptly stood and moved restlessly to the window, shaking her head. "No, no, Ann, this is *not* good! Honestly, this is Trevor Hamilton! He was the most sought after bachelor in Mayfair the year I made my debut and he scarcely noticed me then. Why now? Why after all that has happened? I cannot help but wonder what he means by it all. Is it my inheritance, do you think? Perhaps he has not heard there is hardly anything left of it after my divorce."

"Oh Sophie!" Ann exclaimed, instantly joining her at the window. She put her arm around Sophie's waist and rested her chin on her shoulder. "There is *much* for Mr. Hamilton to admire. You are entirely too critical of yourself. You're witty, and very clever. You've traveled extensively and seen quite a lot of the world. Why should he *not* admire you?"

"I should debate you on the list of my attributes, but I think the most glaring reason is my past, and as much as I would like to believe it were not true, and as much as I would like to hope that I am not ruined in the eyes of the *ton,* I cannot believe Mr. Hamilton would risk his good name or that of his son for an association with me."

That declaration drew only silence from Ann. Her arm fell away from Sophie's waist; she moved to the dressing table, idly fingered the bottles there. Sophie was absolutely right, and they both knew it.

The awkward silence between them was interrupted by the commotion of Honorine bursting into her dressing room, waving a paper in her hand. "Sophia! You must see this what I have!" she exclaimed. *"Bonjour,* Madame Annie!"

Ann did not respond; she seemed a bit distracted by Honorine's yellow-and-black-striped caftan that resembled a very large bumblebee.

Honorine waved the paper at Sophie again. "Do you see? A picnic! *J'adore* the picnic!" she said, clasping the paper to her breast. "I tell you this, Sofia, and you do not believe! Monsieur Hamilton, he favors you very well!"

Sophie was instantly on her feet; she snatched the paper from Honorine's hand and scanned the invitation with Ann craning to see over her shoulder.

It was a picnic, all right, in Regent's Park the following afternoon, and both she and Honorine had been invited.

"This is *marvelous!*" Ann cried gleefully.

"Oui, très bien!" Honorine eagerly agreed.

"Oh dear God," Sophie muttered, and falling onto the bench at her vanity, pressed her forehead against her palm.

She had no say in the response—"Madame Annie" and Honorine penned it instantly, then sent a grousing Roland to deliver it right away. No matter how much or loudly Sophie insisted she did not want to attend the picnic, Ann and Honorine turned a deaf ear, dismissing her discomfort as maidenly jitters.

Sophie spent a miserable afternoon in her rooms, alternately fretting about the blasted picnic and debating whether or not she should venture to Regent's Park as she did every day on the slim chance that Caleb might come again.

She understood, of course, that her fierce infatuation with Caleb Hamilton was unaccountable—after all, she hardly knew him, really. But she *did* feel a bond, felt it deeply in her bones. There was something between them that seemed right and natural and perfect—she could not believe it was only the eagerness of a lonely divorcée.

But he had not come yesterday, and that had stung her. Although she understood that any number of things might have detained him, it hurt nonetheless. Whatever the reason, she knew with all certainty that if he did not come to the park today, she would not be able to bear it.

So she did not go.

The next morning, she avoided the issue altogether by calling on Upper Moreland Street, dragging Roland and Fabrice in tow.

Naturally, she had debated appearing with the two Frenchmen, lest she ruin her budding friendship with Nancy. But they were two men she could trust, and the fact of the matter was, they had a wonderful eye when it came to clothing. They were frustrated modistes, she had decided, particularly because Honorine refused their considerable help.

The two had been rather suspicious when she told them of the outing, but curious as to what she was about, and bored with the happenings at *Maison de Fortier,* now that they had settled into some sort of unspoken arrangement with Lucie Cowplain, they donned their best coats and came along.

Nancy did not do a very good job of hiding her shock when Sophie introduced Fabrice and Roland to her, and seemed very apprehensive about showing them to the small attic room where the clothes were kept. But the moment they crossed the threshold, Fabrice let out a shriek and pounced on a china-blue silk gown. He held it up to himself, whirled around to Roland, and cried, *"Magnifique!"*

"Aye, I rather thought so myself," Nancy said.

Both men jerked around to her. In French, Roland said to Fabrice, "but she is perfect." Fabrice nodded. Together they advanced on Nancy, who, trapped behind the small door, had no means of escape. Yet she was smiling at her image in the mirror a half-hour later, admiring the elegant coif and gown in which Roland and Fabrice had dressed her.

When it became apparent to Sophie that they thought to dress themselves in the gowns next, she sent them on to a cobbler with a box of slippers to be repaired. They left chattering excitedly—something to do with a ball, she noted wearily.

She and Nancy sat in the tiny room on the third floor amid the donated clothing and sorted through a pile of slippers and shoes as Sophie told Nancy about the supper party, and the subsequent invitation to the picnic this afternoon.

She did not mention Caleb. He was her secret.

Nancy laughed heartily at her distress over Hamilton. "Ah, luv, why are you so determined to find ill will in your Mr. Hamilton? Perhaps he is wiser than you know."

"Meaning?" she demanded.

"Meaning," Nancy said with a look, "that perhaps he don't give a whit what the high and mighty society folk think. Perhaps he would judge his acquaintances by their good character."

Sophie snorted loudly to that, for which she received a withering look from Nancy.

With a sheepish shrug, she tossed another shoe aside. "All right then, what have we left?" she asked, changing the subject, and surveyed the room they had cluttered.

"The bonnets. Ah, but we'll sort through them in no time at all, we will. Where do you think to sell all these things?"

"I'm not certain," Sophie said. "We could sell them to a proprietor on High Street, but I rather believe we'd see a better result if we sold them ourselves. The only question is, where?"

"Covent Garden. We should do nicely there, I would think," Nancy offered.

"Yes, I thought of that, and I have the funds to construct the booth. But I must ask my brother to broker a lease agreement for it—he should not object. I will speak with him soon."

Satisfied with their plan, Sophie and Nancy finished putting the clothing in some order. It was early afternoon when Sophie bid her friend a good day—promising to return with Fabrice and Roland soon—and walked to the corner of Essex Street to wait for a hack.

She glanced at her watch; the Hamilton picnic would begin soon. She could, if she were of a mind, walk by the pond on her way to this blasted picnic. Perhaps he would be there. Perhaps he would be waiting for *her*.

Ridiculous! Men did not wait for her. Caleb Hamilton had enjoyed her company for a space of time, but it was over.

A hack appeared in the bend of Essex Street and pulled to the curb alongside her. "To Regent's Park," she called to the driver, and climbed in, busied herself with arranging her skirts as she waited for the hack to pull forward. But instead of moving, the door opened and someone came inside, landing heavily on the bench beside her and on her skirts.

Frowning lightly, Sophie glanced at the intruder from the corner of her eye—*Caleb!*

The shock of seeing him sitting beside her left her momentarily speechless; she simply could not comprehend how he could be in this hack, at this hour, in this part of London.

He grinned cheerfully.

And Sophie realized his thigh was pressed along the length of hers. The *full* length. She could feel the heat of his flesh through their clothing, spreading quickly, coursing along her spine. Heat inflamed her face; she abruptly looked down to hide it as she attempted to find her tongue.

"Yes, well, I suppose I deserve that."

"Deserve what?" she asked stiffly, amazed that she was able to say any thing at all.

"Your shoulder instead of your beautiful smile. You are angry with me."

"Angry?" She rolled her eyes, looked out the window. "Why on earth should I be angry?"

Caleb laughed, grasped her hand tightly in his. "Ah, then you *have* missed me!"

"I did *not* miss you—"

"You did!"

"I did not!"

"I missed you."

That shut her up. Catching her surprise in her throat, she stole a glance at him. He was holding a small nosegay. A nosegay! Where had *that* come from?

He held it out to her, his smile brightening.

What a handsome man he was . . . and she was keenly conscious of every fiber where they touched, the scent of leather and horse and faint cologne that clung to him. This was awful, completely wretched! Yes, but something had awakened in her, something that had lain dormant for far too long, burning her from the inside out and making her shiver with the heat of it.

The very base truth was that she longed for a man's touch, longed to be held, to be caressed, to be kissed again as he had kissed her. She looked down, to where his hand covered hers, his fingers tightly encased in leather gloves, long fingers that had undoubtedly pleasured a woman . . .

She suddenly pressed her palm to her cheek, jostling him in the process.

"Thank God, you are smiling—I was beginning to fear your mouth was permanently affixed in a frown."

Was she smiling? This was madness! She was aroused, could not ignore the feel of his leg or his arm against her, could not stop imagining his hand on her breast.

"How did you find me?" she asked as she reluctantly took the nosegay he offered and brought it to her nose.

"You wouldn't believe me if I told you—a bit of dumb luck, really. And now that you have ended my misery with that smile, I am desperate to know if you intend to walk about Regent's Park today."

"Desperate?"

"Yes, indeed, madam," he said earnestly. "I have been deprived of the pleasure of your company for two and one-half days now, and I am quite certain I shall expire if I am to be deprived of a full third."

"Deprived!" Sophie snorted at that.

"You don't believe me?"

"I believe you have been in your usual company, sir."

"My usual company? What do you mean?"

She squirmed a bit, shoved the nosegay to her face again. "You know very well what I mean . . . the company that you are rumored to keep. Particularly at night."

"At night," he echoed, sounding as if he were sorting out some puzzle. "I'm afraid I don't understand."

Sophie sighed, glanced heavenward. "The *ladies*," she insisted.

"Oh?" He sounded surprised. "Is *that* what is said about me?"

Honestly, now he sounded pleased!

Caleb laughed, grasped her hand. "Oh come now, there is only you, Sophie Dane. If there are rumors of others, it is nothing more than that—a rumor."

She frowned, sniffed the nosegay again. "I am not a schoolgirl."

"You are hardly that, I would agree. Really, if there were others, do you think I would spend every day with you in my house? Would I not drag scads of admirers through? No, there is only you, and I shall say again, if you deprive me of the pleasure of your company a third day, I will expire, I promise you."

Sophie couldn't help herself; she laughed. "You'll hardly expire, sir."

"How do you know? You won't want to chance it, I assure you. Come on then; say you will walk with me."

The Hamilton picnic. Her destination rudely interjected itself into her thoughts; her shoulders sagged. "I . . . I'm sorry, but I have accepted another engagement."

"Oh." He looked a bit bewildered by that. "Another engagement. I see."

Sophie twisted the nosegay in her hand.

"And you thought *I* was the gadabout?" He flashed her a weak smile, then shrugged and looked out the window as the hack pulled alongside the entrance to Regent's Park. "And what is this engagement? Perhaps I can suggest to the old boy that I found you first—"

"No! I mean . . . perhaps we might walk another day."

Caleb frowned. "Another day? I can't imagine that I might wait so long as 'another day.' I should really find this chap and have a bit of conversation—"

The thought of Caleb suggesting anything to Trevor Hamilton sprouted a whole new panic in Sophie, and as the coachman opened the door, she jerked forward in her haste to disembark, but in her squirming, she had managed to get the hoops of her underskirt latched onto the iron bed of the bench. Just when she might have sailed gracefully out the door, she bounced back onto the bench.

"See there? You don't want to meet this bloke."

"He's not a bloke. Oh dear, I have managed to catch myself—"

"Yes, I see the problem," he said, and turned to the coachman, who held the door open for Sophie. "If you would be so kind, sir, as to give us a moment. It would seem the lady has caught her heel." He winked at Sophie, leaned over, and lifted her skirt. "Ah yes, you've done it up right, haven't you? If I may be so bold, I believe I can dislodge you if I am allowed to acquaint myself with your foot."

"That won't be necessary—"

"I'm afraid it will," he easily countered, and his hand wrapped around her ankle.

Sophie all but came out of her skin. His touch fired the heat in her belly to a boiling pitch. As he stretched her leg out, her heart tumbled and began beating against her breast with the force of ten men.

"There you go. Free as a bird," he said, but instead of letting go, he caressed her ankle with the heel of his hand.

The sensation was like lightning. Liquid lightning across her skin. Carefully, slowly, he turned her foot, stroked it with his fingers. "What a lovely ankle you have," he murmured. His fingers trailed up her calf, toward her knee, tracing little figures on her skin, his touch feather light—and highly erotic.

"Beggin' yer pardon, sir!" the driver called up through the open door.

Her foot fell to the floorboards with a *thud*. Caleb adjusted his neckcloth and cleared his throat. "So he's not a bloke, eh?" he asked again, his warm green eyes fixed steadily on her.

She had to get out of that hack, *now,* before she melted. "Um, no, not really. Thank you, Caleb," she croaked, and pushed away from the bench, stumbling awkwardly into the coachman as she shoved through the small opening, and nearly twisting her ankle as she landed hard on the street. Marvelous. Once again, she had made a complete goose of herself. She looked back as Caleb very gracefully exited the hack.

He smiled. "At least give me the pleasure of saying you'll meet me in the park on the morrow."

All her feminine wiles—what few of them she possessed, anyway—told her not to respond too eagerly or quickly. She smiled, nodded politely. "If my schedule permits," she said primly. "Good day." She began walking across the park before he could say more. Sprinting, really. Fleeing was more like it. Only once did she turn to look behind her, and her heart climbed to her throat. He was still standing there, watching her walk away. Still smiling.

And what was *that* smile supposed to mean? Blast it, she was so unaccustomed to men and their smiles that she hardly knew which end was up. She had done the right thing, had she not? It would have been horribly un-wise to throw her arms around his neck and cling to him as she had most certainly wanted to do. But that was ex-actly something Honorine might have done, and *she* never lacked for suitors.

She was not Honorine. She was Sophie. Drab, stupid Sophie who believed anything a handsome rogue might say to her. She waved at Caleb and continued marching forward.

Thankfully, her party was easy to find in the park, given Honorine's particularly festive tangerine-and-olive-green day dress. From across a wide slope of grassy lawn, Sophie could see her standing next to Lord Hamilton, who, with the use of two hands and a cane, was standing next to his wheeled chair, ignoring the two footmen who hovered just behind him. Just down the slope from there, Mr. Hamilton was frolicking with Ian. Next to the trees, a handful of servants milled about a table laden with serving dishes of all shapes and sizes.

Sophie slowed down, took several breaths, dabbed at the dew of perspiration on her forehead as she forced the image of Caleb from her mind. She harshly reminded herself that she was a complete ninny to be driven to such volatile emotion from one ride in a hack. On top of that, if she had in mind to make a match, it was *this* Hamilton she should be impressing with her feminine wiles, not the other one. It hardly mattered that she did not particularly care for him. That would come in time—everyone said so.

She was so successful in berating herself for that slip in judgment that when Mr. Hamilton caught sight of her and smiled, she easily returned his smile, even lifted a hand to wave cheerfully, as if she had not a care in the world.

With one last deep breath, she marched onward, into the midst of that dreaded picnic, determined to enjoy every moment of it if it killed her.

When she reached Honorine and Lord Hamilton, her

faithful employer smiled brightly and looked up at her bonnet. "What is this you do with the *chapeau*?" she asked innocently.

Sophie reached up and felt her bonnet. Bloody rotten fabulous. Just how long it had been hanging so askew? It was amazing she was still able to wear it at all, given that it had inched completely over to the left side of her head and was hanging by little more than a wisp of ribbon. She quickly snatched it from her head, and ignoring Honorine, flashed a very bright smile at Lord Hamilton. "HOW DO YOU DO, MY LORD?"

"Mon Dieu!" cried Honorine, covering her ears. "His ears, they hear!"

Lord Hamilton shifted awkwardly, propped himself on his cane, and offered her a trembling hand. "Rather w-well," he said.

"Lady Sophie, how good of you to join us!"

It was Hamilton, come up the slope with Ian to greet her. Sophie plastered what she hoped was a winsome smile on her face, and not the imbecilic one she was in the habit of showing Caleb. Drat it all, there she was thinking of *him* again! "Thank you, Mr. Hamilton. Your invitation was too kind."

"Nonsense. We quite enjoy your company," he said as his gaze slowly traveled the length of her.

What now? Surely nothing was amiss, although her day thus far hardly engendered any faith in that. Self-conscious, she looked to Ian. "Master Ian, how do you do?"

"Very well, mu'um," he answered, but his eyes were fixed on Lord Hamilton, who had carefully resumed his seat. Honorine was making sure the lap rug was tucked tightly around him.

"It is a beautiful day, is it not?" Hamilton asked, drawing her attention once again. "I should very much like to introduce you to the gardens just below. They are quite lush this time of year."

"Splendide!" Honorine chirped, and fairly ripped Sophie's bonnet from her grip. She happily ignored Sophie's glare and grabbed Ian's hand, yanking him into her side. "Come to your grandpapa," she cooed.

Hamilton offered Sophie his arm. "You will enjoy the gardens, I am sure of it."

"Ah, yes. Yes, sir," she said, and carefully placed her hand on his arm, tossing one last glare at Honorine as he led her away.

As they strolled down the grassy slope to the gardens, he casually made note of the fine weather. When they were out of earshot of the others, he covered her hand with his and squeezed lightly. "I am so very glad you came. I was beginning to fear you would not."

Sophie merely smiled. This was a dream, she thought, some sort of strange little dream where suddenly she had two men wanting her company. It was so extraordinary, so completely unexpected, that she almost burst into hysterical laughter.

"If I may, you look quite fresh this afternoon. Quite sunny."

That was a little much—she was hardly *sunny*. "Thank you."

"I have remarked on your taste in clothing. I find it refreshingly simple. Frankly, I am relieved you have not acquired Madame Fortier's dressing habits in your years as her companion," he said, and chuckled at his own remark.

But he sounded so perfectly snide that Sophie was momentarily taken aback. Hamilton smiled again, and she thought perhaps she had misunderstood his tone. Of course she had—a gentleman would not make an unkind remark. "Indeed, Madame Fortier is quite colorful," she agreed with a little laugh, and felt the tension beginning to ease as they strolled farther away from the picnic.

They entered the garden path walking slowly, admiring

the flowers to either side of them. He carefully pointed out the different flora, for which he had, apparently, memorized every botanical name.

"I must confess, Lady Sophie," he said after a time, "I am quite pleased to find you safely returned to England." He stopped in the middle of the path and glanced at his feet. "Sophie—may I call you that?— I should very much like to say—although I may very well regret it in a moment—but I find myself rather drawn to you and I . . . I hope endlessly that you will decide to stay in London."

All right, then, she was flabbergasted—absolutely, unequivocally flabbergasted. First and foremost, that he was *drawn* to her. Secondly, that he would admit such a thing, given her background and standing in the community—or lack of it. And thirdly, Mother of God, that he *wanted* her to stay in London. How could he possibly have reached this conclusion? It wasn't as if they had spent more than a moment in one another's company—

He gripped her hand tighter. "I shouldn't say this, but I want you to know that I have thought of little else but you from the moment I saw you in the orangery. You have changed, Sophie. You seem . . . I don't know how to explain it, truly I don't, but I find it terribly enchanting. I can only hope that you find me appealing in some small way . . . enough that you might consider staying on in London past the Season."

Was this really happening? Had she perhaps walked into one of those magical gardens? Men like Trevor Hamilton did not make such declarations to her! Never! It was too fantastic to be believed, and frankly, she couldn't.

"Dear God, I've gone and made a mess of things. You don't find me appealing a'tall, do you?" His smile suddenly turned sullen.

"No! I mean, *yes,* of course I find you appealing, Mr. Hamilton—"

"Trevor, please—"

"But I am at a bit of a loss to understand your interest, I truly am—"

"As am I, Sophie, but I cannot deny what I feel."

"Perhaps you do not actually *feel* these things, Mr. Hamilton—"

"Trevor—"

"Perhaps you are merely missing your wife," she said, pulling her hand from his.

He startled her by abruptly grabbing her shoulders and kissing her. Her mind went blank; she felt the firm pressure of his lips on hers, the sensation of his tongue against her teeth, and the world suddenly froze.

His arm snaked around her back; he pulled her into his chest as he increased the pressure firmly against her lips until she was forced to open her mouth beneath his. His tongue swept inside, almost gagging her. His kiss was too strong, too demanding. She was so stunned by it that she hardly knew what she was doing—but her hands were suddenly between them, pushing hard against his chest.

And just as suddenly, it was over.

Breathing hard, he lifted his head, stroked the pad of his thumb across her lower lip. "My wife has been gone more than two years now, and she was quite ill for many months before she died. I assure you, I have made my peace with her passing. My esteem for you has nothing to do with her, Sophie. But say nothing, not now. Just promise you will consider what I have said, will you?"

Still reeling from his kiss, Sophie nodded dumbly. "W-we should return now," she managed to say.

"Of course," he said quietly, and his hand went possessively to the small of her back.

They returned to the picnic, although Sophie had no memory of how. It wasn't until they had reached the others that she was able to come out of the disbelieving fog that shrouded her brain. When she finally began to recover, she was seated at the table the servants had set

up, picking at a game hen, nodding absently at those moments Honorine pressed her, and stealing glimpses of
Trevor as her skepticism grew.

He was handsome in a distinguished sort of way, she
thought, several inches taller than she was—but not as
tall as Caleb. A more refined build than Caleb's rugged
one, and his eyes were hazel, not the crystalline pale
green of Caleb's. But more important, she supposed, he
seemed rather thoughtful, doting on his father and son
with equal care. Yet it was impossible to imagine how
she might settle into something with Trevor Hamilton,
impossible to believe the things he had said to her. It was
so unlike the Trevor Hamilton she had known eight
years past. But then again, perhaps he had changed. She
certainly had.

If it were true, her family would be ecstatic. The world
would rejoice in perfect harmony. The kind, thoughtful
Mr. Hamilton had taken an interest in poor, damaged
Sophie Dane. They would say it was a miracle, shake
their heads and marvel at his largesse.

And all she could think of was Caleb.

The entire day had disconcerted her so completely
that she scarcely heard the commotion at first. Mildly
cross that she had been aroused from her thoughts, she
looked up, saw that Lord Hamilton had become quite
agitated. Honorine was at his side, gripping his good
hand, and Trevor . . . where was Trevor?

Sophie swiveled in her chair to look behind her.

Ho there—Caleb was standing behind them, speaking with Trevor. Sophie suddenly sat up, gripped the
edge of the table as she realized Caleb and Trevor were
exchanging heated words.

The gasp of alarm from Honorine caught her attention, and Sophie jerked around, to where Honorine
was now standing, her hands on Lord Hamilton's shoulders. The viscount seemed to be in some sort of distress.

"What is it?" Sophie exclaimed as she hurried to Honorine's side.

"I do not know! He begins when this man comes!" she cried, gesturing wildly to where Caleb stood with Trevor.

Sophie looked to Lord Hamilton again; he strained to see around her to where Trevor and Caleb were standing. She went down on her haunches next to the viscount. "Lord Hamilton, is there something I can do?"

He looked at her with clear light brown eyes, but the words would not come. He screwed up his face, strained so greatly that he turned red before spitting out the word "*son.*"

"Trevor," she said, nodding, but Lord Hamilton reached across his unmoving body and clamped her forearm tightly with his good hand. "N-no, no . . . *son,*" he said, his voice stronger, the word clearer.

Confused, Sophie looked up at Honorine, who shrugged helplessly. Lord Hamilton's grip on her arm tightened painfully and Sophie nodded, tried to pry his fingers from her arm. "Son," she repeated, nodding.

Lord Hamilton let go.

Sophie exchanged a look with a troubled Honorine. "I shall fetch Hamilton," she said low, and reluctantly hurried to where Trevor and Caleb were speaking.

Both men turned to her at once, Caleb smiling sympathetically, Trevor frowning.

"Forgive me for interrupting," she said hastily, "but your father—he seems to be in distress."

"I shouldn't wonder that he is," Caleb said, and stood calmly as Trevor raked a heated gaze over him.

"I'll thank you to take your leave now, sir. My father's health cannot tolerate such wild claims as yours," he snapped, and without waiting for a response, pivoted sharply on his heel and marched away.

Amazingly, Caleb did not seem at all fazed by Trevor's admonishment. He smiled again at Sophie; she felt the

peculiar warmth of it in spite of the strained circum-
stances, and unthinkingly put a hand to her nape.

"He's every right to be distressed," he said calmly,
stepping forward. "But I think Father shall be right glad
to see me all the same," he added, more to himself, and
began walking to where Lord Hamilton was now standing, his weight balanced precariously on the cane.

Chapter Eight

LORD WILL HAMILTON, Viscount, had been known all his life as a man of action and deed. He had lived dangerously in his youth, crossing to the Continent on many occasions and finding himself in questionable situations before his duty as a gentleman, husband, and father obliged him to settle down. In the last few years, he had been living peacefully and quietly in the country with his son Trevor.

He never dreamed he would become a prisoner in his own body.

He could still recall the feeling of it as it came on him one blustery January day—something evil, a demon, an illness of the mind, who knew?—first tingling in his arm, then a tightening of his body . . .

To be bound, for all intents and purposes, to a wheeled chair was the most humiliating thing he had ever endured, and the worst of it was that he could not seem to make his son understand that was so. His stuttering fell on deaf ears—he never received anything more than a sympathetic smile and a pat on the shoulder from Trevor for all his efforts.

He could not speak as clearly as before, could not

remember all the words he needed to explain, but by God, he could think, and he was alive in the shell that was once a man's body.

How very odd that the only person who seemed to recognize that was a pleasingly peculiar Frenchwoman. Honorine Fortier was a pretty one, he would give her that. Luscious black hair and red lips, a gorgeous smile, the most arresting blue eyes he had ever seen. And when she touched him . . . well, he was rather ecstatic to learn that not *all* of his body had seized up. Thank God Honorine had burst into his life when she had. The despair had almost killed him, *would* have killed him, perhaps by his own hand, had she not come when she did. Thanks to her, he realized that life was, potentially, still very much worth living.

Not only was it worth living, but he had noted an improvement in his speech and his ability to move since the day she had approached him in the park. Improving, yes, but he was still suffering occasional setbacks, most often at home, most often when he was agitated, like now. It was these moments his entire mind seemed to freeze.

He looked down at Honorine's hand, so delicate but strong on his. He could see the worry in her eyes as Trevor strode toward them, could see that she believed he was suffering another seizure. It felt as if some invisible vise gripped his heart so tightly that he could not breathe, and the dead side of him began to quiver of its own accord. But all that had evaporated into a monumental struggle to tell her exactly what he must: That the man who followed behind Trevor now was his Caleb, the bastard son he loved above all else.

Trevor pushed past Honorine without even realizing he had done so, his mind a savage chaos of thought and emotion. How *dare* the lying bastard come into their midst! He had already turned him away countless times, sending him from the steps of his father's home like the scoundrel that he was. He would not allow this man to make his outrageous claims, would not allow him to touch his father's fortune. Unthinkingly, he grabbed his father's hand. "Father, listen to me! This bastard would make false claim to you!"

His father glanced at the Frenchwoman; Trevor shook his arm, hard. "Did you hear me, Father! He claims to be your *by-blow!*"

"Papa," the man said behind him, and Trevor felt the rage boil within. It was so obvious, so blatantly obvious that this man was out to steal a fortune that by all rights belonged to *him*. How could anyone stoop so low as to take advantage of the mere vegetable Will Hamilton was now?

"Papa," the man said again, and went down on one knee beside the viscount. "Dear God . . ."

"*No!*" Trevor snarled, and pushed him away. "You do not belong, sir!"

But the imposter ignored him, calmly righted himself, and reached again for the viscount's hand. "What can I do?" he asked the viscount, and by God if he wasn't able to muster a tear.

"Unhand him," Trevor said through clenched teeth. "Unhand my father."

The imposter glanced up at him, his eyes narrowed. "He is my father too, sir."

"He is *not* your father!" Trevor exploded. *"You are an imposter!"*

He merely shook his head and shifted his gaze to the viscount again. "Ask him if you don't believe me. Ask him who is his son."

One look at his father and Trevor faltered; the expression on his twisted face was remarkable. It was as if he had understood the bloody bastard . . . but when he forced out the word *mine*, Trevor felt the world shift beneath him.

The viscount was looking directly at the imposter.

The extraordinary conclusion to the picnic was matched
only by the *ton's* extraordinary ability to spread gossip. It
was so astoundingly efficient and swift that it once again
took Sophie's breath away.

She first heard the titillation surrounding the alterca-
tion in the park the very next day from the most unlikely
source of Lucie Cowplain, who, having ascertained from
Honorine that Lord Hamilton himself would be joining
them for afternoon tea on Thursday, asked, "Just the old
man, then? Or will he be accompanied by any of his
sons, legitimate or otherwise?"

"Lucie Cowplain! What in heavens do you think to
mean by that?" Sophie had immediately chastised her.

Lucie Cowplain merely shrugged and began her
crooked walk out of the morning room. "It ain't as if it's
a secret. He's even setting up house just a stone's throw
from the old man."

Sophie stared at Lucie Cowplain's retreating back;
the mere mention of his house reminded her of the kiss
she had shared with Caleb and made her blush like a
virgin. She slowly turned her gaze from the door through
which Lucie Cowplain had disappeared, and inadvertently looked at Honorine.

Honorine looked back with one brow cocked high
above the other.

Sophie unconsciously lifted a hand to her neck and
quickly looked down at the table.

"Umm," was all Honorine said. But it was enough.

Sophie stood abruptly and looked at the door. "I've
some correspondence I must finish," she muttered, and
quickened her step at the sound of Honorine's quiet
chuckle.

As there really was no correspondence, and she was in
desperate need of something to occupy her time and her
hands, she made her way to the kitchen, and finding it
deserted, rooted about until she found a large porcelain

bowl, some flour, a few eggs, and some freshly churned butter. Without having any idea of what she might do with it all, Sophie donned an apron, pushed up the sleeves of her morning dress, and dumped the flour into the bowl.

She was pulling the first batch of fig tartlets from the oven when Ann found her. "I thought you'd gone out!" she exclaimed, pausing to look around as if seeing the kitchen for the first time. "What on earth are you *doing*?"

"Baking fig tartlets."

Ann looked at the tartlets as if she were surprised to see they actually came from a kitchen. She blinked, looked at Sophie again. "Well then?" she asked breathlessly, the tartlets apparently forgotten. "Is it true what they say? The imposter showed himself at your picnic yesterday?"

Sophie nodded.

The sparkle in Ann's eyes was instantaneous. "I had it from Lady Paddington directly, just this morning! Do tell! It's all *so* titillating!"

Her zeal was a little unnerving; Sophie gave her the briefest sketch of what had occurred in Regent's Park yesterday.

When she had finished, Ann sank onto a stool, picked up a tartlet, and munched thoughtfully. "Lady Paddington believes his claim to be true, you know."

Now Ann had Sophie's undivided attention. "Does she?" she asked anxiously, trying very hard to appear nonchalant.

Ann nodded, went on to say that Lady Paddington—who, by all accounts, was the chief purveyor of gossip among the *ton*—believed Lord Hamilton to be rather attached to his illegitimate son and had desired to leave a sizable portion of his estate to him.

"Indeed?" asked a skeptical Sophie. "Lord Hamilton confided all this in her?"

Ann shrugged, helped herself to another tartlet. "I

suppose. She has called the viscount friend for many
years now."

"But what of Trevor?"

"I don't rightly know. But I rather imagine Lord
Hamilton has quite enough to provide rather hand-
somely for all his offspring."

"Oh really, Ann," Sophie said, laughing. "How could
you possibly know such things?"

Her sister's spine stiffened. "I know such *things*," she
said indignantly, "because I *listen*. But enough of that!
Come on then, tell me everything about Trevor Hamilton!
Did he say anything to indicate his feelings? Anything
a'tall?"

Sophie tried to bite back the truth, but Ann saw the
evidence of it on her face. With a squeal of delight, she
lunged across the table and grabbed Sophie's arms,
jostling her in her enthusiasm. "Ooh, but this is *marvelous!* Sophie, Sophie, do you realize what this means?
We had so hoped and oh Lord, how we *prayed* you
would be accepted! This is more than we even dared
dream!"

More than they dared dream? Putting aside, for the
moment, that her family was apparently quite mortified
that she might remain on the shelf all her natural days,
Sophie wasn't entirely certain there was anything to *"dare
dream"* just yet. And she could not help her laughter as
Ann began to regale her with how wonderful life would
be as a Hamilton, wondering what her proper older sister might think if she knew it was Caleb Hamilton who
invaded her mind's eye as she spoke, not Trevor, or Caleb
Hamilton who had melted her all over the floor of the
house he was building with a single kiss. Or that Caleb
Hamilton was the subject of her wanton, risqué dreams,
he who filled her every waking moment, particularly
since the extraordinary events of yesterday. There was
something about the way he had looked at Lord Hamilton,
something poignant in his expression that made Sophie

believe he was telling the truth—he *was* Lord Hamilton's son.

It was that image that filled her mind long after Ann had taken her leave and long after she had finished making more than four dozen fig tartlets.

There had been quite a lot of figs.

Standing in the dressing room of her suite later, she surveyed her wardrobe, wishing that she possessed a gown in some bright color. Claudia was right—she could stand to add some color to her wardrobe. *Any* color. Her clothing reminded her of her life—drab and dull. But in the last few weeks, something different was fluttering to life within her, desperate for release. It was as if her blood had started to flow again, stirring feelings that had been dead for so long that she hardly recognized them.

And those feelings required color.

The best that she had at the moment, however, was a rose-colored gown devoid of any ornamentation. Making a mental note to see a modiste straightaway, Sophie donned the thing. She then critically assessed her few bonnets. Very practical. Very nondescript. Honestly, her bonnets were as tediously uninteresting as her gowns. She might as well walk about wearing a box on her head.

None of them would do.

Her next thought was so astounding that she wondered briefly if she shouldn't send for a physician, but marched out of her dressing room nonetheless, turned right in the corridor, and proceeded purposefully to the far end, to Honorine's suite of rooms.

She paused at the door.

No. This could not be right. She was anxious, all right, but was she insane? Had she gone so far round the bend she would actually consider . . . *bloody hell.* Sophie shoved open Honorine's door with gusto.

A half-hour later, with the tamest of Honorine's bonnets tucked securely beneath her arm, Sophie descended to the main foyer. She knew a moment of panic when she saw Fabrice there, holding an umbrella as he struck various poses in front of the large mirror, in spite of the day being brilliantly sunny and blue. This felt dangerously familiar, as if she were sneaking about when she knew she should not. Well she *was* sneaking about, not unlike she had eight years ago in her frantic efforts to meet William Stanwood in some clandestine place. But this was different. This time, she at least knew how to go about it, she thought with a wry smile—but more than that, she was not the naive young girl she was then. This time, she knew what she was doing . . . she was almost 95 percent certain that she did.

Drawing a deep breath and holding it, Sophie sailed right past Fabrice, calling out a cheerful *"Good day!"* Fabrice was too quick for her, however, and whipped around, immediately spotting the bonnet. Sophie sprinted for the portico landing, ignoring his warning that the bonnet was not the appropriate color for her gown, and she kept walking, right through the gates of the house, not stopping until she was in Bedford Square, where she paused to don the thing.

One look at the bonnet and the enormous blue flower it sported made Sophie wrinkle her nose and fit it firmly on her head. She spent a few moments trying to adjust the overly large flower, but impatience made her leave it to flop about as she continued her march across Bedford Square, her only worry now, of course, that Caleb would not come, proving, once and for all, that she was indeed a fool.

But Caleb did come. In fact, he had been waiting three quarters of an hour for her at the pond feeling particularly anxious after what had happened yesterday.

He came instantly to his feet when he saw her on the main path, the flower flopping over the brim of her bonnet. Hat in hand, he walked quickly forward to meet her, reaching for and grasping her hand tightly in his. "I thought you would not come," he said earnestly, his eyes roaming her face.

"Did you?" she asked, and smiled softly, so softly that it permeated straight through to his heart.

"After what transpired yesterday afternoon, I thought . . . I must apologize, Sophie. I did not intend to ruin your picnic. But when I saw my father sitting there, I could not let the opportunity slip by."

"Oh," she said softly, her smile fading.

He sighed heavily, looked away for a long moment. "I owe you an apology and an explanation. Come on then, will you walk with me?"

She nodded; he put her hand protectively in the crook of his arm. They walked in silence for a few minutes, around the pond, to his house. As they climbed up the knoll on which it sat, he noticed that it was beginning to take shape, to grow and mold itself into the image he had held in his mind for so many months—a house of happiness. Perhaps even one day, a house with children, and his father.

His father.

"I have made several attempts to see him," he said at last.

"Have you?"

He nodded solemnly. "I am unable to count the number of times I have tried. Trevor has turned me away at every opportunity. I've even gone so far as to follow him around the park here, but the one time I attempted to see him, the so-called footman kept me from him. I did not want to make a scene publicly, so I have kept my distance."

"A footman kept you from him?" Sophie asked, clearly confused.

"Yes. Trevor is determined our father will not see me."

She withdrew her hand from his, forcing him to stop, and peered up at him with wide brown eyes. "But . . . why should he be so determined to keep you away? You've no *real* claim to your father."

Meaning no legitimate claim. It was funny that after thirty-five years, those words could still affect him so, make him feel somehow less a man.

Caleb sighed, took her hand in his. "There is much I would tell you, Sophie." He began walking, led her inside, to the ballroom again, where sheets of muslin were draped over workbenches and the floor.

Sophie walked to the middle of the room and impatiently pushed the sagging flower from her temple. "The work is almost done," she remarked, and looked at Caleb.

He tossed his hat aside, onto a workbench, and hands on his waist, returned her gaze for a long moment before speaking. "I beg your patience, Sophie, as I must start at the beginning."

She turned so that she was facing him fully, and nodded solemnly.

What he told her was that he was the product of a true love match between a Frenchwoman—his mother having died several years ago—and Lord Hamilton. After his birth, Lord Hamilton returned to France several times to see his son; through the years, they formed a deep attachment to one another. He told her he had understood at an early age who he was, that as the illegitimate son of an English nobleman, he had no claim to his father's wealth. He even knew there was another son, Trevor, and had even seen the miniature portraits of his half-brother through the years. And while Caleb confessed he had often envied Trevor his legitimate name, he had never begrudged him the Hamilton estate. That was because, he insisted earnestly, his mother had some wealth in her own right. They had lived comfortably—not to the degree of his father, certainly, but it was enough. He insisted that he wanted nothing more than a relationship with his father, and had exactly that up until a year or so ago, when the viscount's visits to Caleb's home in the Scottish borderlands had abruptly ceased.

What Caleb did not tell her was how panicked he had felt when the first letter had been returned to him under Trevor's bold signature, unopened. How he had felt the world falling out from underneath him, for he had realized at that moment his father was the only thing he held dear in this world, and he could very well lose him. Nor did he tell her how angry it had made him, *still* made him, or how his anger had built into an unrelenting, helpless fury when he had endeavored to find out why his father was being taken from him, only to be blocked at every turn.

"I learned he had suffered a seizure quite by accident, from an acquaintance who happened to be in Edinburgh. I went to Hamilton House straightaway, but was escorted off the estate by a constable."

"Oh my," Sophie muttered, the empathy evident in her voice.

"I had no choice but to leave," he said, looking off into the distance. "Trevor has quite a lot of power in Nottinghamshire. If he had wanted to see me locked away for good, I daresay he could have done it."

"How awful for you!" Sophie exclaimed, and reached for his hand.

Caleb grasped her hand firmly. "Would that you had been there. I was in desperate need of a friend." *I'm still in desperate need of one . . .*

"What happened then?"

"Oh," he said, flashing a wry smile. "Trevor thought to move Father to London, presumably to seek better medical treatment." He did not add that he suspected Trevor wanted the world to see his father infirm, for reasons that still escaped him. "The moment I heard he had brought him to London, I followed. And again, I have made several attempts to see him, but Trevor refuses me entry. I must see for myself that he is receiving the proper care—I don't trust my brother."

That admission clearly surprised Sophie. "I beg your pardon?"

Caleb gazed at her sweet face—she didn't understand the cruelty of man, how could she? "I don't trust him," he said again. "My father seems to have gotten worse in his care from what little I have seen, not better."

"Surely you are not implying—"

"I don't know what I would imply, truly," he interrupted, feeling the exasperation of his situation. He was a bastard—to some, that equated to blackguard, swindler. "All I know is that my father's health seems to have deteriorated, and Trevor refuses to allow me access to him. What can I think?" He looked at Sophie again. "What must I think?" he muttered again. *What could he think yesterday, seeing her with him, realizing that she had declined his offer for Trevor?* "Do you understand me?"

"I don't know," she answered truthfully.

As much as he had wanted her to say yes, she understood, her candid answer was another one of the many things he loved about her. Caleb smiled, reached up to push the flower from her temple. "Lovely bonnet, Miss Dane," he said, chuckling when Sophie blushed. "*You* are lovely . . . far lovelier than I have a right to want. I will not lie. When I saw you with him, I was envious. Deeply envious."

Her blush deepened to a dark rose; she nervously fidgeted with her glove. "Really?" she asked shyly.

His smile faded; his gaze caught hers and held it. "Really," he said softly. "I've come to understand how mad my passion is for you, Sophie. I think you beautiful and charming and—"

"I am divorced."

Her words stunned him; it was the last thing he had

expected to hear, the last thing he would have suspected of *her*. He tried to speak, but no words would come. It was so unheard of—

Sophie's face fell—she abruptly turned on her heel and walked purposefully for the door.

Chapter Nine

THE DOOR SUDDENLY seemed miles away. Why, *why* had she said it? She should have known how he would receive such news, and it was humiliating.

But Caleb's quick reaction startled her; he caught her before she reached the door, his hand clamping firmly on her arm. "Just a moment, where are you going?" he demanded.

"I have obviously offended you," she said tightly.

"Offended me? You have surprised me, Sophie, but you could never offend me." His answer astonished her—she was so sure . . . Caleb relaxed the pressure of his grip on her arm, but he did not let go. "I want to know, Sophie. I want to know what happened to you."

The tenor of his voice was sincere. It was almost unearthly, but he seemed to know instinctively that something terrible had happened to her, that hers had not been a match of convenience that had become inconvenient for her husband. Cowering from his intent gaze, Sophie looked down. She had said the worst of it, hadn't she? Admitted she was a pariah? Could she bring herself to say more than that? She had not spoken of it to anyone in years.

He slipped his arm around her shoulder, and the comfort of it was almost more than she could bear. She wanted to bury her face in his collar, cry one last time at the ancient events that had ruined her, cry for the damage done to her life.

"Come on then," he said soothingly. "I'll make a pallet. We can sit there." He led her to a spot just below the windows of the ballroom, took several muslin cloths, and bunched them up to make a sort of padding on the polished wood floor. They sat, Sophie's legs crossed under her skirts, Caleb's legs stretched out in front of him, his back propped against the wall.

Unable, at first, to speak her shame in more than a whisper, she began softly. But as she spoke, as the memories tumbled out of her mouth and soul, her voice grew stronger. She told him how she had met William Stanwood, how he had courted her in earnest and convinced her that her brother Julian was her enemy. It had been an easy charge to believe when Julian had taken her to Kettering Hall and left her there. And when William had come, she had thought him so terribly gallant—she told Caleb how she had fled Kettering Hall with him, how they had run to Gretna Green and married there.

When he did not seem particularly disgusted with that, she continued cautiously, hinting at what had been a nightmare, a marriage in which her husband had loved her money, not her, and how, when things became unbearable, she had finally escaped with her maid Stella and had gone with Claudia to the house on Upper Moreland Street.

What she did not tell Caleb was that she had discovered the violent horror that would be her marriage on her wedding night, when he had forced himself on her then slept like a baby. Nor did she tell him that William had paraded her, broken and battered, in front of Julian to extort her inheritance, pound by pound, until there was hardly anything left of it.

He remained silent when she told him that Julian had sent her to France while he sought a divorce on her behalf. "A parliamentary divorce," she clarified. "The most cumbersome and public of them all. But it was the only way I could be completely free of him."

His reaction was strange—he did not seem repulsed or even shocked by her confession as she had expected, but indignant. Terribly indignant. For a moment, he sat gazing at her, as if seeing her for the first time. After a long moment he grimaced and asked, "Do you know where he is now?"

Sophie shook her head, fidgeted with the bonnet in her lap. "I have heard he is in Spain. Julian once mentioned America. I don't know really, and I daresay I don't *want* to know."

"I want to know," Caleb muttered. "I want to break his neck."

Sophie smiled weakly at his bravado. "You mustn't say such things. It's over—"

"The hell I shouldn't," he interjected irritably. "To think that someone did that to you, lifted even one finger . . ." He paused, glanced heavenward as he ran his hands through his hair. "God, Sophie, to look into your sweet face and know that you were so egregiously duped—it is *maddening*. Infuriating! Of course I realize there is nothing I can do to change it, but it does not lessen my fury in the least. You are simply too beautiful, too charming, and—"

The laughter caught in Sophie's throat, sounding more like the honking of a goose than a shriek of disbelief.

Caleb jerked his gaze to her in alarm. "Dear God, are you quite all right?"

That only caused Sophie to snort with more laughter; she instantly covered her mouth with one hand, waved the other one at him as if to convince him she was all right until she managed to get a grip of her hysteria.

When she at last stopped laughing, he arched one brow. "Better now?"

She nodded.

"Do you think you might be able to speak?"

She nodded again and held her breath, raising one finger in a silent request to wait until she was certain the next gale of laughter had subsided. "There," she said at last. "It's quite gone, I think."

"Then perhaps you might share what you find so amusing?"

She reached for his hand, squeezed it affectionately. "What I find amusing," she said with deliberate care, "is that you find me beautiful . . ."—the laughter was bubbling in her again—"or *charming* . . ." She giggled, clamped a hand over her mouth again.

Caleb smiled wolfishly. "Do you doubt me?" he drawled. "Then I must be allowed to convince you." He caught her by the wrist and pulled her across his lap, into his chest and arms, dousing her laughter quickly and fluidly with his lips.

Sophie was lost in the moment before it had even begun. His lips were soft and full, gently gliding over her mouth, molding hers. His touch was so light yet so heated that she felt as if she were floating, her body suspended somewhere just beyond his lips, anchored only by the weightless pressure of his hand on her back. He touched her with his tongue, languidly slipped inside her mouth.

Sophie couldn't help sighing with pleasure; that seemed to turn his kiss molten—she could feel it dripping down, pooling in her breasts and her groin. Never had she felt a kiss to the very tips of her toes. Never had she felt a yearning run so quiet and deep within her, stirring the chaos.

He reluctantly lifted his head, stroked her cheek. "Have I convinced you?"

Oh, he had convinced her, all right. Convinced her that she had never desired a man so thoroughly. Her mind was racing with wickedly provocative thoughts. She leaned deeper into the circle of his arms, longing to know his weight on her, feel him move inside her, feel his warm breath on her breast. It was a lust that was beginning to consume her, one she thought of constantly when she was with him, constantly when she was not. A desire so strong that it made her weak, impossibly weak. *Who was she?* What sort of woman felt such prurient yearning? And how was it possible for her to feel it? Had she not all but shriveled up in the last eight years? Was there anything left of her but this craving?

Caleb stroked her cheek. "Well then? Are you convinced?" he murmured.

Who was she? "Not entirely, sir," she said in a low voice she did not recognize. "I think it will require greater effort."

Her response took him aback—she felt her smile go deeper, and a slow, lopsided grin graced his lips. "Then please, madam, allow me to make a greater effort," he said, and drew her down beside him.

He kissed her gently, feathering her eyes and cheeks with a rain of kisses, moving then to her ear, his tongue darting inside and out, his lips suckling her lobe. But his tongue quickly became a flame, licking and tantalizing her beyond explanation, leaving a trail of fire down her neck that burned in her groin and built to an intolerable pressure inside her.

Sophie was keenly aware of the dampness between her thighs, the ache of her breasts as his hands explored her body through her brocade gown. His kiss grew more urgent; he was delving deeper, plumbing her depths. With his hands, he cupped her breasts, squeezed the round of her hip.

She wanted him. She wanted to feel his hand in her dampness, his mouth on her breast. Her thoughts were wildly lustful, sinful—but she felt herself out of control, pushed into the well of longing and drowning in it, sinking deeper and deeper into its depths.

It did not seem to be her who suddenly pushed up

onto her knees and shed the jacket of her walking dress. Nor did she feel herself when she untied her chemise, then lifted his hand and pressed it against her breast.

Caleb's gaze pierced hers; he must have seen the passion boiling beneath her surface, for he released his breath in one long agonizing sigh and tenderly kneaded the flesh of her breast. *"Perfect,"* he murmured. "God in heaven, you do not know what you do to me, Sophie. You do not know how desperate is the passion you create within me. I cannot touch you like this and not have all of you . . . I might very well perish from the wanting of it."

With his hand on her breast and the thirst so clear in his eyes, Sophie could almost believe she did that to him. She arched her back, pushing her bare breast into his palm, and whispered, "So might I."

Caleb's breath was ragged as he reached for her chemise and slowly, deliberately, pushed the straps from her shoulders, his fingers singeing her skin, his eyes feasting on her breasts. The peaks of her dark brown nipples stood rigid, and when Caleb brushed the pad of his thumbs across them, she felt the draw from deep within her belly. Unsteadied by it, she caught his arm, held tight.

"I feel so . . . so desirable in your arms," she murmured. "You make me feel like a woman."

"Sophie, *God,* you do not know, do you? You do not understand . . . you are the most desirable creature I have ever chanced to behold." His voice fell away as he drew one rigid nipple into his mouth, sending another dizzying wave of heat spiraling downward. As he suckled one breast, Sophie closed her eyes, felt herself floating again, adrift on a sea of erotic sensation.

"I want to make love to you," he muttered against her skin. "I want you to know just how mad with passion you have made me, show you how a man might pleasure a woman. Let me make love to you, Sophie. Let me come inside you."

His words were so beguiling that Sophie could not

seem to catch her breath; she gasped softly as he shed his waistcoat and shirt. Free of the garments, he gathered her in his arms and pulled her into his chest, pressing her body against his as he buried his face in her neck. One hand dropped free, groped for the bottom of her skirt.

The touch of his hand on the soft, bare skin of her leg was electrifying. His hands, roughened with the labor of building his house, created a sensuous friction that left a burning trail on her skin. He moved higher and deeper beneath her skirts, scorching her when his fingers brushed her damp undergarments. His breathing quickened; using both hands, he pushed the drawers down, and unthinkingly, Sophie maneuvered out of them. Guiding her with his hands on her waist, he pulled her forward, until she was straddling his lap. She could feel his erection straining against his trousers beneath her, and she moved slowly across it, tantalizing herself.

"How radiant you are," he whispered as he lifted one hand to her face and slipped the other beneath her skirts again, cupping her fully this time, and slowly, agonizingly so, slid his fingers between the slick folds of her sex, watching her eyes as he carefully explored her. Sophie gasped at the raw sensation; her head lolled helplessly to her shoulder. His fingers slid into her tight sheath while he continued the gentle, swirling assault over and around the nub of her arousal.

She listed on the waves of pleasure he gave her, bracing herself against his shoulders, her fingers digging into his flesh to anchor herself as her body writhed on his hands. Such pleasure was not part of this earth; it was wildly carnal, shimmering in every fiber of her with a furious fever.

"I want to be inside you," he said hoarsely. "I want to feel you shudder all around me."

His hoarse utterance pushed her over the brink; her climax erupted in his hand, rippling through her body. She cried out, threw her head back, felt the pieces of her raining down around them.

"How beautiful you are," she heard him say, felt his hands on her waist, felt him lift her . . . felt him gently, slowly, impale her.

In the lush cloud that surrounded her, Sophie heard herself laugh as he slid deep inside her, a guttural sound of pure pleasure. Burying his face in her breasts, he began to move. It was an exquisite feeling, both emotional and physical all at once. The joining of their bodies, the feel of his hard cock deep inside her made her reel. All her defenses had been shattered with the first silent explosion; she began to move on him, wanting to feel him deeper, feel him harder, feel him melt into her, become part of her.

"*Sophie,*" he muttered raggedly as she lifted her breasts to his mouth and moved up and down along the rigid length of him. "You are an inspiration, a dream . . ." Sophie moved faster, sinking as deep as her body would allow before rising again.

Caleb moaned deeply, then grabbed her around the waist and smoothly maneuvered her onto her back. Suddenly he was above her, gazing down at her, slowing the tempo of their primal waltz to a smooth glide. He lowered his head, touched his forehead to hers, slid gently in and out of her in long, patient strokes, prolonging the experience and torturing her with the sheer pleasure. Moaning softly, Sophie's knees came up around his waist; she arched into his body, silently begging for more, for another explosion within her.

He shifted his weight, the stroke and pace lengthened, reaching for the very core of her. He began to move with the urgency that she felt, thrusting deep inside her, reaching for her womb, releasing all the hope that had lain dormant in her for so many years, until it filled her and strained to the point of bursting. Sophie clawed at the muslin sheets; her hips rose to meet him. Caleb groaned deep—he was past the point of gentle strokes, was now swimming in the current she had created, moving harder and deeper, and then he was stroking her, his fingers once again dancing upon her sex.

Julia London

Desire and longing spiraled tighter and tighter, building to a dangerous, mind-numbing release that crashed over them in one tremendously violent wave.

She heard Caleb cry out, felt him convulse inside her.

Then she felt his ragged breath on her neck, the staccato beat of his heart against her own. He lay with his forehead against her shoulder as he sought to drag air into his lungs, his fingers blindly searching for her, his hand caressing her arm.

They lay silently that way for several moments before Caleb spoke. "You have stolen my heart, Sophie." He pushed himself up onto his elbows, brushed the loose hair from her face, kissed first one eye, then the other. "I am yours. Irretrievably yours."

Too spent to speak, she cupped his square jaw in her palm and smiled into his pale green eyes, and hoped to God he spoke true, for he certainly had her heart.

They lay entwined in one another's arms, caressing each other, speaking low. Neither of them wanted to leave, but Caleb at last insisted, fearful that someone might turn a search party out for her. They dressed quickly and solemnly; Caleb made every attempt to fix her hair, but in the end, he stuffed Honorine's bonnet down over her head with a soft admonishment to comb it before anyone saw her.

They paused at the door of the ballroom, shared one last, long kiss, then walked hand in hand out of his house, down the path and to the edge of the park, oblivious to the world around them. At the park entrance, Caleb kissed the back of her hand, made her promise once more that she would meet him again on the morrow, and slowly, reluctantly, let her fingers trail through his before dropping her hand completely.

She was smiling, her hand tapping absently against the side of her skirts as she wandered back to *Maison de Fortier*. Their lovemaking tingled throughout her body with each step; she recalled every place his fingers had touched her, every breath he had drawn, every moment he had looked at her with those pale green eyes. *Every thrust, every drop of his seed in her belly.* It had been a highly volatile experience—after eight years, her body had been primed, had quivered at the mere touch and had come quite undone with the feel of his body in hers.

The world as she knew it ceased to exist the moment he had put his hands on her body. He had lifted her to some higher plane, and on that plane, she could truly believe he had a mad passion for her, could even believe she was beautiful. It was not a state of existence she ever wanted to leave again, and strolling lazily along as she was, she amused herself by imagining more lovemaking.

As she walked into the foyer, she smiled at Roland and scarcely noticed that he held an umbrella in each hand. He looked at her curiously and demanded, "What is this look of yours?"

Sophie chuckled quietly to herself and shook her head.

Roland shrugged. "Madame Fortier, she awaits in the salon for you," he said, and with another intent look at her, walked away in the opposite direction with his pair of umbrellas.

Carelessly tossing her bonnet onto a console, Sophie made a halfhearted attempt to repair her hair, then shrugged, and glided on her cloud to the salon.

But she came crashing back to earth the moment she opened the door.

It wasn't that every conceivable surface was covered with her fig tartlets, biscuits, and some sort of ill-shaped little meat pies—it looked as if Honorine intended to feed an entire army in her festive attire of a purple turban and peach caftan. No, what shook Sophie from her dreamy state as Honorine came hurrying forward was that Trevor Hamilton was a step behind her.

And behind them, Lord Hamilton and the boy, Ian, who looked up at Sophie with a sullen frown.

Trevor was the last person Sophie wanted to see at the moment. The mere sight of him marred the tremendous

sense of happiness she felt and gave reality entry to creep
back into her world.

"Bonjour, bonjour!" Honorine said happily, and grabbing Sophie by the shoulders, kissed her roughly on both
cheeks. When she reared back, she looked at Sophie
strangely, her blue eyes peering deep.

"Lady Sophie," Trevor said warmly. "How do you
do?"

How did she do? Ooh, quite *wonderfully*, thank you,
very well indeed . . . "Ah . . . very well, thank you," she
responded, reluctantly extending her hand. Trevor instantly brought it to his lips, glancing up at her hair as he
pressed his dry lips to her knuckles.

When he let go, Sophie resisted the urge to rub the
feel of his lips from her hand. "I . . . I did not expect—
Have you tea? Might I offer you tea?" she asked, ignoring another curious look from Honorine as she turned
back to Lord Hamilton.

"That would be lovely. I believe some has already
been brought round."

Aha, so it had. Sophie motioned dumbly to a settee,
unconsciously smoothing her hair as she preceded him
and sat herself gingerly.

"How fetching you look in rose," he remarked as he
sat next to her. "A sprig of violet for your hair would
complement it well."

It was an innocent comment, meant nothing . . . but it
sounded so very much like William Stanwood that it
made her feel suddenly unsteady. Sophie faltered; ancient feelings of inadequacy bubbled up from the murky
depths to which she had buried them. William had never
approved of anything she wore. It was never bright
enough, pretty enough, fashionable enough—

She caught herself and turned away from Trevor,
pouring a cup of tea, amazingly, without very much clattering.

"I have looked forward with great anticipation to being in your presence again," he said as he accepted the

cup from her. "I very much enjoyed our walk in Regent's Park." He smiled strangely and purposely brushed her hand with his.

Sophie's face flamed. "Ah," she mumbled, and hastily poured a cup of tea for herself, anything to avoid his gaze, and most certainly his touch.

"I don't suppose Madame Fortier keeps up her gardens, hmm?" he asked, sipping his tea.

In a moment of panic, Sophie looked at him. He was gazing at the bodice of her gown. "*Ahem.* She does."

"She does what?"

"Keeps a garden," Sophie said, raising her cup so as to obscure his view of her chest. "The Fortier vintner, Roland, is here with Madame Fortier, but of course there is no wine, so he has undertaken the occupation of gardener."

Trevor glanced up at that; when he saw she was serious, he snorted. "Rather ridiculous, isn't it? A vintner in London?"

"In truth, they are friends," Sophie clarified. "Fabrice and Roland have been with Madame Fortier for many years."

Trevor placed his teacup firmly on the table and leaned back on the settee, casting one arm casually across the back as he shot Honorine a glance across the room. "A rather peculiar arrangement. I cannot imagine befriending someone in my employ to such an extent, but then again, I am not a Frenchman."

His tone seemed harsh, too harsh. But Trevor suddenly laughed. "My father always said the French were a colorful lot. He spent quite a lot of time there as a young man—I am sure that is why he so enjoys her company."

The way in which he said *French* sounded slightly hostile, too. Please, what was the matter with her? Why was she finding fault with everything he said? He might not be Caleb, more was the pity, but he was hardly the Devil. Sophie forced a bright smile, held up a plate of tartlets. "Honorine Fortier is nothing if not colorful."

"I suppose," he said, shifting his gaze to the windows. "The weather is awfully dry for this time of year, wouldn't you agree?"

Dry? The only thing Sophie had noticed was how glorious it was—bright sunshine, deep blue skies, crystal clear air.

"We've better weather in the country, all in all," he added.

Sophie sipped her tea, tried not to smile at the unexpected image of Caleb at her breast.

"In spite of the early spring rains, which of course we need for the growing season, it seems to me better suited for the body."

"Ah." In a valiant attempt to not focus on the realization that her petticoat was hopelessly twisted, she attempted to concentrate on watching his lips move as he spoke.

"It can be rather dry in summer, although we did have quite a lot of rain in eighteen and forty, as I recall . . ."

Her mind inadvertently drifted back to the image of Caleb holding himself above her, the curve of muscle in his shoulders and arms. Her struggle to maintain her composure was hopeless. As Trevor droned on, she nodded intermittently, but she heard nothing he said—she was too occupied with hiding a half-dozen little smiles behind her teacup as she relived every moment of her extraordinary, beautiful afternoon.

When Honorine announced a card game, she fairly vaulted from her seat—Trevor followed more slowly—and dove into the game with gusto and a hope that it would consume what was left of the late afternoon.

Unfortunately, it did not last nearly long enough—as Honorine put the cards away, Trevor quietly asked her for a stroll about the gardens.

Sophie thought frantically for a polite way to decline, but his hand was on her elbow, pulling her away from the others, and unaccustomed to such attention, unaccustomed to making her own assertions, she dumbly followed.

As they stepped out into the gardens, he didn't say much, but seemed rather lost in the flora surrounding them. His pensive demeanor and her great distraction were making Sophie a wreck, and she realized she was filling the space around them with chatter. It was so unlike her—she was not one to talk without purpose. But talk without purpose she did, as if she could somehow keep him from speaking if she kept her mouth moving, or worse, *kissing* her. She spoke of Honorine, and of the Continent, Italian olives, and Spanish figs and how one might use them in delicious sauces for fish. She spoke of Christiania—*Christiania*? As if Trevor Hamilton had any concept of a place as remote and foreign as Christiania!

She was just beginning to relate the minute details of Honorine's skating party when Trevor turned from his review of a lovely hydrangea bush and impulsively grasped her hand.

It rattled Sophie out of her discourse on the habits of Scandinavians.

"You enchant me," he murmured as he tried to pull her into his arms.

That announcement roiled in her belly; she did not want to hear *that,* not from him, and most decidedly, not now! "I . . . I really—"

"I think of you often, Sophie," he said, overpowering her. "I find myself desiring to hold you . . . to kiss you . . ."

"But—"

He silenced her protest by pressing his lips against hers. His mouth was hard, his tongue a stiff prod, forcing her to open her mouth. Sophie struggled in his embrace; Trevor merely gripped her tighter. Her sudden panic was swift and terrifying; she struggled until he finally let go, then stood before him, gasping for breath.

Trevor had the nerve to laugh. "You are so shy, my

dear! There is no need to be shy." And he reached for her again.

From his perch on the window seat above, his face pressed against the thick pane of glass, Ian frowned and announced petulantly to Honorine and his grandpapa, "Papa is kissing Lady Sophie."

"*Bien!* This girl, she needs *d'amour,*" Honorine said matter-of-factly as she carefully examined Will's latest attempts to write. "Come from there now, *mon petit*—it is not nice to see this kiss. Come, come and look at your grandpapa! He writes his name!" she declared triumphantly and grinned at Will as she held up the paper for Ian to see.

Will watched as the boy cocked his head to one side and seriously considered the chicken scratch before shrugging his shoulders and wandering off to peer out the window again. How Honorine managed to see his name in that was beyond Will. Yet he could not deny that two weeks ago he could not so much as grasp the pen, much less make any effort at writing. There was no denying it—with Honorine's persistence, he *was* improving. There were still things missing, however; select thoughts, a notion of how to do things. And the vague anxiety he felt about Caleb and Trevor—it stemmed from something, but what? All he knew was a vague dissatisfaction with . . . *what?*

As if she could sense his frustration, Honorine turned toward him, her ever-present smile beaming. "Ooh, *mon frère,* you have many thoughts in your head, *non?*"

Will chuckled deep in his chest, felt his lips lift in his twisted smile. He forced a word out over his thick tongue. "Few."

"This is better than too many," Honorine said in all seriousness.

Yes, but there was something about Caleb and Trevor that he simply had to remember. A sudden, fragmented idea occurred to him; he awkwardly picked up the pen and, willing his hand to remember the letters, he scratched out the name Caleb and showed it to Honorine.

She looked at him, confusion in her blue eyes.

How did he explain? How could he make her understand so that she might help him? *But help him what?* He didn't know; it just suddenly seemed imperative that Honorine understand him.

"Caleb?" she asked uncertainly.

Will frowned, gripped the pen harder. Why couldn't he remember? If there were ever a time he needed Him, it was in these last few days. He moved the pen, showed his effort to Honorine.

She laughed, clapped her hands gleefully as she looked at the paper. *"Merveilleux!* You see? You write English *and* French!" she exclaimed, and gave him an exuberant kiss on the forehead. *"Mon fils Caleb,"* she read, and looked up at Will. "Aha! Caleb is your son, *non*?"

At last! Will thought, and took the paper from her, eager to tell her more.

Chapter Ten

As the Season hit its high point, Trevor Hamilton and Sophie Dane were suddenly the talk of the entire *ton,* the curious centerpiece in the maelstrom created by Honorine, Lord Hamilton, and Mr. Caleb Hamilton, otherwise known as the Imposter.

This, Sophie learned courtesy of one Lucie Cowplain, who, as luck would have it, could claim only one true friend on this earth, who just happened to be the cook in Lady Paddington's household, of all places.

Lucie Cowplain apparently received reports from Millicent at the early morning market, and promptly served up tidbits of those reports over breakfast to an enraptured Sophie, Honorine, and on occasion, Fabrice and Roland, if they happened to have arisen to greet the day.

It seemed the *ton's* sentiments were firmly divided over the veracity of Caleb Hamilton's claim. Many believed he was indeed Lord Hamilton's son, having heard the many rumors through the years of a torrid romance on the Continent. Still others labeled him a wretched imposter, come to prey on an infirm man. All agreed only one person could set the record straight and he had lost too much of his memory.

All agreed on one other point—Caleb was a handsome man, even more so than Trevor, and rumor continued about his female acquaintances, of which there were, apparently, many. He was forever reported as having been seen somewhere in the company of one beauty or another, although usually those with a less than an acceptable reputation.

Regardless of the truth, there seemed to be another faction altogether that simply could not resist the sport of trying to put the two alleged sons together in one setting. According to Lucie Cowplain, neither man had taken the bait as of yet.

The Imposter was, by all accounts, quite unaffected by it all. He was, as Lady Paddington said, insufferably cheerful in the face of his detractors, even while being rather adamantly firm in his claim of being the illegitimate son of Lord Hamilton, after nothing more than his father's welfare.

But, as he told Sophie during their daily meetings in Regent's Park, seeing after his father's welfare was not so easily accomplished—Trevor was just as adamant in his belief that he was a thief and a swindler of the highest and most diabolical order. He refused to allow Caleb to step foot in his father's house. As Caleb did not want to create an ugly scene at his father's house, he continued in his attempts to see Lord Hamilton in the course of his daily outings to Regent's Park.

His cheerful tenacity in the face of all that turmoil was another thing Sophie so genuinely admired about him.

The mutual adoration was growing between them, and any lingering doubts Sophie had about him quickly faded beneath the warmth of his laughter and jovial conversation, which they shared over the mouthwatering dishes she would prepare. They stole every moment they could, both of them acutely aware of their desire and ignoring their conflicting standings in society. They struggled to hold the world at bay, playing house in a partially constructed home. In fact, Sophie had not, as yet, inquired as to where Caleb actually lived, and he had not offered, other than to remark it was in or around the area of Cheapside. Knowing something as simple as that allowed reality to seep into their little world, and she did not want that.

So on the evenings that she could get away, they would dine by candlelight on the floor of what would one day be his dining room. These moments Sophie enjoyed above all other moments in her life—it was as if there were no one else in the world but the two of them. He was her secret lover and their world was magic.

So too was his touch—his hand to her cheek, to the small of her back, made her giddy. The feel of his lips against her skin, against her mouth, was enough to drive her quite mad with desire. There was, she had discovered, a voracious beast living within her. Years of longing, of wanting to be held . . . of wanting to erase all images of William Stanwood from her mind had created the beast. Caleb was her one true pleasure in her life, the tendrils of his affection surrounding her heart, the roots growing deeper each day.

He was, however, an increasingly difficult secret to hide.

Fabrice and Roland knew something was different with her—they were always peering at her curiously when she returned from the park, as if they expected her to do something, like stand on her head. Lucie Cowplain was much less uncertain about her suspicions. "Blimey if ye don't look as moon-eyed as these silly gels," she observed one afternoon, motioning to Fabrice and Roland, who were sprawled in overstuffed armchairs.

Fabrice clucked and glared at her, but Roland boldly retorted, "Better the eyes of *la lune,* than no eyes, *Madame Cowplain!*"

That drew a derisive cackle from Lucie Cowplain,

and fortunately, for Sophie, started a row that enabled her to quietly quit the room before anyone questioned her further.

Honorine suspected, she knew. Caleb had made some headway with her in his many attempts to see his father, and had actually befriended Honorine. When she wasn't so wrapped up in Lord Hamilton, she noticed Sophie's frequent absences and very much enjoyed making remarks that had Sophie squirming—*"Ah, the bloom of love, it is good for this face!"*

Sophie began to avoid her.

If Honorine suspected, it could only be a matter of time before Ann or Julian would begin to question where she went every day. She tried not to think of that—she did not want to imagine how disastrous it would be for her and Caleb if her family discovered her secret love affair. She didn't want anyone to know, really, lest they wake her from her dream. And sometimes she wished Caleb would not finish his house, lest she lose all the wonderful memories they had created there.

It didn't help that her family was so very hopeful that Trevor would offer for her. Ann was the most wishful, chattering endlessly about the gossip, citing source after reliable source that Trevor Hamilton was indeed quite smitten with Sophie Dane. In the privacy of Sophie's suite—where she often came to critique Sophie's wardrobe—she confided that it was more than the family could have hoped given Sophie's unfortunate background and lack of . . . well, finesse. But Ann would brighten and cheerfully remind Sophie that Lady Paddington had said to Alex Christian, who had said to Adrian Spence, who had said to Julian that Trevor Hamilton was willing to let Sophie's past lie.

But Sophie seemed to be the only one curious to know *why*.

Ann also took great delight in the fact that some among the *ton* were beginning to hint that perhaps they had misjudged a youthful Sophie, that perhaps she was deserving of a man as fine as Trevor Hamilton. That was enough to make Sophie ill, but even worse, Ann let her know that Julian was making it known among the men's clubs that he strongly favored a match between them, so much so that he might enhance what was left of Sophie's inheritance.

Oh how bloody grand!

Sophie listened to her sister's chatter but said very little, afraid anything she might say would be construed as being in favor of the match. Of course Ann did not ask *her* opinion, but why should she? Naturally they all assumed she would leap across the Thames just for the mere chance to be connected to a man of Trevor's stature and credentials, particularly in light of his willingness to ignore her past. They certainly would, in her shoes. Sophie could hardly fault Ann for her enthusiasm—it was their way, how they had been taught to think. She was merely doing what she thought best for Sophie and the family. And honestly, had Sophie not spent eight years abroad opening her eyes and her mind, she *would* have jumped at the chance of a match with Trevor Hamilton.

But she *had* spent those years away, and she had changed. She was not the same Sophie who had left under a cloud, that much she knew. But in moments of private reflection, she wasn't completely certain she was the new Sophie, either. It seemed she hovered somewhere in between, in a sort of no-man's-land, second-guessing herself constantly, feeling the chaos churning into a storm.

All she could do was sit quietly when Ann was talking, fretting what she should or could do about her predicament, the irony of it too rich—she had gone from society's little misfit to a woman with the unusual burden of too many men. She loved Caleb, tolerated Trevor. But to love Caleb meant to disgrace her family, and she wanted to make them proud of her for once in her life. To tolerate Trevor meant she pleased her family and society.

Yet she was so different from the plain and ungainly girl who had made her debut and hoped for Trevor to look her way. How could she make her family see that? As they told her over and over again, their utmost concern was her happiness. They wanted her to have the best life had to offer. They thought the path to reaching that goal lay in Trevor. She could not begin to imagine the recriminations if they ever discovered that she was, in fact, quite in love with the other Hamilton, and in fact, involved in a rather torrid love affair. Naturally, they would instantly believe she was the old Sophie, so desperately naive that she had fallen for the charms of an imposter. God only knew what they might do—they had sent her away before.

Which is why Sophie continued to struggle to hold her little secret, endeavoring to keep her countenance serene through the course of Trevor's frequent calls.

His visits were unbearable.

If he wasn't deploring Hamilton the Imposter, he was making some remark about Honorine's monopoly of his father's waking hours. Yet in spite of what he deemed his disastrous situation, Trevor remained a gentleman and attentive of Sophie, apparently intent on wooing her with talk of his empty home in the country, his many ideals, *too* many, really, and his desire to find just the right feminine influence for Ian.

Whether or not he meant this to influence her, Sophie hardly knew—the only thing of which she was certain was that young Ian did not care for her in the least.

That was painfully obvious. The child squirmed uncomfortably in her presence, openly cringed each time she came near him, scarcely looked her in the eye, responded with monosyllabic answers when she inquired after him, and then quickly went about the business of determining just where he might find Honorine.

Worse, Sophie was hardly any better in her behavior. It wasn't intentional—she loved children, she truly did, and surely her nieces and nephews could attest to

that. She even wanted her own, *imagined* her own, with
Caleb. But she was hopelessly inept when it came to
Ian—honestly, what did one say to such a sullen child?
He seemed to harbor some glaring resentment for her
and it amazed her that Trevor did not see how astoundingly poor her rapport was with the child, or how she
bungled each interview with Ian. Surely he would eventually see that any hope he might harbor that she could
influence the lad at all would be put into its proper
place—the rubbish heap.

But more than that, Sophie could not dismiss the
vague feeling that something was not quite right with
Trevor. Nothing wrong, exactly, but . . . it was just a feeling, nothing more, based on nothing concrete, for certainly he was a gentleman. Nevertheless, she could not
shake her intuition about Trevor and felt it keenly one
morning when Lucie Cowplain recited her latest opinion
of the news received from Millicent.

"Ye'll see yourself married by the end of summer,
mark me," she said, wagging her finger authoritatively at
Sophie over a plate of steaming eggs. "Mr. Hamilton,
he's been alone with that child for far too long."

"You make it sound as if he seeks a nursemaid," Sophie
said as she took the eggs from her.

Lucie Cowplain snorted disdainfully. "Why in God's
name do ye *think* he'd marry? It ain't for position or
money, obviously."

"Mon Dieu!" Honorine exclaimed hotly, roused from
her concentration on a plate of delectable pastries. "You
do not say such things, Lucie Cowplain!"

The woman rolled her eyes and pivoted on her twisted
leg. "I ain't saying there's anything wrong with Lady
Sophie, I ain't. But she's got the burden of her past, you
cannot deny it," she said, and lurched through the servant's door.

Clearly stunned, Honorine tried to smooth it over, but
what she said came out in a mishmash of French and
English. It hardly would have mattered had she man-

aged to say something in flawless English, because Sophie knew that the old cook was quite right.

Everyone knew it.

Everyone except Honorine, that was, and unfortunately, Honorine could not seem to grasp any of the nuances of the latest gossip surrounding Sophie and Trevor, or worse, herself and Lord Hamilton. On those occasions when Sophie tried to make her understand the furor she was creating, Honorine would cluck her tongue. "These *Anglaises,* they know nothing of life," she would say, and refuse to hear any argument Sophie tried to put forth regarding English propriety.

Honorine's nonchalance and Sophie's frustration collided with fury one afternoon when Honorine announced her very disastrous notion to have a ball in the orangery.

"*Ooh, oui, oui!*" clapped Fabrice.

"Why on earth would you want to host a ball?" Sophie demanded.

"Why not?" Honorine asked nonchalantly as she exchanged cards with Roland in the course of a game. "London, she is very good to us. Very nice, *non*? We should give this ball. Will likes it."

"Honestly, Honorine! Have you no idea what is being said about us? *All* of us?"

Honorine looked up from her card game and smiled. "*Oui. You* they speak about, and *Monsieur* Trevor Hamilton . . . but I like this other son," she said, looking pointedly at Sophie.

"Ooh, *oui,* this other son, he is *very* nice," Fabrice said dreamily, earning an impatient glare from Roland.

"Oh no, you can't invite them both!" Sophie cried with alarm.

"*Non,* I do not do this!" Honorine said indignantly, as if she were suddenly the queen of society protocol. "You think only *you* are concerned for these things? For Caleb," she said matter-of-factly, "I will be concerned, too!" Fabrice and Roland paused at that and looked at Sophie.

That sort of remark usually sealed her lips—but Sophie was beside herself. "I am not concerned, Honorine, but I think you do not understand. These people, the society here, they are not sincere. They will come to your house to gawk."

"Gawk? What is this *gawk*?" Honorine demanded. Fabrice quickly translated for her, and Honorine laughed. "At what do they gawk?' she asked as Lucie Cowplain entered the room carrying a vase of freshly cut flowers.

"At you! And them!" Sophie cried, motioning impatiently to Fabrice and Roland.

A collective gasp went up among them; they all gaped at her as if she had spoken blasphemy. Even Lucie Cowplain seemed taken aback. Honorine carefully placed her cards aside and stood from the table, pausing to look down at her with all superiority. "I do not care what they will think, Sofia," she said haughtily. "I will have this ball. They do not come, *c'est la vie!*" she added, and sailed out of the morning room to discuss the ball with the winsome trio of Lucie Cowplain, Fabrice, and Roland on her heels.

Fine then, bloody-well fine. The whole Hamilton debacle was at least absurd, not to mention calamitous. Having had enough with the lot of it, Sophie donned her bonnet in a huff, grabbed her reticule, and set out to do something more productive than mull over the latest gossip and Honorine's insistence on disaster, or moon over Caleb for endless hours.

It seemed to her an excellent time to speak with Julian about leasing a booth at Covent Garden.

Julian and Claudia were both at Kettering House on St. James Square, in the gold drawing room with their two young daughters. Claudia was attempting to repair Beth's tail of ringlets that had come loose. Bridget, whose long black curls already hung loosely, romped about the room, pretending to be a knight and waving a wooden sword about fiercely. At the far end of the room, Julian looked up from his paper and removed his spectacles as Sophie was shown into the room. "Pumpkin! How good to see you!" he said, smiling warmly. "My, my, how well you look, Lady Sophie. Hamilton's courting apparently agrees with you, hmm?"

What, was the entire city of London following Trevor's every move? And since when did a drab brown gown look anything but ill advised? Sophie could feel herself pinkening under his scrutiny, but her discomfiture was hidden by a collision with Beth. The darling, just freed from her mother's attentions, flew across the room to her sister, Bridget, intent on retrieving her sword—Sophie winced at the impact of the child to her person and immediately reached for her smarting knee.

"Pardon, Auntie Sophie," Beth said as she skipped around her.

"Oh dear, you haven't gone and hurt yourself, have you?" Julian asked.

"No," Sophie said, biting her lip, "really I am—"

"Must be those stars in your eyes," he said, and laughed appreciatively at his own jest.

"Really, Julian, I thought you above all the gossip," she retorted pertly.

"It's hardly gossip!" Claudia chimed in. "Hamilton has indeed called on you a dozen times now, and that can only mean one thing—"

"It can only mean that we are neighbors. But never mind that, please?" she asked, limping to the grouping of chairs in the center of the room. "I've come to speak about much more important things."

"Oh no," said Julian with a playful moan. "I am always quite ill at ease when a woman wishes to speak of something 'more important.' Go on then, let me have the worst of it."

"Oh, Julian!" Claudia clucked.

"It's about the Upper Moreland Street House."

"Ooh! How wonderful!" Claudia exclaimed. "Nancy

Harvey told me herself how much time you have spent helping her these last few weeks. I am so very glad you've taken such a keen interest in the house—Lord knows I've not been able to give it the attention it deserves."

"Upper Moreland Street?" asked Julian, clearly surprised.

"I really haven't been much help a'tall, but I should very much like to do more," Sophie said eagerly.

"More? Do you think that wise, pumpkin?" Julian asked, frowning lightly. "After all, your past association with the house—"

"Julian, whatever do you mean?" Claudia asked indignantly. "Her past association with that house makes her all the more sensitive to the needs of the women there. I, for one, am very proud—"

"I did not say I was not proud, Claudia. I am merely thinking of what is best for Sophie, and I cannot help but think the less reference made to her past, the better."

"Oh no, Julian, you really mustn't mind; I am quite—"

"What reference is it to her past?" Claudia demanded, interrupting Sophie.

"An obvious reference!" Julian snorted.

"Why should you mind so? Trevor Hamilton doesn't seem—"

"*Stop!*" Sophie exclaimed, holding up her hands to them. Startled, Julian and Claudia turned twin looks of surprise to her. "Please," she said more calmly, lowering her hands. "Julian, no one knows I attend the house on Upper Moreland Street, and Claudia," she said, preempting the remark of triumph Claudia was undoubtedly about to make to Julian, "I have not spent a great deal of time there. Nancy is being kind. But in the little time I *have* spent there, I could not help noticing they are without sufficient funding to maintain the house properly, much less clothe the women and children as they should."

"What? But I sent several gowns just one month past!" Claudia exclaimed.

"Yes, so you have—but those gowns are too fine. The women there need garments that are more practical for their daily work. Yet there are two dozen ball gowns and accoutrements if there is one, all stowed away in a small room on the attic floor."

"Oh," murmured Claudia, deflated. "I had no idea . . ."

"I had a thought, however—what if we were to hire a booth in Covent Garden or a small shop on High Street and sell the gowns that have been donated?" Sophie moved to the edge of her seat, excited about her idea. "Surely there are other women in London who would appreciate the quality of clothing they might have for a fraction of what they would pay in commission to a modiste. The proceeds from the sale of the gowns could be turned over to the house, and Nancy could purchase what was necessary. You needn't worry about a thing— Nancy and I would do everything. I have the funding necessary, but I need help in acquiring the space."

No one said anything for a moment; Claudia and Julian both looked at her with equally dubious expressions.

"You would sell these gowns?" Claudia asked her, the disapproval evident in her voice.

"Yes," Sophie said, trying to ignore the sinking of her gut. "It should not require a very big booth, really, just enough space where Nancy could display them."

Julian and Claudia exchanged another look; Julian frowned. Claudia shifted her gaze to her daughters, who were now fascinated with something on the Aubusson carpet.

"Sophie, that is an admirable notion, truly," Julian said carefully. "But you cannot think to sell the gowns women of the *ton* have donated to a worthy cause, particularly at Covent Garden or on High Street. That would be unseemly."

"Unseemly?" she echoed, uncertain how it could possibly be unseemly to sell cast-off garments to women who would truly appreciate their value. Julian cleared his throat as he withdrew his spectacles and carefully put them on. Not a good sign, that, and well Sophie knew it. "Perhaps I did not make myself entirely clear," she quickly said, but Julian was already shaking his head.

"Sophie, you must consider that our friends have given some very fine gowns to a worthy cause. But to take them and sell them to persons who might actually be in their *employ* would be indecorous. I cannot allow you to do this. I cannot allow you to be known for selling the clothing of the *ton* to . . . to—"

"Women," she quietly finished for him.

Julian shrugged lightly and looked at Claudia.

Incredible. They would seek donations to the house on Upper Moreland Street, but now they would fret if the women were of the right class to *wear* those things? What had happened to her brother in the eight years she had been gone? He was one of the infamous Rogues of Regent Street, a group of men who had flaunted their disdain of societal convention—and now he would *protect* such arcane convention?

"I don't understand," she stubbornly insisted. "How could selling the gowns possibly be any different from *giving* them away?"

"It's just that it is rather *base* to sell them, dear." This, practically whispered from Claudia Dane, the undisputed champion of underprivileged women.

It was all too unbelievable. And she had thought her idea so sound, so perfect . . . "I cannot believe this," she said low. "Both of you profess to believe in charity, do you not?"

"We'll think of another way to help them, darling," Julian said kindly. "Is it money you need? I shall—"

"No," Sophie said, shaking her head. "It's not your money they want." That was one thing she instinctively understood, but she had no idea how to impress that on her brother. "They are proud women, all of them, and anxious to be on their feet again. They appreciate the help they receive at Upper Moreland Street, but they would prefer to make their own way."

They wanted to make their own way as fiercely as she wanted to at that very moment.

"Oh darling, try not to look so cross. The house will be fine," Julian said.

"Yes, of course," Claudia anxiously agreed. "And besides, you have your Mr. Hamilton to occupy your time."

Now the indignation was beginning to choke her. Not that she was surprised, particularly—it was the way of the *ton,* the values they cherished. They would dismiss her request and suggest that she occupy her thoughts with something more appropriate for a spinster like herself—the prospect of a match. Even in that, they valued someone who was possibly the most tedious creature on the face of God's green earth merely because of his credentials. It was all about appearances, and her family was just like everyone else in that regard. Of course they were! The ordeal over her escape and divorce from Sir William had all been about appearances, had it not?

"Yes, you are right," she said slowly, and came to her feet. "The house will be fine." She forced a smile to her face. "Well then, if you will excuse me—"

"Sophie, wait—where are you going?" Julian asked as he took the spectacles from his face. "Sit down, please. We were just about to ring for tea."

"Thank you, no, I wouldn't impose. I really must be on my way," she said, backing away from her brother and sister-in-law. "Besides, I promised Honorine to help her with some, ah . . . painting."

An atrocious lie, and she could tell from their expressions that Claudia and Julian recognized it as such.

"You won't stay for just a moment?" Claudia asked, coming to her feet.

"No, really, I—" Sophie jumped when she backed into a round table, jerking halfway around to catch a vase before it toppled to the floor. From across the room, Beth and Bridget giggled.

"At least let me have a carriage brought 'round," said Julian, who was standing now, too.

"Its such a glorious day, I prefer to walk."

"Sophie, come now," he coaxed her, arms open. "Please don't be cross."

"Oh no, you misunderstand me!" she said cheerfully. "I am not in the least cross. I am . . ."—*lost!*—"It was a silly idea, truly. I must be going—I should not keep Honorine waiting overlong."

And before anyone could say likewise, she called a cheerful *ta-ta* to her nieces, waved at Julian and Claudia, and quickly retreated from their pained expressions, stepping out of the salon and rushing down the corridor before spilling out of Kettering House onto St. James Square.

She walked quickly across the square in the direction of St. James Park, her head down, lost in thought. *How was it possible her family had become so like the* ton? There was a time she believed the Danes were far too compassionate about the plight of the less privileged to care what society thought. What else had she believed of her family that was not true? They said they wanted her happiness—perhaps they wanted respectability more. Why else would they push the idea of Trevor without so much as asking her wishes?

Because they had never asked her wishes. They had made her decisions for her from the time she was a little girl—she was always the one to be guarded, to be looked after, as if she were infirm, incapable of making the right decision. Worse, they had made her believe it, too. Wasn't that precisely the reason she had not dared breathe a word of Caleb to anyone? He was not the right decision.

Sophie ran quickly across the crowded thoroughfare of Pall Mall and into St. James Park, slowing her step until she was wandering idly, her disappointment growing with each step. So lost in thought was she that she almost collided with the pair walking toward her. Startled, she stepped abruptly to one side without really looking at them.

"Sophie!"

The voice washed over her like silk; Sophie's heart immediately leapt to her throat, and she glanced up at Caleb with a broad, irrepressible smile. "Caleb! What a pleasure to meet you!"

He flashed her an impossibly white grin as he tipped his hat.

"Lady Sophie Dane—a surprise, if I do say so myself. Why, I haven't seen you smile so brightly since the Season of your debut," a woman said.

Sophie's heart sank to her feet as she forced herself to look to Caleb's right.

With a smirk that seemed permanently twisted, Melinda Birdwell stood on his arm.

Chapter Eleven

T HROUGH SOME HERETOFORE undetected and miraculous will, Sophie managed to keep smiling in spite of her shock and great sense of betrayal. In fact, she *beamed* at Melinda as if they were long-lost sisters united at last. "Miss Birdwell!" she exclaimed cheerfully. "An even greater surprise to see *you* taking a turn about the park!"

Melinda's smirk dimmed a bit; she glanced sidelong at Caleb, but he was still smiling at Sophie.

Ha.

"I am a great proponent of daily walks," Caleb said cheerfully. "I believe it keeps one feeling rather youthful, wouldn't you agree?"

"You must know my thoughts on the subject, sir," Sophie said pointedly, and stepped around the pair. "And certainly I would not want to keep you from it. Good day," she said pertly. With a passing look at Caleb, she continued briskly on, moving so quickly that within moments, she was beginning to labor a bit in her breathing. She hardly cared—an apoplectic fit wouldn't stop her now. She would flee that park at once because she was quite certain she had never been so humiliated in her life.

How dare he? How dare he consort with Melinda Birdwell, of *all* people? Oh God, oh God, how could she have been so bloody stupid? She had practically *thrown* herself at him.

An ancient feeling of betrayal twisted in her gut before a thought suddenly occurred to her, and groaning, she paused, closed her eyes. She could well imagine the scene behind her now—Melinda would inquire as to how Caleb knew her, then pounce delightedly on the opportunity to tell him the whole sordid story of her past, leaving nothing unsaid. Around the park the two of them would go, whispering feverishly—

Sophie's eyes suddenly flew open.

Just one blasted moment—what was Melinda doing on Caleb's arm? She would hardly associate herself with someone rumored to be a swindler. Furthermore, even if she *did* believe him to be the unfortunate but illegitimate son of Lord Hamilton, she would never align herself with someone with tainted credentials. That much, Sophie knew very well—Melinda Birdwell was precisely that sort of woman. But then again, Melinda was very close to being put on the shelf permanently. It could be that she was desperate for a match . . .

That thought enraged Sophie. She would rather die than see a man as fine as Caleb Hamilton shackled to that fat cow all his days. Yet it would serve him right, the bloody blackguard! Sophie stomped across a footbridge and onto the main walkway bordering Pall Mall, uncertain exactly who made her more livid—Melinda or Caleb.

How could she have fallen in love with a known philanderer? Really, as annoyed as she was at the moment, she was hardly certain if it was love or merely infatuation. Perhaps this was why her family never allowed her to do as she wished—perhaps she could not trust herself to know the difference and had succumbed to the first man to show her affection in eight years. *Oh, that rotten bounder!*

She could scarcely wait to get to Upper Moreland Street.

But wait, apparently, she would, as there were no hacks in sight, not a single solitary one. Sophie stood impatiently, her general frustration growing with every passing moment. Suddenly everything in her life was topsy-turvy. From the moment she had set foot on English soil, it seemed as if everything she had come to know was called into question. She had no idea who she was anymore—to some, like Melinda Birdwell, she would never be able to discard the mantle of her scandal. To others, like Trevor Hamilton, she was the unlikely candidate for a second wife, a notion she found repugnant. To her very own family, she was a still a little girl.

And to Caleb Hamilton, apparently, she was nothing more than an amusement. *Bastard!*

Her life had been far too simple the last eight years to bear all of this. Really, she had not realized *how* simple. During her years of travel with Honorine, she had been free of entanglements such as family and society, free to be herself. And the longer she was forced to stand on Pall Mall and think of it all, the closer she came to exploding into confused little pieces of herself. If a conveyance did not come along soon, they might very well find the pieces of her scattered all over London.

The tap on her shoulder very nearly did it.

She jerked around; Caleb quickly threw up his hands in supplication. "I beg your pardon, I did not intend to startle you," he said, and watching her carefully, slowly lowered his hands.

Feeling suddenly awkward and ungainly, Sophie fidgeted with the ribbon at her waist. "I beg your pardon, you did not *startle* me," she said stiffly, and unconsciously glanced around him to see where Melinda Birdwell had hidden herself.

Caleb followed her gaze, glancing around, too. After a

moment, he looked at her from the corner of his eye. "I handed the battle-ax over to her cousin moments after you left."

Shocked and embarrassed that he had read her thoughts, Sophie shrugged and looked up the thoroughfare again for a hack.

He sighed loudly. "I suppose I shall be commended to Hades for saying so, but she's a rather difficult woman all in all, and frankly—" he paused, looked around to see that no one could overhear—"one can't be entirely sure that isn't a galleon hidden beneath those hoops."

A thought that had occurred to Sophie, too, even if it was beside the point.

"Ah, come now, where is that lovely smile of yours? I have determined it is the most winsome smile to ever grace a woman. I hope you don't mind me saying so."

Well. Perhaps she didn't mind too terribly—she was many things, but insane was not one of them. Nonetheless, she was not a fool who would allow compliments to turn her head. "Quite a circle of acquaintances you keep," she muttered low.

"I don't keep acquaintances. I have none really, except you."

"Oh really? Then you must enjoy walks in the park more than I understood."

"I beg your pardon?"

Sophie shot him a look of exasperation.

A frown creased his brow; he looked at her strangely for a moment, until something dawned in his green eyes. "Ah . . . You are upset about Miss Birdwell. That is why you are treating me so coldly," he observed matter-of-factly.

What, did he think it perfectly acceptable to consort with the shallowest woman of the *ton*? "Not coldly, Mr. Hamilton. Indifferently. You must think me quite stupid, or quite inexperienced—"

"I do not think so."

"—but I am well aware of a man's proclivities!"

"I know."

He said it so quietly, so gently, that it stopped Sophie cold. Something fluttered in her belly; she brushed the back of her hand across her cheek. She had shown too much, exposed too many of the jagged edges of her life to him.

"There is your hack."

"Pardon?"

"Your hack. You were waiting for a hack, were you not?"

Her disappointment was swift; she glanced over her shoulder as the old carriage slowed to pull alongside the curb. Naturally, she'd be forced to wait an eternity just so the bloody thing could appear *now*, of all moments. "Yes. Yes, I was waiting for a hack." She roughly adjusted her gloves.

"A rather thrifty mode of transportation," he said as the hack coasted to a halt alongside the curb.

Righto. He probably didn't know that an heiress who had lost a good part of her inheritance had to be thrifty. She dug in her reticule for a crown.

"But not quite as thrifty as my cabriolet."

Sophie glanced up at him. "Oh." She said it stupidly, but looking at him just then, at his green eyes, she felt a kick in her gut, the deep regret that it *was* love she felt for him, not infatuation. It could only be love, because the loss of trust hurt her deeply, as did the sense that she had lost the magic. "I, ah . . . I am really going too far to impose."

"I rather doubt that."

"Where to then, mu'um?" the hack driver called down to her.

"Essex," she called back up to him, and dug deeper into her reticule for a coin.

"Drive on, sir! We've a more economical mode to Essex!"

Sophie gasped, waved her hand at the driver to gain his attention. "No, no, just a moment, please!"

"Keep your coin, Sophie," Caleb said firmly, and grasped her elbow tightly as he waved the driver on. "Drive on!"

The driver shrugged, cracked his whip at the team of four. As the hack eased away from the curb, Caleb pulled Sophie into his side. "Firstly, my dear Sophie, I am mortally wounded that you would refuse my offer. Secondly, I very much enjoy your company and am loath to surrender it just yet. And thirdly, I did not intend to hurt your tender feelings with Miss Birdwell's presence, but I should think it painfully obvious how I feel about you," he said, guiding her away from the curb.

Well, yes, it *should* be obvious how he felt—that's why she was so confused at the moment, and perhaps a little delirious. "I know what you feel—"

"No, apparently you do not," he said, his tone betraying his frustration. "Apparently you do not know that I live for the few moments I might steal with you in Regent's Park. Nor do you seem to understand that you are the *one* bright spot in my otherwise dreadfully dull days," he said as he led her toward a neat, one-horse coach tethered on the edge of St. James Park.

"I *am*?" she asked, wincing at how breathless she sounded as he helped her up.

"Please, Sophie. I am just shy of worshiping the very ground upon which you walk. I have shared the most extraordinary lovemaking with you; I feel another piece of myself disappear each time we must part, packed tightly away in your basket. I dream about you, I think of you constantly, I see you in my house and I think, dear God, is this woman really here? With me? And you would believe I have some affection for Miss Birdwell? Frankly, I'm of a mind to be a bit petulant myself," he grumbled as he tossed the reins up to the bench and gracefully pulled himself up.

"I am not petulant," she muttered.

"Yes you are, my love. If you must know, Miss Birdwell's cousin foisted her on me, I rid myself of her annoying presence the very moment I could, and frankly, madam, you have your nerve thinking the worst of me when you receive my brother on a regular basis."

That caught her off guard. "I harbor no affection for Trevor Hamilton, you may rest assured!" she exclaimed.

He looked at her then, his green eyes shining with exasperation. "*Precisely*, Sophie."

Speechless, she blinked.

"Well then? Might I have your destination?"

This was ludicrous. She should escape while she could and put an end to this secret affair before it destroyed her. But the small smile playing at the corner of his lips was enough to turn her to butter. And as quickly as that she thought that perhaps she had judged him too harshly.

"Upper Moreland Street," she muttered. "But you mustn't think for a moment I've forgiven you."

He grabbed her hand and brought it to his lips. "You must not ever forgive me. You must not ever let me be less vigilant of your happiness than I am at this very moment."

All right, how could she *not* love a man who spoke so beautifully?

With a lopsided smile, Caleb flicked the reins and sent the horse trotting.

The drive to Upper Moreland Street was something Caleb would remember all his days, he was quite certain. In spite of the congestion of man and horse, he could see only Sophie, hear only Sophie. In fact, he couldn't be entirely certain that it wasn't her heartbeat he heard in that cacophony of street noise.

The sense of panic he had felt in St. James Park when he realized he had offended her somehow was something he had not felt since he was a boy. But then again, he had not known anyone who had become quite as important to him as Sophie, particularly since Lady Paddington had told him everything about her past. But hearing it from Sophie's own lips that day in the ballroom had haunted him. To know she had endured such hardship was almost more than he could bear. It was impossible to believe that a woman as uniquely charming as Sophie Dane could have suffered so much at the hands of the bloody bastard Stanwood.

It was odd, really. The moment he understood what she must have endured, his good opinion of her had escalated right up through the clouds to God and back. It was her quiet dignity he admired the most—she was gentle and unassuming, but one had a sense that if challenged, she refused to be beaten down by anyone or anything.

Yes, his esteem of Lady Sophie Dane was very high, impossibly high, and the moment in St. James Park he realized he had hurt her had been torturous. He could not relieve himself of that parasite Miss Birdwell quickly enough—he had not sought her companionship, had certainly tried to dissuade it, and had all but thrown her off his arm the moment Sophie went marching away from them.

He knew exactly how Sophie felt, for he had certainly felt the same and more each time he heard the rumor of the potential match between her and Trevor.

When he had asked her, Sophie had told him about Trevor's frequent visits, saying they were quite tedious. He believed her, believed she had a certain distaste for his half-brother. Nonetheless, the idea that Trevor could call on her when *he* dare not darken her door, for fear of the gossip that would certainly follow, made for a terrible envy. And he would be untruthful with himself if he didn't admit that he wondered from time to time if he could trust her completely. She was, after all, a woman of the *haut ton*.

Her trust in him had faltered when she had seen him with Miss Birdwell. That, somehow, was not surprising—people rarely trusted him. It was as if being born out of wedlock somehow compromised a person's integrity. The

world expected a bastard son to behave a bastard, and
God knew there were times he had. But not with women,
never with women, and especially not Sophie Dane. He
would be a fool to toy with her affections, even if he
could.

There was no pretense about her; she was sincerely
warm and wryly witty. When she spoke, it was with a
genuine animation that he found lacking in others. And
those wide brown eyes—when they talked, he could feel
himself sinking into their depths, being pulled into a
strong current of pure, unadulterated passion. The afternoon they had spent in the ballroom had been an incredible experience, far richer than any other he had
ever experienced. Her reaction to him, the passion flowing through her was as gratifying as a man could possibly hope. They had flowed together like water until it
was impossible to tell him from her. He had felt that for-
bidden emotion too keenly, felt his love for her spilling
over them, dousing them. They were two scarred people,
two outcasts in an imperfect world.

But they were perfect for each other.

There had been a time in his life, before his mother's
death, when he would have entertained prettier, more
experienced women. But he had been a different man
then—the man he was now preferred the plain beauty of
Sophie Dane, the intelligence of her conversation, the
easy, lilting laughter that splashed around him like rain-
drops.

Thankfully, he heard it as they made their way to
Upper Moreland Street as he regaled her with the tale of
how exactly Miss Birdwell had been forced upon him.
She began to relax a bit, began to smile again.

Their talk soon shifted to Honorine, whom Caleb had
met a handful of times now in the park. "Rather . . .
vivid, isn't she?" he remarked.

Sophie laughed. "Vivid, yes. Lustrous, like sunshine.
There is nothing that can dampen her spirits, I think."
She credited Honorine with having helped his father to

improve. "I've seen the improvement in him," she avowed. "He has even begun to write again." She smiled softly at that, looked wistfully up the road. "Honorine," she said on a sigh, "is undoubtedly the most exasperating woman I have ever known. But I adore her." Caleb instinctively understood the bond between the two women, could sense an abiding and mutual respect.

As they turned onto Upper Moreland Street, Sophie told him more about the small townhouse with the green shutters. It fascinated him—and the plight of the women there concerned him greatly. He knew what it was like to have no place to turn, knew what it was to be an outcast. Sophie's compassion for them obviously ran deep. Tentatively, she told him of her idea to sell the donated ball gowns and he instantly recognized the brilliance in her scheme.

It made him impossibly proud. "That's very clever of you, Sophie, a splendid idea! When shall you start?"

"Umm . . ." she fidgeted with the ribbon at her waist. "There is a slight problem."

"Problem?"

"I've no place to sell them. I can't lease a shop front alone, you know."

He immediately offered to help. There was not much he could do for a woman of Sophie's means, but lending his name to a hiring agreement was definitely something he could and would do. Not only that, he could build the blasted thing if necessary. "I've a strong back, and I rather enjoy that sort of work."

His offer clearly surprised her. Her cheeks colored; she laughed and thanked him.

Reluctantly, he helped her down from the cabriolet, his hands lingering on her waist. She smiled up at him, her gaze piercing him down to his boots, and Caleb did not want to let her go, never wanted to let her go. He wanted to drink the smile from her lips, taste her laughter in his mouth. There was a current running between them, the same coarse desire.

"I can't thank you enough for driving me. It is rather a long way."

His gaze dropped to her lips, lingering there. "I would drive you anywhere, Sophie," he said truthfully. "To any-place your heart desires."

She made a small sound in her throat that ran like white heat all through Caleb. "Anywhere," he muttered, and descended to those plump lips, devouring them hungrily as she rose up on her tiptoes to meet him. He held her tightly to him, wanting the kiss to last forever, wanting to hold her forever, feeling the desire tighten in his groin.

When at last she slipped from his arms, his heart was racing. "I can't wait to see you. When will I see you?"

"Tomorrow," she whispered.

He nodded, squeezed her hand one last time before reluctantly letting go. "I will not disappoint you," he said earnestly, and fairly leapt onto the bench of the cabriolet. With one last look at her smiling face, he urged his horse on, already counting the moments until the morrow.

Chapter Twelve

ANY DOUBTS SOPHIE had about Caleb evapo-
rated over the next several days until she no longer had
any question—she was wild about that man. She felt like
a girl again; he was her sun, her night. The moments she
spent with him winged by; it seemed he was standing to
go almost the moment he sat beside her on the wrought
iron bench.

But what wonderful moments they were! They laughed
together, spoke of everything and nothing, recounting
their lives and travels. They strolled through Regent's
Park in quiet companionship, sometimes not speaking,
simply being with one another. They spent countless hours
working on his house, painting the walls, or just wandering through the rooms and imagining what would be
where. Imagining they were someone else, two people
whose lives had intersected normally and not in secret.

On some days, Caleb insisted on accompanying her to
the house on Upper Moreland Street, where he put himself to work repairing what needed it, chatting amicably
with the women as he did so. What Sophie most admired
was that there was nothing judgmental in his manner—
he treated the women as if they were all equal, as if

money and stature and life's experiences did not separate them all in some way. Naturally, the women adored
the handsome devil; some openly swooned when he
rolled up the sleeves of his shirt and went to work. One
afternoon, he worked to repair the pantry door, gone
crooked after years of use. As he worked, Nancy, Sophie,
and two other women who were residing at the house—
Catherine and Bette—prepared the evening meal, watching him surreptitiously, admiring his masculine form and
cheerful demeanor.

"Aha," Caleb said to himself at one point. "I'll need to
insert a peg here."

"I've got a place you might insert a peg, luv," said
Bette, to a howl of laughter from the other women.

Caleb laughed. "I beg your pardon, ladies, but there
don't seem to be enough pegs to go 'round."

The women dissolved in laughter, but it seemed to
Sophie that more than one looked rather wistfully at
him.

So did Roland and Fabrice, who became frequent
callers at the house on Upper Moreland Street, too. Fascinated by the endless possibilities the many gowns and
accoutrements presented for the ladies and themselves—
Sophie did not want to know how many possibilities,
really—the two Frenchmen could not seem to tear themselves away from the little townhouse. They had, naturally, been quite surprised by Caleb's presence at first,
but they soon grew accustomed to seeing him about, just
like the women, and would watch him covertly from beneath the veil of their lashes. Just like the women.

Caleb also insisted on building a suitable booth at
Covent Garden. Fabrice and Roland successfully located
an ideal spot for the sale of the gowns, and Caleb leased
it for them. The very next morning, he arrived with two
workmen borrowed from the construction of his house
and began building the booth.

Feeling enormously pleased with herself, and rather
liberated of the *ton*'s stifling mores about such things,

Sophie bounced about the market square, directing the men as they began to erect her booth, handing them tools as if she knew something about the construction of booths. Caleb watched her, grinning, and at one point, surprised her by grabbing her wrist and abruptly yanking her around to face him. Smiling wickedly, he had anchored her to him with one arm around her waist. "I cannot abide it another moment," he said, and kissed her so fiercely that he literally snatched the breath from her lungs. As always, the moment his lips touched hers, she was melting into him, wallowing in the pool of desire he created in her as he devoured her lips. He kissed her thoroughly and completely in the middle of Covent Garden, in front of his workmen, the crowds, and even Fabrice and Roland, then left her standing in the middle of all that chaos in something of a daze, still feeling the softness of his lips against hers, the taste of his mouth, and the bold touch of his tongue as Fabrice clapped delightedly.

Sophie stopped worrying about the appearance of it and gave way to the exquisite feeling of being in love.

The man knew how to kiss. He knew how to make love. And her body yearned—no, *pleaded*—for more, much more. His mastery drove her higher—he knew when to be gentle, when to be hard, where to touch her, where to kiss her. He knew every inch of her body that could elicit pleasure, and laved each place until she surrendered to her own private madness.

Unfortunately, those moments were rare. Their shared fear of a pregnancy and its consequences was quietly spoken between them, but there were those days they could not deny the intense desire flowing between them, and succumbed to their emotions.

Oh yes, she loved Caleb Hamilton, loved the way he looked at her, the way he touched her, the way he listened when she spoke. She loved the way he treated everyone around him with respect. She loved everything about him, and the man he was.

The one thing she did *not* love about Caleb was the

fact that it was his half-brother who was attempting
to court her. She had been truthful with Caleb about
Trevor—she told him she had no interest in him, despite
what the *ton* rumored, and he seemed to believe her. Yet
her assurances could not remove the pall Trevor cast
over them.

Which made Trevor Hamilton's calls increasingly intolerable.

Sophie was beginning to realize that Trevor imagined
nothing more than a woman seated at his table, a figure
that made his little family complete. He did not want a
companion, he wanted someone to watch over Ian. Worse,
his vision of the world around him, and even his future,
was astoundingly narrow—not broad and colorful and
with a view of the entire world, like Caleb's. He seemed
to have few outside interests, and on those rare occasions
she attempted to engage him in conversation by asking
about his day, he would grow cold and noncommunica-
tive, as if he did not want her to know what he did.

Nor did Trevor have much tolerance for Sophie's attempts to broaden their conversations. He told her very
pointedly one day that he did not care to listen to the
tales of travel with Honorine as he found that woman's
character to be questionable and preferred not to think
of Sophie in her employ.

It had taken her aback; she had no idea how to respond to something so blatantly cold. She replied unsteadily that his preference was all well and good, but
she most certainly *was* in Honorine's employ, and that
for all her idiosyncrasies, she was a kind person and a
dear friend. "And," she added curtly, "I should think it
obvious how giving she has been with your father. Look
at the improvements he has made!"

"My father," Trevor replied tightly, "is a sick man. She
aggravates him." Trevor did not seem to recognize the
improvements Lord Hamilton had made under Honorine's
care. He didn't seem to recognize anything except his
own needs.

But what truly astounded Sophie was that no one seemed to notice *his* character. The only thing anyone seemed to notice at all was that Trevor was the legitimate heir to the Hamilton fortune and therefore, a prized catch. Not a day went by someone didn't remind Sophie how fortunate she was that a man of his caliber had noticed her.

She was so very *fortunate*, her sister Ann told her time and again, to catch the eye of a man like Trevor Hamilton. How very *fortunate*, said Claudia, that Sophie had chosen this particular time to return to England, for she never would have met the gentleman who everyone speculated would offer for her. What good *fortune*, Julian said, that this man would overlook her unmentionable past.

Her blood boiled when they openly speculated about Caleb's character and his claim. "Seems rather coincidental, does it not," Julian opined one day, "that he should make his claim now, when Lord Hamilton cannot legitimately confirm or deny it? Ah well. There is little he can do to further his scheme, not with Trevor handling it so very cleverly."

"Cleverly?" Sophie asked. "What is so very clever about his handling of it?"

"That's unkind to Mr. Hamilton, darling," Ann quickly chastised her. "This is most trying for him, you can be sure. He is handling it as well as anyone could under the circumstance."

"Yes," Julian agreed. "He is handling it all quite well— now *there* is a man worthy of your esteem, pumpkin."

Sophie ignored that. "Why should you be so certain Caleb Hamilton is a swindler?" she demanded.

Her brother and sister looked at her with some astonishment that she would challenge them.

"Has he inquired about a fortune? Made any claim at all?"

"What has come over you, Sophie?" Ann asked. "You are betraying Trevor's goodwill."

Beside her, Julian's dark scowl penetrated her pique.

Sophie shrugged. "It just seems unfair to judge him," she muttered, and avoided any further eye contact with her brother.

Of course she knew *why* they were so desperate for her to embrace Trevor's overtures. For years they had assumed she was destined for the life of a spinster, surely Julian most of all, who now beamed brightly anytime the Hamilton name was mentioned. And truthfully, Trevor's interest in her *was* incredible, if not unbelievable. For the first time in her life, she was being courted— an extraordinary turn of events, something no one had expected.

Certainly nothing had prepared her for the outrageous possibility of *two* men courting her.

It baffled her, amazed her—she was Sophie Dane! The plainest of the Dane sisters, the one who had to be sent to a Swiss finishing school if there was to be *any* hope of a suitor. She was the clumsy one, the foolish one—*not* the desirable one. But here she was in London again and in the unimaginable position of being courted by one of the *ton's* most eligible men.

And on the other hand, by the world's most handsome man.

That delighted her beyond compare.

What did not delight her was Honorine's ball, for which they had now received almost two hundred confirmations.

It was, without a single doubt, a disaster in the making, a looming storm on the horizon. With the strangely united forces of Fabrice, Roland, and Lucie Cowplain to help her, Honorine was in the throes of joyous planning for a ball that was quickly turning into what could only be *the* event of the Season. The four of them argued over every detail, right down to the color of the flowers on the tables and the wine that would be served. (*"Mon Dieu! What does she know of wine?"* Roland complained of Lucie Cowplain.) The food, the music—nothing was left to chance.

"Dear God, Honorine!" Sophie had exclaimed one day as they counted the latest replies. "How shall we ever hold them all?"

Honorine clucked, nonchalantly waved a hand beneath the voluminous sleeve of her cranberry red caftan. "Here and there! You must not fret of these things!"

Here and there indeed. "How can I not fret? It seems as if the entire *ton* is determined to attend this ball!" Little wonder, since Trevor had sought sole guardianship of his father in the high courts.

Sophie only knew this from the gossip mill, for certainly neither Trevor nor Caleb had discussed their growing feud with her, save an occasional remark. It was Ann who told her what Trevor had done, and Ann had it all from Lady Paddington herself. Up until that point, Caleb had not acted on his claim, except to try and see his father. But when rumor reached him that Trevor sought to obtain legal guardianship over his father, the gloves purportedly had come off.

Caleb denied any such goings-on when Sophie told him the latest gossip over luncheon one afternoon. She had heard just that morning from Ann that he had supposedly lost his temper, publicly proclaimed Trevor would obtain that right over his dead body, and then had promptly gone about the hiring of a solicitor. "Now everyone is waiting on tenterhooks for the challenge they feel sure Trevor will issue you," she finished.

Caleb laughed roundly. "All lies, sweetheart," he told her, and laughed with great amusement again.

But it was clear that the Hamilton story, complete with speculation of romance between Sophie and Trevor and the bizarre companionship of Honorine and Lord Hamilton, was better than any novel currently being passed about the ladies' drawing rooms.

And it was only going to get worse, Sophie realized two days before Honorine's ridiculous notion of a ball, when she received Trevor and Ian in the salon.

As usual, Trevor spoke of Ian as if the child were not

physically present. Sophie glanced at the boy—he was frowning at her, of course, seemingly fixated on her hair. Why the child found her so objectionable was beyond her—any attempt she made to gain his trust was quickly rebuffed. And he had become particularly good at avoiding her. But he couldn't avoid his father's conversation any more than Sophie could and sat rigidly as his father had instructed him, with only his small foot moving, back and forth, back and forth, as he absently shifted his gaze from the window to frown at Sophie and back again.

She rather doubted Ian heard a word his father said of last year's harvest, and God only knew how impossibly bored she was with Trevor. His conversation was stifling, and to make matters worse, Sophie had the feeling that he had an unusual drive for perfection. There was something about Trevor that gave her an uncomfortable reminder of William.

Even his kiss was devoid of any feeling—not that she didn't avoid *that* occurrence like the plague, but from time to time, she could not escape the hard and almost motionless buss of his lips.

All in all his attentions left her feeling very restless; she found his calls excruciatingly hard. Her mind wandered from his speech to how she might end his visit without hurting him or bringing the entire wrath of the Dane family down on her head.

And when Trevor mentioned Honorine's ball with almost childish glee, Sophie thought she might be ill. She could very well imagine the scene—everyone watching him watching her, her brother beaming with unconquerable pride, her sister crying from sheer relief.

The thought suddenly propelled her from her seat, startling Ian and causing Trevor to stammer. "Sophie, my dear? Is something amiss?" he asked, quickly gaining his feet.

"No. No, nothing. I thought I would take some air."

"Shall we walk in the gardens, then? Come, Ian—"

"Umm, actually," she said hastily, preferring torture to

walking in the gardens, "I've a bit of headache. I don't mean to offend, but—"

"Nothing serious, I hope?" he asked anxiously, attempting to reach for her hand.

Sophie moved abruptly—the thought of him touching her, if only to hold her hand, was repulsive. "Nothing serious," she readily assured him. "But I think perhaps I should rest a bit."

"Of course, of course," he said, and impatiently motioned for Ian to come to him. "You should rest. After all, Madame Fortier's ball is soon upon us."

As if she could possibly forget *that*.

Trevor put his arm around Ian's shoulders. "Well then. I hope with some rest you will find yourself much improved."

"Thank you."

He glanced at the door, then to Sophie again. "If you should need anything, anything at all . . ."

"You are too kind," Sophie said, and looked meaningfully at the door. Trevor frowned, gently pushed Ian in the direction of the door. The boy was only too happy to oblige his father; he walked as quickly as he could without running, pausing only to push the heavy door open before disappearing into the corridor.

Trevor hesitated, then took several steps toward Sophie, catching her elbow. "I do not like to see you unwell," he murmured, and dipped his head to kiss her.

Sophie turned her head; he caught the side of her mouth. It surprised him; he lifted his head, blinked down at her for a moment before forcing a smile to his face. Her face flamed; she looked away, toward the window as Trevor ran his hand lightly down her arm. "Rest, then, my dear," he said simply, and quietly took his leave.

She waited until she heard the door shut behind him, then sank onto the settee. *What was she doing?* Did she think to push away the one man who might offer her marriage? And for what? An affair with his brother? But she *loved* Caleb—they were kindred spirits. Trevor was a gentleman, an upstanding member of Britain's elite, a good provider . . . but he did not spark the deep heat in her like Caleb did. He did not make her sigh, did not make her feel anything but restless and cross. Sophie was long past trying to convince herself that she could, somehow, grow to care for him.

She could not.

And she wasn't convinced that he cared for her. There was more to his interest, of that she was certain—or was she only imagining things, manufacturing what her heart wanted her to think? Nevertheless, no matter how hard she tried, she did not particularly care for Trevor or his thinking. She did not want to be told what to do, by him or her family. She did not want to be shackled to him or his son for all of eternity. How ironic it was that she had spent the last eight years convincing herself she was miserably enslaved to her scandal, when in truth, she had been *free*. She did not want to give that freedom up to anyone, and most of all, Trevor Hamilton.

How she dreaded Honorine's ball.

The one saving grace, she supposed, was that Caleb would not be there. He had not received an invitation. Thankfully, Honorine was not nearly as deaf to the gossip as Sophie had feared. True to her word, she had not invited Caleb, deferring to the possibility of scandal. "How cruel is this *société*! I wish very much I should have all of Will's sons to come to my ball," she lamented one evening.

"*Oui*, the handsome one," Fabrice said on a sigh.

"*Tsk-tsk*, Fabrice, are you to duel with Sofia for his favor?" Honorine asked, and laughed roundly at herself while Fabrice and Sophie turned several shades of red and Roland pouted.

The next afternoon, Will Hamilton watched his son leave in a gig and wondered if he hadn't had a grander conveyance at one time—he seemed to remember one.

Honorine sat beside him, peering closely at the paper in her lap. He appreciated her efforts, he truly did, and he struggled daily with a way to tell her so. But there was something that didn't seem quite right, something in the far reaches of his mind that taunted his inability to grasp it.

The only thing he knew for certain was that it had to do with his sons.

What? What could he not remember?

"Aha! You see, Will Hamilton! You write now very well!" Honorine praised him as she held up the paper on which he had scratched his full name and title. "Now. You write what you want," she said, and pushed the paper back beneath his hand that held the pen.

What did he want? The answer was *there,* just there on the tip of his tongue. He grasped the pen again, tried to force his mind to form the words.

After several minutes of frustration, he scratched his answer out and pushed it to Honorine.

She studied his scratching, her head cocked to one side. After a moment, her face lit up with a beautiful smile. "Ooh, I see this now!" she exclaimed brightly. "This is what you want. To go home!"

"Y-yes, Honor. I want to g-go home."

Chapter Thirteen

THE EARLY EVENING of Honorine's ball was a brilliantly sunny one. Naturally, Honorine saw that as an excellent omen and proclaimed the evening a grand success before it had even begun. She flitted from one room to the next to inspect the preparations in a gown made of pink, purple, and grass-green silk brocade. Roland and Fabrice were anxiously on her heels, dressed in identical black tails and matching red waistcoats and neckcloths. The three of them were sure to catch more than one eye.

As for her gown . . . Sophie surveyed herself in the forest-green brocade Claudia had worn before her pregnancy. It was simple; a flounced hem with no adornment, suitably austere, the cut of the bodice very modest.

"Perfect," Ann had proclaimed earlier. "Not *too* risqué, I think," she had added, eyeing the bodice critically. One could not help but wonder exactly what coverage Ann would deem appropriate for a spinster. She had then fussed with Sophie's hair, displeased with the curls over her temple. "Too tight," she muttered. When she was satisfied Sophie was appropriately dressed—"Oh my, won't Hamilton find *you* appealing,"—she had left Sophie to finish dressing on her own.

Sophie stood in front of the full-length mirror, frowning. She looked too austere, too rigid. Someone's governess. The *ton's* most famous spinster. She thought of Caleb, felt a strange sense of resentment. She did not *want* to be a spinster, and moreover, she certainly did not want to look like one. Ann meant well, but Sophie was tired of all the decorum given her scandal, tired of the prudish manner in which Ann expected her to conduct herself.

The image of Caleb flashed in her mind's eye again, and something snapped. She walked to her wardrobe, threw it open, and looked at the pale cream silk she and Nancy had found among the donations at the Upper Moreland Street house. Sophie had added a translucent pink silk organza to overlay the skirts, and Nancy had embroidered the bodice in pale pinks and browns and greens. The result, much to Sophie's great pleasure, was one of the most beautiful ball gowns she had ever seen. She had kept it hidden in her wardrobe, however, because she was certain Ann and Claudia would not approve, principally because it had come from the Upper Moreland Street house.

Well, it was *her* life, and *her* reputation. If one gown was going to ruin it, then so be it—there were certainly worse things that could happen to a body. In a sudden fit of frustration with her inability to stand up to her family, Sophie squirmed out of the forest-green gown, carelessly tossed it aside, and donned the pale cream silk. She struggled with the buttons, finally managing to fasten them all, then stalked to the mirror.

Whether it was the candlelight or the flush of her exertions, Sophie was actually astonished by her appearance. The gown was beautiful—and she looked like a princess in it. Her only regret was that the previous owner had been a bit smaller than she; the dress fit snugly, and the sleeves dipped so that her shoulders were bare, and . . . really, she might very well fall out of the thing. But determined to wear a gown of her own choosing, Sophie

yanked the bodice up for all the good it did, and finished
dressing.

She dreaded the evening. All eyes would be on her, including those of Trevor—a notion which made her skin
crawl. Being a veteran of this sort of event, she knew
very well that the gossip would be rampant. But for all
her fear, there was a rebellious side of her, a side that
could scarcely wait for this ball, if for no other reason
than to show the *ton* she was not the old Sophie, but the
new one . . . *this* one. Her only regret was that Caleb
would not be there to see her in a gown as fine as this.

As there was no way to avoid the inevitable, Sophie
tugged one last time on the gown, took a deep breath to
steady her nerves, and walked out of her suite, head held
high, wearing her hand-me-down princess gown.

Sophie was not alone in her misgivings.

At his temporary home in Cheapside, Caleb dressed
carefully, brushing the lint of disuse from the formal
black tails he wore. He straightened his neckcloth once
more, smoothed an unruly wave of hair above his temple, and wondered for the thousandth time what he was
doing.

He had no business, no business at all attending this
ball. Lady Paddington's invitation to escort her was not
entirely sincere, he was well aware of that. Everyone
wanted to see him in the same room with Trevor, including Lady Paddington, but it was a potentially explosive
situation, particularly after Trevor had so coldly informed
him, through an intermediary, that he would seek to
have him permanently barred from ever seeing Lord
Hamilton again. Why Trevor was so determined in this,
Caleb could not be sure. He had tried on more than one
occasion to explain through the same intermediary that
he sought nothing more than his father's well-being—it
wasn't as if he had made any claim, public or otherwise,

to the viscount's fortune. Whatever Trevor feared, it was baseless.

Nonetheless, misguided notions or not, Caleb's contempt for the man was growing. Admittedly, part of him relished the thought of being a thorn in his side this evening; but the desire to put Trevor Hamilton in his place was not enough in and of itself for Caleb to subject himself to a public display he was so certain he would endure. Sophie, on the other hand, was. He could not abide the thought of Trevor anywhere near her, or touching her . . . or *dancing* with her. Even when Sophie had assumed he would not be attending the ball, as Madame Fortier had not sent him an invitation, he had let her think that and had avoided an inevitable argument. He had simply smiled, assured her all would be well, and tried to force the ugly image of her in Trevor Hamilton's arms from his mind. He could not.

He sighed, thrust his arms into the coat.

Damn it to hell, what had happened to him? What depravity had so invaded him that he would think he might be in love with the woman? *Love.* A foreign word. Did he even know this emotion? Hadn't he avoided it all his life and quite successfully at that? It hadn't been hard to do—from the moment Miranda Snipes, the object of his great esteem at the tender age of ten years, had informed him his lineage was not of a suitable caliber, Caleb had instinctively understood what he was to the world. A bastard, nothing but the by-blow of a rich and important viscount and naturally unworthy of society's esteem. Nothing his mother could say would divest him of that notion—Miranda Snipes had been painfully clear in what society thought of people like him.

Once the boundaries had been set in his young mind, Caleb had adjusted well. There had been plenty of willing women through the years to ease the needs and desires of his male flesh, some of whom he still considered friends. But there had never been a woman who had made his heart pound with the anticipation of seeing her, or empty his mind of all useful thoughts and responsibilities just so he could remember her laugh or the sparkle in her eyes. There had never been a woman he could believe was genuinely interested in him beyond what he could give her, certainly no one who was particularly interested in what he thought or felt, what moved him, what made him laugh. What hurt.

And truly, Caleb had never once believed he had missed any of those things. He never once thought he needed the touch or companionship of a woman. He had scattered himself about the world, making his own way, leaving one wench for the next as it suited him.

Until he met Sophie Dane.

Caleb straightened his cuffs, took one last look at his besotted self in the beveled mirror.

He had not expected to feel anything for Sophie. He simply had been intrigued by the woman who appeared every day across the pond, had found her peculiar, solitary habits amusing. He did not know then that he was desperate for love. *Her* love. Sophie had, somehow, reached the deepest part of him. He needed her, needed to feel the warmth of her smile when his struggle seemed hopeless. He needed her sweet kiss hello, her sultry kiss good-bye to remind him that he was quite alive.

She was pretty, in an unconventional way, free of cosmetic artifice, seeming to prefer the natural state God had given her. He found that terribly appealing. Her carriage was graceful, as if she were quite content to move about in her skin. Her figure was perfectly shaped in all the right places and she seemed fitter than most; her arms and face were slightly tanned, as if she had spent a great deal of time out of doors. She thought nothing of physical labor. The time he had spent with her working on his house or her booth at Covent Garden had been some of the most enjoyable of his life. And the woman looked radiant with a bit of exertion.

But it was more than the physical attraction he felt

toward her. He had fallen in love with Sophie because she seemed to accept him for exactly who he was. There was no judgment about his birth that he could detect, nothing but what seemed to him a genuine interest in his person and his life. She made him laugh, shared his view of the world around them. Her interest in his work, his house, in everything he did, made him feel as if she truly cared about him. He very much enjoyed the time he spent with her, enjoyed it so much that he was beginning to imagine what it would be like to spend all of time with her.

It certainly compelled him into agreeing to attend Honorine's ball with Lady Paddington. As disastrous as his gut told him the evening could or would be, the forces drawing him there—Sophie and his father—were too great to ignore. But his instincts were strong—he was flirting with disaster.

That instinct had his gut in knots by the time he and Lady Paddington arrived at Bedford Square. Carriages lined the streets and as they slowly wended their way to the house; he could see that the guests had already spilled out onto the veranda. Strains of the music from a quartet lifted softly into the evening sunset; the sound of voices and laughter and crystal upon crystal could be heard in the street. All of London seemed to be crammed into that house.

"Ooh, it seems as if *everyone* is here, does it not?" Lady Paddington whispered excitedly, and plumped her gray ringlets one more time.

"It does indeed," Caleb muttered as he offered her his arm. He looked up at *Maison de Fortier;* the urge to flee while he could was almost overwhelming—but he thought again of Trevor and the rumors of his intentions toward Sophie. He sucked in his breath, smiled down at Lady Paddington. "Shall we?" he said pleasantly, and led her up the walk.

Judging by the stir of people as he entered the foyer— and in particular, Lady Paddington's titter—he surmised he had arrived before his father. Lady Paddington's beaming smile created folds of plump flesh as she surveyed those around her, obviously pleased with the reaction they were getting.

Mrs. Clark, another elderly woman who Caleb had surmised was her closest friend, was the first to remark on his presence. "Mr. *Ham*ilton! And they said you would not come!"

"Not come?" he drawled, bowing over her hand. "But I would do my friend Lady Paddington an insult if I were to refuse her kind invitation."

"Oooh, do you *see*?" she fairly shrieked to Lady Paddington. "He's such a *charming* young man!"

"Very charming," Lady Paddington hastily agreed, and thrust her hand in the crook of his arm just as Honorine sailed into their midst.

"Monsieur Hamilton, soyez le bienvenu! Très heureux de vous, mon frère!"

"Thank you. I am delighted to be here," he lied.

Honorine laughed and grabbed his hand, oblivious to the twin looks of disapproval at her brashness from Lady Paddington and Mrs. Clark. She promptly turned and yanked him aside.

"I did not expect you," she murmured in French. "Are you quite mad?"

"Perhaps," he admitted.

"Unfortunately, your father has not yet arrived," she said as she led him down the corridor to the main salon. "But there are many others here who look forward to making your acquaintance. My friend in particular I think."

She paused as they stepped across the threshold and looked around, ignoring the many people who were suddenly moving toward them. "Ah, there she is now," Honorine said, and inclined her head across the main salon before greeting the first guest to reach them with a very cheerful *"Bonsoir!"*

Caleb did not immediately see her. It wasn't until he

had greeted several of Honorine's gawking guests, that he caught sight of her across the room. He didn't recognize her at first; her hair was done up in a very appealing style, and her gown . . . bloody hell, that gown hugged every curve. His gaze boldly swept the length of her; a slow, very appreciative smile spread his lips. Sophie seemed to sense him, or perhaps the raw heat in his gaze; she turned suddenly. A glorious smile lit her face, and she laughed gaily, her delight evident. The sight of it made him burn slowly from the inside out.

He nodded pointedly in her direction, tried to relay what he was thinking. Several around him turned immediately to see whom he would acknowledge.

A fan tapped on his arm; Caleb reluctantly dragged his gaze from Sophie to Lady Paddington. "Mr. Hamilton, would you be a dear and fetch a punch for a parched old woman?" She followed that request with a coy smile.

Right. His charge for the evening. "I'd be delighted, Lady Paddington." He set off in the direction he had just come, but not without overhearing Lady Paddington remark to Mrs. Clark, "He is *so* nicely mannered in spite of everything, is he not?"

Yes, that was right. A nicely mannered bastard, he was.

Caleb found the dining room, which had been set up with all manner of punches, wines, finger sandwiches, and an amazing number of fig tartlets. He fetched the punch like the good little bastard he was, thinking he would deliver it and then make his way through that insufferable crowd to Sophie. God, but she looked radiant tonight. He had not seen her smile quite like she just had or felt the weight of it quite so strongly.

He strode back to the main salon, prepared to take a temporary leave of Lady Paddington, but the moment he stepped over the threshold he was distracted—by almost walking directly into Trevor's back.

His half brother stood stiffly behind his father, who had, apparently, entered the room on his own two feet, albeit unsteadily, aided by a cane. He seemed oblivious to everyone around him but Honorine, who was instantly at his father's side, helping him navigate the throng to a huge, leather wingback chair she had arranged in a prime location. Caleb watched as she helped him to sit, then fussed about him like a hen. Even when Father waved her away, she continued to stand close by, her hand lightly on his shoulder as she regaled the guests around them with some story Caleb could not make out.

He stared blindly at the punch in his hand and swallowed a lump in his throat. It was painful to see his father like this—he had always been larger than life to Caleb, a big man with a big smile. His hero. Seeing him like this, so physically undermined, was almost unbearable, and Caleb was almost lost to his memories for a moment, until a palpable tension began to seep into his consciousness. He looked up; Trevor stood before him, staring daggers.

"Good evening, Trevor," he said, and watched without surprise or emotion as his brother turned sharply on his heel and disappeared into the crowd, to the great titillation of the many guests around them.

From across the room, Sophie watched the exchange between the two men and felt a stirring in the cold dread lying in her belly. She had warned Honorine of the disaster that awaited them, but had never suspected it would have to do with Caleb. Although the sight of him elated her, she was not prepared for this. She wondered madly why he had come, and with whom? What did he think to do here, knowing the entire *ton* would be in attendance? But there was no time for that now—Trevor was pressing through the crowd toward her now, his gaze boring a hole right through her.

Sophie managed to force a smile to her lips, but by the time he had made it to her side, her smile had degraded.

Trevor nodded curtly, glanced at her bare shoulders, and she could see the displeasure in his eyes. She did not care for his expression at all, not at all. In fact, his whole demeanor made her uncomfortable, and as they exchanged an obligatory greeting, she began to feel as if she had done something wrong. There was something ugly about his manner, the way he stood so rigidly, looking at her shoulders so disapprovingly—it reminded her of William, an abrupt and almost violent reminder that kicked her in the gut.

She suddenly felt a desperate need of air.

"You look rather peaked," Trevor said authoritatively, and grasped her elbow as if he had the right to do so.

Sophie surreptitiously tried to dislodge it from his grip, but his fingers sank into her flesh. "It's the heat, I think," she said. "I am quite all right, really."

"You could use a breath of air. Let's walk on the veranda, shall we?" He did not wait for her answer, but began to propel her through the crowd.

Sophie unconsciously looked over her shoulder, to where Caleb had been standing.

She could not see him anywhere.

Trevor moved purposefully, pulling Sophie along with him, his eyes locked on one of four pairs of French doors leading onto the veranda. The music for the second set of dances was just beginning to drift across the lawn from the orangery as they stepped out onto the veranda. Couples who had come out on the lawn to cool off began to move languidly toward the music, their laughter spilling out onto the night air as Trevor led Sophie to the railing. She thanked him, turned her head to the gardens and took a deep breath. *Where was Caleb?*

Trevor said nothing, but stood by as she breathed in the cool air, then sighed impatiently. "Feeling better?"

"Yes, thank you." She looked away from his frown, to the crowd moving toward the orangery.

"Splendid. Then perhaps you will do me the honor of a turn about the dance floor?"

Sophie closed her eyes, tried to shake off the feeling of aversion.

"My dear?" he pressed her.

She turned halfway toward him; he was already holding out his arm for her, impatient to move on. There was no graceful way out of it, nothing she could do to escape this dance, not without causing a scene. "Umm, yes. Yes, of course," she mumbled, and put her hand very lightly on his arm.

Trevor quickly covered it with his own and squeezed possessively. "I understand that you are a bit anxious. After all, it has been many years since you turned a waltz in London. As I recall, you did not turn many then, hmm? But you mustn't fret—I am an expert dancer and I will not let you falter with so many eyes upon you." He patted her hand.

Sophie almost bit through her tongue in her effort to keep her mouth shut.

Apparently unaware of her resentment, Trevor led her down the veranda steps and across the lawn, crowding in behind the others into the orangery.

The room had changed dramatically from the dusty old structure it had been several weeks ago, transformed into a kaleidoscope of color and opulence. Gone were the cobwebs and old drapes, and in their place, crystal chandeliers that hung from the ceiling. The large floor-length windows were bare, reflecting the light of dozens of candles back into the room. The women moved about in brightly colored, jewel-encrusted gowns, softly muted by the candlelight. At the far corner of the room, the string quartet sat surrounded by various potted plants. A host of servants moved about with crystal flutes of champagne on sterling silver service trays. But not Fabrice and Roland. They were openly enjoying the ball as if they were invited guests, each with a flute of champagne in his hand.

Trevor immediately swept Sophie into a waltz that

had just begun, looking down at her with what could only be an expression of great surprise. "My, my, you dance very well, Sophie, very well indeed!"

"Did you expect that I would trip and fall?" she asked, unable to bite her tongue another moment.

Trevor blinked, then laughed lightly, and, Sophie thought, insincerely. "I suppose I rather thought you had not had opportunity to perfect your skill these last few years."

Sophie merely nodded, choosing not to tell him precisely how many balls she had attended and in how many corners of the earth. Instead, she hoped fervently that the first waltz would be done with quickly.

Under Trevor's guidance, they moved woodenly about the dance floor. He was smiling now, his gaze rather wistful. "The evening is quite fine," he remarked.

Sophie nodded.

"But all in all I'd say the summer has been rather stifling."

What, the weather *again*? Well, she could hardly fault him, could she? After all, they had not had a discussion of it in what, two full days now? "Yes, quite hot," she agreed, her gaze wandering to the people standing along the wall.

Trevor suddenly twirled to the left, taking them out of her line of sight. "I don't recall a time it was quite so unbearably hot," he continued.

She nodded absently.

"Ah, there now, you mustn't be distressed," he said. "Naturally you are the object of great curiosity, what with the old scandal and all."

That certainly caught her attention; Sophie jerked a horrified gaze to Trevor.

But he merely smiled. "If I may be so bold, Sophie— a private life in the country would surely afford you a peace and a distance from the scandal that you will not easily achieve in London."

"I beg your pardon?"

"The scandal would not follow you there, I would see to it."

"There? *Where?*" she asked, incredulous.

"Surely you have noticed my interest in you, my dear. I think that in spite of your unfortunate past you would make an excellent wife to me in the country . . . and a fine influence for Ian. I can rather imagine you quietly reading or sewing at Hamilton House."

The suggestion was so unexpected, so absurdly inconceivable that Sophie swallowed down a burst of hysterical laughter.

"And frankly," he blithely continued, leaning into her so that he might whisper in her ear, "I can rather imagine you in another, less pure, circumstance."

Sophie instantly jerked backward, away from him, but Trevor held her tightly to him. She squirmed, tried to be free of his grip. "The waltz, sir, it has ended!"

Trevor looked up, smiled sheepishly. "So it has," he said, and abruptly let her go in the middle of the dance floor.

Feeling the dozens of eyes on them, Sophie clapped politely, too flabbergasted to know what to say or do next. The next dance would undoubtedly be a quadrille— she could not abide the thought of any further discussion of this topic, at least not now, not *here*.

"I think I should like a champagne," she said, and began to move off the dance floor, hardly caring if he followed her or not.

"I'll fetch it for you," he said, and in a move that was becoming all too familiar and all too resented, he grasped her elbow, leading her to the edge of the dance floor. "Wait here for me," he said, as if he already owned her, and walked away.

Incredulous and somewhat panicked, Sophie stared at his back, still unable to believe what he had said, *how* he had said it. And she was still standing there when Trevor returned, paralyzed by her repugnance and the growing realization that she would be pushed headlong into a match if he should ever utter those words to anyone else. But as he handed her a cup of punch—she had asked for champagne—Sophie heard the voice that made her heart pound.

"I beg your pardon, sir, but I should like to stand up with Lady Sophie, if she will do me that great honor."

Trevor spasmed oddly at the sound of Caleb's voice behind her; in her haste, Sophie almost spilled the punch on her gown as she whirled about. *Oh my . . .* He was heavenly, terribly handsome in his black coat and immaculate white shirt. His forest-green waistcoat perfectly matched his neckcloth, making his green eyes more vivid than usual. She had never seen him in such finery; she had not expected to have her breath taken away by his magnetism. She smiled warmly, hungrily, at him, wanting to feel his arms around her, his breath on her lips. For a blind instant, she was deaf to the growing murmurs of the crowd as they strained to hear the exchange between the two would-be brothers, deaf to Trevor's heavy breathing.

"What in the *hell* do you think you are doing?"

The low tenor of Trevor's voice dragged Sophie back to a cold reality.

"Asking Lady Sophie for the honor of a dance," Caleb said calmly. "You've had your turn about, old boy. Why not step aside and let someone else have a go of it?"

"What bloody nerve," Trevor snapped through clenched teeth. "You don't belong here! Run along now and return yourself to whatever rock from under which you crawled!"

Caleb chuckled, belying a gaze as hard and cold as ice. "I beg your pardon, sir, I did not understand that *you* were hosting this affair."

Trevor's breathing turned horribly ragged; Sophie instinctively moved, positioning herself between the two men. *"Please,"* she whispered. "Do not think to disgrace your father!"

That earned a growl of pure disdain from Trevor, and

part of her withered instantly, reacting to an ancient, buried fear. "Make no mistake, madam," he said coldly, "this man has no father here!"

The contempt dripping from his voice sent a chill down Sophie's spine, but Caleb chuckled lightly as he took Sophie's hand and removed the punch. "Oh, now, really, sir," he said cheerfully to Trevor as he placed the cup aside and put her hand on his arm. "You cannot be entirely certain of that, can you?" He did not bother to receive Trevor's response, but simply smiled down at her as if everything were perfectly normal. "As for that dance, Lady Sophie, might I have the honor?"

A hush had fallen over the room—everyone seemed to stand in rapt attention, feasting on the scene between the two brothers. Sophie could feel Trevor's fury, could feel everyone watching her, holding their collective breath. For the first time since she had donned her princess gown, she felt her old awkward self, the center of unwanted attention, uncertain what to say, how to act. But when she looked up at Caleb, the warmth of his smile seeped into her skin, the distractions around them began to fade to distant noise. With his hand locked firmly around hers, she could almost believe there was nothing but the two of them, no one standing in their way.

She drew her courage from the gentle squeeze of his hand. Unthinkingly, she nodded. She did not hear the hiss of breath Trevor drew, or the gasps behind her as Caleb led her to the middle of the dance floor and took his place across from her. She did not even sense the awkward moment when everyone looked frantically about, wondering who would join them on the dance floor. Caleb held her gaze as one couple joined them, then another and another, the smile in his eyes mesmerizing her.

As the music started up, Caleb stepped forward to begin the dance. "Smile, then," he said, as he moved around her in the steps to the dance. "Or else they will think I forced you to abide me."

Sophie laughed then, let the rhythm of the quadrille carry her forward, into his arms, and out again. Let them all see that she *wanted* to stand up with Caleb Hamilton, that she did not care who he was, other than the one man on this earth who could make her smile, make her feel beautiful, and so very glad to be alive.

At the edge of the dance floor, still holding a cup of punch, Trevor watched them, felt the rage in him begin to boil like a cauldron. He could scarcely believe it—how dare that bastard think to insinuate himself with Sophie, of all people? Who in God's name did he think he was? He would ruin everything. *Everything!*

His anger escalated as the Imposter casually clasped his hands behind his back and smiled down at Sophie when the music began.

But it soared when he saw Sophie smiling so warmly in return.

Chapter Fourteen

SHE WAS EXQUISITE; he could not take his
eyes from her. Sophie laughed as they stepped about in
the familiar pattern of the quadrille, her chocolate brown
eyes dancing with merriment. The gown she wore made
her look resplendent, her shape that of a man's desire,
and Caleb could feel the tug at his heartstrings as he
touched her hand, the small of her back, and released
her again.

He ceased to see the dancing around him, or hear the
voices of the crowd and the music of Haydn playing in
the background. His focus was only Sophie; her breath,
her voice, the only thing he could hear. It was odd, he
thought, as they went round again, that she had captured his imagination so completely, made him so moon-
eyed. He was so enthralled with her that he would—and
did—make the unpardonable mistake of asking her for a
second dance, feeling enormously pleased with himself
when she, too, ignored all ballroom etiquette and eagerly
accepted his invitation.

And as he led her into a waltz, she smiled, whispered,
"Hold me close, Caleb. Make me sway." The memory of
their private ballroom dance rushed over him; he was

holding her close before he realized it, wondering what it might possibly matter. After all, both of them were already marked—Sophie by scandal, he by illegitimate birth. What was one more dance or holding her too close in the greater scheme of things? Besides, he could not let her out of his sight, could not let go of the feel of her in his arms, or the memory of what it was to hold himself above her, thrust deep inside her. No, he could not see that one more dance could matter.

But it apparently did matter to one Lady Ann Boxworth, who Sophie quickly and furtively identified as her sister as the dance ended. The moment Caleb escorted Sophie to the edge of the dance floor, she was accosted, her sister's fingers digging into Sophie's arm as she politely but firmly begged their leave of him.

Sophie scarcely had time to react; she muttered a quick *pardon* to Caleb and gave him a look she hoped he would understand as Ann marched her toward the ladies' retiring room like a child being removed from play for some terrible misdeed.

Sophie resented it greatly.

When the door shut behind them, Sophie jerked her arm from her sister's grip. "I am not a child!"

"You certainly act like one," her sister retorted, folding her arms tightly across her middle. "Have you any idea how this looks? Have you forgotten everything you have ever learned about social propriety?"

"For heaven's sake, Ann! I merely danced with him!"

"*Twice.* One, two in a row, paying him particular attention while Mr. Trevor Hamilton stands by and watches you dance with a man who may very well be a swindler!"

"He is not a swindler," Sophie muttered, and turned away from Ann, pretending to fuss with her hair in the mirror.

But Ann's face was instantly looming behind hers in the mirror's reflection, her dark eyes narrowed with ire. "I don't know what you are about, Sophie, but you will *not* humiliate Mr. Hamilton! He has shown you nothing but his goodwill since you arrived, and this is how you would show him your gratitude?"

Gratitude. She hated that word! As if she were some beggar woman desperate for Trevor Hamilton's favorable attention. It was degrading and it angered her. "I am a grown woman and I may dance with whomever I please!" she snapped. "I do not need or want Mr. Hamilton's permission!"

Ann gasped; she stared at Sophie as if she could not fully comprehend what she had said. "You would do well to endeavor to be less querulous and think beyond your desire to make a show of yourself this evening, Sophie. Mr. Hamilton has very graciously ignored your past! We all expect him to offer for you, and you cannot hope for better than that, can you? Do you want to remain a spinster all your life? If you do, then carry on your present course. But if you wish for a home and a family, then you had best behave!"

Sophie groaned, closed her eyes as she pressed her fists to her temples. "I am not nearly so intent on marrying as my family is on marrying me away."

"Then I suppose you think to cavort about the world with Madame Fortier all your life?"

Sophie opened her eyes, glanced at her sister's reflection. "Honestly? I rather don't know *what* to think about the rest of my life."

"That has been your misfortune for many years now, Sophie. You do not think. I'm of a mind to go at once to Julian, if you must know."

"Oh marvelous, Ann!" she said with a derisive laugh. "Run to Julian and tell him how I have disgraced the family once again by dancing *two* dances with one man. Oh my, what a tragedy for Kettering!"

Ann said nothing; she pressed her lips tightly together and lowered her gaze. When she looked up again, her eyes were shimmering with tears of frustration. "I surrender. I have tried my best to help you, but you will not allow it. What can I do?"

"Ann, *please,*" Sophie begged her, feeling immediately contrite. "At least try to understand me."

But Ann wasn't listening; she threw up a hand in a gesture of surrender as she turned and walked to the door. "Do as you will, Sophie," she said wearily. "But please do not deceive yourself. You cannot carry on with a man of questionable birth and not expect there to be consequences. Never mind the sound advice of your family—you will only have yourself to blame for what may come." With that, she walked out the door.

Sophie sank onto one of four velvet-covered stools and buried her face in her hands. How could she hope to make anyone understand? She did not *want* to be Mrs. Trevor Hamilton, even if that meant she would at last have a respectability she had lost eight years ago. She wanted to be with Caleb, but that was just as impossible, albeit for completely different reasons.

The door opened behind her; two debutantes whose names she did not know bustled in, giggling. When they saw Sophie sitting there, they stopped cold and stared at her for an awkward moment. Sophie sighed, gained her feet. She walked past the two girls, nodding curtly as she did, then into the orangery, where the ball was once again in full force. There was no sight of Ann, or Trevor. Honorine was absent, too.

So was Caleb.

Sophie quit the orangery and moved quickly across the back lawn to the veranda, where the silhouettes of several couples dotted the railing. She glanced around as she climbed the veranda steps, stopping midway when her gaze inadvertently landed on Melinda Birdwell.

She was standing off to one side with the same woman Sophie had seen with her at Lady Worthington's garden tea so many weeks ago. Melinda calmly regarded Sophie with the familiar, lopsided smirk of her thin lips. "My, my, Lady Sophie, how elegant you look this evening."

Sophie barely managed a polite smile. "Thank you,

Melinda." She took another step, fully intending to continue on.

"Mr. Hamilton must be right proud."

The remark caught her off guard; Sophie shot her a
look, curious as to *which* Mr. Hamilton Melinda meant
to deride her with.

Melinda's smirk turned into a snort of derisive laughter; she exchanged a look of superiority with her friend.
"Don't know what to think? Well. I confess I am as mystified as you. In fact, I rather imagine the entire guest list
is mystified by your apparent preference."

Her laugh was cold and brittle; Sophie could hear the
entire *ton* in that laugh. Her pulse pounding, she did not
spare Melinda another glance, but ran up the steps, ignoring her mocking laughter as she passed her and
stepped into the main salon.

She was instantly greeted by a dozen or more heads
swiveling in her direction. As her gaze met those around
her, Sophie felt her skin crawl. She looked wildly about,
saw the top of Honorine's head on the opposite end, in
the place she had set up for Lord Hamilton. Head down,
she pushed forward, anxious to be near someone she
knew, someone she trusted.

As she made her way through the crowd, she could
see Honorine's colorful gown swirling about. But when
she reached the far end of the room, her heart plummeted. Honorine was sitting on Lord Hamilton's lap,
laughing with him like a dockside wench. It wasn't done
in the salons of Mayfair, it simply wasn't done. Nearby,
Trevor watched, his jaw clenched tightly shut. Several
people stood gaping at the spectacle.

Only Lord Hamilton seemed to enjoy her company.

It was plainly evident that the novelty of the Frenchwoman was wearing thin; Sophie could not help but see
the censure on so many faces. The woman meant no
harm; she merely loved life and all that accompanied it.
Sophie pushed forward, mindless of Trevor or anyone
else around her, and caught Honorine's arm.

Honorine turned a broad smile to Sophie. "*Sofia!* I tell you this is good, *non?* See my Will, how much he enjoys this."

Sophie glanced down at the viscount, who flashed her a grin. "Lovely evening. V-very lovely."

"You see?" Honorine said proudly to Sophie, then smiled at Lord Hamilton and slid off his lap. "Come now, my Will, you have feet, *oui?*"

"*No,*" Sophie whispered harshly, glancing covertly around them. "Can you not see how everyone looks at you?"

Honorine shrugged as she helped the viscount to his feet. "What care do I have that they look?"

The viscount wobbled a bit as he moved his cane around to steady himself, but grasped it firmly with two hands and looked at Sophie. "Your friend," he said, nodding at Honorine, "she has h-helped m-me very m-much."

"Lord Hamilton, you mustn't overtax yourself," Sophie pleaded with him, but he didn't seem to hear her, and instead held out an arm to Honorine.

Delighted, Honorine instantly attached herself to him. "*La Orangerie, monsieur. We dance in la orangerie.*"

"I . . . want to . . . t-try," he said, and striking the cane firmly in front of him, took a strong step forward, Honorine encouraging him.

Perhaps she was dreaming. Perhaps she had fallen into some horrible nightmare from which she could not awake, Sophie thought, as she watched the pair move through the stunned crowd.

"That woman is making a laughingstock of my father."

Apparently, she was *not* dreaming. Sophie glanced over her shoulder at Trevor. His jaw was set stiffly, his eyes like two nuggets of coal as he watched his father pause to attempt to speak with an acquaintance. He slid that hard gaze to Sophie. "And you are making a laughingstock of *me.*"

His words sliced the warm, moist air between them.

"*I* am?" she asked, despising herself for sounding so tentative.

"You danced with a man who would steal my rightful fortune from me," he said with not a little disdain. "Did you think I would not mind it?"

The sheer arrogance of that remark infuriated her. "Pardon, sir, but I was not aware I required your permission."

Trevor's frown deepened; his gaze roamed her face, lingered on her hair for a moment. "Perhaps you have been so long in her company that you have forgotten proper etiquette. I cannot hold it against you, Sophie. I regret that you did not think before you acted. But I suppose I might take comfort in the knowledge that we likely won't have any more frivolous behavior as the Imposter has gone and cannot harm you further."

His announcement stunned her. How could he be *gone?* Without a word? No, no, she didn't believe him; she went up on her toes, her eyes frantically scanning the room for Caleb. But Trevor's low chuckle made her stomach roil.

"You may trust me, he has quit his charade for the evening. My father was not of a mind to speak with him at all, I am grateful to say, and since he could not press his claim further, the Imposter departed. I think he came merely to make a scene and discredit my father's good name even further. Now why do you look so disbelieving, my dear? Did you expect differently? Or is he perhaps as charming as they say?"

She would not dignify that stab with an answer. Her head ached with confusion—where would he have gone? How could he leave without so much as a word of good night? How could he leave her *here,* with Trevor, with all eyes upon her?

"I rather imagine he is," Trevor said.

"Is what?" she asked, almost on a whisper.

"Charming. His reputation with women is well known.

But I should think a woman of your tender sensibilities would not understand how a man may use his charms."

Oh, but didn't she?

Trevor put his hand on her arm. "Come, let me fetch you something to eat. You are looking quite pale again." He wrapped her hand around the crook of his arm, pulled her close, and began to lead her toward the dining room.

Sophie followed mutely, too disconcerted to do differently.

Trevor brought her a plate of sandwiches and a glass of punch, then stood by as she tried to force herself to eat. But she couldn't; she stared at the plate, already full with her dismay and the swelling sense of dread. Ann and Victor came into the dining room and took seats around her, but Ann barely spoke at all. The only thing she remarked upon was Honorine and Lord Hamilton. "I'm certain it is not good for him a'tall to be moving so awkwardly about the ballroom."

Even that remark was said with a tone of disapproval, the same tone she had heard in so many of the voices around her. It was enough to drive Sophie quite mad. As Victor and Trevor began to speak of the events surrounding Parliament, Ann avoided her gaze, and Sophie wondered if she hadn't already gone round the bend.

All her life, she had dutifully done what her sisters and her brother told her to do; she never dreamed of doing or thinking otherwise, with the notable and disastrous exception of William Stanwood. Apparently, they would hold that over her head for the rest of her life, using it as an excuse to question her judgment about every little thing. Even someone who had been as kind and as gracious to her as Honorine would be subjected to their scrutiny and their impossible rules. Yet what they failed to understand, all of them—all of *London* for that matter— was that in the last eight years, she had discovered there *was* a Sophie inside her, a living, breathing being with thoughts and desires and opinions all her own. A Sophie who was capable of making her own decisions.

Then why in God's name didn't she make a few? Angry with herself for being so meek, for letting Trevor lead her around like a prized calf, for allowing Ann and Claudia to enhance her wardrobe—*enough!* Ann was right—it was time she acted like a grown woman. If she would only stop pretending to be one and stand up for herself!

She wanted the ball to end. She wanted it to end so badly that she picked up a flute of champagne from a passing waiter, frowned at Trevor's grunt of disapproval, put down the strong urge to toss the contents of the flute into his face, and drank it. Then she helped herself to another.

When Trevor insisted on accompanying her to the main salon, she took another flute, this time smiling boldly when he gave her a questioning look. That third flute of champagne was the one that made her feel rather light on her feet, and she realized it was *she* who was laughing gaily when Fabrice and Roland collapsed, exhausted, on the throne Honorine had made Lord Hamilton. When the viscount returned, flushed and smiling from his attempt at dancing, Trevor spoke with his father for a few moments, at which point Sophie took the opportunity to help herself to an unprecedented fourth flute of champagne.

As she lifted the flute to her lips, she caught sight of Caleb, alone in the back of the room, leaning insouciantly against the wall.

He hadn't left.

He hadn't left! In her hazy, intoxicated state, she realized that Trevor had lied to her. Unthinkingly, she started for Caleb, but a firm hand on her arm stopped her.

"Sophie, where are you off to? There is something I want you to hear."

Trevor's voice was sickeningly sweet. "Wh-what?" she said, peering up at him. "Hear what?"

"Give me the champagne, will you?" He took the flute from her hand, then lifted it over his head and in a strong voice, called out, "Pardon! Pardon, please, everyone! If I might have a moment of your attention!"

What in heaven's name was he doing? Sophie took a wobbly step backward, looked at Honorine. She was staring at Sophie, her expression a curious mix of terror and bewilderment. Trevor's hold on her arm slipped to her hand, which he grasped tightly in his. So tightly, that it hurt.

"If I may have your attention for just a moment!" Trevor called again, and waited till the din of the many conversations had died and all eyes were looking at him. Sophie looked to Caleb and tried to smile, but his expression was so dark, terribly dark—

"First, if I may, I would thank our lovely hostess, Madame Fortier, for this evening and providing such a splendid venue for an announcement."

How odd, Sophie thought dreamily as a polite round of applause rose up, that Honorine should look so deathly pale. She adored compliments.

"Most of you know I have been alone with a young son for two years. He is in need of a loving woman to guide his passage to manhood, and I am in need of a loving wife. It is therefore my great honor to publicly offer for the hand of Lady Sophie Dane."

Whatever else he might have said, if anything, was lost in the sudden swell of voices and cries of surprise. It took several seconds for his words to sink in through the chaos that was suddenly Sophie's brain. Ann's unmistakable cry of relief was what shook her; she looked up at Trevor in horror. He stared down at her with a smile that appeared forced, then lifted her flute of champagne to his lips and drank, draining the entire contents. How could he? *How could he?* Revulsion, astonishment, humiliation, and champagne all began to mix in the pit of her belly, sickening her.

Caleb.

She jerked around to where he was standing; he was still there, staring at her, his expression one of fury and . . . *did she imagine it? . . .* despair.

She moved forward, but Trevor's hold on her hand tightened painfully, and he held her back. "You will stay, Sophie," he said through clenched teeth. "I just publicly offered for you. You will at least do me the courtesy of not humiliating me by running off."

He had just yanked the world out from under her feet, and he worried she would somehow humiliate *him*? Dumbstruck, mute, and unbalanced by the champagne, Sophie stared across the room at Caleb, feeling her despair mix with his.

Amid the chaos, Honorine struggled to lead Will Hamilton from the agitated crowd in the stuffy salon and onto the veranda. Will had asked her to, having felt suddenly powerless upon hearing his son's announced intentions. Once Honorine had managed to free him from the melee inside, he stood leaning against the wall for support. She marched to the railing, punched her hands to her hips, and dragged the night air into her lungs.

Will felt his body sigh—he did not blame her for being so terribly upset. Trevor had no right to do what he did, no right at all. But it was always that way with Trevor, wasn't it?

Wasn't it?

There was something he wanted to remember, something that seemed to swirl around his broken mind, something he was not quite able to grasp. A mystery for which the answer lay at home, he was certain of it—he had no idea how he knew it—he just instinctively knew the answer was there, at Hamilton House, his country estate.

Will looked again at Honorine, still at the railing. "Honor," he said.

She turned immediately at the sound of his voice, came to him, and put a comforting hand on his shoulder. *"Oui?"*

"I want to g-go home," he said, more clearly than before, his voice stronger these last few days. "Please. T-take me home."

Honorine nodded instantly. *"Oui, oui . . .* home. This you want now?"

Will reached a twisted hand to her waist. *"Now,"* he said.

Chapter Fifteen

F ROM HIS POST in the shadows of the alcove, Caleb watched Sophie as she took another flute of champagne and lifted it to her lips, nodding to something one rotund woman said. His heart was silent now, perhaps even dead, having somersaulted in his chest a dozen times when Trevor announced his intentions. He didn't want to be angry with Sophie—after all, she hadn't made the announcement—but frankly, he didn't know what to think or believe anymore.

It just seemed impossible that the woman who had met him each day in Regent's Park could have deceived him. The one thing he thought he knew above all else was that she was guileless. And he had believed with all his heart . . . *still believed* . . . that she loved him. So how could she just stand so obediently and let Trevor do it? Why didn't she throw up her arms, cry out, do something, *anything*, to stop him?

Unless Trevor had employed her help to somehow destroy *him*.

It was a thought that had flitted across his mind more than once in the last half-hour since the stunning announcement was made. Although he could readily believe it of Trevor—there was no point so low to which he would not stoop—Caleb could not believe it of Sophie. But her complacence—what had she done to them with her complacence?

Whatever else might happen tonight, he would not leave until he had that answer. It was simply a matter of waiting until he could speak with her alone, even if it took all night.

He had no idea how long he had been standing in the shadows of the alcove just outside the main salon, but he had done so undetected as many guests began to make their way home. The rotund woman finally left Sophie; she took the opportunity to leave the salon, wobbling down the corridor on the legs of a woman who had drunk too much champagne. Shoving his hands into his pockets, Caleb followed her.

He walked silently, two or more lengths behind her, past the hat that someone had left lying carelessly on the floor, past a woman's cape draped over a console, the jeweled clasp glistening in the dwindling light of the candelabras. Past the gaming room, where four men still held cards and cigars, turning right at the door to the morning room as Sophie had done, into a corridor that was dimly lit.

Light spilled out from one open door just ahead. He paused there to look inside, surprised to see Roland sprawled across a settee, staring up at the ceiling while his fingers idly thread through Fabrice's hair, who sat on the floor, propped against the settee.

He moved on quickly, to the end of the corridor, to a pair of French doors that were opened onto the veranda. As he stepped outside, a rush of cool air hit his face, made him release the breath he had held that was burning his lungs.

He strolled to the railing. There was a handful of people milling about the expansive lawn; lights still glittered in the windows of the orangery, but the music had long since ended. There was no sign of Sophie, although he was certain she had come this way. He walked to the edge of the veranda, letting his eyes adjust to the darkness beyond the light that spilled from the house. He scanned the grounds, could make out no one who even remotely resembled Sophie, no one who was wearing the pale, shimmering color of pearls. All right then, it was to the bedroom suites above, if he must, and Caleb pivoted on his heel, almost colliding with Sophie.

Her sudden appearance gave him quite a start; he reared back, put his hand over his heart.

Sophie cocked her head to one side and peered at him curiously.

"You startled me out of my wits," he said gruffly, lowering his hand.

She seemed not to hear him. "Why did you leave?" she asked, the pitch of her voice a measure of her inebriation.

"As there was hardly anything left for me after hearing my brother's astounding announcement, I thought to take some air," he said caustically.

Her eyes narrowed. "I mean *before*," she said carefully, swaying slightly with the effort. "Why did you leave me here, Caleb?"

"Leave you here? What on earth are you saying? *You* dashed off upon the conclusion of our dance. I waited for you for a time until I was finally forced to consider that you were perhaps permanently indisposed! I merely accompanied Lady Paddington to the dining room. After all, it was she who invited me to escort her tonight."

For some reason, that seemed to incense her; she snorted with displeasure and looked down at the lawn. "You didn't leave."

She said it as if she were surprised. "I did not leave you, Sophie, is that what you thought?" he asked, reaching for her hand.

She nodded absently, frowning.

"Why would you think such a thing?"

"Trevor said that you had left."

How he hated the sound of that man's name on her lips. "Do you think me a boor?" he asked, the indignation swelling, and dropped her hand. "I should hope you would know me better than that."

"I am not certain I really know you at all," she said, and awkwardly gripped the railing to steady herself.

"Meaning?"

"Meaning . . . meaning you have a rather strange habit of disappearing. Or appearing, as you did tonight. You disappear, then you reappear—"

"What in God's name are you talking about?" he demanded.

She shrugged, lifted her chin.

The fury was stirring deep inside him. He, too, gripped the railing in an effort to maintain his composure. "Please do me the courtesy of clarifying your accusation, Lady Sophie."

His tone apparently startled her; Sophie took a step backward and stared up at him. "What was I to think?" she demanded uncertainly. "He said you had left, and I thought you had gone without a word. I didn't know what to think . . ." Her voice trailed off; she grimaced, put a hand to her forehead.

What was she supposed to think? Had he imagined the hours spent between them? Had he imagined the way she had looked at him on those warm, sunny afternoons? The way she had laughed, had spoken of her travels with great animation? And had he been the only one to feel the sense of togetherness they shared as they worked side by side on the booth for Covent Garden?

"You are drunk, Sophie," he said evenly, "or else you would have known to think that I adore you. You would think that perhaps I care a great deal for you, so much that I attended this event with Lady Paddington in spite of my better judgment. You would think that I would devote myself to you entirely until the end of time if it were necessary. But you would *not* think that I was playing you for a fool!"

"Oh," she said softly, dropping her gaze so that her long lashes formed dark crescents against her skin. "I . . . I did not dare to think all of that."

The indignation in him soared. "I am sick unto death of your mistrust. Why won't you believe that I love you?" he demanded.

"Because I can't!" she blurted. "I don't understand why you do! I am not the sort to inspire men like you!" she cried, sinking down to her knees, clinging to the railing with one hand. "Don't you know? I loved a man once, but he loved my fortune. I am afraid to trust you, Caleb, I am *afraid*."

How was it that he could love her so much when she could doubt him so? He leaned down, gripped her wrist, and pulled her up to her feet. "Listen to me carefully, Sophie. Hear what I say to you. I *love* you. No other! There will never *be* another, do you quite understand me?"

She started, looking up in alarm as he pulled her forward, into his embrace. He did not let her speak, but kissed her fiercely, hoping insanely that he could pass his heart to her, make her feel his love flowing through it, making it beat.

Sophie's body relaxed in his arms; she tilted her head back to better reach him, returning his kiss with tenderness in spite of his attempts to make her *feel* him.

But the ugly image of Trevor standing in the salon invaded his mind's eye, his chest puffed as he looked at Caleb and made his grand announcement. Caleb abruptly lifted his head and turned away from Sophie's beatific face, to the east, where the sky was beginning to lighten.

"What was I to think, Sophie?"

"What?" she asked, sniffing.

He forced himself to look at her. "Was I a fool to believe in the promise of us?"

Her look of bewilderment grated on him; he clenched his jaw. "Trevor, Sophie! What am *I* to think? The hours we have spent in one another's company making love . . . they have led me to believe you held me in *some* esteem.

What is the truth? Did you traipse from one picnic to the other? Laugh at my attempts to capture your fancy while you dine with him?"

She was shaking her head, denying it. He stepped away, suddenly not wanting to hear any excuses.

"I told you, Caleb, I did not encourage his suit," Sophie said. "I gave him *no* reason whatsoever to believe I would consider marriage!"

The cast of repugnance in her voice rang true. Yet she had not turned him away from her door, and Caleb stubbornly persisted. "If you did nothing to encourage him, then why should he announce an engagement?"

"He announced his intentions, not an engagement! He has not bothered to ask *my* opinion on the subject, and I can assure you, my intentions are quite the opposite! Please believe me, Caleb! I most certainly will *not* accept his offer, not under any circumstance!"

She took a step toward him, but stopped, seeming uncertain what to do. He did not reach for her. He wanted to believe her. But there was a small nagging part of him that understood Trevor could offer her so much more than he could, a standard of living above his own. *A legitimate name.* Would he truly shackle her to a bastard? The woman had suffered enough.

"What were you to think?" she all but whispered. "You were to think it is *you* I want, you I think of every waking moment, you I long to hold, to love."

The words reverberated in his heart. *She loved him.* The knowledge emboldened him, made him swell with hope.

"Then accept *my* offer," he said impetuously, grabbing her hands in his, catching her elbow when she stumbled. "Accept *my* offer, Sophie! Marry me! Come live with me. *Dance* with me, laugh with me, *be* with me—"

"Please don't do this," she pleaded, choking on a sob.

His voice fell into nothing. Sophie's eyes were suddenly shimmering with tears, and he instantly regretted his foolish impetuosity. "What, Sophie? Don't do what?"

"I *cannot* accept your offer, Caleb." She very ungracefully wiped the back of her hand across her mouth. "I cannot!" The sobs erupted again; tears made rivulets down her cheeks.

But he hardly noticed; she *could not* accept his offer . . . old feelings of inadequacy and despair were clanging in his brain, his heart. Had she been any other woman . . . but he could not bear to believe that of Sophie. Oh, but he had thought she was different from the others. He had thought them two pariahs, destined for one another. He stood mutely, staring at her, convincing himself that he had not heard her correctly at all as he tried to make sense of it. *"Why?"* he finally demanded.

"Because, I . . ." her voice trailed away; she wiped tears from her eyes, avoiding his gaze. "Because . . ."

"Because you do not care for me as much as this?"

"No!"

"Then *why*? Tell me why, Sophie, make me understand how you might profess to love me, then turn about and refuse me!"

She gulped on her tears, hugged herself tightly, and Caleb suddenly did not want to hear her answer.

"Because I . . . I simply cannot," she murmured weakly. She lowered her gaze to his neckcloth, stared dumbly at it.

There it was, then. The one person he thought was above society's rules as to whom one should or should not consort with was not above them at all. "Did you think it a game?" he asked hoarsely. "Did you think to keep your secret lover like a pet? Let me out of my cage when you wanted me to pleasure you? Amuse you?"

"No!" she cried. "Don't say such horrid things! I love you, I *do*—"

"I am hard pressed to believe that at the moment."

"Oh God," she said, and closed her eyes, put her fists to her temples. "I don't know what I am saying."

"Let me assure you it is quite ugly," he said, and

moved backward, away from her, but Sophie abruptly grabbed his hand, clinging to it.

"Caleb—"

"No," he said gruffly, shaking her hand from his. "You've made yourself perfectly clear, Sophie. I find it ironic that you should accuse me of being faithless when you would do this."

"You don't understand!"

"No!" he said again, more sharply, as she tried to take his hand again. "I don't understand, but what does it matter? There is nothing more to say, except that I . . ." The pain was choking him, making it difficult to speak. "I wish you the best," he said sincerely, and turned away from her, began walking across the veranda, consciously putting one foot in front of the other as he silently prayed she would call him back, tell him that he was wrong, that he had misunderstood her—*anything*.

But she did not utter a word, just let him keep walking, until he had rounded the corner, disappeared from her view.

And her life.

Chapter Sixteen

WHEN THE SUN had reached the top of the sky the next day and cast a bright sliver across Sophie's face, she made the mistake of moving. The instant pain was excruciating, forcing her eyes open. As her vision adjusted to the midday sun, another sharp pain shot across her forehead.

Oh God, she hoped she was dying.

Only death could possibly make her feel better than this. Her head felt enormous, one hundred pounds or more, and her mouth tasted like dirty figs. Little wonder, given that she had consumed a half-dozen or more in something of a frenzy, washing them down with two glasses of champagne before finally succumbing to mind-numbing sleep.

The sound of the door being shoved open sliced painfully through the fog on her brain; she closed her eyes, hoped death would come sooner rather than later.

"Do ye intend to lie about all day, then?"

The grating sound of Lucie Cowplain's voice only made the pain worse. "I am dying," she muttered thickly.

"Ye ain't dying, although ye ought after all that champagne. Come on now, be up with ye."

Swallowing back a wave of nausea, Sophie murmured, "I can't. If I move, I shall expire."

"London would not be so fortunate as that. Here now, take a sip of this."

She opened her eyes, winced at the pain in her head as she slowly turned to focus on Lucie Cowplain. The old woman was standing next to her bed, holding a glass of some milky concoction.

"What is it?"

"Raw egg, goat's milk, and a bit of whiskey—sure to mend what ails ye."

Lucie Cowplain was trying to kill her—the nausea was so great that she quickly closed her eyes, swallowing hard.

"Drink it. Ye'll feel yourself again."

But she didn't *want* to feel herself again, not that befuddled, mousy, helpless little spinster!

Slowly, gingerly, Sophie pushed herself up on her elbows, felt her stomach roil in protest, and quickly lowered herself down again. *She had never drunk so much in all her life.* Bloody hell, she had never *drunk* in her life, save a glass of wine with dinner and the occasional Yuletide nog. Yes, well, she had never had such a night in her life, what with Trevor practically marrying her in the main salon and Caleb . . . *Caleb!* . . . looking as if he hoped he would never be forced to lay eyes on her again. Honestly, she had the two of *them* to blame for her misery—it had been the most perfectly wretched, ghastly evening of her entire life.

Had it really happened?

A firm hand on her shoulder forced Sophie up. At least she managed to sit up without dying.

"Drink," Lucie Cowplain said, and forced the glass to her lips. The substance went down uneasily; Sophie could hardly swallow it. But she managed to choke it down, then sat hunched over, her hair shielding her from the sight of Lucie Cowplain's self-satisfied smirk until she felt her stomach might settle.

Perhaps it was all Honorine's fault. It was a wonder she hadn't come banging in here, full of vigor and new French ideas this morning. Perhaps she was abed herself—perhaps even she was feeling a bit embarrassed that Sophie had been so very, *very* right in her assessment of the ball—a complete disaster, just as she predicted, thank you very much.

Food. What she wouldn't give for something substantial, something to take the taste of fig from her mouth. At the moment, she rather thought she would never so much as look at a fig again, much less eat one.

"I've drawn a warm bath for ye, lass," Lucie Cowplain said in a voice that was uncharacteristically sympathetic. Sophie nodded, shoved one leg over the side of the bed, and carefully inched the other one over before testing her full weight on her wobbly legs. She stood slowly, moaned at how the room was spinning, and gripped the bedpost until the spinning had stopped. When she at last felt as if she could maneuver about well enough in her body, she limped to her bath.

When she emerged a full hour later—fifteen minutes of which had been spent with her face floating in a basin of cold water—Sophie felt somewhat more herself, physically speaking. But her mood had not improved in the least, and as she stomped heavily down the long corridor, a deep frown furrowed between her eyes.

The guilt was consuming her, eating her from the inside out. Caleb, dear Caleb—she *loved* him! But marriage? It was impossible. Julian, her sisters—they would never allow her to wed a baseborn man, no matter how charming or gracious or very handsome he was. So what exactly, then, had she believed would come of their daily meetings? What had she been doing, tempting fate so openly and brazenly? Had the foolish little Sophie really thought that she could live in her make-believe world with her secret lover and expect him to do the same?

She despised herself. Her actions had been no worse or no better than William Stanwood's, really—he had lured her under false pretense. Had she not done the same to Caleb? It was a nauseating thought, and tears filled her eyes as she imagined what Caleb must think of her now. The whole thing made her wholly miserable— her heart was literally breaking into pieces.

It wasn't the first time it had broken, but it certainly felt like the worst.

Tears blinding her again, she determined she could not think of it now, not with a headache the size of England. Grabbing the railing, she bounced unevenly down the winding staircase, silently berating herself with each heavy step. But when she landed on the ground floor, she forgot her woes as she looked around her.

The house looked as if a violent ocean wave had crashed through it.

She moved slowly through the foyer, being careful not to step in the spilled champagne, or on the expensive, gold velvet cape that had been carelessly dropped on the marble tile foyer. The corridor was worse—empty crystal flutes, china plates littering the consoles was to be expected, and even the occasional hair ribbon and neckcloth, she supposed, but the gentleman's shoe in the middle of the floor was an object of some curiosity. She picked her way around the debris until she reached the door of the main salon, where she paused to debate whether or not she dared to look inside.

She dared.

The room didn't seem quite as battle-strewn as the rest of the house, but the furniture was all askew and an abundance of pillows were scattered about. More important, Fabrice and Roland were lying at opposite ends of one long couch, their stocking feet entwined with one another's. She watched them for a moment until Fabrice snorted in his sleep and she was certain they were quite alive.

And exactly where was Honorine?

Food.

Sophie moved on, making her way to the kitchen, where she stood, hands on hips, frowning at the lack of immediate food sources. With a sigh of great irritation, she threw open the cupboard and began to rummage.

Claudia and Ann found Sophie slicing a loaf of bread. Butter and preserves were piled into bowls in front of her, and she had just removed boiled chicken from the kettle hanging over the hearth. Hardly in the mood for callers, Sophie mumbled a greeting as they walked in.

Claudia's nose wrinkled slightly as she looked around; a hand went protectively to her swollen stomach. "We looked all over for you."

"I was hungry."

"Really, don't you have someone who can prepare that for you?" Ann asked. "It's so unseemly for a lady to be rooting about a kitchen."

"I should think it more unseemly for a lady to expire from hunger," Sophie muttered irritably.

"Now Ann, don't be so stern," Claudia said as she examined the jam. "Trevor Hamilton won't have his wife toiling away in a kitchen, will he?"

That remark earned a glare from Sophie; Ann and Claudia chuckled. "Oh come now, you mustn't be so cross!" exclaimed Ann, still laughing.

"And you mustn't think Mr. Hamilton will have a wife," Sophie returned smartly.

That effectively chased the smile from their lips. Both women looked at her as if she had lost her mind. Sophie shrugged, tore a piece of boiled chicken from the carcass, and stuffed it into her mouth.

"You could not possibly mean what you imply," Ann said incredulously.

"I could and I do."

"But why on earth would you refuse his offer?" Claudia asked, confused.

"What offer? He has made none to me. I heard of his desire just like everyone else—in the main salon with dozens looking on," Sophie flatly informed them, and went about the business of spreading jam on a slice of bread.

Ann and Claudia exchanged a wary look. "Naturally, he should have spoken to you first," Claudia said carefully. "But what harm is there really? He meant well, I am certain. Perhaps he was carried away with the excitement of the moment."

"And perhaps he had simply lost his mind!" Sophie exclaimed, waving her bread and jam in the air to emphasize her emphatic belief of that. "But it hardly matters, for it will be his own shame to bear. I had no say in it a'tall."

"But what if he were to give you a say in it?" Ann asked, pushing the jam bowl away from the edge of the table. "You would most certainly accept his offer, would you not?"

Sophie shook her head, munched on a bite of bread and jam.

Ann made a sound of exasperation and muttered something unintelligible under her breath. Claudia sank onto a stool, propped her chin on her fist, and studied Sophie thoughtfully for a moment before asking, "Why would you not accept? His credentials are impeccable."

"His credentials?" Sophie exclaimed incredulously, and tossed down the bread and jam. "Is there nothing else than that? A man's pedigree is all that should recommend him to me?"

"I didn't say—"

"Why should I not hope for more? Why should I not expect to admire and esteem the man I would marry?" she demanded.

"You do not admire and esteem Trevor Hamilton?" Ann asked, looking very perplexed. "But why on earth *not*?"

"He is quite tedious and boring!" Sophie all but shouted, and yanked another piece of meat from the chicken carcass. "He speaks of nothing but the weather! And that child of his despises me!"

"But he is only a boy, and Trevor is an upstanding citizen—"

"I don't care!" she interrupted Claudia.

"And someone who would care for you well, Sophie, you mustn't overlook that. Your inheritance after all . . ."

"I shouldn't worry about that if I were you. Honorine compensates my companionship quite nicely, thank you."

Ann snorted at that; she yanked a piece of chicken from the bird and popped it into her mouth, chewing fiercely as she glared at her younger sister. "That may be, Sophie Elise, but you'd be a fool to refuse an offer because you think him a bore!"

"Why would you ask me to marry someone whom I could not make happy? Why should you want me to marry for anything less than love? *You* did!"

Ann moaned, shook her head. "Of *course* I didn't marry for love! I have come to love Victor over time, but I married him because he was a good man, a good provider—"

"And met the expectations of society," Sophie said, mimicking her sister.

"Sophie!" Claudia exclaimed disapprovingly. "Ann is right! You must think of your future. You must realize that you likely will not have an opportunity like this again!"

That, in a nutshell, was the sum of it for them—she was nothing if not married to someone of suitable stature. She was a burden, an embarrassment, an old spinster who would need to be looked after all her days. She carefully put aside the knife she was holding and looked Claudia in the eye. "What you must think of me, Claudia. How pathetic I must appear to you—do you think I will perish an old spinster? That I shall have no opportunity to experience love? Am I as hopeless as that?"

The color drained from Claudia's face. "Of *course* I don't believe that! I just know society—"

"I have had opportunity," Sophie continued, ignoring Claudia's attempts to explain herself. "Honorine has shown me a world of opportunity, actually, and I need not settle for a tiresome country gentleman."

"I should have known Madame Fortier was behind all this," Ann muttered as she picked at the sliced bread.

Sophie suddenly lost her appetite. Honorine, with a heart the size of the moon, was not tolerated because of her unique person, not even by her own family. And that same attitude, that same closed-mindedness, had caused Sophie to send Caleb away last night, out of her life and out of her heart. The clarity was almost blinding—at last, at long last, she understood. Having been part of the society that would, among other things, condemn a man for the uncontrollable circumstance of his birth, having been a prisoner of that society, then cast out of it, only to be miraculously welcomed into their fold once again for the sheer novelty of it . . .

Sophie finally understood.

And she did not want to be a member of that society, not now, not ever.

Caleb, oh Caleb. Her head was pounding . . . or was that her heart? She began walking for the door.

"Wait . . . where are you going?" Claudia called after her.

An excellent question—she felt adrift, no sense of direction, not certain of who she had become overnight. "I couldn't really say," she said truthfully, and walked out of the kitchen, leaving her family and the *ton* behind.

Chapter Seventeen

Sophie found herself at the house on Upper Moreland Street that afternoon.

It was that or propel herself into complete insanity. As the day had worn on, she had grown more ashamed by what she had done, particularly since her actions were exactly what she despised about the *ton*. It had been a rote reaction; she had been thinking the way she was supposed to think, behaving the way she was expected to behave.

The hypocrisy between her thoughts and deeds had forced her to take a hard look at herself today, and what she saw made her, impossibly, even more miserable.

She had toyed with the idea of going to Regent's Park, if only to catch a glimpse of him. That was the only place she knew to go, for in all her brilliant maneuvering in her affair with Caleb, she had never asked him where he lived, knew only that it was generally in the area of Cheapside. Knowing the exact direction would have been too concrete for her carefully constructed fantasy, wouldn't it?

But she could not go to Regent's Park, at least not yet.

She simply didn't have the courage to see the look of disappointment—or disgust—on his handsome face.

She had instead come to Upper Moreland Street, the one place she felt free of scrutiny. And Nancy knew the entire story of the two brothers—she was the one person Sophie had trusted with the truth. Well, at least half of it. When she told Nancy the events of Honorine's ball, she had left out any mention of cleaving Caleb in two.

She sat in the tiny parlor, slumped in an old and worn overstuffed armchair, watching morosely as Nancy made small repairs to the batch of gowns she would sell the following morning at Covent Garden. In its first day, the little booth Caleb had built met with astounding success—six of the seven gowns Nancy had taken had sold to women for more than she had hoped, and all of the hats and slippers had been snatched up before midday.

Nancy was quite pleased with the success of Sophie's idea, but made it clear they were no longer in need of her help. "We'll manage on our own, thank you," she had said when Sophie had offered to accompany her to the booth the next morning. "We've scarcely room for Bette and myself, in truth. And you've undoubtedly more important matters than this."

"Hardly," snorted Sophie, and idly picked at the bit of stuffing that was peeking out of a hole on the arm of her chair. "Other than, I suppose, determining how one goes about refusing an offer of marriage made to a room full of society's most favored people."

"Why, you say to the bloke, 'No thank you, milord, for my heart belongs to another,' " Nancy offered, clasping her hands dramatically over her heart, then laughed at her own jest.

Sophie frowned.

"Oh there now, luv, you mustn't look so sad. The bloke will pick himself up by his bootstraps, you'll see."

"I really don't know how he will accept it, but I rather think my family will never forgive me . . ."—she

winced, glanced at Nancy from the corner of her eye—
"or Caleb."

That caught Nancy's attention. "Caleb?" She put
down her sewing and looked curiously at Sophie. "*Our*
Mr. Hamilton? But he should be very pleased indeed!"

Sophie shook her head, picked even more intently at
the stuffing. "He isn't very pleased with me a'tall. Actually,
I will be quite surprised if he should ever speak to me
again."

Nancy's brow wrinkled in confusion. "Why ever
should he not?"

She did not want to say it aloud, did not want to hear
her betrayal again. "Because I refused him, too," she
muttered.

That was met with stunned silence from Nancy. She
peered hard at Sophie, as if she were trying to see what
was in her mind, and a distinct look of aversion crossed
her features as she slowly leaned back in her chair. "Mr.
Hamilton, he loves you. You *know* that, do you not?"

Oh yes, she knew it. Knew it by heart.

"And you love him, it is plain to see."

Of course she did. With all her heart. But—

"What a wonderful man he is, your Mr. Hamilton.
Really, I thought you were different than the rest of that
lot," Nancy uttered irritably as she picked up her sewing.
"I thought you understood that there is more to this
world than the fancy parlors of high society, and their ti-
tles and servants—"

"But I *do* understand it!" she protested, knowing how
empty that sounded. "That is why this is so very hard,
because I *do* understand it, and all too well!"

"Apparently not as hard as doing the right thing by a
body, it would seem."

The truth of that stung. Sophie abruptly shoved to
her feet and moved restlessly to the bay window. All rational thought scattered into oblivion as she sought a jus-
tification for her actions that Nancy would understand.

But there was nothing, no excuse, no reason for her to turn Caleb away. She loved him; he loved her. Theirs was a meeting of the minds, a joining of spirits. How could something as simple as the manner of his birth change that?

And, lest she forget, there was plenty about *her* Caleb could find objectionable. Yet the ugly taint of her past actions had never deterred him, had never seemed to even enter his thoughts. He genuinely loved her for who she was, and she had returned that respect by refusing him. She had been too afraid to stand up to her upbringing, to make her own decisions. Too uncertain of herself to believe she could.

Sophie had never in her entire life felt so low as she did at that very moment.

She glanced over her shoulder at Nancy. She was busy with her work, the needle flying angrily in and out of the fabric.

"If there is nothing more for me to do here, there is something I really must attend," she said.

Nancy did not look at her; she merely shook her head.

"Well then. I'll come again in a day or two."

"As you wish," Nancy said, and glanced up. Her disappointment was clearly evident, and it sliced across Sophie like a knife.

She could not escape that house or her shame quickly enough.

At Essex Street, she waited impatiently for a hack to take her to Regent's Park. By the time a hack arrived, she knew it was too late; the sun was already beginning to slide into the western horizon. But when they reached the park, she nonetheless hurried to the little pond, hoping that by some small miracle, he would be there.

He was not.

His house stood as a silent behemoth, dark and empty. Cold.

How long she stood there, she had no idea, but she

had no right to go inside without him. Yet she did, compelled by an overwhelming need to be near him —or at least, the essence of him. She found the key he always left for her beneath a flagstone and stepped carefully in the dim afternoon light, wandering from one unfinished room to the next, feeling her heart constrict with every step.

Every moment they had spent in this house came rushing back to her. She remembered each place they had picnicked—in the foyer, the ballroom, and the library. She remembered their gay conversations, where they had pored over plans and tried to imagine what the finished rooms would look like.

In the ballroom where the muslin sheets still covered the floor, they had lain on their backs and looked at the newly finished ceiling, studying the elaborate frieze like so many puffy white clouds. In the master suite, they had succumbed to their mutual desire, and he had made tender love to her there, taking his time to bring her to fulfillment, then just as tenderly taking his own . . . a memory that made Sophie shiver.

But it was the morning room that undid her. When she stepped into the room, she gasped lightly and stood, her mouth agape, staring at the west wall. He had planned to hang a portrait on that wall, let the light come in from the east. But the north wall looked out over the little pond, and Sophie had jokingly suggested that he put a small window there so that he might watch for her.

Caleb had chuckled at her idea, idly mentioning the expense of adding another window.

But there it was. Her window. Caleb had put it in for her.

Sophie walked slowly to the window and peered out at the little pond, felt the tear sliding from her eye down her cheek. What a mess she had made of everything!

Caleb, Caleb!

Sophie sank down on her knees in the empty morning room and covered her face with her hands, sobbing. What would she do without him? How could she live?

It was an hour or later that she finally emerged from the dark and empty house, replaced the key, and slowly made her way home, feeling the weight of her life on her shoulders. She climbed wearily up the steps and into the foyer of *Maison de Fortier,* pausing to deposit her bonnet.

"I've been waiting for you."

Trevor's voice startled her; Sophie whirled around to see him standing at the edge of the corridor, in the shadows. It was funny, she thought for a single mad moment, how she had hardly spared him a thought all day, other than the need to remove any notion of marriage from his mind.

"H-how long have you been here?" she asked, despising the quiver in her voice.

"Long enough to know that Madame Fortier and my father are not here," he said coldly. "Where has she taken him?"

"Taken him? I don't know—have you inquired—"

"I have not had the pleasure of actually *seeing* a servant here, other than your housekeeper," Trevor snapped, and walked out of the corridor into the light of the foyer. "Not that I should have any reason to hope any one of them would be particularly useful."

The bitter edge in his tone was disquieting; she noticed that he looked ragged, with dark circles beneath his eyes. Something about his appearance caused an old spring of fear to rise in her and she unconsciously took a step backward, bumping into the entry console. "I have not seen Madame Fortier today. I would surmise they have gone picnicking as they often do. Did you not see your father this morning?"

A strange expression fell over him; Trevor planted his hand on his waist and glared at her. "I said I do not know where he is!"

"I am sure there is no cause for worry—"

"No cause for worry, indeed? And what would you know of worry, Sophie? My father requires medicine for his condition, and I shudder to think what might happen if he doesn't receive it."

Frantically trying to think when she had seen Honorine last—the ball, but *when?*—Sophie shook her head. "Surely they will return very soon, Trevor—they always do."

He made a guttural sound of disagreement and stalked past Sophie toward the door. "I pray that you are right," he said, and reached for the door. "Father is unwell."

"Trevor, wait! I . . . I—"

"What?" he demanded sharply.

"I thought we should speak of last night."

That seemed to stun him as much as it apparently aggravated him. "I beg your pardon, but this is hardly the best moment for that. I shall call in the morning." He yanked the door open. "Good evening."

He disappeared through the open door without another word, closing it loudly behind him. Hardly the sort of exit a gentleman ought to make—Trevor did not seem himself. But who did? Certainly not her.

With a weary sigh, Sophie turned from the door and glanced around. Someone had picked up the debris from yesterday's ball. She assumed Fabrice and Roland had somehow managed to survive, and with Lucie Cowplain's rather obnoxious prodding, had gone about the business of cleaning up.

Where was Honorine? It really wasn't like her to be gone so long. Sophie walked to the curving staircase, trudging up to her suite of rooms as she pondered the question. Certainly wherever Honorine had thought to take Lord Hamilton, she would return this evening. She always did. And please, God, let her be fast asleep when Honorine did come blustering in, for Sophie was in no mood to discuss the events of last evening or today with anyone.

She went through the motions of her evening toilette and sneered at the early evening sky, wishing the sun would go ahead and slip behind the earth so that full night would come. After brushing her hair and braiding it, Sophie read for an hour. When she glanced at the window, she groaned with dismay. The sky was a slate gray; the sun had not yet taken its leave. In a fit of pique, she stood abruptly, marched to the window, and drew the shutters tightly closed.

When she at last laid her head down—after taking her great frustration out on her pillow—she offered up one more prayer, begging God for a few hours of complete respite, a few hours of a sleep so deep that nothing could find its way up from the dark pool of her conscience to torture her in her dreams.

Apparently she got what she had hoped, for the next thing Sophie knew, someone was banging on something quite loudly.

With a moan, she pushed herself out of bed and padded over to the windows. Pulling open the heavy shutters, she blinked at the morning sky and pushed open the heavy counterpane window. Below her, Roland was toiling away in the garden; Fabrice was sitting nearby, his legs casually crossed, a book open in his lap. He glanced up when Sophie leaned out over the sill and waved cheerfully.

The banging persisted—it was coming from the front door. "The door!" she called down to Fabrice, but he merely waved again, pretending not to hear her.

"Oh for heaven's sake," she muttered irritably, and hurried to her dressing room, where she donned a simple day gown, passing up the petticoats and crinolines in favor of tackling the dozen or more buttons as she rushed out of her room.

As she stepped onto the staircase, the banging got louder—it sounded as if a king's army wanted entry. She flew down the staircase—where was Lucie Cowplain? Honorine? Honestly, had she not hired a host of servants?

She reached the door, yanked it open, expecting to see at least a troop. But the army consisted of only Trevor and Ian.

"Trevor!" she exclaimed, surprised. "When you said you would call, I—"

He startled her by pushing past her into the foyer, dragging his son behind him. "Do you know what she has done?" he demanded, his hard gaze sweeping the length of her.

"Who?" she asked stupidly.

His eyes narrowed menacingly. *"Madame Fortier."*

Sophie's gut twisted; she mindlessly fingered the end of her long braid as she quickly ran through a mental list of all the things Honorine might have done. "W-what?" she finally asked, quite certain she did not want to hear it.

"Kidnapped him!" Trevor all but shouted, and clamped a hand down so hard on Ian's shoulder that the boy winced.

That was ridiculous. Patently absurd! Honorine might have taken Lord Hamilton somewhere, but she most certainly had not *kidnapped* him. "Trevor, you are overwrought," she tried, but he was quick to interrupt her.

"Very astute, Sophie, I *am* overwrought, for it is not every day that one's father is kidnapped!"

"Your father has not been kidnapped! I am certain—"

"You might hear this before you go off defending her," he said, and roughly shook Ian. "Tell her. Tell her what she's done!"

The boy looked up at his father in fear—an expression Sophie knew very well, knew as her own, having experienced it so many times herself. When William Stanwood was in a black mood, the entire house feared for their safety, and she saw the same look of terror on

Ian's face. She instinctively reached for the boy, but Trevor jerked him backward, beyond her reach. "Trevor, please—"

"Tell her!" he demanded.

"M-madame Fortier, she and Papa w-went on a holiday," he stammered uncertainly.

Impossible. The child was obviously lying. "I don't believe you," Sophie said instantly. "Honorine would not leave without saying something . . . at least to *someone*."

But Ian was nodding his head furiously. "They *did!*" he insisted. "She came and took Papa's little carriage," he said, and looked up hopefully at his father.

Trevor, however, ignored him—he was staring daggers through Sophie. "There you have it," he said low. "What have you to say for your Frenchwoman now?

How she despised the tone of his voice! "I do not believe it!" But did she believe it? It was so unlike Honorine— then again, Honorine never ceased to surprise her.

Sophie suddenly picked up her skirts and pivoted about, determined to have the truth from Fabrice and Roland.

"Where are you going?" Trevor demanded hotly.

She did not respond; she was too intent on speaking with the pair of Frenchmen. If Honorine hadn't said anything to her, she would have at least said it to the two men who had followed her around the world all these years.

She hurried down the corridor and through the doors leading onto the terrace, Trevor on her heels, Ian struggling in his father's grip. From there, she ran down the steps, picking up her skirts higher still to better run across the dewy grass. Trevor strode across, dragging Ian behind him. Sophie reached the wrought iron gate that marked the gardens before Trevor and sailed through, marching to where Fabrice was still sitting. Roland hardly looked up from his work.

"Where is Honorine?" she demanded.

Fabrice shrugged.

Oh no, she would not have this now. Hands on hips, Sophie leaned over him, just inches from his face. "You will tell me where she is, *mon frère,* or Mr. Hamilton will certainly call the authorities to have it from you!"

Fabrice lifted one brow, casually glanced around her to where Trevor stood, and after contemplating him for a moment, shrugged again. "*Je ne sais pas.* We do not see *madame* for more than two days," he said, and as if that were a perfectly normal state of affairs, picked up his book and continued to read.

Chapter Eighteen

Thanks to Trevor, word spread with amaz-
ing celerity among the *ton* that the Frenchwoman had
kidnapped poor Lord Hamilton.

Trevor apparently railed at anyone who would listen,
alternating between his poignant concern for the fact
that his father did not have, in his possession, the very
medicine he needed to live, and an increasingly public
rage at "the Frenchwoman."

The Bobbies were summoned to *Maison de Fortier;*
Sophie was questioned with strained civility in deference
to her status as the sister of the Earl of Kettering, but
Fabrice and Roland were interrogated as criminals.
Although no amount of bullying by the London authorities could force the two Frenchmen to know what they
clearly did not know—the whereabouts of Honorine—it
left them feeling terribly vulnerable. The two men began
frantically packing to leave for France, taking hysteric
turns to watch Bedford Square for signs of any more
would-be interrogators.

Two days after the strange disappearance of Honorine
and Lord Hamilton, Lucie Cowplain nonchalantly informed Sophie that the entire *ton* was suddenly speaking

of Honorine as if she were some sort of strumpet-turned-felon. "They call her Madame Miscreant, I'll have ye know. Say her depravity comes from the beatings she used to receive from Monsieur Fortier."

Such ugly remarks about Honorine's character angered Sophie. The very same people who had taken advantage of her hospitality now turned on her at the mere mention of scandal. It wasn't just the insinuation of lawlessness, it was the blatant remarks intended to conjure up images of lewd behavior. It seemed to Sophie that if a woman chose to follow her own unique spirit—instead of the *ton's* interpretation of what was pure and correct—she was quickly branded a harlot, an immoral wanton.

An outcast.

That she fared only slightly better than Honorine in the gossip spreading rapidly through the *ton* inflamed her fury. "They say you've been seduced by her ways," Lucie Cowplain casually informed her. "They say one could expect little more, what with your past and all."

Would she never be forgiven the mistakes of eight years past? Would that decision to elope, that single moment in time, follow her for the rest of her bloody days?

According to Julian, it would. He had called on her that same morning, his face drawn and his expression grim behind his spectacles, quietly demanding an explanation for Honorine's behavior.

Sophie wished she *had* one. "I don't know where she is," she responded coolly, weary of answering the same questions over and over again.

Julian released a sigh of exasperation and thrust a hand through his hair. "Help me, Sophie! Might you at least try again to imagine where she might have gone?"

As if she hadn't thoroughly racked her brain for *any* answer for what Honorine had done, where she might be! "I am as astounded by this as you, Julian, but I do not know where she is, nor can I *imagine* where she is."

Julian came to his feet then, pacing restlessly before her. "This is unfortunate, to say the least," he said irritably. "Her conduct naturally reflects on you, and just when I was beginning to hope that your reputation could perhaps be mended."

"And what, exactly, does *my* reputation have to do with any of it?" Sophie demanded, just as irritably.

He did not deign to answer that, but bestowed a very impatient look on her. "Think hard, Sophie. Where might she have gone?"

To the moon for all she knew. And no amount of prodding from her older brother was going to give her any clue as to Honorine's whereabouts, or the inexplicable reason she had not at least left a note, a fact that bothered Sophie greatly. "Why must everyone assume Honorine has done something wrong?" she demanded of Julian. "*She* is missing too, is she not? It's not inconceivable that someone has abducted both of them."

Much to her surprise, Julian nodded. "Yes, I had thought of that, too. The man claiming to be his son was the first person I suspected, but as he has been seen at his favorite haunts, I cannot give that theory credence."

Her heart suddenly pounding, she asked, "His favorite haunts? What are they?"

Julian looked at her curiously. "I wouldn't know. I've just heard it said. But I rather think it safe to assume your friend Madame Fortier is the culprit, Sophie, for who would possibly think to gain from harming a batty Frenchwoman and a rather debilitated man?"

Her heart went crashing to her feet again. She turned away from Julian to hide the flush of her disappointment from him; she was no closer to knowing where Caleb might be, except that he was still in London. Fat lot of good that did her.

"Sophie?"

"Whatever you might think of her, Honorine has a heart of gold," she said softly.

Behind her, Julian snorted his opinion of that.

"I know her, Julian. Whatever she did, she had good reason for it, I can assure you."

He said nothing, but it was plain from his expression he did not share her good opinion of Honorine. By the time he left, Sophie wasn't entirely certain he kept a good opinion of *her*.

She followed him to the door, watched him toss a leg over his mount and haul himself up, then gather the reins. "If you perchance think of where she might have gone, I hope you will send for me straightaway. I am doing everything in my power to keep your name from this debacle, but I don't know how long I can do that. Do you understand me?"

Oh, she understood him only too well; she nodded slowly. Seeming satisfied with that, Julian tipped his hat and spurred the horse to trot out of the courtyard.

She shut the door, turned around and leaned heavily against it, staring blindly at the chandelier above her. *Where was Caleb?*

How she missed him! She could not sleep, could not eat, could not think without him. And she couldn't even attempt to find him—leaving *Maison de Fortier* at the moment was impossible, given the number of callers seeking some word, or having a new idea as to what might have happened. She felt herself under particularly harsh scrutiny, as if the entire city were watching her.

Nevertheless, Caleb had remained at the edge of her consciousness, his image jarring her over and over again. She wondered if he had worked on his house, or did it still stand silent? Perhaps Julian was wrong—perhaps he had left for Scotland. Maybe France? She could not begin to imagine where he was, no more than she could imagine where Honorine had gone. The only thing she knew was that she missed him terribly, would sell her soul to see him again, if only for a moment, if only to say, *I am sorry, so very sorry.*

What she wouldn't give to take it all back now.

She spent the rest of the morning waiting . . . for what? Word from Honorine? From Caleb? Fabrice and Roland were also out of sorts, arguing between themselves about where Honorine might have gone, becoming so adamant in their respective viewpoints that they each locked themselves away in their respective bedrooms. As the minutes and hours passed, however, every plausible explanation evaporated. There was nothing. Nothing but the torturous thoughts of Caleb, the sharp pain of her devastation sinking in, the slow shattering of her heart with the realization her deed had destroyed the raw love she had for him, love that was too large, too deep, to fathom.

Exhausted from a lack of sleep, Sophie tried to nap, but her dreams surrounded Honorine. They were at the ball again, Honorine in her wildly colored gown, twirling Lord Hamilton around in his wheeled chair as everyone gaped at her in dumbfounded horror. *"Shameful,"* whispered one. *"She's mad,"* said another. In her dream, Sophie had run from person to person, trying to assure them there was nothing wrong with Honorine . . . until they began to whisper that *she* was the one who was mad.

She was exhausted when she awoke that afternoon.

Slowly, she dressed and wandered down to the morning room. Lucie Cowplain was not long behind her, jerking through the door with a tray of tea.

"No word?" she asked.

Sophie shook her head.

Lucie Cowplain slapped the tray on the table in front of Sophie, shoved a cup and saucer toward her. "What rubbish it all is! It has the lads quite upset! I hear they've got the authorities searching the countryside for her. They'll not be lenient, I reckon."

"She has done nothing wrong," Sophie sharply reminded the housekeeper. "They have no reason to be lenient or otherwise."

Lucie Cowplain lifted a sparse brow. "Indeed? Well, to hear Miss Birdwell tell it, Madame Miscreant might very well be capable of murder."

Sophie sprang to her feet; clutching her fists at her

sides, she glared at the diminutive housekeeper. "Watch your tongue, Lucie Cowplain! Madame Fortier may be many things, but she would never do anything to harm Lord Hamilton!"

That earned her the usual shrug from Lucie Cowplain. "Suit yourself," she said as she hobbled toward the door. "I merely repeat to ye what I hear."

When the door closed behind her, Sophie sank into her seat, buried her face in her hands. There had to be an explanation. There had to be a note, a message they were missing. She suddenly glanced up, stared blindly at the wall.

Ian.

The boy had seen Honorine and Lord Hamilton leave—surely they had said where they were going. It was so simple, she was amazed she hadn't thought of it before.

Sophie was greeted at the door of the Hamilton House by a stately old butler who curtly informed her that Mr. Trevor Hamilton had left earlier that morning.

That piece of news hardly registered. "Yes, well, I have come to call on Master Ian Hamilton."

The butler frowned ever so slightly. "Master Ian?" he said in something less a question and more a statement.

"Master Ian," Sophie repeated.

The butler eyed her suspiciously.

"I beg your pardon sir, but is Master Ian within?" she asked pointedly, hoping to high heaven he could not see the solid and rapid thump of heart against her chest.

The man sighed, then smoothly stepped aside, holding the door open. "Master Ian is with his governess in the morning parlor. If you will follow me."

Miss Hipplewhite was known to Sophie—they had met in Regent's Park a time or two, and of course, in Honorine's salon. She smiled uneasily as Sophie was shown into the parlor, her gaze darting nervously to Ian and back again. Ian scarcely looked up as Sophie entered the room, seeming more interested in the wooden locomotive he rolled about the Aubusson carpet.

"Good morning, Miss Hipplewhite."

"Good morning, my lady," she said softly, her gaze darting to Ian again. "Master Ian, please extend your greeting to Lady Sophie."

Reluctantly, the boy came to his feet. "Good morning, mu'um."

Sophie forced a smile to her lips, glanced at the toy locomotive again, her mind unable to release the image of Caleb for even a moment. "Ian, how well you look!" she forced herself to say brightly. "What have you got there, a locomotive?"

He nodded, scratched his nose.

"How lovely," she said, and looked again to the governess. "I don't suppose . . . that is to say, if you wouldn't mind terribly, might I have a word with Ian?"

Miss Hipplewhite looked surprised by her request; a hand wavered at the prim collar on her throat and she glanced nervously at her charge. "Umm . . . I really don't know if I ought, Lady Sophie. His father, well, Mr. Hamilton is quite insistent that I not leave him alone, particularly when he is away."

Away? Sophie had no idea what she meant by that, but it was hardly surprising that Trevor would be meticulously restrictive with Ian's activities. "Surely Mr. Hamilton will return soon?"

Miss Hipplewhite shook her head. "I can't rightly say, mu'um. He's gone to have a look about for his father."

The information caught Sophie off guard. She was so accustomed to his daily calls that it had never occurred to her—"Did he say where?" she asked suddenly.

Miss Hipplewhite's eyes rounded slightly; she quickly shook her head again.

Sophie looked at Ian—the child was making a concerted effort not to look at her, and in fact, had managed to maneuver himself all the way to the other side of the carpet, his back to her. He didn't *want* her to ask him a question.

Too bad for the little bugger.

Sophie smiled sweetly at Miss Hipplewhite. "You needn't leave the room. I meant only to inquire after him, what with his father away."

Miss Hipplewhite considered her request. After a moment, she picked up her book and nodded. "I'll just be there," she said, nodding toward the far end of the room.

Sophie smiled her thanks, waited until the woman was at a sufficient distance that she might not hear a harsh word or two if necessary, then turned her attention to Ian again. He was slowly rolling the locomotive about the carpet. She strolled to where he was playing, stood with her hands folded before her, waiting for him to look up. When he did not, she nudged the locomotive with her foot.

Ian frowned at her slipper and shifted away, taking the locomotive out of reach.

"Ian, if you please, there is something I'd like to ask you," she said softly.

Ian ignored her.

"It's about your grandpapa," she added hopefully, but he shifted even farther away.

"Perhaps you can help me," she tried again, but Ian surprised her by whipping his head around to glare at her. "I shan't help you!"

"Why not?" Sophie demanded, genuinely surprised.

"I won't, that's all!"

"That isn't terribly nice, is it, Ian? I would help *you* if you asked."

"I wouldn't ask you!"

"Not even to help your papa?"

"Papa doesn't care for you in the least, either! He loves Madame Fortier!" he cried.

Aha. At last, the roots of the little heathen's dislike toward her. He wanted Honorine for a mama, not her. "Wonderful!" she exclaimed cheerfully. "Perhaps he will persuade her to marry him one day. In the meantime, Madame Fortier is with your grandpapa, and I must find her."

He said nothing, merely shrugged his slender shoulders as he pushed the locomotive back and forth, back and forth.

Sophie took another step forward, squatting down beside him. "I am actually rather desperate to find my dear friend Madame Fortier," she said softly. "I fear she might be in a spot of trouble."

The frantic movement of the locomotive increased; Ian pressed his lips tightly together and refused to look at Sophie.

"You wouldn't want Madame Fortier to meet with any unpleasant trouble, would you?"

He shook his head.

"Then might you tell me where they have gone?"

The locomotive paused for a moment as the boy considered her. After a moment, he began to move the locomotive very slowly. "Papa has gone to fetch her."

Sophie's heart skipped a beat. *"Where?"* she whispered, putting a hand on Ian's shoulder.

He reacted strongly to the touch of her hand, jerking away as he began to move the locomotive back and forth with increasing fury. "I won't tell you!" he said loudly.

Miss Hipplewhite raised her head, craned her neck to see around the furniture. "Lady Sophie?"

"It's quite all right, Miss Hipplewhite," Sophie called, and suddenly frantic, slapped her hand down on top of his locomotive, prohibiting its movement.

Ian yelped with surprise, but Sophie ignored him. "All right, then, Master Ian, you have plagued me from the moment we met. I *know* you do not care for me, I *know* you do not want me to marry your papa, and you may trust me in this—you have nothing to fear. I also know that you care very much for Madame Fortier and so do I. I do not know where she is and I am very fearful of what might await her. I am asking you—*begging you*—to tell me if she said *anything,* anything at all when she got in that coach, or if your grandpapa conveyed to you where they might be going!"

The boy struggled to free his locomotive, but Sophie would not allow it and grabbed his wrist.

"Lady Sophie!" Miss Hipplewhite cried from behind her, but Sophie held fast, her gaze boring into Ian's.

"Where, Ian?" she demanded, aware that Miss Hipplewhite was fleeing the room for help. She had only a matter of moments before she was tossed out on her ear. *"Where?"* she almost shouted.

"I think to home!" he cried, and suddenly yanked his locomotive free of her grasp.

"Home?" she repeated dumbly.

"I don't know," he said, and clamped his mouth shut, pushing his toy back and forth again.

Sophie stared at him—was he speaking the truth? Had they gone to Lord Hamilton's home, wherever that might be, or was the child lying to her?

Ian did not even bother to look up as the butler and a footman rushed into the room ahead of Miss Hipplewhite. One of them grabbed her shoulder, but Sophie was already gaining her feet, and shook him off. "There is no need, sir. I have what I came for," she announced, and straightening her skirts, caught Ian's eye once more. "Thank you kindly, Master Ian," she said pleasantly, and marched from the room, her head held high, refusing to acknowledge the gape of horrified shock from Miss Hipplewhite.

And as she marched down the front steps of the house, she didn't even wince at the sound of the door being slammed behind her. Let them think her a pariah again, for what did it matter? She had already made up her mind. It couldn't be too terribly difficult to learn where "home" was, if Ian was telling the truth. Once she did, she'd go fetch Honorine, and they would return to France.

Only this time, it would be forever. Any hope she had

of perhaps salvaging her tattered reputation had been permanently impeded by Honorine's disappearance and her bullying of a seven-year-old child.

She continued on, past *Maison de Fortier* and across Bedford Square, her feet moving ahead of her conscious thought.

As she passed into Regent's Park, she reminded herself that any hopes of happiness she had harbored were gone, too—smashed by her own insecurities, destroyed by her own supercilious beliefs as to who was acceptable and who was not.

How she regretted that now, she thought miserably as she neared Caleb's empty house. It was silent—no one had worked on the house for two days now, and Sophie suddenly felt very foolish for coming. He wouldn't come back, not as long as there was any danger of encountering her nearby. Bloody fabulous—she had destroyed his dreams, too.

She abruptly turned away, forced herself to walk on.

It was her own rotten fault. She had, in a moment of knee-jerk, *haut ton* reaction, dismissed a man she adored above all others as some sort of being beneath her. It sickened her. And what made it particularly revolting was that there was no way to correct it—she couldn't even apologize.

Her resolve to find Honorine and leave London was overwhelming now. Only this time, she was not running. She was walking away, by choice.

In Cheapside, at a gentleman's club of second order, Caleb heard the gossip that Trevor Hamilton had gone in search of his missing father. It was rumored that the Frenchwoman had kidnapped the viscount. The men openly discussed her motives, all quickly coming to the conclusion that she meant to harm him by extorting money from him somehow. Perhaps even to cause injury to his person. The discussion bothered Caleb greatly.

They certainly did not know Madame Fortier, or that
she had almost single-handedly led his father to improvement in spite of Trevor. But neither did he know
her, not really. Was she capable of such a crime? It was
hard to imagine, but as of two days ago, nothing was as
it seemed.

Yet it was the second piece of gossip that truly disturbed
him: that Lady Sophie Dane, formerly Lady Stanwood—
an emphasis that raised more than one eyebrow—had
apparently left on her own search. What Caleb found so
disquieting about that was the fear that seemed to over-
take him and constrict his breathing in an odd sort of
way.

He feared for Sophie.

The fool woman had gone running after Madame
Fortier and with Trevor in the apparent state of mind
that he was, Caleb could only imagine the potential danger for Sophie. Regardless that she had all but destroyed
him, he still loved her. Would go to his grave loving
her—he could not scrape that burn from his heart. How
very odd, he thought in a detached way, that he still
loved her so much he would do anything to see that no
harm came to her, including chasing her halfway across
England.

The irony of that was almost laughable, he supposed,
but nonetheless, with a weary sigh of defeat, he tossed
two crowns on the table, strolled out of the club, and
headed home to pack a satchel.

On the banks of a gurgling stream, approximately fifteen
miles north of the village of Gedling, Honorine spread jam
on a thick slab of fresh-baked bread she had purchased
in the village and handed it to Will. *"Voilà, mon petit
ami."*

"Thank you, darling," Will said, and taking the bread
with his good hand, sank his teeth into it. It was, without
a doubt, the most delicious bread he had ever tasted. He

smiled at Honorine, then looked up at the azure-blue sky, silently naming the shapes he saw in the clouds, ecstatic that he *knew* the names. A few months ago he had not even known his own name. Since Honorine had come into his life, he was stronger every day, finding words in his brain he had thought lost to him forever, finding strength in his legs, his arms.

It was amazing and humbling, really, this miracle that had come to him by the grace of God.

Beside him, Honorine flopped onto her back on the blanket they had spread and folded her arms behind her head as she gazed up at the sky. "This day, it is *très joli,*" she sighed.

Will nodded, munched his bread. "Not as p-pretty as you, l-love," he said.

Honorine laughed, ran her hand seductively along his leg, which instantly stirred all the passion he felt for her. "You speak this English better than me!"

He grabbed her hand and squeezed it. She was a true godsend; he had not adored someone so completely since Caleb's mother more than thirty years ago.

He adored her so completely that he put her hand to his groin, let her feel the hardness there. Her blue eyes sparkled; she came up on one elbow, shaping her hand to the rigid length of him. "Umm . . . but this love, is it better than me?" she asked low, and suddenly pushed him on his back, coming over him with a gleeful laugh, her smiling face blocking the clouds from his sight.

Chapter Nineteen

LUCIE COWPLAIN DID not divulge the information he needed until he pressed ten pounds into her palm.

After that, it had been easy to find Sophie's trail. Caleb was making good time, given that she had almost a full day's head start on him.

The village of Stevenage had been the most productive so far. The tavern at which he devoured an unremarkable luncheon was immediately adjacent to the coach station. That station, he had guessed, supplied a steady stream of travelers in and out of the Hawk and Dove on a daily basis. This notion was confirmed by the woman who served the common room patrons, and fortunately for Caleb, she had an excellent memory.

"Oh me, aye, we seen 'em, we did," she said when asked about Madame Fortier and his father, bobbing her head so eagerly that thin wisps of her hair seemed to float about her face. "Thought it rather odd that the lady was driving. She gave the hostler *five* crowns to care for the horse, and the gent didn't seem to mind a'tall."

"Did anyone happen to notice their direction?"

"Oh, north, sir. They all go north from here." She nodded, started to walk away, but Caleb put his hand on her arm.

"I beg your pardon, madam, but I am also in search of two other people. A gentleman, about my height, perhaps a notch or two shorter, a bit of silver at the temples? A wealthy gentleman—"

The woman grinned with all three of her teeth and wiped her palm on the dirty apron she wore. "Oh *aye,* I remarked him, I did—not many gent through here; a handsome one he was, too. And that coach, Lord! Never seen a coach so fine, not 'ere. Ask Mr. Litton—"

"Yes, I've seen the coach," Caleb interjected wryly. "Headed north I suppose?"

She nodded. " 'E'll have a time of it, that fancy coach on *these* roads!" she added with a delighted cackle.

"And lastly," Caleb said, withdrawing five crowns from his pocket and placing them on the table. "Have you perhaps noticed a woman traveling alone today? She's quite attractive, perhaps a head shorter than me." He paused—how exactly did one describe Sophie? How did he capture the spirit within her?

"Aye?" the serving woman prodded as she slipped the five crowns into her pocket.

Caleb cleared his throat, drummed his fingers on the edge of the table. "A woman of slender frame . . ."—*so slender that she fit perfectly within his embrace . . . and beneath him*—". . . and dark brown hair. And her eyes . . ."—*bottomless wells of passion*—". . . her eyes are dark brown, like chocolate. And . . . and she has a certain essence about her, a sort of radiance if you will." He glanced up at the woman. "Do you perhaps recall her?"

Grinning, the woman chuckled low. "Luv, had I seen a woman as you describe, I'd not forget her, I promise you that. But no, I ain't seen her, not 'ere. She sounds too fine for the likes of this," she said, gesturing to the common room around her. "Another ale, then?"

"No, thank you."

She shrugged, adjusted the tray at her hip and wandered off.

At the dry goods shop, Caleb had better luck. He bought a sack of oats for his mount and some hardtack, then inquired after Sophie. The proprietor there remembered her, remarking that she seemed rather prim in selecting two hard candies and some bread and cheese for her journey north. He had thought it odd, he told Caleb as he polished an empty jar, that a woman of her obvious stature was traveling alone, to Nottinghamshire, on a public coach.

To Hamilton House, then.

They were all headed for his father's estate, to the place where Caleb had once longed to live, longed to be accepted. His father and Madame Fortier may have already reached it, or would in a matter of one or two days. As for Trevor—assuming he knew where they had gone—he could conceivably arrive within twenty-four hours of his father with the viscount's coach and team of four grays.

Sophie, however, was another matter, particularly given that Caleb wasn't entirely certain she knew where she was going. Moreover, having availed himself of the public coach system on more than one occasion, he rather thought Sophie would be lucky to reach Hamilton House by the end of the week, and in one piece.

At least there was only one viable road going north, only one that the public coaches would take, and if he rode hard enough, he could conceivably catch her by nightfall.

As he rode out of town, Caleb marveled that he could not recall a time he had been of such single-minded purpose. Even the construction of his house had not consumed him so, in spite of the many hours he had devoted himself to it. That was, he had come to realize, only a diversion, something to occupy his hands and his thoughts, a monument to his success in the rail industry, a symbol to show the world that he was worthy.

But since Sophie had refused him the night of the Fortier ball, the house had left him feeling curiously empty. After two days of brooding over it, he had finally understood why that was so. For all his hard work, it was nothing more than a house. It was not a home, nor would it ever be, not without Sophie, not without her laughter and warmth to fill every room, every corridor. By chance, she had sat across the pond one day, and his life had been changed forevermore. He had begun to believe in life again, had begun to believe that love was possible for a man like him. He had begun to see her in every room of his home, of *their* home.

Now, he would never be able to look at the house in the same way. He rather doubted he'd even be able to live in it. Sophie had scored him deeply with her refusal, had lacerated feelings so old and so deep that he had wondered in the last two days if he might ever recover from it. The rejection had left him feeling heavy and old. Alone. Forsaken.

Yet here he was, chasing like a dog across the English countryside after her. *Why* he felt compelled to do so, he wasn't entirely certain, other than he vaguely understood, on some remote level, why she had refused him. It did not lessen the sting, did not ease his suffering in the least, and he thought that perhaps he had convinced himself he understood so that it might somehow deaden the pain. Yet the pain remained, nibbling away at the corners of his heart.

So why, then, was he chasing after her?

Because he loved her, adored her so completely that in spite of her rejection, he could not bear to see any harm come to her. It was that simple, that primal.

It wasn't hard for Sophie to learn where "home" was. Naturally, Lucie Cowplain knew everything about Hamilton House, right down to the fact that Millicent's cousin's sister was a maid there and found it excruciatingly tiresome, as there was hardly anything with which to occupy one's time. Somehow, that did not surprise Sophie in the least.

Having secured herself passage on a public coach, Sophie made herself as comfortable as she could on one hard wooden bench, directly across from an elderly couple who proudly informed her they were on their way to visit their son, a solicitor in Birmingham.

But in Biggleswade, the coach collected a woman and two children, which forced Sophie to squeeze onto the bench with the elderly couple. The two children began bickering immediately, and continued on for the entire journey, seemingly without so much as taking a breath. Their mother attempted, in her near shouting, to silence the two, but she only managed to make them louder. Sophie exchanged more than one look with the elderly couple beside her, who looked as appalled as she felt.

When it became apparent that the two children were determined to make their journey miserable, Sophie settled herself in as best she could and tried diligently to block them, and everything around her, out of her mind. Unfortunately, all her attempts met with dismal failure— if she wasn't feeling the throbbing at her temples, she could not stop thinking of Caleb. Or her argument with Ann.

She was exhausted beyond reason; her journey had begun on the heels of a terrible row with Fabrice and Roland, who did not want to be left alone in the middle of a hostile *ton*. They wanted to accompany Sophie, but she could not afford the time it would take the three of them to travel. She had finally convinced them to return to France if they must, leave the house to Lucie Cowplain. If and when she found Honorine, she would send word and arrange to meet them in Burgundy, at Château de Segries, the Fortier estate.

Her suggestion had caused Fabrice and Roland to howl with dissent; they all but clung to one another like frightened children, but Sophie had held firm, much to the amusement of Lucie Cowplain. "Ah, go and do what ye must then. I'll keep an eye on the lassies," she said with a sardonic smile.

As if that ordeal weren't enough to send her straight over the edge, she next had a terrible argument with Ann, who discovered her stuffing sundries into a portmanteau, and demanded an explanation.

"I am determined to find Honorine before something horrid happens," Sophie had flatly informed her older sister.

Ann's eyes rounded. "I beg your pardon, you mean to do *what*?"

"You heard me. I intend to find Honorine."

Surprise caused Ann to fall into an armchair. She gaped at Sophie, then at her bag. "It is *unseemly*," she began, gesturing wildly at the portmanteau. "This *will* not do. All of London will think you have run off with Trevor Hamilton. God, Sophie, can you not see how improper it all will seem? Have you considered what Trevor will think?"

What *Trevor* would think? That was, without a doubt, the final straw. How had they all come to care so much for appearances at the expense of all else? She returned Ann's glare. "I am sick unto death of caring how everything *appears* to everyone else, Ann! I could not possibly give a whit what Trevor Hamilton will think, much less high society! And I cannot abide another untoward remark on Honorine Fortier's character—she has done nothing but show her kindness and support to Lord Hamilton when his own son considers him too infirm, and her thanks for that is to be denounced a criminal by all of England!"

"Her behavior has brought this on her! She has taken an ill man from his family without permission—"

"He is not so infirm—"

"He is hardly capable of making his choices, you cannot disagree! But be that as it may, you have your *own* reputation to think of, an offer from a gentleman—"

"I couldn't *possibly* care less about my reputation!

And *you* mustn't worry about any offer, either, for as I have tried to tell you, I have no intention of marrying Trevor, not now, not ever!"

"Sophie!" Ann had cried with alarm. "You cannot mean that!"

"I can and I *do!*" she responded sharply, slapping the portmanteau closed. "I do not *care* for Trevor Hamilton; I think him a pompous, boring ass!" she continued, ignoring Ann's gasp. "If you want to know the truth, I am in love with his brother, Caleb. Completely! Thoroughly besotted with him! I have been such a bloody fool about it all—he is a far better man than Trevor, and were it not for the circumstance of his birth, you would think so, too!"

Her admission had shocked Ann into momentary silence. She stood slowly, her gaze unwavering. "No," she said low. "You cannot possibly mean what you say."

"I bloody well do."

"You foolish chit! Have you lost your mind? Do you think these affections are returned, or has the Imposter duped you into believing he loves you so that *he* might have a chance at your fortune?"

The implications of her question stung so deeply that Sophie felt it all the way to her toes. She stared down at the portmanteau, her heart and mind reeling with the hurtful and overwhelming sense of inadequacy and failure in her family's eyes. Slowly, she lifted her gaze to her sister, saw the genuine concern there, and felt betrayed by it.

"He is not a blackguard."

"You didn't think so of William Stanwood, either."

Sophie struggled not to dissolve into tears, swallowing hard. "I am not a child, Ann. I am a grown woman. Granted, I have made mistakes—but you could at least do me the small courtesy of believing that I have perhaps learned from them instead of treating me like a simpleton. Caleb Hamilton is an honorable man and I love him. And I am so very tired of everyone believing they know what is best for me, because they don't! *You* don't! You haven't the faintest idea who I am, Ann! But I am through pretending, I am quite through trying to be part of the *ton* with all its disingenuous hyperbole and hypocrisy! I cannot remain true to myself, not like this, not in London, and most certainly *not* with Trevor Hamilton!"

"Oh Sophie, how can you do this to us again? To Julian?"

That was the moment Sophie had picked up her portmanteau and walked purposefully to the door. "I did not *do* it to *you* the first time, Ann. I did it to *me*. This is not Julian's life, it is not your life, it is *mine*. When will you accept that?"

Ann opened her mouth to speak, but Sophie quickly threw up her hand. "Please save your breath. And please don't worry overmuch—I refused Caleb's offer for the sake of propriety, just as you would want me to do. Surely that should please you, and by God, I hope it pleases you for years to come, as I have no intention of returning to London or marrying again!"

The declaration had spurred her onward, made her more determined than ever. Ann had, of course, tried to stop her, but Sophie had pushed her sister's hand from her arm and marched down the stairs. With Ann fast on her heels, she marched past a fretting Fabrice and Roland in the foyer, past a smirking Lucie Cowplain who held the door open for her, and onto Bedford Square, leaving behind Ann's frantic threats to find Julian before she left.

The public coach came along before Ann could have possibly reached Julian. Sophie was bound for Nottinghamshire and Lord Hamilton's country estate long before Julian could have learned that she had left everything behind. She regretted that she did not have the opportunity to take her leave of Julian, but she had to go. She could not live the lie that had become her life even one more day.

It was over the course of several hours and an excruciating drive from London that she realized exactly what she had become. She regretted the argument with Ann—not what she had said, exactly, but perhaps the way she had said it. Her family *had* always wanted what was best for her and she could hardly fault them for that. It was just that somewhere along the way, she had allowed herself to lose her voice, to let them bang out the rhythm of her life, out of step with her own wants and desires. All her life she had tried to please her brother and sisters, and anyone else who happened to enter her world. She had to please herself now, and she hoped desperately that they would understand, but could not ignore the rather desperate feeling that they never would.

When the coach stopped for the night, she took a room at a public inn. Unable to eat, she retired immediately, tossing and turning on the very thin mattress. The next morning, she filed out into the courtyard with the other passengers at dawn. The elderly couple did not board, leaving Sophie, the mother and two children, and a rather large fellow with hands that looked like beefsteaks to sit beside her. He took up as much room as the elderly couple had, and Sophie sat squished between him and the small window.

That day of travel was doubly miserable. Sophie had reconciled herself to her argument with Ann, knowing in her heart that she was justified in what she had said.

Which left her with the image of Caleb to haunt her.

The more miles between her and London she traveled, the more imperative it became that she accept the fact she would never see him again. The despair that welled in her was enough to drown her; it filled the emptiness, the dull ache that would not go away, would not let her sleep. How she had managed to let propriety and protocol and all the little rules of the *ton* guide her heart was now unfathomable to her. It seemed so shallow . . . but it had been so easy to do.

She could have learned from Caleb instead of hurting him—he had accepted who she was, and had shown more regard for the person she was than her family ever had. Her gift in return was an outright rejection of his love because of who *he* was. She missed him. Missed him so much that she felt she was dissolving under the weight of it.

By the time the coach pulled into the tiny courtyard of the Ravenfield Inn in the hamlet of St. Neots that evening, Sophie thought she was on the verge of being ill. The throbbing pain in her head was enough to drive her to her knees. The children were pouting and restless, and the man sitting next to her had fallen asleep, his arm a dead weight on her leg.

"All out for the night. We resume the drive to Petersborough at precisely seven o'clock on the morrow," the driver called up as he opened the door.

That announcement caused one of the children to whine. Their mother—who looked as exhausted as Sophie felt—pushed first one, then the other, through the door, wiggling out behind them. The man went next, slowly and carefully, causing the coach to tilt dangerously to one side. When Sophie finally disembarked, it felt as if she were standing on hundreds of needles, her legs and feet were so numb.

She wandered about the courtyard for a few minutes, trying to circulate her blood. The sound of laughter and cheerful voices filtered out into the courtyard through an open window—the inn was obviously very crowded. Curious, Sophie walked to the window and peered inside. The place was filled to almost overflowing; the entire village of St. Neots had come for a tankard of ale.

When she stepped through the entrance, her senses were immediately overwhelmed by the smell of ale and fish and human flesh. Several heads turned in her direction, then quickly away again when the patrons realized she was no one they knew. Sophie walked farther into the room; a small little man hurried over to her, stood hopping from one foot to the next as he wiped his hands on a rag.

"From the public coach, are you? We've an attic room for the night, if it suits you, milady. A little close, but the bed is clean, it is."

That was, remarkably, a rather strong selling point after last night. "Thank you, that will be fine," she muttered, finding several coins in her reticule for him.

He pocketed the coins. "I'll fetch you a key. In the meantime, you need not put up with this rabble. We've a private room in the back if you'd like—or a table in the corner just there." Like a bird, he motioned with his head in the general direction of the table.

The last thing Sophie wanted was a private room where her misery could swallow her whole. "Thank you, but the common room will be fine," she said, and pushed through the crush of tables and people toward the small table he had indicated. Shoved up against the wall as it was, she could see the entire room. As she removed her gloves, a young girl no more than fourteen or fifteen years of age stepped to her side.

"What will ye 'ave, mu'um?" she asked.

Taking a page from Honorine's book, she said, "A tankard of ale, if you please, and a large one at that."

The girl nodded and hurried away, pausing to slap one man's beefy hand from her skirts when she passed by.

As she waited for her ale, Sophie noticed another set of rooms just beyond the common room; several men wandered in and out. A gaming room, she guessed. Such arrangements were popular on the Continent.

After the girl brought the tankard, Sophie quietly sipped the dark ale, lost in her own despondent thoughts, idly watching the crowd swell and bustle around her.

After a half tankard, however, she grew weary of her despondency, and looked up, searching for something to look at, to think of, until she could climb the stairs to the attic room above and attempt another night of sleep. As she wearily surveyed the crowd, her eye caught sight of something dully familiar. She lowered the tankard, shifted her gaze . . .

Trevor.

He was standing on the threshold of the other rooms, boring a hole right through her with his narrowed gaze.

Chapter Twenty

SOPHIE'S PULSE QUICKENED as Trevor shoved his way through the crowd toward her wearing an expression far too reminiscent of William Stanwood's. It sent a familiar chill up her spine; she pushed the tankard aside, clutched the edge of the little table as he reached her, halting there, towering above her. His jaw clenched tightly shut, he eyed her from head to toe, folding his arms tightly across his chest as an impatient father might.

"What in bloody hell are you doing here?" he demanded.

"I might ask the same of you."

His jaw clenched tighter still. "Who brought you here . . . the Frenchmen?"

Sophie shook her head. "A public coach."

"A *public* coach?" He spat the word like it was rancid. "What exactly are you about, Sophie?"

The very suggestion that she somehow owed him an explanation washed over Sophie in a wave of indignation. There was a time she would have been cowed by it, but sitting there, watching the bulge in his cheek—as if he had a *right* to be angry—snapped her fear like a twig. Whatever she might become, she had had enough of being held to arcane standards that were not her own. Who was this man who thought he might announce to a crowded parlor that he would offer for her without so much as mentioning it to her? Who was *he* to question her presence in St. Neots? What, did he think he owned the bloody hamlet?

She was standing before she realized it, bracing herself against the scarred tabletop, leaning forward so that he would not miss a single word. "I stopped in this quaint little inn for an ale. That is *exactly* what this is about."

Her curt response obviously surprised him. He blinked, seemed to suddenly wake from his pique, and glanced nervously about them. "All right, all right," he hissed beneath his breath, and reached around her to hold her chair. "At least sit, will you? I prefer not to attract a crowd."

"I beg your pardon, but it would seem too late for that."

He glanced apprehensively over his shoulder at the several patrons who had turned toward them. "Come on then, be a good girl and sit so that we might discuss this like adults, will you?"

"I am not the one who is being childish," she said. Then she sat. Hard.

Trevor sat, too, much more carefully than she, and gingerly ran his palm across the tabletop as he considered her.

Defiant, Sophie sipped her ale.

"You seem to be a bit agitated, my dear," he said, taking a smoother tack. "Perhaps if you told me whatever you think to do here, I can help you."

Patronizing buffoon. "That's quite all right, Trevor. I don't need your help," she said, and lifted the tankard to her lips again.

He lifted a brow. "What is your destination? Kettering? I'm afraid you're a bit east of it. I confess, I am a bit perplexed—you did not tell me of any travel plans."

The tankard came down on the table harder than she intended. "I did not *have* travel plans until two days ago. But let me be perfectly frank—had I planned this little sojourn as much as two weeks ago, I had no obligation to tell you. You have no right to me, sir!"

The blood drained from Trevor's face. He moved suddenly, grabbing her wrist and pressing it against the table in a painful vise. "Watch what you say, my dear, because I cannot vouch for my patience!" The harsh tone of his voice belied his composed expression, donned for the benefit of the crowd. "I have no *right* to you as yet, but I daresay you will not speak to me thus when we are wed!"

Sophie jerked her arm up and away from him, yanking back hard until he let go. With a quick, surreptitious glance around them, he casually straightened his neckcloth. But as he leaned back in his chair, his gaze was one of fury.

So was Sophie's. She angrily rubbed her wrist where he had gripped her. "As to that, there is one small matter you have overlooked."

"*Is* there?" he snarled. "Then by all means, please astonish me with a sane explanation for your foolish behavior."

"Haven't you forgotten something? Haven't you forgotten to *ask* me to be your wife?"

An incredulous bark of laughter escaped him. "Do I understand your meaning, madam? Are you implying that you have chased halfway across the countryside so that I might perform the formality of *asking* you to be my wife?" Again, he laughed with the disbelief of it.

Sophie's fury was quickly giving way to a full-bodied rage. "Let me assure you I have most certainly *not* followed you. I am in search of Honorine—"

"A bloody waste of time. I'll see that madwoman imprisoned before the week—"

"Not if I find her first," Sophie said low.

"I beg your pardon—"

"And secondly," she continued, not allowing him so much as a breath, "asking a woman if she would like to marry is not a formality—"

"A formality, please! It is not as if you are dripping with suitors, Sophie. It's not as if you have any prospects at *all,* save me. In this instance, I would suggest that yes, it is a *formality,*" he snapped.

The insult literally stole her breath. Sophie stared at him, watched the smirk grow in his eyes. "Perhaps you are right," she said slowly, marveling at the cruel smile that turned the corners of his lips. "But you have my solemn vow I shall die an old and penniless spinster before I will ever consent to marry you, Trevor Hamilton."

For an instant it seemed as if the air were sucked from the room—the din around them was suddenly gone, the smell of ale and flesh gone. For an instant, there was nothing but Trevor and her, and in that instant, Sophie feared for her life.

The look on Trevor's face was one of vicious rage, a look so intense and piercing that she could feel it through her bones. The sickening heat of anticipation spread rapidly through her, the anticipation of being struck, again and again, until she vomited. She lurched backward, knocking up against the chair back, almost unconsciously prepared to curl into a ball like she had with William.

But miraculously, his expression faded to raw anger. *"Bitch,"* he said low. "I offer you a chance to save your tattered reputation, and you would throw it back in my face? You will regret what you have done here tonight, mark me! Your childish temper will not spare you from my offer!"

"But *why?*" she exclaimed incredulously. "Why do you want me as your wife when I so obviously despise the idea?"

Oddly enough, the question seemed to confuse him. He frowned, twisted a cuff link as he considered her. "I have my reasons—and I am quite certain your brother will convince you of your good fortune in such a match. He's as encouraging of it as anyone."

Sophie's rage was on the verge of spiraling out of control. Did they *all* think to barter her away like some old cow? "Well look around you, Trevor. Julian is not here. *I* am here."

His jaw bulging with his anger, Trevor suddenly shoved up from the table, then leaned down so that his face was mere inches from hers, his eyes burning with resentment. "I'll forgive you your stupidity once, Sophie, but not again," he breathed angrily, and slowly straightened. He sneered with disgust as he looked down at her. "Go to your room—you look like a whore sitting there. You'll ride with me on the morrow."

With that all too superior pronouncement, Trevor stalked across the room, practically pushing the serving girl aside as he disappeared into the connecting rooms.

Only when he had stepped through the dark opening did Sophie breathe again. She looked down; she was gripping the table so tightly that her knuckles were stark white. Slowly, she let go, drew a ragged breath, but could not stop her hands from shaking.

She had done it. She had, for once in her bloody life, stood up to someone, to a *man,* to the *ton,* the world, and everyone in it. It left her feeling wobbly and giddy all at once. With both hands, she held the tankard, lifted it to her lips, felt the warm liquid sluice down her throat.

She lowered the thing, and with a small inward smile of victory, watched an old man put a fiddle to his chin and begin to play a festive old Gaelic tune.

The fiddler's music drifted out into the courtyard of the Hawk and Dove as Caleb handed the reins to the hostler's young son. "There's a crown for you if you'll rub her down and feed her," he said, rubbing the slender neck of his Arabian. The boy's eyes lit up; he nodded eagerly and instantly began murmuring to the horse.

Caleb watched him lead the mare toward the stables, then turned to look at the inn. Light streamed from the small bay window; the strains of a Scottish jig pulled at his heartstrings, reminding him of home.

Home. *Scotland.* How he longed to be there, particularly those moments when he felt adrift and rudderless in this world. Moments like now. Fatigue and hunger made him question his sanity as he moved slowly toward the inn. He had ridden like a madman across England after the woman who had broken his heart. And for what? She was in there now, he was certain of it, and he hadn't the vaguest idea what he would say.

That he loved her, would always love her.

As he moved across the courtyard, the confusing sense of betrayal and longing muddled what was left of his brain—he could make no sense of his actions now, other than an overwhelming need to see her, to touch her hair, to kiss her.

Hardly noticed as he stepped across the threshold, Caleb found the common room exceedingly familiar, having been in dozens just like it across England in the course of building the railroad. At one end, a fiddler stroked a lively tune; a dozen or more folk danced a jig, their heels kicking higher with each refrain. The darkened door to his left undoubtedly led to the gaming room; a tail of smoke streamed from it into the common room. The stale air was thick and heavy—there were at least four dozen souls stuffed inside, their tankards held high, their voices rising above the music.

His gaze swept the crowd; he did not see her. Was it possible the coach had gone on? Was she perhaps trying to sleep above the racket?

Then he saw her.

A lump swelled in his throat as he gazed at her slender back. Seated at a tiny little table in the corner of the room, he watched her lift the tankard, lower it again, her knee moving in time to the music, almost unnoticed beneath her voluminous skirts. He was moving before he knew it, moving toward her, the desire to touch her over-whelming the fear of further humiliation and the need to hide his heart from her. He had to touch her, had to breathe her in, assure himself no harm had come to her.

Then he would determine what he would say.

Sophie felt him before she saw him. The feeling came over her like a rush of cool air, sharpening her senses, waking her from her ruminations. How she knew was impossible to fathom, but she *knew* it, knew Caleb had come into the room, was coming to her.

The tankard slipped from her grasp; she shoved to her feet, uncertain what she should do with herself, which way she should turn, what she should *say*. But she could feel him approaching her, feel him almost at her back, and all thoughts of reason or propriety or even common sense flew out of her head.

She whirled about, saw him standing ragged before her, his clothes dirtied with the grime of the road, the shadows of fatigue on his face. She had never seen a more beautiful man in all her life—the smile, the shining of his green eyes, sent her reeling. She had thought she would never see him or touch him again. Without think-ing, Sophie lurched forward, threw her arms around his neck, buried her face in his collar, and inhaled the scent of him. His arms surrounded her, squeezed her tightly to him.

"Caleb," she murmured tearfully onto his shoulder.

"Don't. Don't say anything," he whispered into her hair. "Just let me hold you, let me breathe you, let me fill my soul with you once more."

The tears spilled from the corners of her eyes as he squeezed her to him. "I'm sorry!" she rasped. "I'm so very sorry!"

"Don't cry, please don't cry."

"How very wretched I have been! I have thought only

of you, have dreamed only of you, have prayed and begged God to let me take it all back! Caleb, Caleb, I thought I'd never see you again, that you were lost to me forever! I didn't know where you lived, and you didn't come back to the park, and I thought you had left—"

"I am here now," he said, and she felt herself being lowered into a chair. "Don't cry, darling—I am here."

She fumbled for his hand, afraid to let go, lest he disappear. Reluctantly, she opened her eyes.

He *was* here.

In a curious state of shock, she looked at him seated across the table from her, almost afraid to believe this miracle. She shakily wiped the tears from her cheeks, unable to tear her gaze from him. Caleb put a kerchief into one of her hands; the other he clasped tightly in his own. Sophie wiped her nose with the kerchief, looked up, and smiled at the several people around them who were watching with considerable interest.

Caleb took the kerchief from her and smiled warmly. "How good it is to lay eyes on you. I thought . . . I thought . . ." He expelled his breath harshly. "I've been trying to imagine what I might possibly do without you," he said awkwardly. "And I confess, I could not very well imagine anything a'tall."

After what she had done, he would say something so sweet? "How can you be so kind after what I did?"

He smiled sheepishly. "I love you."

The explanation was so simple and heartfelt that Sophie felt her entire being lift to some preternatural realm, one where she felt instantly comforted and safe. *Loved.* If only they could keep going, deeper into that realm, away from here and England . . . but they were here, in the middle of England. Nothing had changed. "W-what are you doing here?"

"I came for you. I heard you had left after Madame Fortier and I could not rest knowing you were out here somewhere, alone."

Sophie's heart constricted. "Oh Caleb," she whispered, looking down at her lap as tears spilled. "I would give the moon and the stars to take it all back if I could! I was so foolish, so terribly vain to refuse you—"

"Let's not speak of it now," he said, grimacing as if her words had pained him. "I just want to behold you."

"How can I not speak of it?" she muttered miserably.

"Sophie, darling, you are upsetting yourself," he said gently, motioning to the serving girl. "Two ales," he called to her.

The music was louder now; several around them had lost interest in Caleb and Sophie and had turned toward the dancing, a few more deciding to join in. But Sophie was almost oblivious to the noise around them. Caleb's appearance had given her a chance she had not thought she would have again, and she was suddenly desperate for it. "Caleb, I—"

He squeezed her hand, silencing her with a broad smile. "My darling, there is much we would say to one another. But at this particular moment, I am so very grateful to have found you well that I feel a bit like dancing."

"What?" she asked, incredulous, and looked at the dancers, then back to Caleb. *"Dancing?"* He nodded. "But I don't know how!" she quickly protested as Caleb stood.

"Ah, certainly you do," he said, and pulled her up. "Just kick up your heels. Come on, then, dance with me . . . make me sway." He threw his arm around her shoulder, kissed her hard and long, then just as abruptly lifted his head and caught her hand, pulling her behind him, wading into the fray of dancing with an ebullient grin.

"Come on, *kick*!" he shouted to her over the noise, and with the grace of a swan, folded his arms across his chest and kicked up his heels.

Frozen, Sophie stood in the middle of the crowded floor, watching Caleb and everyone else dance a jig around her. It was surely a dream . . . after days of wretched misery, it seemed so unreal, this crowded room, the dancing, and Caleb, his feet moving so quickly that he seemed to float.

Something about that made her laugh; Sophie grabbed her skirts, watched Caleb for a moment, and then kicked up her heels, mimicking him.

They danced for hours, kicking and spinning away what had gone on between them, fortified by long draws of ale. They laughed, kissed long and deep, then laughed again, as if nothing had happened between them, as if they were old and married and had danced a thousand jigs together. They spun round the room over and over again, their heels going higher and higher, their spinning more frenzied with the increasing tempo of the music.

In the early hours of the morning, they stumbled outside, hand in hand, for fresh air. The moon was full, spilling gray-white light over them and the courtyard. Sophie looked up at Caleb standing beside her, at the fine lines around his eyes, the square cut of his jaw. He must have felt her gaze; he looked down, his smile so heartwarming. "I have exhausted you, I am afraid," he said.

Funny, but she felt more alive and vibrant than she had in days.

"I should be a gentleman and insist that you retire for the night, or what is left of it."

Ah, but her blood was stirring as it always did when she was near him, and Sophie smiled coyly. "Perhaps you should be a gentleman and *see* that I retire for the night . . . and what is left of it." It didn't even sound like her—but a light sparked deep in Caleb's eye and Sophie flashed him a terribly wanton smile. "I mean, there are so many people about . . ."

He leaned down, nibbled her earlobe. "You should think twice before inviting me to your bed, madam, for I am the greatest threat to your virtue." His lips moved from her earlobe to her neck, sending a rain of sparks down her spine.

"Perhaps you should think twice before accepting, sir," she murmured, bending her head so that he might have better access to her neck, "for I may very well be the greatest threat to *your* virtue."

Caleb laughed softly against her neck, pulled her into a strong embrace. "You may have my bloody virtue, madam. You already possess my heart."

More seductive words were never uttered, and Sophie melted into his chest, kissed his chin as she grasped his hand. And just like that, with the touch of his fingers, the old Sophie disappeared. Gone was the cowardly, timid sister of the Earl of Kettering, and in her place, the new Sophie—the one who had traveled the world over, the one who knew the man she loved and wanted to show him just how much that was so.

She stepped out of his embrace, pulled on his arm. Still smiling, Caleb took one heavy step toward her. A seductive little giggle escaped her throat—with him, she felt capable of being the seductress, of enticing him to bed with her smile alone. Apparently, she was not far from the mark, because Caleb followed her back into the common room, through what remained of the dancing crowd, and up the wooden stairs to the room Sophie had acquired earlier.

When they stepped inside, Caleb quickly shut the door behind them, then trapped Sophie against it, letting his hand and mouth eagerly explore her body. The sensation was exquisite; smiling decadently, Sophie arched into him, guided his hands to feel all of her. She was floating, buoyed by his strength and his determination to have her, the pleasurable sensations overtaking all conscious thought.

Only vaguely did she feel herself being lifted; their collective weight made the bed moan as it sank. Caleb laughed. His hand skimmed the outline of her breast, to the buttons of her bodice. A moment later, Sophie felt the breath of cool air on her skin. She sighed as he pressed his lips against the hollow of her throat and pulled the pins from her hair, reaching for him as he moved lower, pushing the white cotton frill of her chemise below her breast as he went, laving the dark nipple. Sophie whimpered at the slow but urgent caress of his tongue on her breast. "You are beautiful," he whispered.

What Caleb uttered in the dark was terribly erotic—Sophie actually *felt* beautiful, so beautiful that there was not even a glimmer of self-consciousness when he pulled her up, dispensed with her gown and her chemise and petticoats. She fell back on the bed, onto her elbows, her legs stretched out in front of her as she watched him undress beneath hooded eyes. His was a magnificent body, entirely masculine, from the breadth of his muscled shoulders to the taper of his lean waist, the full thighs and buttocks. And of course, there was *that* standing erect before her, long and sleek.

Standing naked before her, Caleb openly admired her as she admired him, then smiling wolfishly, he leaned over, grabbed her waist, and pulled her forward, until her legs were hanging off the edge of the bed. He went down on his knees before her, his lips grazing her thigh, his breath grazing the apex of her legs.

Moaning, she let her head fall back and closed her eyes as his tongue slipped between the folds of her sex, languidly at first, carefully tasting her, exploring each crevice. But then the lap of his tongue took on new urgency, the strokes harder, his mouth covering her. Her writhing seemed to inspire him; his fingers gripped her hips, holding her firmly as he stroked and licked, suckled and nibbled her into a frenzy of delicious torment, until the dark suddenly erupted into brilliant starlight. She was falling and soaring all at once, drifting on a cloud of pure pleasure, away from everything. Except Caleb. *Caleb.* How she loved him!

She groaned, gulped for air.

Caleb came over her, kissing her cheek, her throat, as the aftermath of the eruption washed over her in a whisper. *"Beautiful,"* he said again. "I want you, Sophie. I want to love you." With his knees, he spread her legs wider, moved so that his cock was pressed against her, begging entry.

She moved, lifted her knees. "Come inside me," she whispered, and gasped with exhilaration as he slipped inside her, slowly sliding into her depths.

"Ah God." His voice was ragged, full of emotion, as he began his seductive movement, tantalizing her with his breadth and the depths to which he smoothly stroked. As he lengthened within her, her passion was swelling again, as was the primal need to meet every thrust. "Harder," she heard herself mutter, heard Caleb groan, bury his face in her neck. Sophie's knees gripped him; she lifted her pelvis to reach him, matching his rhythm, until she was bucking wildly beneath him, begging him with her body to stroke faster, harder. The tantalizing pressure began to mount in her again, and as his strokes deepened within her, the pressure became unbearable.

"Come now, darling, *now,*" he urged her, watching her eyes as she did. "Now!"

"Caleb!" she panted, wildly anxious, and gripped his shoulders, her nails digging into his back, lifting herself higher, meeting each hard stroke, until the tidal wave of pleasure crashed through her, carrying her swiftly away from all reality but the magic of Caleb inside her. She arched her neck, grabbed helplessly at the coverlet beneath her as the release flooded from every pore.

Caleb cupped her bottom with both hands, lifting her from the bed as he drove into her twice more, releasing his own passion with a powerful thrust and strangled cry. He filled her completely, his seed pouring deep inside her as he softly called her name, then collapsed beside her.

They lay for several minutes with his flesh inside her, panting for breath, both blissfully sated. After a time, Sophie slowly opened her eyes and turned to look at Caleb.

He was watching her, an unfathomable look in his pale green eyes. Without speaking, he reached up and smoothed a strand of hair from her eyes. "I love you," he said. "I have never loved a woman as I love you. Do you know that?"

"I love you," she whispered, cupping his face in her palm. "With all my heart, my soul, my flesh."

He smiled, stroked her hair once more before pulling her protectively into his embrace.

They slept in one another's arms. Caleb awoke sometime in the night, his gaze drawn to the moonbeam that spilled through the small attic window. It cast a pale light over Sophie's face; she was so serene in her sleep, so pretty, and he was reminded of the night in London, in his half-finished ballroom—the first time he had ever truly made love to a woman. *This* woman. He wished now that he could reach up and take the moon in his hand, hold it exactly where it was, and freeze this moment for all eternity so that he might forever gaze on her like this, his heart full to bursting with love. He watched until the moon slid away, and only then did he gather Sophie close again and close his eyes.

The next morning, Sophie awoke him with a shower of kisses. He opened one eye—she was up and dressed and beaming from ear to ear. He yawned, scratched his chest, and pushed himself up on one elbow. "Top of the morning, my darling."

She laughed, kissed his cheek, then bounced up, tossing his trousers to him. "You've caused me to quite miss my coach, Mr. Hamilton."

"Did I indeed? Well then, there is nothing to be done for it," he said as he swung one leg over the edge of the bed, then the other. "Having brought this travesty on you, I now must personally see you to your destination." He winked, shoved one leg in his trousers, smiling as

Sophie stole a glimpse of his nakedness before stepping in with his other leg.

"My destination is quite a distance, I should warn you."

"I am well aware," he said, and fastening his trousers, walked to where Sophie stood, grabbing her in a strong embrace and kissing the top of her head before continuing on to the basin to wash. "Might I ask *why* you decided to strike out on your own and follow Madame Fortier? It is hardly the sort of thing a lady is suited to doing."

"And why isn't a lady suited for it?" she demanded, punching her fists to her hips. "I can ride in a coach as well as any man."

Her zeal surprised him; Caleb blinked. "All right," he said slowly.

Sophie blushed a very becoming shade of pink, bit her lip sheepishly. "Besides," she said, shrugging, "I had no choice. Trevor intends to accuse her of kidnapping and any other crime he can think of. I do not condone what she has done, but Honorine is no criminal. Her intentions are good."

He did not choose to debate that at the moment, but instead opined, "I would rather imagine Trevor is halfway to Nottinghamshire by now."

"Why, no! Trevor is here!"

That announcement struck him. He paused in his bathing and looked at her, half-certain she was jesting. *"Here?"*

Sophie nodded.

"What do you mean, here?"

"Here. At this inn. I had the misfortune of encountering him last night," she said, and abruptly turned away, but not before he saw the look of disgust on her face.

Caleb glanced in the mirror before him, noticed his scowl. The mere mention of Trevor's name had effectively ruined the mood for him, the heady sense of love and the feeling that they were the only ones in the world.

"We've got to leave this place," he muttered. "Hurry with you now," he said, grabbing his shirt and waistcoat from the floor, dispensing with any ideas of shaving he might have had. "We can reach Hamilton House before him—if you can ride, that is."

"Yes. Yes, I can ride."

He nodded, dressed quickly, uncertain as to the exact nature of his sudden anxiety, other than recognizing a monumental fear of doom should Trevor find him here with Sophie like this.

"Come on then," he urged her. "I'll see to my horse and a separate mount for you. Meet me in the courtyard, will you?" He started for the door, his mind on the business of finding another horse. He started at the feel of Sophie's hand on his arm, and abruptly stopped in midstride, looked around to her.

"I . . . I did not know he was here until I saw him."

Caleb forced down the ancient feelings of rejection, of envy. It wasn't her fault, he knew. But he resented the hell out of Trevor at the moment, and knowing that he had been here, somewhere on the same floor as they had made such passionate love, did not improve his disposition in the least. The best thing to do was leave St. Neots as soon as possible.

He kissed her forehead. "Hurry," he said simply, and quit the room.

In the stables, he arranged for a serviceable mare and even an old sidesaddle for Sophie. Having agreed upon what he thought was a reasonable price, Caleb walked past the stables and around to the back, where several carriages had been pulled. Nothing overly ornate or black, he noticed with a sigh of relief. Trevor had undoubtedly left with daybreak.

He was wrong.

As Caleb walked into the courtyard, he saw his half-brother standing beside his father's ridiculously appointed coach, looking as pompous and as obnoxious as ever. He

thought to skirt the edge of he courtyard and remain unnoticed by Trevor—but then Sophie stepped out into the
bright sunshine.

Trevor's jaw tightened noticeably.

Caleb reached her first, managing to step in front of
her before Trevor could accost her. His sudden appearance obviously startled Trevor; he took an involuntary
step backward, his eyes hardening at the realization of
who would stop him.

"Good morning," Caleb said evenly.

His brother did not speak for a moment. His hard
gaze flit to Sophie, then back to Caleb. "What in the hell
are you doing here?" he demanded.

"Passing through, like you."

"Then pass through. But stand away from me, sir."

Caleb did not move. He braced himself for a fight, not
even flinching when he felt Sophie's hand fall on the
small of his back.

"You missed your coach," Trevor said flatly to Sophie.

She stepped up to stand beside Caleb. "No. I didn't."

It was a moment before Trevor understood; the realization slid over him so slowly that Caleb could see it
drain the blood from his face. Scowling, he shifted a
murderous gaze to Caleb. "You have wrought too much
harm, sir. Do not think that I will allow an imposter and
a blackguard to steal from an infirm man and compro-
mise a lady of the *ton* with his bastard seed."

"At any time or place you name," Caleb responded
low.

"No—" Sophie started, but Trevor cut her off with a
murderous gleam that made Sophie shrink into Caleb's
side.

"As for *you,* madam . . . if you think you have experienced the sting of scandal before, I think you will find
the label *whore* a much deeper wound."

Sophie merely lifted her chin at the insult. Raking one
last glare across Caleb, Trevor turned on his heel, stalked

to his coach. Barking an order to the driver, he climbed inside, slamming the small door behind him.

Caleb and Sophie stood side by side, watching the coach pull away. Sophie found Caleb's hand and squeezed gently. "We've nothing to fear from him," she said pleasantly.

Caleb smiled. "Of course not."

God help us both.

Just west of Huntingdon, on the banks of the River Nene, beneath the wide boughs of an old oak tree, Honorine and Will sat admiring the buttercups that blanketed the slopes. Will brushed Honorine's hair slowly, his mind struggling to capture the thought he knew was there. It definitely concerned Caleb, that much he had come to remember. He also knew with some certainty that the answer to whatever was lurking there in the shadows of his mind was at Hamilton House. The sooner they could reach it, the better, for Will had a sense of unease, a sense that something wasn't quite right.

He finished brushing Honorine's hair, bent forward to catch the scent of it before leaning back against the tree.

Honorine moved to rest against his chest, staring thoughtfully into the flowers around them, her bare feet sticking out beneath her gold-and-blue skirts.

"What has your . . . thh-thoughts, m-my love?" he asked.

She shrugged, smiled up at him. "My thoughts, they are simple," she said, looking a bit confused when he laughed. "I have these thoughts that you are more well without *la médecine.*"

Will stopped laughing. "What? What do you m-mean by this?"

Honorine pressed a finger against his lips, then leaned up to kiss him. "*La médecine,* it does not help, *non*? Your head is more well without it," she said, gesturing to his forehead.

Will nodded, looked away. There it was again, the urgent thought on the periphery of his mind, the sense that something wasn't quite right.

Honorine was correct. His capacity to think and reason had improved tremendously in the last several days. The only difference—aside from being with Honorine and in the clean air of the countryside—was the absence of any medicine. That, he found quite interesting. But also deeply perplexing.

Chapter Twenty-One

RURAL ENGLAND

SOPHIE AND CALEB chose a rarely traveled back road, hoping to gain some ground on Trevor.

It had been years since Sophie had ridden horseback, and while it took her a few miles to find her equilibrium, she soon rediscovered the exhilaration of riding with the wind in her face. She felt free, wanted to ride faster, harder, into the space before them.

The events of the last three days had, by some miracle, transformed her into the woman she had always wanted to be. She felt invincible, unconquerable, the queen of her own world—an independent woman, capable of making her own decisions and turning her back on the collective prejudices of the *ton*. She had never felt quite so strong in all her life—if she wanted, she was certain she could lift mountains.

They decided to stop in the small village of Peakirk and inquire if anyone might have chanced to see the gig carrying Honorine and Lord Hamilton, and assure themselves that they were on the right path. After all, Sophie reasoned, they had only the word of a small boy, and he had been rather angry. Caleb agreed that it was conceivable that the child might have lied.

Feeling quite formidable, Sophie insisted on conducting the interview of the dry-goods proprietor herself. Prepared to make quick work of him, she marched into the small shop.

The proprietor, as it happened, was not a man at all, but his large and jovial widow.

"Have you perhaps encountered a woman about my height, her hair dark with a bit of silver? She is wearing it long and unbound, I am quite certain," Sophie explained with a slight roll of her eyes, "and a skirt of . . . ah . . . very vivid colors. You've undoubtedly never seen such colors on one bolt, I'd wager. Oh yes, she is driving a gig for a gentleman who can't come down off the bench—he's had a seizure of some sort, you see—and she was probably speaking half-English, half-French. You'd surely know it, because you must listen very carefully to make any sense of it at all."

The shopkeeper blinked.

"She's French," Sophie added.

The woman's burst of laughter startled Sophie; her large belly jiggled as she laughed. "You are quite serious, are you, mu'um? Oh no, we've not had anyone of that description through Peakirk, I can assure you, for we'd all know it." She laughed again with her hands on her belly, as if to contain the jiggling. "Ooh, I must compliment your bonnet! Rather colorful, isn't it?"

Sophie touched the brim of the hat borrowed from Honorine and smiled.

She became so engrossed in the telling of the story of Honorine in Dieppe and the dozens of hats distributed there that it was several moments before she or Mrs. Clevely saw Caleb, his arms folded across his chest, leaning casually against the door frame. Mrs. Clevely's pudgy hand floated to her double chin. "Oh *my,*" she said, blushing. "Won't you come in, sir?"

"Thank you, madam, but I've just come for my ward there."

"Oh." Sophie glanced at the watch pinned to her breast and realized she had been talking more than a quarter of an hour. "Oh dear," she muttered, and smiled sheepishly at Mrs. Clevely. "It would seem I have taken too much of your time."

"Not at all, not at *all*," the woman crowed as she eyed the full length of Caleb, sizing him up like a side of beef.

Sophie hurried to the door, bustled Caleb out in front of her before he could respond. "Thank you again, Mrs. Clevely! A lovely day to you!" she called over her shoulder, and practically fell through the door in her haste to get outside.

Laughing, Caleb caught her by the elbow. "Did you perchance learn anything, or was the entire visit focused on your hat?"

"Yes, I did indeed," Sophie responded with mock arrogance. "I learned that Mrs. Clevely's husband has been gone for five years now, and she desires a new mate." She glanced at Caleb from the corner of her eye. "Judging by the way she looked at you, I would advise you to set your mount to a bit of a gallop."

Their luck was not improved in Thurlby or Morton. But in Ingoldsby, a diminutive fishmonger remembered Honorine quite vividly, describing her perfectly in great, poetic terms.

"Did she happen to mention where they were bound?" Sophie asked, cutting off his rather lengthy description of Honorine, the lone daisy in a field of dead grass.

The man placed a finger alongside his nose, and thought hard. "Yes, yes . . . I *do* recall! They were to Billingborough and the pottery market there! She had in mind some platters."

"Platters?" Caleb asked, his skepticism evident. "But Billingborough is in the opposite direction of Nottingham."

"Yes sir, it was Billingborough," the fishmonger said, nodding adamantly.

Caleb looked to Sophie; she was as skeptical as he

was, but it was a true fact that one never knew quite what to expect with Honorine. The woman definitely did whatever suited her. "I wouldn't be terribly surprised," she said truthfully.

With a glance at the midday sun, Caleb sighed. "All right, then. To Billingborough."

They thanked the little man, fetched their mounts. As they began to ride away, the fishmonger called after them. "You'll give her Mr. Ickham's kindest regards, will you? *Mr. Ickham of Ingoldsby!*" he shouted.

Sophie nodded and waved; she and Caleb rode on, their laughter trailing behind them.

At Billingborough, no one had seen a Frenchwoman with an ailing man.

They agreed they obviously had been thrown off track. The only plausible explanation, Ian's uttering aside, was that they were headed for Nottinghamshire and Hamilton House. They returned the way they had come, veering to the north in Ingoldsby, toward Nottinghamshire. Neither of them remarked on the time they had lost and rode at a comfortable pace, quietly relishing one another's company in spite of the circumstance that had brought them here. Without conscious thought, they slipped into the fairy-tale world they had created all those afternoons in London and had found again in the English countryside. It was not hard to do; the day was simply gorgeous— bright sunshine, summer flowers blanketing the fields, picturesque vistas of hamlets and an occasional old keep. Neither of them wanted to leave the magic.

Outside of Grantham, they stopped for a time to feed and water the horses. Sophie took the opportunity to stretch her limbs, wandering around the little meadow picking flowers.

As he watched her, Caleb fell into a thoughtful silence. Last night's lovemaking had bewitched him, stayed with him all day. He wanted to believe it had been the same for her. Sophie had a way about her, a subtle air that swept a man in, allowed him to rest, to feel safe. But while he felt all those things and more about Sophie, she had refused his offer of marriage. In all his thirty-five years, he had never so much as had the inclination to offer for a woman, much less act on it. He realized, of course, that was in part because he had never loved like he had come to love Sophie—completely, deeply, and with all that he had.

Which was why part of him now feared this warm, dreamy association, for another rejection such as she had handed him before would be devastating, if not paralyzing, destroying a piece of him that he could never reclaim. *Still* . . . she had apologized, had made him believe with her words and her body that she would rescind the words she had uttered that night, return them both to the blissful happiness they had known in London.

He watched as she stooped to pick a handful of wild daisies. When she stood again, she was smiling at him as she had the first time he had ever seen her across the little pond. He loved that smile, loved it with all his heart. Moreover, he had *trusted* that smile.

He trusted it now, didn't he? Last night had restored his faith, had it not?

She was walking toward him, her skirts lifted in one hand, free of the cumbersome petticoats, which she had, apparently, discarded in the course of her liberation. She stepped carefully, her trim calves lifting above the tall grass. Her bonnet dangled, forgotten, down her back. She had tied her hair simply at her nape; it trailed almost to her waist in shimmers of gold and mahogany. As she neared him, she dropped her skirts, let them drag the grass behind her, her smile growing brighter as she handed the wild daisies to him.

Caleb took them, examined the small petals for a long moment.

"Are we quite ready to continue?" she asked. "The horses are feeding—"

"I would know something, Sophie," he blurted, and lifted his gaze from the flowers, feeling the grip of uncertainty close around his heart. "There is something I must know. The night of the Fortier ball, I asked that you marry me." He paused, gathered what was left of his courage. But Sophie said nothing, simply drew her bottom lip between her teeth and looked at him with no small amount of trepidation.

It was too late to go back, too late to snatch his heart back from the abyss into which it had suddenly plummeted. "You refused me," he said flatly. "You rejected me on the grounds of my birth, I think."

A small sigh escaped her; she bowed her head. "Oh my, I've made quite a mess of things, haven't I?"

God. Oh God.

"I suppose you will never forgive me, will you?"

"Pardon?" he asked dumbly. *Breathe.* He could not seem to breathe.

"You shall never forgive me, I think, nor would I, in your place."

Forgive . . . could she not forgive him the circumstance of his birth? "There is nothing to forgive, Sophie. If you feel strongly in your conviction—"

"But that is just the thing, Caleb, I *have* no conviction. Not about that, at any rate. Quite honestly, I feel hardly anything a'tall about the circumstance of your birth, other than I am rather glad you are here. I have no excuse for what I did, not after what we shared, but I would ask that you please consider my upbringing and please forgive me this terrible mistake. *Please* forgive me."

Caleb's heart leapt to his throat; he tried to swallow it, tried to keep the hope from surfacing because he could not quite believe her—he had spent too many years a bastard, known too many ladies of the Quality.

"It's just that . . . it's just that appearances are quite important to members of the *haut ton*," she continued, obviously flustered, "and while I would not want to dishonor my family again, I cannot be unfaithful to myself, can I? Oh honestly, I am making such a mess of things! What I am trying to say is that what matters most of all is that you love me, exactly for who I am. And while I won't pretend to understand it, the past seems not to make a whit of difference to you. Actually, I'd rather not delve *too* deeply into why, because the Lord knows I am desperately in love with you, and I could not bear to hear a single disapproving word. Do you see?"

Caleb nodded solemnly as he took a step toward her.

"Honorine always says, 'Love is like good French wine—one simply cannot live without it, whether it comes in a brown bottle or a green bottle.' I understand that—well, in one way, perhaps—but you might therefore ask yourself, 'Well then why would you refuse the offer of a man who loves you if you believe all this talk of bottles?' I don't know other than to say I reacted as I supposed I ought. I said what I thought would meet everyone's approval, what everyone would expect of me . . ." She paused to catch her breath and looked up at him with great longing. "I did not speak my heart, Caleb—I spoke the *ton's* drivel. I hope you will forgive me. I hope you will allow me to speak my heart now, and believe me when I tell you that I love you, more than I love my very own life."

His heart was pounding now with hope fresh and raw. He caught Sophie by the hand, pulled her into his embrace. "Then may I take it that if I were to ask again, you would accept the offer to be my wife?"

She startled him by firmly shaking her head. "There remains the problem of *me*. Have you considered how your own good reputation might be compromised by consorting—*marrying*—a divorcée?"

It was so absurd that the laughter rumbled up from his chest, bursting and spilling into the meadow around them. "Sophie, the things you say! I may be rest assured I shall never want for laughter! *No,* my darling, I do not worry that my reputation will be compromised. Quite the contrary—every gentleman from here to the moon shall wish himself so fortunate as me!"

Sophie opened her mouth to speak, but Caleb seized her, kissing the very breath from her lungs. When he lifted his head, the glitter of happiness had returned to Sophie's eyes.

"But you must know there will be talk. What Trevor said this morning is only the beginning," she warned.

"I have been the subject of gossip and unkind conjecture all my life, Sophie. I hardly care anymore." He kissed her again, and reluctantly looked at his timepiece. "Come on then, we must be on our way."

But as they rode away from the meadow, his thoughts full of her promise, Caleb remarked idly, "I rather think Kettering will not approve."

Sophie sighed wearily. "I suppose not. He's always been quite rigid about these things."

"Will he forbid you?"

"Ha!" she exclaimed defiantly. "And what if he does? I am a grown woman—he cannot dictate my life to me."

"Nonetheless, he is your brother. And the Earl of Kettering. I suppose he could dictate *my* life if he were of a mind."

She shrugged. They rode in silence for several moments before she asked, "Where shall we go, do you suppose? To the house at Regent's Park?"

Caleb did not answer immediately, as he rather imagined that would be impossible now, his dream of it notwithstanding. The two of them would cause quite a stir there. But where *would* they go? He had been so intent on his heart's desire that he hadn't really thought through the details of it, had he? His house in Scotland, in dire need of repair, was little more than a hovel by Sophie's standards. There was his mother's property in France, but he hadn't seen it in years and scarcely knew if the château was still standing. His work, the railroad—it kept him moving. Did he keep Sophie moving, too? And what of children? How would they bring a family into this world with his name and her reputation and no home?

"I don't know," he admitted at last. "But we'll find our way, I promise you." Or he would die trying.

And they rode on, each wondering what a pair of outcasts could do in this world.

The skeleton staff left behind at Hamilton House had taken to lazy afternoons of napping and a little friendly wagering on card games. On occasion, such as this fine summer day, they would challenge the groundsmen to a game of cricket on the south lawn. The stable master was just taking his turn at bat when they heard the shriek. All of them whirled around as one, straining to hear the sound and identify it. Another one immediately rent the air, then another.

Everyone was suddenly running in pandemonium— the men toward the house, the women to gather up and hide the implements of their game, the butler anxiously directing them. One maid suggested it was perhaps little Ian returned to them, but an older, wiser cook shook her head. *That,* she said authoritatively, was the sound of a ghost. It was Elspeth Hamilton come to chastise them for playing instead of working.

None of them could have guessed it was a madwoman. None of them had ever seen the combination of sea green, orange, and pale blue swirling about one set of ladies' skirts, or a woman of mature age and bearing run across a lawn barefoot.

And certainly none of them had ever seen Lord Hamilton looking quite so . . . happy. Or, in these last few months, quite so lucid. Praise God, the underbutler said. The housekeeper adjusted her cap and squinted once more to ensure she wasn't seeing things, then proclaimed it a bloody miracle that he was even walking. All of them cautiously crept forward as they attempted to determine what to make of the woman.

She smiled brightly, waved and wished them all a fine day in half-French, half-English. She then whirled about and put her arm around Lord Hamilton's waist, strolling casually beside him as he moved forward to where the staff was blindly assembling.

"How you do, D-Darby," he said politely to the butler. "M-may I introduce Madame Honorine Fortier. I intend to m-make her m-my wife," he said, and smiled so brilliantly at the woman that they all felt the force of it. More than one felt the smile spread to their own lips.

A dozen or more pairs of eyes peered at Honorine Fortier, who nonchalantly brushed the grass from her hem, then at Lord Hamilton again. Impossible. At least improbable. Perhaps a true miracle, because the old man was actually smiling and talking.

The same dozen pairs of eyes shifted to Honorine Fortier again. And they smiled.

In the village of Grantham, Trevor instructed his driver to pull into the courtyard of the Willowbough Inn, where he took a room for the night. He was exhausted, having bounced around in that bloody coach all day long. He was also furious. An old crow in Essendine had told him a small gelding meet would be held in Peterborough that afternoon. *That* had cost him several hours and several hundred pounds, paid in the form of two of his team of four grays. The meet had been rigged, fixed to favor the owners. It was so bloody obvious.

He should have known better than to listen to a woman, for Chrissakes, and much less a withered one hawking vegetables.

Trevor angrily tossed his hat onto what looked to be a very lumpy mattress, then withdrew his purse. The contents looked quite bleak. The bastard at St. Neots had cleaned his pockets last night; Trevor remained convinced the man had swindled him. He exhaled his exasperation and dropped heavily onto the mattress. He had to find his father. If he didn't find him soon and force him to sign another banknote, he would be ruined. The very thought sent a chill up his spine—he was on the verge of losing everything. *Everything!* His creditors could not be long behind him now—the situation was impossible, the only answer being the old man's shaking hand when he needed it.

But what if he was wrong? What if they hadn't gone home at all, but she had instead whisked him away to France? Christ God, what would he do then?

Trevor angrily snatched up his purse again. Twenty crowns. With a little luck, he could double that. That was all he needed, a bit of luck, that was all.

And his father.

Chapter Twenty-Two

As the eastern sky was beginning to show a faint hint of light, a small, tenacious group of men surrounded the card table in the back room of the Willowbough Inn, their eyes bloodshot and their whiskey glasses empty as they stared down at the cards being dealt.

None of them noticed the gentleman from London slip out the front door of the common room, instead of climbing the stairs to retire, as he had said he would do.

Trevor ran almost soundlessly across the courtyard toward the stables. Carefully, he pulled the door open, freezing when one horse lifted its head and whinnied. He waited a moment until he was certain the horse's rustling hadn't sounded any alarms. When the horse turned its head away from him, Trevor walked calmly into the stables, down the center of the pens, in the direction of a single door leading to an adjoining room, where a handful of drivers slept on pallets.

No one stirred when he opened the door; a faint snoring set the rhythm of their sleep. A lamp at the far end of the room was burning low—but it was enough light to find his driver. The man was quite large; in the darkness, his shape rather resembled a cow carcass. Careful not to disturb the other drivers, Trevor moved quietly to where he slept and nudged him with his foot.

The man did not move.

Trevor nudged again, harder, making contact with the soft flesh of the man's bum. With a small cry of alarm, the driver rolled and sat up all at once, blinking hard before grinding the heels of his hands into his eyes and looking up.

He blinked when he saw Trevor. "Milord?" he asked, incredulous.

Trevor went down on his haunches, put a finger to his lips. "How quickly can you ready the team?" he whispered.

"The hostler comes at daybreak. Then it's not more than a quarter of an hour," he whispered in response.

Having no intention of waiting for the hostler, Trevor leaned in closer to the driver. "I mean *now*."

The driver winced sharply. "*Now?* But it's the middle of the night, milord!"

The idiot obviously could not grasp that was precisely the point. "I am well aware of the time! I would leave *now,* and the sooner and more quietly you can be about it, the better!" Trevor rose to full height, stared down at the groggy driver. "Get to your feet," he whispered harshly, and turned on his heel.

The driver followed him a few moments later, stuffing his shirt into his trousers as he stumbled through the door. When he saw Trevor standing just inside the stable he started, pressed his hand to his heart. "God's blood, milord, you gave me another fright!"

"Where are the grays?" Trevor asked, impatient. The driver nodded toward several stalls on the right. Trevor looked over his shoulder, saw the head of one, and looked to his driver again. "And the coach?"

"Behind the stables, milord," he said, nervously wiping his hands on the sides of his pants.

"Bring it round."

The driver looked as if he might speak, but then apparently thought the better of it. Trevor waited until he had disappeared through the stable doors, then walked to where the grays were penned and began to methodically bridle them.

In spite of the cool night air, a sheen of perspiration dotted his forehead and neck as he worked. It was not, however, the slight exertion that had him perspiring, oh no. It was fear, a raw, gnawing fear, a sense of impending doom that had been eating away at him for weeks, growing stronger every day.

The situation was hopeless. He had sunk so deeply into the morass that it seemed impossible he would ever extricate himself, even with his father's considerable, but unconscious, help.

It still amazed Trevor that he had ever managed to ensnare himself in such a predicament to begin with. It had happened so quickly, so silently—he had not understood what trouble brewed until a man purporting to be the rather dubious "friend of a friend" accosted him on a dark road in Nottingham one night. That man told Trevor, in no uncertain terms, that if he did not requite the nearly two thousand pounds he owed a moneylender, that he might potentially find his young son missing. That threat had chilled him to his marrow—certainly he had had his fair share of gambling debts in his life, but he had never found himself in the position of having to borrow money, not like he had begun to do.

It was all because of one particularly ugly game of cards; he had lost a bloody fortune. But his finances were in terrible disarray—he had suffered an astounding loss at the parish horse races in the spring of that year when the mare on which he had placed a small fortune went down with a broken femur. That, coupled with Elspeth's dying and directing that the remainder of her small inheritance be settled in trust for Ian, had left him with scarcely anything on which to live.

So he had gone to the moneylender about whom he had heard in gaming rooms around the parish. The man lived in a small, rundown house on the edge of Nottingham. Its dilapidated appearance belied the rich appointment within its walls—the parlor to which Trevor had been shown was full of valuable artwork. The lender himself, dressed in a blue velvet smoking jacket, was dripping in gold rings and a pocket watch. He had nodded sympathetically as Trevor had explained his predicament, then smiled reassuringly when he had signed over the banknote, urging Trevor to take all the time he needed to repay the debt.

Apparently, three months was too long for the moneylender.

Truly, Trevor had never meant it to drag on so long, but it happened that he experienced the most incredible string of bad luck—he couldn't win a hand of cards or a horse race to save his sorry life. Whatever he tried, he only managed to lose more money while the interest on his debt to the moneylender mounted at an extraordinarily rapid pace.

When the man had accosted him in Nottingham, Trevor had no place else to turn but his father.

His father. The viscount had condemned gambling as long as Trevor could remember. This point he had made abundantly clear when Trevor was a young man. He had foolishly bet his finest horse on a game of cards and had lost. When he asked his father for the money necessary to buy it back from his friend, his father had flatly refused. "Let this be a lesson to you, son" was all he had said. Trevor lost his horse. He had never spoken to his father about his gambling again, although his father knew from others that he continued to do so, and let it be known that he did not approve in action and in deed.

Nonetheless, desperate times called for desperate measures. Trevor had been duly frightened by the threat against Ian and was prepared to ask the old man for a loan, if only for his son's sake. The seizure had taken that opportunity from him. The viscount was hardly capable of seeing after his accounts, much less making a loan on them.

Trevor had devised his scheme one evening after giving his father a dose of the opiate the doctor had prescribed to ease any pain. As he had watched his father drift into the oblivion of the drug, he had been struck with the idea of perhaps forging his father's signature on a banknote.

He hadn't really meant to steal from his father, he'd really only meant to borrow. As he was certain his father would have loaned him the money, given the threat against Ian—and assuming, of course, that Trevor could make him understand it. But seeing as how he could not make him understand it, he couldn't really see the harm in signing for his father. After all, the man was incapable. Why not simply *help* him sign the banknotes? Then it wouldn't be stealing, not really.

That night, Trevor had placed the pen in his father's gnarled hand, pressed it against the paper, and helped him form the letters. It had dumbfounded him when his father actually began to sign the document of his own accord. Trevor had dropped his hand, stood back in horror as his father completed his signature without so much as looking at the paper. It was as if some part of him had not died with that seizure; some part of him understood what he was to do and even remembered how to go about affixing his name to a document.

Looking back on it now, as he led the first gray out of the stable, Trevor marveled at how easily that one wish to repay a disreputable moneylender had escalated into the machination that was his scheme now. His father had signed literally thousands of pounds over to him. Even as he began to improve, to regain the use of his limbs, parts of his memory, Trevor continued. It was astoundingly easy—giving a man who cannot remember most things a strong dose of opiate night after night had the desired effect—his mind remained incapacitated. And Trevor had, somehow, rationalized it time and time again in his own mind.

There was a part of him that would never regret the deceit. It was only fair, to his way of thinking. *He* was the legitimate son of Lord Hamilton. He was spending *his* inheritance. When he thought of that goddamned imposter, how he would attempt to take what was rightfully his, Trevor fumed—the man had no right, no claim to what was his, and he would die defending that if he must!

Which meant, of course, that he had to reach his father first, reach him before the swindler managed to do it and somehow convince the old man that he *did* have another son. *Rubbish!* Oh yes, he'd die first before allowing that man to have a single pence of what was rightfully his.

Trevor quickened his step.

By the time he and the driver got the team harnessed, the night was beginning to lift. There was no time to go in and retrieve his things from the dingy room at the top of the stairs—it would be a bloody miracle if they were able to drive out unnoticed, much less get down the road before the authorities were sent after him.

With a strict warning to the driver to be quick, Trevor climbed into the coach and sent him along with a sharp rap above. The coach lurched forward; Trevor held his breath, waited for the sound of shouting, something to indicate that the innkeeper was demanding payment, or the gent from Coventry was realizing he had slipped away without paying him the one hundred pounds he had lost and had given his word to pay this morning.

But the coach kept rolling, and when it was apparent that they had, by some wondrous measure, managed to slip away, he buried his face in his hands and squeezed his eyes tightly shut, mortified that he was, for the second time this week, fighting tears.

The strain was unbearable—he had almost crumbled

into madness when he returned to Bedford Square from the gaming club and realized the French whore had stolen his father away. He had already signed too many bank-notes without his father's assistance; their London banker had looked at him rather suspiciously the last time he had been in, had made some remark about the drain on his father's accounts.

God, he needed the viscount, needed him to lend his hand to the notes!

But that was, he knew, a door that was slowly swinging shut. He could not continue much longer before another banker took notice.

Which was why, in part, the prospect of a match with Sophie Dane had looked so desirable.

Certainly he had been, quite simply, amazed by the transformation in Sophie since her scandal. She was no longer the mousy little thing who had hovered in corners of ballrooms. She had matured; even her features seemed less plain than they did then—she was actually quite attractive in an unassuming way. In his estimation, she was a well-mannered, docile woman who was perfect for Ian and him.

And it certainly did not hurt, in his present dilemma, that she was an heiress in her own right.

His offer for her hand was a stroke of brilliance, he thought. He had solved her problem of being so undesirable—with her reputation and scarred past, it was inconceivable that another gentleman of the *ton* would offer for her. No man in his right mind would want her scandal tainting his children or his business dealings. He had also solved *his* problem—he was not in a position to be overly selective. He needed a wife. A wealthy wife. And Sophie Dane fit that description. Quite frankly, she fit that description so well that he was rather looking forward to their conjugal relations. Looking *very* much forward to that.

Damn her all to hell, then.

Her refusal of him had brought his fury crashing down on him, muddling his mind. The foolish chit had come chasing after him and the French whore and his father. And she was drinking ale like some doxy, a sight that displeased him enormously. A woman of the *ton* did not sip ale like a commoner. She apparently had no regard for her reputation, a flaw he would have quickly corrected once they were wed.

But more than those astounding facts, when he had stepped out of the game room for some air and had seen her sitting there, as if it were perfectly acceptable to go chasing across all of England, the chit had not been contrite in the least. Lord no—she had summoned up the audacity to refuse him, to throw his offer in his face. And all because of some female pique that he had not spoken with her privately about the offer. No doubt she envisioned some terribly romantic moment with him on one knee, her on some gilded swing.

He would have, in due time, corrected her overly romantic notions and wild ways. He would have delighted in teaching her how a Hamilton would behave, in more ways than one. But Sophie had ruined it all, had effectively made herself so untouchable that even *he* could not come near her. She had thrown it all away for one romp in the sack with the bastard imposter.

The very thought of her standing in the courtyard . . . next to *him* . . . made Trevor choke with anger. A tear inadvertently slipped from the corner of his eye, trailed down the stubble of his unshaven face.

He slammed his fist into the side of the coach.

She had ruined it, ruined everything.

Ruined him.

Another miserable day, and Trevor and his driver arrived at Hamilton House, exhausted and ravenous, well after midnight. He sent the driver around to the stables, and limped to the door of his father's house, his legs gone numb with disuse. He did not bother to knock, but retrieved an old door key they kept under the rain gutter and let himself in.

He paused in the foyer, listening for any sound; the house was silent.

Cautiously, Trevor moved down the corridor to the servant's old stairwell. Sheets still draped the furniture in the main salon and parlor; the library door was closed. Frankly, at this particular moment, he hardly cared if anyone had taken up residence in his father's home—he was too exhausted to think.

He took the stairs two at a time, to the second floor, and his suite of rooms. His bedroom was just as he had left it; the furniture was covered in white muslin sheets, the bed bare. He yanked his neckcloth free of his collar, then proceeded to strip down to nothing. Taking a sheet from one of two winged-back chairs at his hearth, he fell on the bare bed, nude save for the sheet that covered him, and closed his eyes.

But sleep would not come easily; it did not come at all, much to his great exasperation. As exhausted as he was, his mind could not let go the pressures of his indebtedness. Tossing and turning on that bare bed, Trevor tried to sleep, tried to put the vague fear out of his mind, if only for a few hours.

When the clock struck three, he sat up, pressed two fingers to his eyes. After a moment, he rose, stumbled sluggishly to his dressing room, and donned a dressing gown. In his bare feet, he left his rooms, took the main stairwell down to the first floor, and silently made his way to the study. Carefully, he opened that door. The furniture here had not been covered—he supposed that the longtime family butler, Darby, used this room for his bookkeeping. Trevor padded across the carpet to a portrait of his grandfather and lifted the painting from the wall, placing it aside. With a sigh, he stood, staring at the wall safe.

He wasn't certain he wanted to look . . . but he had to. He crossed to the desk, searching three drawers before finding the blasted key.

Fortunately, the safe opened easily. He peered inside, past a stack of currency his father kept for emergencies, past his mother's jewels—what he hadn't sold, that was. What Trevor was looking for was in the very back of the safe. He reached in, took the thick packet of paper, and crossed immediately to the large floor-to-ceiling windows where a bit of moonlight spilled in, and untied the ribbon that kept the papers together. Quickly scanning the documents, he scowled.

Nothing had changed—it was all still there, still boldly penned in black ink. *Bloody hell!*

He stood for several long minutes staring blankly at the packet he held in his hand, his jaw clenched tightly shut. At last he tied the papers together again and walked slowly to the safe, lost in his own tormented thoughts. He carefully replaced the papers, closed the safe, and returned the portrait and key to their appropriate places. Then he made his way back to his rooms, his thoughts torturing him with each step.

In his bedroom once again, he let the dressing gown drop to the floor as he reached his bed, and then fell, face forward, onto the bare mattress.

He closed his eyes, prayed to God for sleep.

Sophie and Caleb spent that night under the boughs of an old elm tree, their mattress a horse blanket, their coverlet Caleb's riding coat.

In the course of their journey that day, their hopeful mood had dimmed, as both understood that the moment they reached Hamilton House, everything would change.

It had been a conscious decision to sleep in the open as opposed to another inn—they wanted to be alone, to hold the world at bay for a few hours more. Neither of them mentioned aloud what they both knew—the spurious realm in which they had lived these last few weeks, and in particular, these last two days, was coming to an end. Once again, they would be exposed fully to the harsh reality of their lives.

Caleb caught some fish in a nearby stream; they cooked the meat over a small fire, ate the flesh with their fingers, and wished for wine. When Caleb had seen to it the horses had plenty of room to graze, they had made sweet love beside that fire and underneath the old elm, clinging to one another as they reached fulfillment, not wanting to ever let go, no longer caring if his seed planted within her.

It hardly seemed to matter—Sophie's reputation had been irreparably harmed and not even time could mend it now. Caleb wanted nothing more than a child who would seal their love for the rest of their natural lives and beyond. Her family could not refuse her the legitimacy of the child's name, could not refuse her marriage to the man she loved.

At least he hoped that was so.

They lay quietly afterward, Sophie curled into his chest, his arm draped protectively around her middle, holding her close. Caleb whispered his love for her once more before drifting to sleep.

But Sophie couldn't sleep—she lay in his embrace, gazing up at the dozens of stars in that summer night sky, twinkling between the leaves of the elm tree. She counted them, wished upon them. Marveled at how far she had come to be sleeping beneath them as she was . . . tried to think of anything but the vague fear in her.

It was only a matter of time before Julian caught up with her and she wondered what he might do this time. She was hardly a young girl without any knowledge of the world—she was a woman who knew very well what she was doing, who had made her choices and was prepared to live with them. At long last, she had determined her course in life, knew exactly who she was.

Julian would perhaps seek to disown her. She pondered that; certainly he would find a justice who would, given her unfortunate history, sympathize with her brother's plight and good name and grant him the dissolution of their blood relationship.

But that seemed too harsh. For all of her brother's faults, he had never been cruel. He had strong opinions of what was right and wrong, but he had always loved her. At least up until now, she thought, absently tracking a path over Caleb's knuckles. God only knew how angry he must be at this very moment.

She sighed, shifted her gaze to the moon. Whatever Julian might succeed in doing, this little glimpse of heaven had been well worth the consequence. She had spent years being numb, years pushing down any desire for romance and companionship. Those years had been a harsh exercise in learning to bury a burning need for acceptance and love. Honestly, she had actually convinced herself that she *didn't* need those things, that she was different from everyone else, given her past.

It had been a lie, of course.

She had secretly watched Honorine through the years, had so often wished she had just an ounce of her courage. But if any man showed her even the slightest interest, she ignored it; she was too terrified of them all, too distrusting of their motives.

But Caleb . . . well, she had known from the start that he was different, that the intensity with which he had worked was unlike the idle men of the aristocracy. He had been so sincerely driven in his desire to build a fine house, so intent on doing it right, and so terribly proud of what he was achieving. There was no artifice in him—he was exactly who he presented himself to be, and when he said he loved her, it was with all his heart, and when he told her he wished for a future, it was his fervent dream.

Would that she were more like him. Would that she

were as simple and sincere in her desires, as intent and as proud in what she did.

As long as she lived, she would strive to love him as unselfishly as he had loved her.

How would they survive?

Did she care? As long as she was with him, would it matter if they slept in an open field or a house? Sophie snuggled closer to him; in his sleep, Caleb moaned softly and tightened his grip around her. Nearby, one of the horses snorted, shook his mane. Sophie smiled, looked one last time at the stars above, and made a final wish: whatever happened to them when they reached Hamilton House on the morrow—and every day after that—she would never regret this time she had spent with him. Never. And on her deathbed, she would remember this night with as much heartfelt happiness as she bore at this very moment.

Chapter Twenty-Three

Hamilton House
Nottinghamshire, England

The distant sound of laughter slowly filtered into Trevor's heavy sleep, so faint and sporadic that he first thought it was part of a dream. But he heard it again, and in his attempt to reach for it, to understand it, he could feel himself swimming leadenly to the surface of his consciousness.

He forced his eyes open, blinked back the blur of not enough sleep, trying to remember exactly where he was. His bedroom. *Hamilton House.* With great effort, he pushed himself up onto one elbow and looked around.

Sprawled across the bed sideways, the sheet draped across a portion of his right leg, he lay naked on the bare mattress. With a groan, he pushed himself up to sitting, rubbed his eyes.

Laughter. There it was again, coming from somewhere in the house.

Trevor stood, stumbled to the windows of his room without bothering to clothe himself, and opened the shutters. The sun blinded him—it was high in the sky, well past noon. *How long had he slept?* The faint laughter drifted up to him again in more than one voice. A man. A woman, too, perhaps?

God, he could not seem to *think*. His head felt heavy; he turned away from the window and gathered his trousers from the crumbled heap of clothing on the floor and struggled into them. He then picked up his shirt, his nose wrinkling at the pungent odor—he had not changed his clothing in three days now. He shoved one arm into a sleeve, then the other, buttoning it as he walked out of the room in his bare feet, hardly conscious of what he was doing.

He strode purposefully down the main stairwell and into the corridor, looking left and right, into any open room, finding no evidence of any one within. *Where was his father, then?* Had he perhaps imagined the laughter? Was he hearing ghosts?

He swung the door of the study open, half expecting to find stiff ol' Darby, laughing at something.

Empty.

Trevor blinked, tried to think. Inadvertently, he looked down, saw his rumpled clothing. He really ought to find a change of clothing. Undoubtedly Darby had stored things away for him. Probably in the attic—

There it was again, the unmistakable sound of laughter. Only this time, he realized, it was coming from outside.

He hurried to the window of the study and strained to see. Nothing. The back terrace, then.

He hastened from the room, feeling a strong sense of urgency, as if he didn't find the source of the laughter it might very well drift away. He reached the atrium, from which one could walk outside, and fairly burst through those doors and onto the terrace. He paused there, straining to hear. A wisp of red flashed across the periphery of his vision; he jerked his head to the right, saw the woman running down the garden path, toward the gate leading into the meadows beyond.

Unconscious of his bare feet or state of semi-dress, Trevor went after her. He half-hopped, half-loped across the gravel path, stumbling into his stride once again as he passed through the gate and onto grass. Running now, he raced down the tree-lined path to the meadows, lurching through the last gate, where he paused at the top of the knoll, his hands braced against his knees as he dragged air into his lungs.

The strange, eerie feeling that someone was watching him invaded his consciousness; startled, Trevor jerked his head to the right.

His breath caught in his throat.

For a single moment, he wondered if he had perhaps gone quite mad, was imagining what he was seeing.

In the meadow, in and around a small stand of trees, was the house staff. Picnicking. *Picnicking.* Blankets were spread about; baskets of fruit and loaves of bread, as well as flasks of wine, were scattered all around. Was he hallucinating in his madness? He had to be—that was his *father* standing in the midst of all of them, taller than Trevor had seen him since before the seizure, wearing an expression of shock.

He was the one who should be shocked. Trevor stared back, too exhausted to know if it was real—until the flash of red caught his eye again. She came slowly to her feet, stood beside his father, the ends of her unbound hair lifting lightly with the breeze. *The French whore.*

He knew it was real then and slowly straightened, facing the absurd little scene fully, his anger mounting with each passing moment.

The woman had the gall to step away from the others, to come forward as if *she* owned this house, as if she had the right to say anything to him at all! She glided forward, eyeing him as if he were some sort of apparition, coming to a halt a few feet from where he stood. Peering closely, she looked him over, as if she could not quite believe what she was seeing, down at his bare feet. After a moment, she glanced up at him through thick lashes.

"Bonjour, monsieur."

Bloody *bonjour*? Trevor's anger soared dangerously; he narrowed his eyes, glaring hatefully at her. "This is all you would say after you have unlawfully kidnapped my father?"

Her brow wrinkled in confusion. "Kidnap? What is this kidnap?"

Now he was scarcely able to contain his fury. He stepped forward. "You have *stolen* him!" he hissed vehemently. "What, did you think you would succeed in your scheme? Did you think to persuade him to sign it over to *you*? Did you perhaps hope that your chances would be improved by refusing him the very medicine he needs to live? You have committed a grave crime, madam, and you are quite caught! Were I you, I would prepare myself for the worst, for I intend to press this crime fully within our courts!"

The French whore recoiled at that, her blue eyes widening with fear.

"Oh yes," he breathed, "you are very right to fear it! English justice will grant you no quarter, not with your rotten French blood!"

"What is this *folie* you speak?" she demanded, taking one step backward. "I do not steal Will! I bring him to his home! What crime is this?"

That response only made him laugh. Hysterically. Her efforts to feign a lack of understanding had been overdone for far too long—she knew *exactly* what she had done, and Trevor was about to tell her so, but he was startled by his father, who moved surprisingly fast to the whore's defense.

"Trevor!" he said sharply and clearly. "M-mind your mouth!"

The admonishment shocked him, not only because it was said with such clarity, but also because he would defend *her*. He gaped at his father, his thoughts swirling in a disordered state of fatigue and panic.

"Father! You have no idea what she has done!" he insisted, balling his hands into fists at his side. "You are distraught, and you've been without your medicine for nigh on a week now! This woman is *not* your friend! Her scheme is vile—she thought to steal you away so that she might ransom you, or even *worse,* I shudder to think!"

"Honor . . ." the viscount paused, put a gnarled hand on her wrist as he tried to force the words out. "She h-has *helped* m-me, tremendously!" he said adamantly. "Y-you've n-no right to c-come here and accuse!"

"*Monsieur,* you look ill," Honorine said to Trevor, cocking her head thoughtfully to one side. "Very ill."

What little was left of Trevor's sanity imploded with that. His fists gripped tighter; he was unaware that his nails cut painfully into his palms as he clung to the tenuous grip he had on his composure.

"Now you would accuse me of being ill? Madam, you have gone too far!" he said behind clenched teeth, and stalked around her, toward the servants, who were all now on their feet. *"Darby!"* he shouted wildly.

The butler appeared almost instantly before him. "Milord?" he asked, his voice betraying his nerves.

Trevor glared down at him. "Why haven't you sent for the authorities? Send for the sheriff at once! Tell him that a French whore has kidnapped my father from London for the purpose of extorting money from him. Tell him to come and take her at once!"

The butler flicked his tongue nervously across his lower lip, slid his gaze to the viscount behind Trevor.

Trevor lurched forward. *"Do you hear me, sir?"*

With a gasp, the butler staggered backward. "Yes, milord! Yes, I heard you quite clearly!"

"Then *go!*" he roared, and stood rigidly, his fists clenched tightly, watching beneath the heavy lids of his eyes as the servants began moving, gathering picnic items, hurrying toward the meadow gate, looking furtively at him over their shoulder. But in the midst of their exodus, the French whore stood placidly with his father, observing him with her witch eyes.

His pulse was beating erratically now; the blood pumped through him so fast and hard that it felt as if it might burst free of his veins at any moment. Unsteadily, he moved to where she stood with his father. "You will pay for what you have done," he said low.

The woman had the audacity to smile. *Smile.* "I do not frighten of you," she said lightly. "Will, he is alive. He knows what you do."

Trevor's pounding heart suddenly skipped a beat and sank like a rock, making him feel queasy. *No.* She lied. His father could not possibly know what he had done. He was a mindless old man! Unless . . . unless he *was* alive somehow, his mind alert in that shell but his mouth unable to speak. Trevor peered closely at his father, into the mirror image of his light brown eyes and wondered, was it possible? Was it possible his father knew how much he had taken from him over the last several months? The question scared him; he suddenly lunged forward, reaching for his father, desperate to take him away from her, and knocking her aside as he did. With a small cry of alarm, she stumbled to one side, tripping over the hem of her blood-red skirt.

"Trevor!" his father shouted. "Unhand m-me!"

Trevor forced a smile as he pushed his father forward, holding him up with the sheer strength of his fear propelling him forward. "Don't worry, Father," he said reassuringly as he moved the old man along, weaving and bobbing with his strangely bent leg. "I am here now. I'll see that no harm comes to you."

His father struggled against him and began to labor in his breathing; Trevor glanced over his shoulder. The whore was on his heels, her gaze intent on the viscount, crying out, reaching out, each time the old man stumbled. *Let her come.* It would make it all the easier when the sheriff came to take her away. He ought to have her hanged for what she had done to him. Yes, he would enjoy that very much, and smiled to himself as he pushed the old man through the meadow gate.

. . .

Darby had been in the viscount's employ more years than he cared to remember. He had known Master Trevor all his life, had watched him grow into a man. But the man that had come to the meadow looking and acting half-crazed was not the Mr. Trevor Hamilton he knew. Madame Fortier was right; *that* man was ill—ill in his head, to Darby's way of thinking.

He walked briskly toward the stables, the note for the sheriff in his pocket, having penned it after assuring himself that the viscount was quite all right. A little shaken perhaps, but all in all, he seemed no worse. As Darby rounded the corner of the house, he heard a female voice.

"Darby!"

He paused, looked around. The housekeeper was standing outside the smokehouse.

"Yes? What is it?"

Wringing her plump hands, she looked nervously behind them. "Are you truly going to bring the sheriff round for her?" she whispered.

Darby hesitated; he looked over his shoulder, then up the path to the stables, then looked at the housekeeper again, nodding.

The woman's doughy face fell. "Oh *Lord,*" she muttered. "Oh *Lord,* you mustn't do that! The woman has done nothing wrong! Do you see how well he is now, Darby? She's to be commended for what she's done!"

"It is not my position to say," he said coolly, aware that anyone could overhear them out here.

"Come now, Darby—"

He quickly lifted his hand, stopping her from saying any more. "I have my instructions. You will not dissuade me from my duty." He nodded curtly, continued walking, ignoring the unflattering utterance the woman made under her breath. He wanted to tell her, but he dared not. In his fifty-fifth year, he was hardly of a mind to find new employment, and he was quite certain that was exactly

what he would be doing if Mr. Hamilton thought he had
disobeyed him.

He walked into the stables, calling for Jamie.

The stable boy appeared instantly, a bucket of oats in
his hand. "Yes sir?"

Darby took the note from his pocket. "You are to deliver this to the sheriff in Nottingham, do you understand?"

The boy looked at the sealed parchment, then at Darby,
nodding solemnly. "Aye sir. I'll get a mount straight
away—"

"No," Darby said softly, and glanced covertly around
to assure himself that no one else was present, then went
down on one knee before Jamie and placed the parchment into his hand. "You are to deliver this to the sheriff
in Nottingham—but not until the morrow. Do you understand me, lad? Not before the morrow."

"Aye sir," he said, and stuffed the note in the pocket of
his waistcoat. "On the morrow," he repeated.

Satisfied, Darby stood, ruffled the boy's blond head,
then turned and walked out of the stable.

He would not, under any circumstance, disobey an order given to him by the viscount or his son. But on occasion, he might see his way to obeying it in his own due
time.

He rather imagined Madame Fortier was going to
need a bit of a head start.

In the main salon, seated on a divan with a lap rug
tucked securely about him, Will warily watched his son
as he paced the hearth. He had never seen him like this,
he was quite certain. In the bits and pieces of his
memory that had started to come back to him, he recalled a young, handsome man, devoted to his wife and
child. Not a madman as was pacing the hearth now,
barefoot and in shirttails.

God, if he weren't so fatigued! When Trevor had pushed

him onto the divan, he had been robbed of the strength to fight him. Although his vitality was slowly coming back to him each day, the seizure had left him remarkably frail; the road to a full recovery needed more time. Silently he cursed his debilitation—there he had sat like a withered old man as Trevor pushed Honorine out the door and locked it. For several moments afterward, she had pounded on the door, shouting in French for him to open. And then the pounding had abruptly stopped. *Where was Honorine?*

"I brought your medicine, Father."

Will's body jerked involuntarily, as if the force of those words had actually hit him. *Medicine.* What was it he should remember about medicine? He had not seemed to need it—

"You must take it or you may never hope to recover," Trevor said, and moved to the sidebar, eyeing the different decanters there. "It's a blessed miracle that no more harm has come to you, really. You cannot imagine what I feared."

Something about his son's voice rang false. Silent, Will watched as Trevor selected a crystal decanter and poured an amber liquid into a glass. From the pocket of his filthy trousers, he pulled a small vial, and emptied the contents of it into the glass, then turned and looked at Will.

His expression was oddly blank; Will felt his blood run cold. As this son approached him, he struggled with the lap blanket, determined to gain his feet. But Trevor was quickly upon him, straddling him with one knee on his lap, one strong arm wrapped around his shoulders, pinning his arms. "I have no idea what that whore might have told you, but you *need* this," he said, breathing heavily.

Overcome by the stench of his son's breath and the growing awareness that something about the medicine wasn't right—*if only he could think for a moment!*— Will struggled. But he was no match for Trevor. He forced his mouth open, poured the liquid down his throat, then let go, falling backward, catching himself before he tumbled to the ground, his gaze never wavering from Will's face.

Panting wildly, Trevor watched him closely. "There now, you'll see. You'll feel much improved, trust me," he muttered. Will's eyelids began to droop; Trevor smiled thinly and moved to a writing table, where he rummaged through one drawer.

The effects of the medicine quickly took hold; the fog was descending on him like the black of night, thickening his tongue, slowing his thoughts, weighting his arms and legs into the divan. His head lolled back of its own accord. Through a heavily hooded gaze, he watched Trevor retrieve a piece of paper, snatch up a pen, and come striding forward, the paper in one hand, the pen in the other.

He could not speak. His mind screamed no, but his lips would not move. Trevor leaned over him, jabbed the pen into his hand. He then grabbed a book from a nearby ottoman, slapped the paper on it, and thrust the book onto Will's lap.

"All right then, Papa."

The medicine . . . there was something about the medicine. *Damn it, why couldn't he remember?*

Trevor squatted down on his haunches, peered up at his father with eyes shining brightly, too brightly. "Come on then, old man, do what you do so well," he muttered.

But Will could not make his hand move, could not make anything move. With an impatient sigh, Trevor grabbed Will's hand that held the pen. "Come *on* then," he said, breathing heavily, and pressed Will's hand down onto the book.

The pressure of Trevor's hand on his snapped something in his feeble brain—Will remembered. Like a light breaking through the clouds, the pressure of his son's hand on his brought it all back to him, everything. *No.* No, he would not sign, not of his own accord.

But Trevor would make him, that he knew, as well as he knew how powerless he was to stop him. And as he helplessly sat there, his body given over to the effect of the drug, Trevor did exactly that.

Finally, it was all beginning to make sense in his scrambled brain. The pieces began to fit together, forming an ugly picture. More pieces of the puzzle that was his memory came flooding back to him as Trevor forced his signature. And Will might have put them all together, then and there, were it not for the pain of his heart breaking.

Chapter Twenty-Four

CALEB HAD A bad feeling as he and Sophie crested the hill above Hamilton House, and paused to look down at the estate. It was an almost eerie feeling of alarm . . . but then again, it could very well be the apprehension he had felt all day. All week, really.

He looked at Sophie; she was leaning slightly forward, staring down the hill at the Hamilton mansion, her long hair tied at her nape, her bonnet on her back. It was amazing, he thought, that she seemed to look more robust every day of their extraordinary little journey. It pleased him enormously to know that this woman was no fragile flower of the *ton*, but a vibrant, thriving woman, very much alive, unafraid to live.

She turned slightly, noticed he was looking at her, and smiled sadly. "I suppose this is it, then," she said, shifting her gaze back to the house. "Where the dream ends?"

He knew, of course, exactly what she meant. Although they had managed to leave it unspoken the last three days, the truth remained like the earth beneath them—silent and unmoving. Their secret had been a dream—and when they awoke from it, they would be forever changed, their lives possibly never returning to the magic that they had been.

There were moments, perhaps, that Caleb regretted that for Sophie. As much as he liked to think differently, their dilemma was his doing, for he had started the wheels in motion with that first kiss.

Yet as he gazed at Sophie's slender neck, the golden glow of her skin, he was not sorry. This woman had walked into his life with her picnic basket and awakened him, shown him the sun and what had been missing from his life all these years. With Sophie had come the elusive wonder of love, the feeling of power and giddiness and contentment with all things and the world in general. Caleb had never known anything like the passion he felt for her. It seemed that for an eternity he had felt nothing but the sting of his birth, the need to prove himself, an all-consuming desire to show the world that he was worthy of esteem.

Worthy of love.

Sophie had made him understand he was worthy of it. He was eternally grateful for it, would go to his grave showing her just how grateful he was for it.

He looked away from her; a lump rose to his throat. *Give me but the chance, God.*

Although he fully intended to be with her until his dying day, the truth—and he would not say so to Sophie—was that he could not help feeling dubious about their future. There seemed so many obstacles!

First and foremost, there was Julian Dane, the very powerful Earl of Kettering, with whom he would ultimately have to contend. Naturally, he had heard in great detail—Lady Paddington having seen to that—how Kettering had dispatched of William Stanwood. Kettering had power and influence that extended far beyond the realm of most mere mortals, and Caleb would be a liar if he did not admit to a palpable apprehension. Certainly he did not fear Kettering, quite the contrary. He *wanted* to speak to him, wanted to prove that he *was* worthy of Sophie's affections, would strive to always be worthy. But he imagined he'd have a rather difficult time of convincing him, all in all—it was bad enough that he was a bastard, but to have been embroiled in such an ugly row with his half-brother and to have traveled across England with Sophie in such intimate companionship, well . . . He could only imagine what he might do in Kettering's shoes.

And there was the nagging question of where they would go, where they would live. England had seemed too small for them *before* this had happened. It seemed impossibly small now—their scandal might very well travel the length of the British Isles and back again. Surely it had already spread like fire all over Mayfair and Bedford Square.

"What if they haven't come? What will we do then?"

The sound of Sophie's voice pulled Caleb from his ruminations. He looked at her, wished he had a good answer for that question. "I don't know," he said, and looked down at the house again, wishing, like a thousand times before, that he was his father's son in truth *and* in name. All of this would have been different then. He could have given her the life she deserved.

How would he give her a life now?

Caleb closed his eyes, drew a deep breath. The feeling of hopelessness invaded him again—too many forces stood in their way. Yet he could not help but think of the love they had made last night beneath the stars, the feel of her body under his, and he knew that he would climb to the moon for her if necessary. Strangely, as he sat there, he felt a draw that started somewhere near the bottom of his heart, the feeling of something blossoming warm and moist within him, and instinctively, without opening his eyes, he put out his hand, toward Sophie.

Her hand met his in the space between them.

Caleb opened his eyes and looked at her. She smiled

warmly, her pretty brown eyes shimmering with affection. "We will make our way," she said simply. "We will."

It was uncanny, the force between them. Moved by it, Caleb could only nod and swallow the lump in his throat. "Let us go and have a look about," he said gruffly, and brought her hand to his mouth, kissing it, pressing upon it all the devotion he felt.

They rode onto the circular drive in the front of the house and Caleb remarked that it seemed odd no one was about.

Sophie was obviously thinking the same thing. "At Kettering Hall, the staff would come running from all corners when Julian came home. They were always so happy to see him."

He wouldn't know if that was the practice at Hamilton House—he had been put away in Scotland or France where there were no servants.

Caleb slid down from his mount, then helped Sophie down and tethered the horses near the water trough. He rejoined her in the drive, pausing to glance up at the old mansion as she was. It was a formidable structure, built a century or more ago, he guessed. Gargoyles dominated the corners and the roof, as well as ghastly carvings of beasts and half-man, half-horse creatures.

"Could it be deserted?" she asked in a half-whisper.

"I can't imagine why it would be." His father had lived here for years; it was inconceivable that there was not at least *some* staff about. He took Sophie's hand in his and together they mounted the steps. When they reached the top step, they stood for a moment, looking at the massive oak door, their gazes traveling higher, to the pair of angry gargoyles just overhead, their mouths pursed, as if they would spew venom at any moment.

Sophie wrinkled her nose. "Not very inviting, is it?"

He shook his head and stepped up to the door. Picking

up the big brass handle, he banged loudly three times, then stepped down beside Sophie again. She moved slightly, into his side, and he put an arm around her shoulders, squeezed reassuringly. They stood for several seconds, staring at the door, waiting for someone to answer.

"Rather odd," Caleb remarked, and stepped up to knock again, but before he could lift the brass handle, the door came open.

He recognized Darby immediately, though it had been several years since he had last seen him on one of his father's trips abroad. The thin butler's face was pale; his blue eyes quickly took them in before glancing nervously over his shoulder.

"Darby, do you remember me? I am Caleb."

The butler's mouth twitched. He glanced again over his shoulder. "Yes. Yes, of course, sir, I remember you. Unfortunately his lordship is indisposed—"

"He is here, then?" Sophie asked anxiously.

Darby seemed to recoil at the question. "I . . . he is indisposed."

His demeanor was awfully peculiar—the feeling that something was very wrong was growing stronger, and Caleb took a step closer, making sure his foot was over the threshold. "We've not come to cause any harm, sir, I can assure you. I would only see that my father is safe. He left London rather unexpectedly, and in the presence of—"

"Darby! Who is at the door? Has the sheriff come?"

The pitch of that male voice sounded almost hysterical, but Caleb would recognize it anywhere. Behind him, he heard Sophie's sharp intake of breath—she knew that voice, too.

"Darby!" he bellowed again, only louder, and Caleb stepped in front of Sophie as Trevor appeared in the door frame.

Sophie gasped. Caleb wasn't certain that he hadn't, too. Trevor's appearance was so shocking—he could not imagine what had happened to him. Although he was dressed in typical fashion—navy coat, plain waistcoat, and trousers—dark circles shadowed his eyes. A growth of beard that looked days old covered his jaw, and his hair, always so meticulously coifed, was in wild disarray. There was something else, too, Caleb noticed—something in his eyes, a strange, almost maniacal light.

He had been drinking.

Which would explain why he staggered so badly when he saw Caleb. The recognition seemed to take him aback; a look of panic washed over his sallow face, and he lurched forward, trying to reach the huge oak door. Darby, however, was in his way.

Instinct replaced all rational thought—Caleb lunged forward, pushing the door aside with all his might, and, unfortunately, Darby. "Where is my father?" he demanded hotly.

Trevor recoiled, looked wildly about him as if he were uncertain what to do. "Y-you have no right to be here!" he stammered. "Before you trespass another step, I should warn you that I have sent for the sheriff!"

The bad feeling he had noticed the moment they crested the hill was raging now—something was *terribly* wrong; he could feel it in his marrow. "Where is he?" Caleb demanded again, moving forward.

"Leave this place at once!" Trevor shouted, stumbling again with the force of his shrieking, and pitched awkwardly toward Caleb, his hands outstretched, as if he meant to grab his throat.

But he missed badly, for he was distracted, like Caleb, by the sudden appearance of Madame Fortier. She emerged like a ghost from somewhere on Caleb's right and flew across the foyer, her yellow-and-gray skirt disappearing into the corridor behind Trevor. He whirled, crashed into the wall in an attempt to catch her, but his hands came away empty. *"No!"* he screamed, and plunged after her.

But Caleb was sober and much quicker on his feet.

He pushed past Trevor and raced after Madame Fortier, saw her duck into a door at the end of the corridor. The bad feeling quickly gave way to a fierce panic. Mindless of everything but his father, Caleb ran, oblivious to Trevor's labored breathing as he followed.

He rushed into the room, coming to an abrupt halt the moment he crossed the threshold, unaware that the small, mournful cry was his own.

In front of him, in a wheeled chair, sat his father. His head was on his chest, his hand curled unnaturally. Madame Fortier was beside him, clutching his good hand, peering intently at his face. "*Mon Dieu!* What has he done?" she cried softly. "*Will,*" she whispered urgently, shaking his gnarled hand. "Will, Will, do you see me here for you? Do your ears they hear me?"

The viscount did not acknowledge her, did not even seem to know she was there. With a sob of grief, Madame Fortier buried her face in his lap. Stunned, Caleb watched as his father slowly lifted his gnarled hand, laid it awkwardly on her head.

Oh God, dear God, how had this happened? How had he regressed so quickly and so terribly from a few short days ago?

At that moment Trevor crashed into the room, knocking something made of glass across the table.

The fury was suddenly pumping through him; Caleb whirled around and pierced his half-brother with a look of sheer contempt. "If you have harmed him in any way, I will kill you," he said low.

"How dare you accuse me! She kidnapped him from my house and you would accuse *me* of harming him? Get away from him!" Trevor snapped, and came striding forward, his eyes blazing. But Caleb intercepted him, grabbing his shoulders in a vise grip. It surprised him that Trevor's struggle was so easy to quell—he seemed sapped of any strength, could hardly summon the might to fight him.

"*Get away from him!*" he shouted over Caleb's shoulder as Sophie ran into the room and quickly went to Madame Fortier's side. "Do you see what she has done?" he breathed hotly. "Father has been without his medicine for days now! *This* is what *she* did to him!"

Madame Fortier lifted her head; her blue eyes narrowed hatefully. *"Bête!"* she cried. "You take my Will from me!"

"Shut up," Trevor said harshly. "You've no right to come here! Any of you! But it's rather fortuitous, all in all—the sheriff can take the lot of you!" he said, and shoved away from Caleb, stepping backward, making no attempt to pass him. "Obviously, you have conspired to take advantage of my father. I should have known, two whores—"

That slur cut deeply through Caleb—he grabbed Trevor's neckcloth, wrenched it tightly. "One more vile remark, sir, and I will twist until your head comes off," he muttered through clenched teeth.

His face turned red; Trevor struggled from Caleb's grasp, slapped childishly at his hand until Caleb let go, then staggered backward, coughing. "Bloody bastard!" he said hoarsely. "He is none of your concern!"

"The *shérif*, he will not come!" Honorine said hotly.

A sneer of contempt spread across Trevor's mouth. "Do you really think this *bastard* will save you?" he snarled. "Believe me, he will not. He is an imposter and will rot in prison alongside you, *Madame Fornicate!*"

That earned him a string of profane French, which seemed to set Trevor back on his heels. Alarmed by how frail his father looked, Caleb strode across the room to him. Just days ago, the viscount was beginning to resemble what he had once been—strong, invincible. His hand shaking, Caleb smoothed his palm over his father's crown and glanced hopelessly at Sophie, on her knees beside him, studying his face carefully. "I think he can hear me," she said.

"Sir!"

The sound of Darby's distraught voice caught all their

attention—the man stood in the doorway of the salon, his neckcloth undone, his hair mussed, his eyes wide. "The sheriff is approaching Longman's Gate . . ."

Sheriff. The word rang loudly in Caleb's consciousness; if he was at Longman's Gate, it was only a matter of minutes before he would be here, at Hamilton House. They had to leave, had to get out of there straightaway.

Trevor knew it, too. "Aha, at last!" he cried victoriously, and rushed out of the room.

Caleb looked down at his father. As worried as he was for him, he had no doubt that whatever had happened to the viscount would be blamed on Madame Fortier and himself. The sheriff would have them all locked away before nightfall, Sophie too, if only for her association with the two of them. He could not help his father if he were locked away in some gaol, that was certain.

They had to leave. *Now.* Caleb reached for Sophie and pulled her away. "Go. *Run,*" he told her. But Madame Fortier refused to go. She broke free of his grasp when he tried to raise her up and clung to his father. Caleb knelt beside her, put his hands on her shoulders. "We must go," he said in French. "We will return again, I promise, but now we must flee, for they will certainly put you away, Madame Fortier. And you will not want to be locked away in an English gaol, I assure you."

"But look at him! How can I leave him? He knows I am here!" She leaned forward. "Will! Will, you tell them, *non*? You remember what to tell the *shérif*! You know this truth! You know of this medicine!" she pleaded with him. "*Remember!* Remember *la médecine!*"

Caleb pulled her up and pushed her toward Sophie, who grabbed her and wrapped an arm around her shoulders as she struggled to lead her sobbing friend away. Caleb paused, grabbed his father's hand and squeezed it hard, choking back the myriad emotions that threatened to drown him. He felt helpless, incapable of saving any of them, but particularly his father. "I love you," he whispered. "I'll come back, Father, I promise you that. Believe me. *Trust* me!"

The viscount lifted his head, fixed his gaze on Caleb. It seemed as if he were trying to speak, trying to tell him something with his eyes, and, much to Caleb's surprise and horror, a tear slipped from the corner of one eye, landed perfectly on Caleb's hand.

"Caleb! You must come now!"

The urgency in Sophie's voice spurred him to move. "I promise," he said again, and let go of his father's hand, feeling the tear burn his hand as he hurried to join the women.

They dragged Madame Fortier between them and moved quickly down the corridor, into the foyer where Trevor stood waiting for the sheriff. Darby stood off to one side looking quite miserable. There were also two footmen standing nervously behind Trevor.

Two footmen with guns.

Trevor laughed coldly, pointed a finger directly at Madame Fortier. "Why, you can't leave now," he drawled sarcastically. "You haven't met our sheriff!"

"Tell your men to step aside, Trevor," Caleb warned.

He laughed at that, then gestured at Sophie. "And you, madam," he said, "I am rather certain the good Earl Kettering would want his wicked sister returned safely from her latest little foray into the English country-side. How indecorous of you—twice journeyed, twice a whore."

The rage passed through Caleb so quickly that he scarcely knew what he was doing. Trevor did not see him coming until his fist connected with his jaw. He went down hard on the marble tile; the blow of his head made a sickening sound. Legs apart, fists curled, Caleb waited, waited for him to say one more word against Sophie, but Trevor did not move.

Caleb glanced up at the two footmen. They looked to Darby.

"Let them go," Darby said quietly.

Caleb did not waste a moment; he hurried the women out the door to where the horses were still tethered. He helped Sophie up first, then a despondent Madame Fortier behind her and, pausing to retrieve his gun from the saddlebag, swung up onto his mount. With a final look at Darby, they rode in the opposite direction of Longman's Gate, Madame Fortier's mournful cries drifting in their wake.

From the veil of his lashes, Will watched the two men watching him, knew they spoke of him as if he were dead for all intents and purposes. He probably would have been dead, had it not been for Honorine. But his love had saved him again, had put the words into his muddled brain that he could not seem to remember on his own.

Remember.

Yes, that was what she had said. Remember the medicine. It had come to him then, clear as a cold winter day. The medicine made him like this; the medicine his son gave him made him a virtual prisoner in his own body. It was horribly frightening; after only a day of it, he could feel the pieces of his mind starting to slip away again, like so many leaves scattered by an autumn wind. And it was maddening—he had come so very close to making all the pieces fit, to solving the little puzzle that had plagued him for weeks now.

The sheriff approached him, leaned down, and eyed him warily. "You're quite certain he cannot understand what is being said to him?"

"No," Trevor said with a sad sigh, and gingerly touched his split lip again. "There are moments of lucidity, but for the most part, he cannot distinguish the things around him."

No, that is not so! Will knew very well what was going on around him; he just couldn't remember the words! It was the *medicine* that made him seem so senseless, not his mind!

"Pity, that," the sheriff said, and straightened, walked back to where Trevor was sitting. "Nasty bump on the back of your head, sir. Would you like me to send for a physician?"

Trevor quickly shook his head. "Please don't bother yourself. I'll be quite all right, I assure you. I am infinitely more concerned about the swine who would do this to my family."

The sheriff nodded solemnly. "You can rest assured that when they are apprehended, they will be brought swiftly to justice."

"Thank you. I cannot ask for more."

Will groaned at that; the two men turned and looked at him, the sheriff's expression curious, Trevor's more of a panic—so much so that he stood, pressed a hand to his forehead.

The sheriff immediately started for the door. "You should rest, Mr. Hamilton. I'll see myself out," he said, and paused. "You mustn't fret over this ugliness. We'll be quite diligent in our search, you may depend on it. You need only concern yourself with your father's care. And your head, of course."

"Of course," Trevor nodded feebly, and sank into the settee again. "Thank you kindly," he muttered, and lifted his hand as the sheriff slipped through the door and closed it softly behind him.

Only then did he lift his head and glare at his father. "Darby let them escape, you know," he said hotly, and came immediately to his feet, striding toward the drink cart. "He should not have done that!" He poured a whiskey, tossed it down his throat, then turned to stare at his father.

"You mustn't worry, Papa. That whore will not bother you again." He poured another drink. "Or that bloody bastard. He *is* a bastard, Papa. There is nothing you can do to change that."

That remark knifed deeply into Will's thoughts—there was something there, something standing at the periphery of his memory again, begging entry. *Bastard* . . .

Trevor sighed. "I will confess, I am *quite* exhausted. This has been a rather trying day all in all. And I haven't even decided what to do with Darby." He drank, contemplated the wall. "He's been in your employ for years, I know . . . but he did not help me today when I needed him most, and frankly, I am a little curious why it took the sheriff so long to arrive."

Not Darby.

"I should dismiss him. He won't have it from me, I suppose, but he'd have it from you," he continued, sipping his whiskey. "Yes, I rather imagine he'd have it from you. The question is merely *how* . . ."

Will tried to speak; he managed nothing more than to move his head and his hand, but it was enough to gain Trevor's attention. His head snapped around; slowly, he lowered the drink glass. "Restless are you?" he said quietly, and strolled away from the drink cart, to the hearth. "It is time for your medicine, Papa."

He retrieved a small vial from the mantel, then turned, walking back to the drink cart, where he poured a finger of whiskey into a glass. He then emptied the contents of the vial into the drink and turned toward Will again, walking slowly toward him.

"I should call on old Dr. Sibley on the morrow. We're a bit low on your medicine." He paused, brushed his hand against Will's cheek. "Yes, we must fetch you more medicine," he muttered, and with his hand, lifted Will's chin, then put the glass to his lips, forcing the whiskey into his mouth. When he had it in, he stood back, watching Will closely.

Will closed his eyes.

It seemed minutes—too long—before he heard Trevor mutter something beneath his breath and quit the room. Slowly, he opened his eyes, looked around the room as far as he could turn his head.

He was alone, he was certain.

Quick now! Moving as best he could, he shifted in his seat until his head was lolling uncomfortably to one side.

Will parted his lips, let the whiskey burning his mouth fall to the carpet.

Chapter Twenty-Five

THEY RODE HARD for the first hour, putting as much distance between them and Hamilton House as they could before the horses were exhausted. When they were at last convinced that no one was following them, they stopped in a small glen to rest and water the horses and to discuss where they would go.

"We return to *Maison de Hamilton,*" Honorine insisted.

"No," said Caleb firmly. "We're no good to him in a parish gaol."

"Kettering Hall," Sophie suggested.

Caleb looked at her as if he thought she had lost her mind.

"No one is there," she said quickly, before he could object. "Julian despises Kettering Hall and Ann never comes, particularly during the Season."

"It sits empty?" he asked skeptically.

"Not entirely," she admitted. "There is Miss Brillhart, the housekeeper—she resides there year-round. And of course the groundskeeper. And Cook, perhaps." Her voice trailed off; she looked off into the distance, struggling to remember who lived at Kettering Hall, her mind inevitably turning to the last time she had been there.

Miss Brillhart.

Sophie had not thought of her in a few years, as her memory of those last days at Kettering Hall was not a pleasant one. It had been the stalwart housekeeper who had watched over her imprisonment after Julian had banished her there. It had been Miss Brillhart who tried to stop her from running away with William Stanwood. Sophie would go to her grave remembering the look of sheer horror on the woman's face as she and Sir William had ridden away, bound for Gretna Green.

The memory of it made her shiver.

"Sophie?"

Caleb's voice instantly warmed her, shook her from the past. She looked at him. "Kettering Hall. We've nothing to fear and we've certainly nothing to lose."

At least she sincerely hoped not.

He sighed, looked again at Honorine, who was leaning against Sophie's back, staring morosely at the ground. "I'm not sure we've much choice, given Madame Fortier's current disposition."

Honorine sniffed, used Sophie's collar to wipe a tear from one eye. "Leave me," she said on a sob. "I would walk to my Will."

"Rather a long walk, that," Caleb said, and in a slight show of frustration, shook his head. "I suppose we ought to continue on before you actually attempt it."

"To Kettering Hall, then," Sophie responded, and spurred her horse on.

They arrived around noon the following day, having been forced by nightfall and sheer fatigue to take a room at a rather shabby inn. Sophie and Honorine shared a very narrow cot; Caleb slept propped up against the wall.

Exhausted and ravenous, they walked the horses down the tree-lined drive leading to the seat of the Kettering earldom, watching the mammoth Georgian mansion rise into view.

The house had the same effect on Sophie that it always had—it was too large, too imposing, and it looked more like a museum than a home. That was because Julian had not made it their home since the death of their sister Valerie years ago. When Valerie died, they had lived in London and abroad, but rarely here, where the memories of his failure to save her had consumed Julian.

Sophie's memories of Kettering Hall were not any more pleasant. Her mother had died giving birth to her in that house. And even though she had been a very little girl, she could recall the death of her father, could recall particularly the grave demeanor of the adults around her, the black drapes and ribbons on the windows. And then Valerie, of course. Valerie, the kindest of them all, the prettiest, perhaps—or at least in Sophie's memory, she was—had died in Julian's arms as he begged her not to go.

How strange it must have been for him—Julian had not been even as old as herself when Valerie had died, yet already he had shouldered the responsibility of raising his sisters for ten years or more. Valerie's death had been impossible for him to bear, for all of them, really, and even now, as Sophie walked past the family cemetery, the angel rising above the other tombs marking Valerie's grave was a gruesome reminder of those horrific days.

Kettering Hall had never been the same after that. Certainly the last time she had been here had not improved her opinion of it. That was because Julian had forced her here, against her wishes, because she had been caught in the company of Sir William after Julian had forbade her to see him. He had no choice, he said. He could not trust her. And he had effectively banished her from London.

She had spent several miserable days plotting escape, but Sir William had come for her, had convinced her they should elope, and had stolen her away in full view of the staff and Miss Brillhart.

Would that she had listened to Julian.

As they walked up the drive to the house, she could see it all again, just as it had unfolded that fateful day— Miss Brillhart on these very steps, pleading with her to stay, to think of her family's name. The two footmen, trying to reach William before she did. The gallop down this very same drive as the servants spilled out onto the front lawn, frantic at what she had done.

She felt Caleb's hand on the small of her back, his breath on her ear. "Are you quite all right?"

Sophie caught herself, shook off the ancient memories, and forced a smile to her lips. "I-I have never told you about that day," she said.

He seemed to read her mind, knew exactly what she meant, and tenderly kissed her temple. "It isn't necessary, my love, unless you want to talk about it. If you prefer not, I will certainly understand."

She needed to tell him. She needed to confide in someone, unburden her soul with what had happened that day and that night. It was a weight that had pressed down on her for years, smothering her, blocking the light from her heart. The need to say that she had realized her mistake almost the moment she had made it, had understood that the harm was irreparable, had immediately felt the panic, the horror . . . Sophie closed her eyes, drew a breath. She needed to say it all.

When she could find the courage to *speak* it all aloud. When she could free herself of William, once and for all.

"This place, what is it?" Honorine asked, awakening from her grief.

"My home," Sophie said softly, and realizing that her return was inevitable, moved forward, to the door. There was no point in avoiding it.

She mounted the steps, faltered at the door, unsure if she should knock like a guest, or reclaim her rightful place here and simply open the door. Fortunately, the decision was made for her when the door swung open and Miss Brillhart filled the opening.

It was her, all right. Her hair was grayer, her arms

thicker, and her face broader. But she was the same Miss Brillhart, the housekeeper who had also served at times as governess, even as surrogate mother to the girls for more than twenty years.

She blinked as she focused on Sophie; the flicker of recognition in her eyes sparked a broad smile, and she held out her arms. *"Sophie!"* she cried happily. "Lady Sophie, you have come home!" Before Sophie could even move, Miss Brillhart had wrapped her in a suffocating embrace, squeezing her tightly to her. "Ooh, Lady Sophie, how *good* it is to see you!' she exclaimed, then suddenly let go, held Sophie at an arm's length. "Oh my, oh *my,* how pretty you are!"

Sophie blushed, tried to push her tangled hair behind one ear, smiling sheepishly. "Miss Brillhart, you flatter me as always."

"Oh no, *no,* my dear, I speak true! How lovely you are! The Continent certainly agrees with you!" She beamed again, looked past Sophie to Honorine and Caleb, standing below.

"Oh, ah . . ." *How did she introduce them?* "Miss Brillhart, may I introduce you to Madame Fortier . . . she is the lady for whom I serve as companion—"

"Ah! Yes, of course! I've heard ever so much about you!" she exclaimed, and letting go of Sophie, reached for Honorine.

Looking confused and a bit dazed, Honorine put her hand in Miss Brillhart's. "They take me from Will," she announced. "But he is needing me."

Judging by the wrinkling of her brow, that obviously confused Miss Brillhart. But always the consummate hostess, she merely smiled and nodded. "I see," she said. "Well then, come in my dear, and we'll pour you a spot of tea."

With a weary sigh, Honorine passed her and stepped into the foyer; Sophie saw Miss Brillhart's double take of the colorful skirts as Honorine passed. She turned a stunned sort of smile to Sophie, then looked to Caleb, still standing in the lawn.

"Ah." Sophie faltered. "May I introduce Mr. Caleb Hamilton. He is . . ." *My secret lover. The man I will marry. The bastard son.* What did she say? Something, anyway—Miss Brillhart was watching her closely. *The truth.* Sophie squared her shoulders, looked at Caleb. "He is the man I love, Miss Brillhart."

Miss Brillhart gasped; she peered at Caleb as he came slowly up the steps, extending his hand. "Miss Brillhart, how do you do?"

She looked at his hand, then at Sophie before taking it. "A . . . a pleasure, Mr. Hamilton," she said uncertainly. "Won't you come in?"

Caleb smiled, put his hand on Sophie's waist, and pressed her to proceed him. Miss Brillhart eyed him closely as they entered the foyer, as if she half-expected him to produce a horse and whisk her away. But the old girl surprised Sophie; she shut the door, walked to the center of the foyer, and turned to face them. Miss Brillhart looked at them for a long moment before a smile slowly spread across her cheerful face. "You look as if you have had quite a journey. Perhaps Mr. Hamilton would like a whiskey?"

"I would be forever in your debt, madam," he responded with a grateful smile.

A swell of old, timeless love filled Sophie as she looked at the housekeeper, and she returned her cheerful smile with one of her own. "Thank you, Miss Brillhart. That would be wonderful."

After they had drunk their tea and whiskey, Miss Brillhart had baths drawn for them. When she discovered that Honorine had no clothes except those which were on her person now, she went immediately to the attic rooms, dug out a trunk that had belonged to Sophie's mother, and found three gowns from a bygone era. Honorine emerged from her bath somewhat refreshed, wearing a gown with an empire waist and a bodice cut so tight and low that she was practically spilling out of it. The fabric, however, while not particularly colorful, was a pale blue with yellow trim that highly complemented Honorine's dark hair and blue eyes.

She complained nonetheless that it was drab and *passé*.

Caleb emerged in a pair of buckskin trousers, a lawn shirt, and waistcoat that accentuated his trim waist. His hair was combed back in long waves that brushed his collar. He had never seemed quite as virile as he did then, striding down the corridor of Kettering Hall, a smile on his face.

As for Sophie, well, the clothes she had packed in the small portmanteau were soiled—Miss Brillhart took them and in their place, gave Sophie a plain black skirt and white blouse that buttoned up primly to the throat. Sophie recognized the skirt—it was one she had often worn eight years ago, was so very much like the old Sophie, plain and austere. But without petticoats, the fabric draped her frame; she fastened her hair up in a twist, and left the tiny little row of buttons unfastened from her sternum and up. At least, she tried to console herself, she didn't look quite the schoolmistress.

It was her idea to prepare a feast. After several days of trailing after Lord Hamilton, she was firmly convinced they needed a respite, a moment in time to feel normal again and replenish their strength. But Caleb was restless; he wanted to move on, before anyone found them there. "Miss Brillhart is bound to send word to Kettering," he warned her.

"Perhaps," Sophie shrugged. "But he won't come tonight. We should rest, Caleb. We should think carefully about what we will do if we are to leave again."

"Hamilton will have the whole of England looking for her," he said, fingering the lace of Sophie's collar. "And me."

"He'll not look here, I'd wager. He'll think we've run to Scotland, to your home."

Caleb nodded thoughtfully. "I suppose you are right. But I don't like this, sitting idle. It makes us quite vulnerable."

She smiled, cupped his jaw in her palm, and winked. "We'll not sit idle, sir, if you take my meaning."

Gathering her in his arms, Caleb kissed her neck. "You have my rapt attention, madam. You look rather fetching in your prim little costume, but Lord, that glimpse of flesh just there"—he brushed his finger along her chest where she had left her blouse unbuttoned—"is enough to drive a man to great distraction."

"Indeed?" she asked, and glanced covertly around the corridor as she stroked his thigh suggestively. "I think you are rather distracting yourself, sir," she said coyly.

Caleb laughed again. "My God, how I love you, Sophie Dane. It doesn't seem real at times, any of this."

"It is real," she assured him. "From the bottom of my heart, it is real, all of it."

She made him follow her to the kitchens then, before he had her right there, on the carpet. In the kitchen, when he attempted to feel her breast, she made him roll up his sleeves and help her. He was still grumbling good-naturedly when Honorine wandered in, a bottle of French wine in one hand. Sophie did not bother to ask where she might have found it.

Much to Miss Brillhart's apparent surprise, she found all three of them in the massive kitchen of Kettering Hall, Honorine sitting at the long wooden table in the center of the room, sipping a glass of wine. Caleb stood across from her, with an apron tied around his chest, chopping carrots with all the finesse of a mule. And at the far end of the table stood Sophie, preparing a sauce for the meat roasting on a spit.

"Miss Brillhart," she called cheerfully. "Will you join us?"

"Oui, oui," Honorine said, waving her over. "It is not good to drink the wine alone."

Miss Brillhart faltered; her pudgy fingers fluttered to her throat. "I . . . I don't know if I ought, Lady Sophie. It doesn't seem right."

As if anything were right with their world at present. Poor Miss Brillhart—she had no idea what they had been through these last few days. The very thought of explaining it made Sophie laugh; she put down her spoon, walked to where the housekeeper stood, and put her arm around her shoulders, urging her forward. "I can assure you, Miss Brillhart, that nothing seems right any longer. You might as well join us."

Reluctantly, she positioned herself on the stool and accepted a glass of wine. Honorine lifted her glass in mock toast to Miss Brillhart. *"Salut,"* she said gravely, then sipped.

So did Miss Brillhart.

After several sips, she was laughing with the rest of them, her face very rosy.

After two glasses of wine, Honorine began to tell them the story of Lord Hamilton, beginning with the moment she had met him at Regent's Park. Honorine was adamant that with very little effort on her part, Lord Hamilton had begun to improve immediately. She told them that she suspected something was not quite right with Trevor from the beginning, for every improvement Will made, he seemed to suffer a bit of a setback after returning home. Nonetheless, he had improved rapidly, transforming from the man in the wheeled chair she had met in the park to one who could move about, who was beginning to remember things. To the man she had fallen in love with.

Yet in spite of those improvements, there was something bothering the viscount, she said, something he could not seem to grasp from the boarded up well of his memory. Something about Caleb that he could not articulate.

That piqued Caleb's interest; he questioned her anxiously about his father's state, what he remembered, what he did not. But Honorine could say no more than what she had, except that he had wanted to go home so badly that she could not refuse to take him.

When Sophie asked why she had left without a word, Honorine was surprised. Ian knew it, of course, but she had also left a note for Roland and Fabrice, which, they deduced after much discussion, had been caught up in the general cleaning after the ball and tossed aside as rubbish.

Honorine spoke fancifully about their languid, carefree journey north, of the sights they had seen, the things they had done. The viscount was, she insisted, quite lucid and feeling better with each day, in spite of what Trevor would have them all believe.

"This, *Monsieur Darby* will say is so," she said emphatically. He was walking well on his own, speaking better than she had ever heard him, and grasping many more pieces of the memory that had been lost to him.

But when Trevor arrived—crazed and irrational, according to Honorine—everything changed. He locked his father away from her, threatened to do the same with her until the sheriff arrived. Darby had shown her where she might hide. And from that hiding place, she had watched Trevor go in and out of the salon where he kept his father, her fear of what was happening confirmed when she had bolted for the salon that afternoon while Trevor was occupied with Caleb.

"This medicine, it makes us believe he is unaware. Trevor poisons him!"

"Poison?" Caleb asked, his disbelief apparent. "But for what purpose? Why should he want his own father to be so incapacitated?"

Honorine stared miserably into her empty glass. "I do not know the answer to that. But he is an evil man."

"I never thought him evil," Sophie offered. "But I thought there was something rather insincere about him. Nothing I could put my finger on, exactly."

Miss Brillhart, particularly pliable at the moment, put her wineglass down and squinted at Sophie. "*Who* is evil?" she demanded.

"Mr. Trevor Hamilton of Nottinghamshire. You wouldn't know him, I should think."

"Indeed I do," she said, bracing her hands against her knees. "He enjoys rather a sordid reputation in these parts."

The room stilled; Caleb, Sophie, and Honorine all looked at Miss Brillhart. The poor woman immediately blushed and waved her hand as if to dismiss what she had just said. "Well, from what I *hear*, that is to say."

"What have you heard?" Sophie asked.

She turned even redder. "Just that he's a bit of a gambler. Actually, he's *quite* the gambler. His departed wife hailed from nearby, and it is said he owes rather a lot of money to men in these parts."

"Ah," said Caleb thoughtfully. "That would at least explain the sudden excursion to Beaconsfield."

"Beaconsfield?" Honorine asked.

Caleb put aside the knife he was holding and wiped his hands on the apron. "Do you recall the afternoon I did not come to the park?" he asked Sophie. "The afternoon of the Hamilton supper party. It was because I had followed Trevor. I had a suspicion—nothing, really, except that his behavior toward me had been too vehement. I had made no claim to Father's fortune; I merely wanted to see him. When I saw Trevor leaving Bedford Square that morning, his manner seemed rather odd, as if he were attempting to hide. I acted on instinct and followed him. He went to Beaconsfield and spent the day betting on the horse races there, then returned in time to prepare for the soiree. I really thought nothing of it, until now."

"Oh yes, that sounds like our Mr. Hamilton," Miss Brillhart said authoritatively. "Never misses a race, to hear it told."

Caleb, Sophie, and Honorine looked at one another. "Do you think that perhaps . . . ?" Caleb asked.

"Yes," Sophie responded authoritatively. "Yet I don't understand why he would keep his own father so incapacitated."

"He is evil, this is why," Honorine insisted, pouring herself another glass of wine. "And we leave Will there!"

"We must notify someone," Sophie said to Caleb. "I am not sure how that might be done, what with the suspicion cast on all of us as it is—"

"I'll tell them!" Miss Brillhart announced, fortified by wine and puffing her chest. "I've no patience for the likes of him, I don't. I'll just pay a call to the parish constable on the morrow, and tell him all about our poor Lord Hamilton."

"The constable?" Sophie asked, surprised. "Perhaps Caleb should accompany you."

"There is no need for that," Miss Brillhart said proudly.

"You know him, then?"

Miss Brillhart suddenly blushed and hastily picked up her wineglass. "You might say the constable is . . . a very old friend of mine," she said, and quickly drank what was left of her wine.

"Ooh, how convenient to keep these old friends about!" Honorine exclaimed, and with a bawdy chuckle, she cuffed Miss Brillhart on the shoulder, almost toppling the housekeeper right off her stool.

Caleb questioned Miss Brillhart further, and was finally satisfied it was indeed the best way to have someone look into the immediate care of Lord Hamilton. It did not, however, resolve their dilemma.

That conversation moved out onto the terrace with supper, continued over a delicious, candlelit meal of roasted beef in a port wine sauce, sweetbread *au jus,* asparagus in crème sauce, and steamed vegetables. But the meal could not alleviate the gravity of their collective situation, and the conversation slowly died from fatigue and a lack of clear solutions.

It was Sophie who broke the somber mood by producing a *meringue à la crème* she had learned from Lucie Cowplain that had Honorine and Caleb swooning, and Miss Brillhart looking at Sophie with great surprise.

"Dear me, I cannot say I am not quite curious, my lady!" she exclaimed as she leaned back, fully sated after her meal. "You never seemed the type, if you don't mind me saying."

"Really?" drawled Caleb. "What type did she seem, Miss Brillhart?"

"Oh my," she said, laughing. "Sophie was such a darling child. But *spoiled*! The earl, he could never refuse her."

"Spoiled?" Sophie snorted at that. "My recollection is a bit different, Miss Brillhart—he could refuse me quite easily!"

"Oh no, he could not," the housekeeper loudly disagreed, straightening her posture to better address Caleb and Honorine. "Sophie was the youngest of them all, you know. She was always following them about, begging to be allowed to play in their games. Eugenie and Valerie, they were horrible to the younger girls. If they determined they would play knights and damsels, poor Sophie was always the black knight and would inevitably be slain in the opening scene of their drama. I daresay Ann did not fare much better, but she seemed to last a bit longer than our Sophie."

Sophie had forgotten knights and damsels, but the memory came back clearly—she laughed softly. "It's true," she admitted. "They would march me out into the center of the bowling lawn and have me stand there, while they ran around me with those wooden swords Julian made. One tap, I was gravely injured and was to lay dying. Two taps, and I could dispense with the acting altogether, for I was dead."

Miss Brillhart laughed. "And do you recall the *ghosts*?"

Sophie couldn't help herself—she laughed fully at the memory. "Of course! Did you think I would ever forget? I still have wretched dreams!"

"What ghost?" Caleb insisted.

"Eugenie and Claudia—Julian's wife—they thought it would be great fun one night to act out a scary story rather than tell one. Eugenie, very dramatically, of course, told the story of the ghost of Kettering Hall. Some ancient ancestor or some such thing. I was too young to notice, I suppose, but Claudia was nowhere to be seen. Ann and Valerie and I hung on Eugenie's every word, and at one point, we were convinced that we had heard the ghost walking overhead. Well . . ." Sophie paused, leaned forward as Miss Brillhart put her hand over her mouth to quell the laughter. "Wouldn't you know, that after we had gone to bed, I felt something tickle my foot. When I opened my eyes, there was a ghost standing at the foot of my bed."

"You've never heard such a bloodcurdling scream in your life!" Miss Brillhart interjected. "Oh my, we all heard it, all through the servants' floor. I went running down the stairs just in time to see little Sophie flying down the corridor to the earl's rooms, screaming all the way. And who should walk out of her rooms? Miss Claudia, draped in a sheet, two big holes cut for the eyes!" she cried, laughing.

"I slept with Julian for a week!"

"*Two!*" howled Miss Brillhart.

The four of them laughed well into the night, relieved with the respite from their troubles if only for a space, recalling various memories from their respective childhoods, reminiscing of days long gone. It was particularly poignant to Sophie that Caleb's memories of his childhood seemed so lonely. Although he laughed at some of his antics, his cheerful telling of it did not banish the image of a lonely boy who had no playmates, apparently shunned because of his birth. It truly amazed her in moments like this that he had become the proud man that he was. Instead of falling victim to his circumstance as so many would do, he grew from it, garnered strength from it. Made himself a man from it.

She loved him. Loved him to the point of devastation.

Which was why, when she later lay in her old bed, staring up at the frieze ceiling of angels she had memorized so many years ago, her heart leapt with hope when she heard the creak of the door.

Rising up on her elbow, she watched as Caleb slipped into her room, taking care to shut the door quietly behind him. Then he turned, fairly flew across the thick carpet, and fell on her, smothering her with kisses.

Sophie laughed; he silenced her with another kiss. *"Ssshh,"* he warned her. "Miss Brillhart may be a jolly good girl, but I rather imagine she'll not appreciate finding a rogue in your bed."

"What would she do, do you think?" Sophie asked playfully. "I rather imagine she'd have a fit of apoplexy and keel over, right where she stands."

Caleb nuzzled her neck. "Then let's give her no cause for alarm," he said, and lifted his head. The playful smile was gone; his gaze searched her face as he brushed his knuckles across her cheek, then her lips. "Let us marry as soon as possible, Sophie. Let us obtain license on the morrow and marry straightaway. I can't go on like this, loving you, *making* love to you, and not having you wholly mine, in truth *and* in name."

Instantly, Sophie sobered. She slowly pushed herself up so that she was leaning against the headboard. Looking apprehensive, Caleb braced himself against the bed with one arm across her body.

How peculiar, Sophie thought, that she should come full circle, come back to the place she had heard similar words before and acted upon them.

"I want it with all my heart, Sophie."

She wanted it, too. But her family would never forgive her. If she thought she had been an outcast before, she would certainly be so now. They could perhaps, in time, come to accept Caleb, in spite of his lack of name. But they would not forgive her for scandalizing them a second time. They would believe her to be the same childish girl who had run away with William Stanwood, would want her out of their lives. Perhaps permanently

But it was *her* life to ruin. It was her life to live. She could no more make this choice for them than she could for Caleb. It had to be for her, and her alone.

Caleb stroked her cheek again; his hand trailed down her neck, her chest, to her lap. "*Sophie*," he murmured.

She smiled, reached for his hand, and pressed it against her heart. "Yes," she whispered. "We will obtain a license tomorrow."

A range of emotion scudded across his eyes; he stared in disbelief. His gaze dropped to his hand pressed against her heart, and then suddenly heavenward, to the frieze of cherubs and angels on her ceiling. "Thank you, God," he said low. "I will not squander this chance, I vow it."

Whatever he might have meant by that was lost to her as he came over her then, kissing her with all the emotion she felt.

At Hamilton Hall that same night, Will waited until Trevor had left his bedroom, then spit out the whiskey and what he was now certain was a very strong dose of opiate. He lay in his bed for several minutes, waiting, straining to hear, uncertain if Trevor might choose to return. He rather thought not. It seemed, in the course of the last forty-eight hours, that he was too intent on drinking. That was rather odd, actually—Trevor had never been one to drink to excess.

A quarter of an hour passed, perhaps more, before he was convinced by the silence beyond his door that Trevor would not return. Slowly, he lifted himself, shoved his legs off the bed, then with some difficulty, came to his feet. Struggling for equilibrium—the hours spent in that damned wheeled chair had taken that away from him— he strained to put one foot in front of the other. Then again. And again and again until he was walking the length of his room, back and forth.

It was, he thought with some satisfaction, only a matter of time now.

Chapter Twenty-Six

Cᴀʟᴇʙ, Sᴏᴘʜɪᴇ, ᴀɴᴅ Miss Brillhart took the cabriolet to the village of Kettering early the next morning, coming to a stop in front of the livery at Miss Brillhart's instruction. She climbed down from the carriage, adjusted her hat and smoothed the front of her gown, then glanced nervously at Sophie. "No need for you to wait, mu'um. I'll take the walk home as I am accustomed to doing."

"Of course we will wait," Caleb said emphatically.

Miss Brillhart stole a glance at the livery where the parish constable worked and cleared her throat. "That's right kind, sir, but it is not necessary. Really."

Caleb opened his mouth to argue, but Sophie put a hand on his arm. "Really," she said quietly. Miss Brillhart was blushing furiously now; she fussed with her reticule, avoiding their gazes, and bid them a quick "good morning" before turning and darting into the livery like a rabbit.

As he watched her disappear inside, a light of understanding washed over Caleb and with a snort, he smiled sheepishly at Sophie. "I suppose I'm so caught up in my own good fortune, I do not think to look around me."

She laughed softly, squeezed his hand. "This means, of course, that we are left quite to our own devices."

"Then may I suggest we find the parish pastor," he responded, and flicked the reins to send the horse trotting.

As it turned out, the pastor, a young man from Coventry, had just received his post and therefore had never heard the name Sophie Dane, much less Caleb Hamilton. He was more than happy to issue a license for their marriage, and even waxed sentimentally about his own desire to marry and father children one day.

Sophie and Caleb had decided, after a whispered discussion in bed the night before, that their wedding would be a very simple and expedient thing, with only the required number of witnesses. They would marry in the chapel at Kettering Hall; the same place Sophie's mother had married her father. They debated whether or not they should tell Miss Brillhart, lest she send word to Julian, but seeing the lunacy in trying to keep something like a wedding from the housekeeper, Sophie decided she would send word to Julian.

When Honorine demanded to know, upon their return from the village, where they had gone so early that morning, Sophie confided in her. For once in her life, Honorine was speechless; her eyes welled, her bottom lip trembled, and she impetuously threw her arms around Sophie, then Caleb, proclaiming she could not be happier.

She was not, however, content with the notion of a simple wedding. She envisioned something much more memorable, such as a garden wedding with dancing and delicious chocolate cakes. Arguing was futile—Honorine was determined and rather certain Lord Hamilton would want it so. And, she added in a supercilious French speech, it kept her mind occupied while they waited for word of Lord Hamilton.

That would, apparently, take some time. Miss Brillhart

returned—midafternoon, Sophie noticed with a smile—
with the good news that the constable was quite keen to
look into the matter. However, he had explained to her
that he could not possibly leave for Hamilton House before the morrow, and the journey would take two days.
His plan was to call on the parish sheriff there, hoping
that they would venture out to the estate together. All in
all, he told Miss Brillhart, she should not expect word
before the end of the week at the very earliest.

Frustrated that he could not do more, Caleb stalked
about the house, complaining of his inability. Honorine,
too, was despondent. She moped about and took to wearing very drab colors and her hair in an austere bun. She
would sit for what seemed hours, gazing out over the
expansive back lawn of Kettering Hall, lost in thought.
It was so unlike her, so very *opposite* of what she had
been, that Sophie worried. The only thing that seemed to
spark a light in her at all was the subject of Sophie and
Caleb's wedding. On that topic, she offered many opinions, whether they wanted them or not. And, she insisted, it would not do without Fabrice and Roland in
attendance.

"But they have gone to France," Sophie tried to explain. "We agreed we should meet at Château de Segries
in Burgundy."

Honorine waved a dismissive hand at her. "You should
not believe they have gone from here, Sofia. These two
men, they cannot attend their own funeral without me,"
she said emphatically, and picked up pen and paper to
send for them.

Likewise, Sophie found a sheet of parchment with the
Kettering seal on it, and sat to write Julian, closeting
herself in her old dressing room while she struggled with
what exactly to say. In the end, her letter was too simple
and hardly relayed all the emotion that filled her. But, she
finally conceded, it relayed the most important message—
that she had made her own decision.

Dearest Julian,

Please accept my humblest apology for having left London as I did. I believed, and still believe, I had no choice, as time was of the essence, and I feared that you would attempt to stop me. As it happened, my decision was the right one for reasons that I cannot fully explain here. I am now at Kettering Hall, as I had nowhere else to turn.

I pray that you will understand when I tell you that I have taken a license to marry and plan to do so by week's end. The man I will marry is not Mr. Trevor Hamilton as you and the family had hoped, but rather, his half-brother, Mr. Caleb Hamilton. In truth, he has been my secret love for many weeks now. I know you believe him to be an imposter and a swindler, but I fervently hope you will trust me when I tell you that he is none of those things. He is the loving son of Lord Hamilton and a man with more integrity in the tip of his finger than Trevor Hamilton possesses in his entire body. He is gentle and kind, he loves me dearly, and he vows to be faithful always.

I do not know where fate may take us; indeed we are struggling with the decision of where we are to go from here. But no matter where we may find ourselves, I know in my heart of hearts that we will love each other madly until we are exhausted and ancient and it is time to sleep. I cannot help but believe, given the course of my life thus far, that the depth of the love we share is the most important reason for which we are placed on this earth.

I hope you will understand my decision and agree that it is, in the end, my decision to make. I do not mean to hurt you or bring dishonor on the family, but I cannot help my feelings or ignore my instinct. I will pray that you find it in your heart to forgive me. Ever yours,

Sophie.

She read the letter several times over before finally sealing it, convinced there was nothing else she could say to ease the blow. She returned to the main salon then, where Caleb had taken it upon himself to inform Miss Brillhart of their decision, with Honorine's help.

Caleb looked strong and secure as she entered the room, striding forward to meet her, grasping her hand and squeezing it reassuringly as only he could do. She looked up into his pale green eyes, saw his conviction shining brightly. He smiled, winked slyly. "It's all right," he murmured as he kissed her temple. "Everything will be all right."

Sophie nodded mutely, shifted her gaze to Miss Brillhart, who was looking at her with an expression of remorse. She immediately went to the elderly woman and put her hand on the two Miss Brillhart held tightly at her waist.

The moment Sophie touched her, she shook her head, and a tear dislodged from the corner of her eye. "It's not right, my lady," she said. "It's not *right*."

"No, Miss Brillhart, it wasn't right the first time," Sophie said softly, "but this *is* right. I am a woman now. I was a child then. The love Caleb and I share is as real as the love you and I share."

Miss Brillhart looked up then, wiped a tear from beneath her eye. "I do love you, mu'um, I have loved all you girls as if you were my own."

"Then be happy for me, Miss Brillhart! Be happy that I have found someone as wonderful and kind as Mr. Hamilton!"

The housekeeper looked at Caleb from the corner of her eye; a bit of a smile tipped the corner of her mouth upward. "Well . . . I suppose he *is* a rather bonny lad," she admitted.

"Terribly so," Sophie readily agreed.

"And I suppose a lady could do worse," she said, holding her head a little higher.

"I *have* done worse," Sophie reminded her with a little laugh.

Miss Brillhart smiled then. "Indeed you have, my lady, indeed you have. Oh drat it all then, I must agree with Madame Fortier. If there is to be a wedding, it ought to be done right."

With a sigh of relief, Sophie embraced her. Miss Brillhart hugged her back, squeezing hard, then abruptly let go. "Leave me be now," she said, flustered. "I've enough to do without all this commotion." With a sad smile, she walked away from Sophie, toward the door.

"Thank you, Miss Brillhart," Caleb said as she passed. "It does a man good to know he is considered bonny."

"Ah now, there you go, Mr. Hamilton," she said, waggling a finger at him. "It's small wonder you've enjoyed a reputation as a lover," she teased, laughing to herself as she went out the door.

Surprised, Sophie asked, "How on earth could she know that?"

Caleb enveloped her in his arms and kissed her before answering. "I had a bit of help from Madame Fortier in breaking the news to Miss Brillhart. She left no detail unsaid," he said, chuckling. "Frankly, I must confess I did not know I had such a randy reputation."

"I do not know of this *randy,* but it is known you enjoy the *mesdames,*" Honorine muttered from her perch on the window seat, where she held her letter to Roland and Fabrice in her lap.

"All right then, let's have your letter," Sophie said, as she slipped out of Caleb's embrace. "We might as well send these on their way so we can begin the business of finding suitable wedding attire."

Honorine looked around at that, eyed Sophie suspiciously. "What do you mean, wedding attire?"

Sophie shrugged, stole a look at Caleb. "You didn't think I'd be married in drab old gray, did you? I was rather hoping you would help me look through the trunks in the attic."

Honorine frowned. *"Qu'est-ce que c'est?* You mean to marry in these?" she asked, gesturing limply at her gown.

"I certainly hope not," Sophie laughed. "There are so many trunks up there, I am quite certain we could find *something* suitable. Will you come then? I would welcome a trained eye."

With a weary sigh, Honorine stood, walked slowly to the door, pausing only to shove her letter at Caleb. *"Oui,* my help you need very much," she said, and dragged herself out the door as Sophie exchanged a silent laugh with Caleb, then trailed behind her.

At Hamilton House, in the master suite of rooms, Will strained to hear Trevor's footfall. After a quarter of an hour, he was convinced his son was not coming back. Darby had confirmed that he spent his evenings in the main salon, drinking whiskey and muttering to himself. Slowly, Will swung his legs over the side of the bed, put his feet to the floor, and stood easily. He began to walk, pacing the floor in front of the bed, watching the clock on the mantel and counting the minutes until Darby would arrive.

At promptly eleven o'clock, Darby slipped through the door, pausing there to listen. After a moment, he turned toward Will and nodded. "I believe he is quite inebriated, my lord. I shouldn't worry that he will appear."

"G-good," Will said, and motioned Darby to the divan at the hearth. "N-now, where were we?" he asked as he began to walk again, moving his legs and his arms.

"Shortly after the death of Mrs. Hamilton, my lord. You recall that she had spoken to you of Trevor's habits?"

"Y-yes," said Will, nodding firmly. He *had* remembered, quite clearly. "Elspeth was quite c-concerned," he said, and began to tell Darby what he remembered, pleased at how eagerly Darby confirmed his recollections.

It *was* coming back to him.

• • •

Over the course of the next few days, Caleb watched as Sophie blossomed with a new depth of confidence he had not seen in her. It seemed as if writing the letter to her brother had freed her from some invisible burden.

Only she was strong enough to make a concerted effort to lift Madame Fortier's spirits and keep them all buoyed. That was a difficult task—every day Miss Brillhart marched to the village, and every day she returned with no word from the constable. Caleb was little help—he was too worried about his father to be of much assistance in the plans for his wedding. So Sophie engaged Honorine in a search of dozens of trunks in the attic, finally producing several costumes for Caleb's inspection. The clothes dated back one hundred years, but Sophie finally agreed with Honorine—a wedding in the dress of the high court of King George II seemed appropriate somehow, given the importance of the occasion. As for Caleb, he discovered there was no shortage of clothing from that era—they gave him the choice of a gold velvet coat or a pale rose, with matching high-heeled slippers, he could not help but notice. He reluctantly chose the gold.

Yet it was impossible for even Sophie to conceive of a formal wedding, much less a feast, with their worry about Lord Hamilton weighing on them. Miss Brillhart did the best she could for them in that regard, plotting a meal appropriate to the occasion when no more than a handful would attend.

It seemed to Caleb that they all waited for disaster. It was hard to add a wedding to the feeling of doom, yet he could hardly continue on with their secret love affair. It was imperative that he honor Sophie, and soon. Nonetheless, there were moments, though infrequent, that he rather wondered if he was doing the right thing. But then he need only look at Sophie and know how devastatingly true his feelings were. There was nothing that

could compare to the depth of passion he felt for her. At
night, when they made love, her natural, heartfelt response shattered him. In the course of their day, the
touch of her hand, the whisper of her lips against his
skin made him long for her with the force of ten thousand men.

He loved everything about her—the way she watched
over Honorine, or seemed to let class distinctions melt
away and embrace Miss Brillhart as a true friend. Her
periods of reflection, when he would see her looking pen-
sively at the fire, no doubt considering the various facets
of her life as it had evolved. She was thoughtful and con-
siderate, kind and loving, and secretly, he could hardly
wait for the moment she would put her hand in his, take
the plain gold band that had been his mother's, and become his wife, his companion, his love for the rest of his
life.

Nothing could douse the sense of wonder he felt when
he was with her, not even the nagging concern for his father's welfare. But he continued to bemoan the fact that
his father would not be in attendance, that he would
marry with his father perhaps in imminent danger.

Unfortunately, there was no news by the end of the
week.

Miss Brillhart and Caleb fretted equally on this point.
Together, they reviewed the time it would take to reach
the parish in which Hamilton House sat. Miss Brillhart
was convinced the constable had met with some misfortune. Caleb wondered if he hadn't simply taken another
route to combine other business with this. But they both
agreed—if the constable had not returned by their wedding day, something must be very wrong.

Caleb discussed that with Sophie and they decided that
if the constable had not returned by the time they were
wed, they would return once again to Nottinghamshire.
It was risky, but far too important. They figured that between his insistence and Sophie's name, which wielded
considerable authority in many parts of England, the

parish sheriff there would not refuse to see after Lord Hamilton's welfare. Further, it was Honorine they wanted, not Caleb. If she remained at Kettering Hall, Caleb believed he had a decent chance of seeing his father, if even for the last time.

That was a persistent worry. He knew Trevor would continue to accuse him of attempting to swindle his father, and while there was no evidence to support such a claim, there was certainly the preponderance of such an assumption based solely on the fact that he was the bastard son. There was nothing he could do to change the way society viewed him, nothing at all.

Which was why he and Sophie had determined they would reside in France. It meant leaving his budding rail endeavors behind, of course, but there was no hope that the two of them would be accepted anywhere within the British Isles. In France, at least, no one need know who they were, much less their histories.

"The work on the rails is only starting there," he said one night as they lay in each other's arms, watching the fire turn to embers. "Perhaps this is a good opportunity."

"What of the house in Regent's Park?" she asked, tracing a pattern on his bare chest.

What *of* the house into which he had put so much of himself? It seemed so distant now, something of a pipe dream he had once held dear. "I'll keep it, I suppose. Perhaps one day, we will feel free to come to London."

Sophie frowned lightly. "I rather think we will not," she said sadly.

Caleb stroked her hair, said nothing. In truth, he had no idea what they might expect. He had seen enough of the *ton's* antics to know that it was probable her family would never openly accept her in their fold again. Still, it seemed impossible to him that anyone who knew Sophie could possibly turn his back on her, regardless of what perceived injustice she might have done.

"I could perhaps open a patisserie," she said idly.

"I beg your pardon?" he asked, surprised.

"A patisserie. We could live above it." She lifted her lashes to look at him and smiled. "Would you like that, Mr. Hamilton? Living above a patisserie?"

He laughed. "And what of you? I should think an apartment above a patisserie is quite a step down from the accommodations to which you are accustomed."

Sophie shrugged, looked at the fire. "If you are there, I cannot imagine what possible difference the rooms will make, Caleb. You are what makes my life meaningful, not the trappings of it."

Ah God, he loved this woman. He kissed the top of her head, but not satisfied with that, pulled her up and kissed her lips. Sophie moved, straddling him as she lifted her bedclothes to her waist, pressing her naked flesh against him. "I would that I could crawl right inside you and live there," she murmured.

"You already do, my love," he said as her mouth came hungrily over his, devouring him until he knew nothing but the feel of her body surrounding his.

It was midnight at Hamilton House, and Will was feeling almost his old self again. He was moving better than he had in months, and with Darby's considerable help, had remembered almost everything.

Not the least of which was the root of Trevor's perfidy.

Will stood, his bad arm folded over his good, nodding thoughtfully as he and Darby discussed his memories. "I remember, of c-course. He l-left me no choice. I had to th-think of Ian."

"Of course you did, my lord," Darby said.

"He has l-lost—" A sound beyond his door stopped Will. He cocked his head, listening carefully. Very slowly, Darby stood, straining to hear, too. They waited for a moment, and hearing nothing, Will shrugged. "M-my imagination," he said sheepishly.

He never heard Darby's response because Trevor

came crashing through his door at that very moment. The intrusion startled Will badly, but miraculously, he managed to keep his feet. Darby was at once in front of him, but Will pushed him aside and took a solid step forward to face his son.

"Well, well, aren't we a cozy pair?" Trevor snarled. His shirttails out and a dirty neckcloth hanging untied around his neck, he stumbled farther into the room. An almost empty bottle dangled from the fingers of one hand; he reeked of whiskey. "I should have known," he said acidly to Darby. "You are nothing more than a weasel!"

"Trevor!" Will said sharply.

That caught his attention, and Trevor shifted his murderous gaze to his father. "You should be abed, Father. You are ill," he said, swaying slightly.

"You'll not d-drug m-me again," Will said tightly.

That seemed to surprise him. He blinked, took one step back, and looked nervously at Darby. "Drug you?" His bark of laughter was high and hollow. "Whatever do you mean? You are not well—"

"It is you who are n-not well, son," Will said low. "I k-know what you have d-done. I know you have b-been stealing from m-me."

The color drained from Trevor's face; he dropped the whiskey bottle. "I've done no such thing!" he shouted, and looked wildly from Darby to his father before making a sudden movement toward Will.

Darby reacted quickly, throwing himself at Trevor and knocking him off balance. "If you touch him, sir, I shall have a host of footmen here to restrain you!"

The look of panic in Trevor's eyes as he backed away told Will more than he had known in months. It was all true, all his suspicions, all his fears. Even though he had finally remembered most of it, a part of him desperately wanted to be wrong, but looking at his son now, he could no longer cling to that thread of hope, and felt his heart slowly tearing in two. He sighed wearily, put a hand on

Darby's shoulder. "Its all right, D-Darby. He will n-not harm me."

Darby did not look terribly convinced, but reluctantly stepped aside. Will looked at his son, wondered again how it had come to this. "I remember n-now," he said to his son. "H-how you f-forced m-me to sign the bank-notes. How you signed m-many yourself."

Trevor blinked, raked a shaking hand through his disheveled hair, and tried to laugh. "Father! What is this nonsense Darby has been feeding you? Of *course* I did no such thing! Why, you accuse me of stealing!" he said with feigned indignation.

"You d-did," said Will calmly. "Your g-gambling has l-led you to steal, son."

Trevor stared at Will as if he could not quite grasp what he was saying. Several emotions seemed to pass over his face, and slowly, his lip curled in a sneer. "My *gambling* led me to steal?" he asked, then laughed coldly. "No, Father, *you* led me to steal! You left it all to that bloody bastard of yours! What was I to do? It was rightfully mine, *not* his!" he said, his voice growing louder. "If there is anyone to blame here, it is you! *You* are the reason I have come to this! You did this to me!" he shouted, red-faced.

Will regarded his son, whose eyes were shimmering with tears of his utter fury, and yes, he *did* blame himself. He wondered again what he might have done to change things, yet he could find nothing at that moment but a deep, deep regret. "I d-do blame m-myself, son," he said softly. "M-more than you know. N-nonetheless, you have stolen from m-me."

"We have sent for the sheriff, sir," Darby said stiffly. "He will arrive on the morrow."

Trevor's expression slipped from furious to despairing, and he glanced helplessly at the carpet. "The sheriff?" he asked, sounding like a boy. "But what shall I do?"

"You shall b-be a m-man," Will told him. "You will f-face your d-deeds like a m-man."

Nodding, Trevor sniffed loudly, ran the back of his hand across his nose, and looked up at his father. "At least allow me to know why, Papa. Please tell me why you left it all to him and forsook me?"

There was nothing Will could say that would ever make Trevor understand. He scarcely understood it himself. On the surface, it seemed simple. He loved Caleb and he despised the man standing before him now. Sadly, it had been that way for as far back as he could remember. "I had to th-think of Ian," he said simply. "You w-would have g-gambled his f-future."

Trevor said nothing. He stared at the carpet for a moment, then went down on his haunches and retrieved the whiskey bottle. Slowly, he stood, and lifted a desperate gaze to Will. "Father, please," he said hoarsely. "A money-lender has threatened my life. If you give me but five thousand pounds, I will leave here and never return. He will see me dead, I know he shall, if I don't give him the money. *Please*, Father!" he said, his desperation clearly evident.

Will's heart was in his throat. "On the morrow, son. We'll determine what must be done on the morrow."

Trevor's cheeks bulged with the exertion of his desperation, but he merely nodded. "On the morrow, then," he said, resigned, and turned, walking unsteadily from the room.

Chapter Twenty-Seven

THERE WAS QUITE a stir the evening before Caleb and Sophie's wedding day when a very nondescript carriage pulled up to Kettering Hall.

Honorine, from her perch at the window seat, where she had spent every evening staring wistfully into the dusk, abruptly came to her feet. *"Mon Dieu!"* she exclaimed, and before anyone could speak, was suddenly rushing for the door of the salon. Caleb and Sophie exchanged a look; Caleb quickly stood and went to the window, but Sophie ran after Honorine.

She reached the front door of Kettering Hall just in time to see the door of the carriage swing open with a bang and Fabrice come spilling out. He landed awkwardly, then turned and shouted up in heated French at a very slow Roland, who stepped gingerly out of the carriage, then paused to smooth the wrinkles from trousers identical to those Fabrice wore.

"Ah, *mes amis!*" Honorine shrieked. "You see? They can go nowhere without me!" she cried, and rushed toward the two men with her arms wide, as they stood arguing, oblivious to Honorine.

"Oh dear," Sophie muttered as Caleb appeared at her

side. "Oh *dear,*" she said again, and flashed a delighted smile at him as Lucie Cowplain emerged and immediately began marching crookedly toward Sophie, demanding to know where the wedding would be held, as she had brought wedding cakes all the way from London.

Sophie and Caleb spent the remainder of that evening with Lucie Cowplain in the kitchens while Honorine spent the evening in the attic with Fabrice and Roland, who, having learned of the plans for the wedding, insisted that they, too, be dressed in costume.

Exhausted, Sophie retired alone that night, sending Caleb off to his room with a kiss that promised their future.

Their wedding day dawned bright and clear, and Sophie smiled at the notion that it was only a matter of a few hours before she would be forever known as Mrs. Hamilton.

She loved the sound of that name, Sophie Hamilton. She imagined it on documents as she dressed, painted in the corner of the window of her patisserie in small, neat letters.

Miss Brillhart, already wearing her old gown of dark red velvet and wide panniers, came to Sophie's suite of rooms to help her dress. They chatted like old friends as she helped Sophie into the tight-fitting corset and quilted gold petticoat. The petticoat was then covered with a dark green overskirt, embroidered in gold. Miss Brillhart strained to lace the bodice—it fit Sophie like a glove, molding her breasts into a mound of flesh rising just above the garment's very low neck. She paused to admire her work, taking care to fluff the flounced sleeves of Sophie's costume just so, and at last she stood back, admiring her. "Beautiful, my lady. You are truly a beautiful bride."

Sophie blushed, nervously tied the forest-green velvet ribbon around her neck. "I confess, I never thought I would hear anyone say so."

"You've changed," Miss Brillhart said solemnly. "So

graceful and pretty. Mr. Hamilton, he is a very fortunate man."

Sophie smiled, donned the tiny teardrop emerald earrings that had been her mother's, and turned to look at herself in the mirror. She couldn't help but laugh—she had never imagined herself in such a dress on her wedding day, but given what they had all endured the last several weeks, the almost surreal effect seemed terribly appropriate.

When she and Miss Brillhart emerged on the back terrace, they could see that all the guests—Honorine, the groundsman and his wife, two footmen, and naturally, Fabrice and Roland dressed almost identically—had already gathered in appropriate costume. Fabrice and Roland had even gone to the trouble of powdering their hair. The only one who looked out of place was the young pastor, who actually looked a little stunned by his surroundings and, most definitely, by Fabrice and Roland.

Caleb looked magnificent in his gold coat, dark brown trousers, and embroidered waistcoat. He had even, after much complaining through the week, donned the high-heeled shoes and pulled his wavy hair into a queue. Sophie had to struggle to keep from running headlong at him, flinging herself into his arms to assure herself that she was indeed about to marry the man who stood so handsome before her.

Honorine assured her it was real by walking up on the terrace so that she might accompany her down to the gazebo, looking more like her old self than she had in days, with a dress of blue and purple and a red quilted petticoat. As she approached, Sophie noticed a sheen of tears in her eyes.

"Ooh, Honorine!" she exclaimed, reaching for her hand. "You mustn't be sad!"

"I wish for my Will to come, but this does not make me sad," she said, shaking her head and smiling affectionately. "This peanut, it is now a coconut," she said, tapping

Sophie's chest above her heart. "I am this day very happy. *Very* happy."

"So am I," Sophie said, and linked her arm through Honorine's. Together, they followed Miss Brillhart to the gazebo.

But as they stepped onto the lawn below the terrace, the sound of an approaching carriage drew them up short. Sophie and Honorine paused, holding unconsciously to one another as they watched the carriage thunder down the long tree-lined drive.

A feeling of sick dread instantly filled Sophie. She knew that carriage—it was as if her life were repeating itself, and she could do nothing but stand dumbly, her knees weakening, as the carriage came to a sharp halt in the circular drive.

Caleb was instantly at her side, his expression grim. "You know who this is." It was more of a statement than a question; he knew, too, she realized, as he grasped her hand and held it tightly.

"I know," she murmured and watched as Julian vaulted from the carriage. He gave her a pointed look as he held his hand up to receive Claudia, then Ann, who was followed by her husband, Victor.

"I'll speak with him, Sophie. I'll not allow him to ruin this day," Caleb said quickly. "We *will* be married."

"He can't stop me, can he?" she asked uncertainly as Julian came striding forward.

Caleb did not have the opportunity to respond, because Julian was already there—he grabbed her by the arms, jerked her into his embrace, and squeezed her tightly. "How dare you, Sophie?" he demanded. "How dare you attempt to marry without me?" He reared back at that, frowning, then kissed her cheek. "Silly girl, I ought to turn you over my knee, I really ought. Exactly who did you think to give you away? Am I to be robbed of the honor?"

Stunned, Sophie and Caleb looked at one another.

Julian dropped his arms from her, punched his fists to his hips, and eyed Caleb up and down, shaking his head disapprovingly. But when he looked at Sophie again, he was trying to hide his smile. "I can hardly say that I approve of his dress—he's in desperate need of a tailor. But I suppose it will have to do as there doesn't appear time to correct it."

Sophie gaped at her brother, speechless. Of all the reactions she had imagined, *this* had most certainly not been one of them.

"Oh dear, please do not stand there like you've no idea who I am," he said, straightening the cuffs of his shirt. "At least introduce me to my new brother-in-law, will you?"

"And me! *I* should have been introduced ages ago!" Ann complained, stepping forward to slip her arm around Sophie's shoulders. "Naturally, I can see why you might have been a bit reluctant to do just that, given how adamantly I tried to push you in the other direction."

Sophie's vision was suddenly blurry; she reached for Ann's hand, then Julian's. "You aren't angry."

That earned a *hmmph* from Ann, but Julian chuckled. "I wouldn't go so far as all that. I *am* angry that you thought to do this without us. And I suppose I am a bit angry that you obviously believed you could not come to me. A bit angry, mind you, but I rather suppose I do understand it. That does not, however, excuse you, not at all, for thinking you might traipse through this day without *me*." He paused then, his expression softening as Claudia slipped in beside him and put her arm around his waist. "I love you, pumpkin. All I ever wanted was your happiness, nothing more, and if I failed to make you understand that, then I am terribly sorry. You are right—you are a woman and this is your decision. I will not attempt to lecture you and tell you what the two of you will face—you know it better than I, certainly. I only want to share in your joy."

"As do I," said Ann. "I was wrong to have tried to arrange your life, wasn't I? Yet I must still insist on being introduced!"

It was more than she could have hoped, more than she had dared dream. With a cry of joyous relief, Sophie threw herself into her brother's arms.

He laughed, rubbed his hand soothingly on her back. "Come now, pumpkin. There will be ample opportunity for wailing when the ceremony begins." Gently, he took her shoulders and set her away from him, toward Caleb.

"Oh really, Sophie, you might at least have said what the dress would be," sniffed Claudia. "I feel woefully inappropriate!"

Sophie laughed shakily, took Caleb's hand in her own, and drew him close to her. "Please allow me to introduce you to the man who will be my husband. Mr. Caleb Hamilton."

And as her family closed around him, greeting him, assessing him, Sophie caught Julian's eye and smiled. He returned that smile, the pride evident in his eyes, and it was in that moment that Sophie finally realized she was one of them, that they did not see her as a child any longer. She had, at long last, come into her own.

The ceremony was mercifully short, and the feast afterward surprisingly sumptuous. They enjoyed an apparently bottomless well of wine, and between Sophie and Lucie Cowplain, there was so much cake that more than one complained of being in desperate need of a place to just lie down for a time.

As dusk crept in and the rushlights were lit, Caleb surprised Sophie with a fiddler he had managed to find in the village. Much to the surprise and delight of her family, the dancing started with Sophie and Caleb leading the Scottish jig they had danced to in St. Neots. It wasn't long before everyone was up and kicking their heels in time of the fiddler's tune, Claudia bouncing about as if she carried a rubber ball instead of a baby, Victor complaining mightily, and Julian nearly laughing himself unto death when Ann kicked her husband in the shin.

Sophie was blissfully happy. She loved to see her family enjoying themselves outside the salons of London, but she could not take her eyes from Caleb, or he from her. She could feel his eyes on her every move, feel them boring down into the deepest part of her. And she sensed that he, like her, was growing impatient with the festivities, wanting the night to end so they could retire for the first time as husband and wife.

And they were getting ready to do just that when Roland noticed a rider galloping up the drive.

The festivity stopped; everyone turned expectantly toward the rider, Caleb and Julian striding forward. As the rider came into their midst, Honorine rushed forward, too, pushing past Caleb and Julian. Miss Brillhart was close behind, her hands clasped tightly at her chest as she looked up at the constable.

"I've come from Nottinghamshire," he announced, his eyes on Miss Brillhart, and dug into his coat pocket. "I've a message for Madame Fortier." Honorine lurched forward and snatched the grimy parchment from his hand. Without hesitation, she ripped it open, scanned the contents, then looked around for Sophie, her face a wreath of smiles.

"It is *him!*" she cried happily. "My Will, he has sent for me!"

Will Hamilton was a little surprised to see two carriages rumbling around the circular drive. He had, of course, believed Lady Sophie would accompany Honorine, and, he had hoped, Caleb. Surely that required only one carriage.

Honorine practically launched herself from the first coach, flying up the steps to him in a gown that was astoundingly provincial for her, and flinging herself into his arms, nearly toppling him over in spite of his cane. Her kisses rained on his face, mixing with her tears.

"Honor," he said laughing, "I am f-fine. I am v-very well indeed."

"I have missed you!" she cried into his collar. "I thought I was never to see your face anymore."

He laughed, squeezed her tightly. "I could n-not be long without my Honor," he said. She closed her pretty blue eyes; tears spilled from the corners. He slipped one hand around her waist and held her to him as he looked to where the others were on the drive. Fabrice and Roland were here, two men whose names he knew very well—it was their relationship to Honorine that baffled him.

But where was Caleb? After all that had happened, he desperately needed to see his son, to touch him.

There. Caleb emerged from the second carriage, pausing to help Lady Sophie step down. He turned then, his eyes on his father, and Will could see the relief wash over him as he came striding forward, pulling Lady Sophie along with him. The Earl of Kettering was right behind them, but what *he* was doing in the midst of all this was a mystery to Will.

Caleb dropped Lady Sophie's hand at the bottom of the steps and took them two at a time until he was standing eye to eye with Will. Honorine stepped away with a smile. "You see, Caleb? He is now well!" she exclaimed.

"I see," he said quietly, his eyes misting. "I had not dared hope for it. How—but where is—"

Will held up his hand. "I've m-much to tell you, with D-Darby's help." He inclined his head, indicating his loyal butler who stood patiently to one side.

Darby bowed perfunctorily, then gestured toward the door. "If you please, sir, his lordship would receive you in the salon," and looking at the others, added, "All of you."

Caleb's apprehension and curiosity were clearly evident—

he looked at his father inquisitively, but abided by Will's wishes, and motioned for Lady Sophie to join him. Will could not help noticing how she slipped her hand into his as if she had done it a thousand times before, and wondered if there was more to their relationship than he could remember.

Ah well. So many memories. With Honorine's help, he'd eventually get to them all.

They all followed him to the red salon, filing in quietly. His physician, Dr. Breedlove, was already in the salon with Ian and his governess, Miss Hipplewhite. Thank God Darby had the foresight to send for them in light of everything that had happened the last several days. They had arrived just this morning, and thankfully, Ian never saw his father.

But when Ian saw Honorine, he abandoned his toy locomotive on the window seat where he had been playing and came flying across the room, latching himself around her waist. Honorine released a cry of joy; she picked the boy up and held him to her as she twirled around. Then she set him down, murmured soothingly in French to him, and finally handed him over to Miss Hipplewhite. "Run with you now, *mon petit,* and I shall come to you soon."

Ian nodded, and watched Honorine as Miss Hipplewhite pulled him along, until he was out the door and could no longer see her.

"Let me have one more look at you, if you please," Dr. Breedlove said authoritatively as Will carefully lowered himself into the old leather winged-back chair.

"Is he quite all right?" Caleb asked, concerned.

"I am f-fine," Will insisted.

"He is now, sir," the doctor said as he checked Will's pulse. "I think we may hope for continued improvement. He is making excellent progress, in spite of everything."

Will gruffly waved the doctor away and motioned Caleb to sit. "I am f-fine. I've m-many answers for you. Sit. Sit now." Caleb reluctantly did as he was told; he

took the settee near his father, seating Lady Sophie next
to him, his hand possessively on her knee, his attention
focused on his father. Honorine and Lord Kettering also
took seats, and Fabrice and Roland, looking a bit uncomfortable, remained near the back of the room.

Will looked at the people surrounding him and offered up another prayer of thanks that he was here,
alive, among friends and family. How close he had come
to losing them, he did not know, because Trevor, in his
deranged state, never realized how far he had gone.
Whatever anyone else might think of his story, Will
would not believe—would *never* believe—that his son
had intended to kill him.

He had thought carefully how he would go about
telling them what had happened, reaching for words in
the deep hole of his memory, going over and over it in his
rooms late at night so that he would not forget a single
detail that he had recovered. When they had discovered
Trevor missing this morning, he had gone over the words
again with Darby so *he* would not forget a single word,
would be able to tell them all that had happened. But as
Will looked at them now, conveying all that had happened seemed overwhelming.

"Trevor has fled," he said, earning a collective gasp of
shock, and looked hopelessly at Darby. "Tell them," he
said.

Darby cleared his throat. "If I may have your attention, please," he called out in a voice worthy of a vicar,
and began to tell them the whole, extraordinary story of
desperation and betrayal.

He told them just what Will had finally begun to remember on those nights he had paced his room, desperate
to maintain the progress he had made under Honorine's
care. How Trevor's horrible penchant for gambling had
ruined his relationship with his wife, whom Will remained convinced had died of a broken heart. Trevor
had never seemed to be able to help himself—he gam-

bled at every turn, driven by some hidden need that Will could not fathom or explain. It was almost as if a demon had him in his grip and would not let him go—he risked everything to gamble, even his wife and child.

It had started innocently, as far as Will could remember—cards, an occasional horse race. But before long, Trevor's stakes grew bigger. Before Will knew what was happening, he had lost all of his inheritance from his mother, Elspeth's pension, too. When he learned of it, Will had been horrified. He had helped his son the best way he knew how—by refusing to give him money, thinking that might wake him from the grips of his madness.

Unfortunately, that did not stop his son—it sent him to a moneylender.

Piecing together his memory with Darby's recollections and bits of gossip, Will had remembered that Trevor continued to gamble by recklessly borrowing money with increasingly higher interest to pay for his losses. Nothing he said could sway Trevor from the madness that had overtaken him. They argued frequently—Trevor accused him of being against him, of having always been against him. Will said things he now regretted. He had finally reached a point where he very much feared Trevor would gamble away Ian's future, and therefore had been compelled to take some very drastic steps.

He started by having a trust established that would go to Ian upon his death—essentially bypassing Trevor. And then he had changed his will, leaving all his holdings to his bastard son, Caleb. The only thing that would pass to Trevor was a modest annual stipend and the title of viscount, for which the entail had long since been eaten up by other holdings and investments.

Leaving everything to Caleb was something Trevor could not forgive or forget.

Will knew now why he had done it. Having struggled

to retrieve the memories, it had come back to him in the course of those long, painful nights. Slowly, he had begun to remember the bond forged with Caleb over the years. It was Caleb whom he had loved; Caleb whom he had wished had been his legitimate son. He was more like Will than Trevor, as a boy and even more so as a man—fit, athletic. Smart and industrious. Caleb had always been proud and true, in spite of the cross Will had handed him at birth. He was a kind soul; always more concerned about the welfare of others than his own. Will had, in the course of those nights, even recalled the care Caleb had given a bird with a broken wing as a young boy. His mother helped him set the wing, then Caleb had nursed it until the wing healed. The morning they let the bird fly away, Caleb had watched it making lazy, uneven circles in the sky, then had said, "I want to be like him, Papa. I want to fly."

Caleb *did* fly. He excelled at all things, never letting his illegitimacy stop him.

Trevor, on the other hand, was a lazy, indolent child, a mediocre student, and lacking in all ambition. It seemed his one desire in life was to gamble.

Those were the reasons Will had made the changes to his will. He had summoned Trevor to his study to tell him of the changes. Trevor had, of course, been angry—Will could now clearly remember his terrible bitterness, how he had accused him of horrible deceptions, of loving Ian and the bastard brother he never knew more than he loved his own son.

It was, unfortunately, true.

How he regretted the turn of fate now! Guilt ate him—perhaps Trevor would have been different had he loved the sullen little boy.

Darby went on to tell the spellbound group that days after Will's ugly encounter with Trevor, on a cold, blustery afternoon, the seizure had invaded his body like a bloody bolt of lightning from the sky. Will wished he could explain the terror—there had been no warnings, no symptoms. He had simply awoken to find himself locked in a gnarled body, capable of thought, but his memory obliterated, and lacking all the words and the ability to act.

"I prescribed the opiate," Dr. Breedlove interjected here. "I confess, I was rather uncertain whether or not Lord Hamilton was in any pain. He was unable to communicate a'tall. I showed Trevor how much of the drug to give him to make him comfortable. Unfortunately, Trevor increased the dosage, and kept him in something very near a perpetual state of paralysis."

"I rather suspect that with the moneylenders threatening Ian's life, Mr. Hamilton apparently realized instantly his dumb luck in his father's seizure. The opiate kept his father in a state that allowed him to steal from him."

"*Steal* from him?" echoed Caleb, incredulous.

Darby nodded and continued on, telling them that Trevor's scheme was simple—Darby had even seen him put the banknote beneath his father's hand on one occasion. As Will listened to Darby, he still held fast to his belief that Trevor had not intended to do it more than once. But it had proven too easy to do—by manipulating the dates and using various venues for the banknotes, no banking authority could readily discern what he was about. Trevor made doubly sure he was safe by gradually increasing the dosage of opiate until it greatly exceeded what the doctor had prescribed. Further, by denying visitors, no one could see just how infirm the opiate made Will.

"Why, then, did he bring Father to London?" Caleb demanded, clearly agitated.

"My personal opinion, sir, is that he grew complacent. Having abused the local banking institution, he thought the height of the Season was a good time to continue his scheme at the Bank of England, where the viscount had considerable holdings. He was moved, in part, by your attempts to see your father."

"But he did not account for Madame Fortier," Sophie said thoughtfully.

"Yes. Honor," Will said, nodding vigorously.

"Madame Fortier?" Julian asked, obviously confused.

"But I have done nothing for this son!" Honorine insisted.

"Yet when you met him in Regent's Park," Sophie explained, "you knew that the viscount's mind was functioning."

"It was not only his mind," Honorine said with a blushing smile.

"That was when she began to work with you, isn't it, my lord? Helped you to move, to learn simple tasks again. The improvement was miraculous."

"Yes, it was," Will readily agreed. "I owe her m-my life. Unfortunately, Trevor s-saw the improvement, t-too."

Darby sighed sadly. "He was quite mad," he said simply, and told them how Trevor had arrived at Hamilton House looking very much like a madman, and worse, acting like one. He had immediately accused Honorine of kidnapping for the purpose of extorting money from the Hamilton estate. This, Darby added of his own accord, he believed Trevor had said to cover up his *own* thievery. Trevor had promptly locked Will away, had administered dangerous doses of the opiate, and had called for the sheriff to have Honorine taken away and charged with a host of crimes.

"What he could not predict, however, was exactly *when* he would have the sheriff to Hamilton House," Darby said with not a little bit of pride. "I delayed the request, hoping to give Madame Fortier time to escape. Fortunately, I was aided in that endeavor by the arrival of Mr. Hamilton."

"Yes, I can attest to the fact that he was quite deranged," Caleb said, frowning. "And Father horribly incapacitated. And knowing Trevor's influence in the parish, I had no hope the sheriff would listen to anyone but him.

I feared for Madame Fortier's safety—we fled to Kettering Hall."

"But we also feared for Lord Hamilton," Sophie interjected. "Miss Brillhart took our concern to the constable in Kettering."

"And we were quite fortunate to have both the constable and the sheriff arrive just two mornings past," Darby informed them. "Unfortunately, not before Trevor discovered his father was not drugged as he had planned, but rather well and remembering more and more each day."

"Where *is* Trevor?" Caleb asked again. "How did you manage to free yourself of his captivity? The drug?"

"Honor," Will said. "She m-made me remember the m-medicine."

"Madame Fortier had, on the occasion of their trip to Hamilton House, already deduced that it was the medicine that was making him so senseless," Darby added. "She told him—just before you rushed her away—to remember what he had learned, to remember the medicine. It jogged his memory, and from that point forward, he merely pretended to take the medicine, disposing of it as soon as Mr. Hamilton had left the room. Then he would force himself to stand and walk, to keep up his strength.

"It so happens that I inadvertently discovered him pacing his rooms one night. He was much more lucid than before and was able to tell me what was happening. In addition, he told me there was something about you, sir," he said, gesturing at Caleb, "that he could not seem to remember but that he knew was important. Seeing what Mr. Hamilton was about, and truthfully, having suspected for some time that things were not quite right with him, I took it upon myself to discover where he kept the opiate. Once I discovered it, I substituted a bit of tea for it, so his lordship was in no danger. At night, when Mr. Hamilton took to his drink, Lord Hamilton

and I were overhead, walking and talking until he recap-
tured his memory. Fortunately, he began to remember it
all quite clearly, and in particular, the will."

"We planned to confront him with his perfidy, hoping
rather to surprise him with the sheriff. As it happens,
Mr. Trevor Hamilton surprised *us* one night, walking into
his lordship's suite as we worked. When Mr. Hamilton
saw his father walking and speaking, he understood that
the opiate had not been administered. The viscount seized
his opportunity, told him that he remembered everything
quite clearly, and that the sheriff would arrive on the
morrow. Mr. Hamilton took this news rather badly, I
must say. He pleaded with his father to understand. He
pleaded for a sum of five thousand pounds, saying that
he was quite certain there were people looking for him
now that would harm him if he couldn't raise it. The viscount promised to consider it the following morning."

"But with morning's light, Mr. Trevor Hamilton was
nowhere to be found. No note, nothing but a few articles
of clothing gone missing, and a bit of cash, and some of
his late wife's jewelry Lord Hamilton had kept in the
wall safe. The rest of the story, I think you know. The
only issue, which remains unclear, is exactly how much
he might have stolen from his father. The viscount has
sent for his man from London to assess it."

The conclusion of Darby's speech was met with silence. The group exchanged glances with one another,
all of them struggling to understand how a man could
find himself in such desperate circumstance as to turn
against his own father.

It was Caleb who finally broke the silence. He rose
from his seat, came and knelt by Will's side. "Thank
God you are quite all right. I have worried so about your
health these last months. It was plain to see, even from a
distance, that you were not improving. It was not until
Madame Fortier began to take her daily walks with you
that I saw a measure of improvement. Sophie and I both

agreed that you looked terribly robust in her company, but frail in your own home."

Will cocked his head at that. He had been ill, and perhaps a bit slow, but he at least recognized it was unusual for his son to address a lady by her given name. "Sophie?" he asked, glancing at the pretty young woman on the settee.

"Actually, I should say Mrs. Hamilton," Caleb clarified, and smiling proudly, extended his hand toward her. "We married yesterday."

Will's heart surged to the point of bursting. But . . . Caleb's lack of legitimate name was more than anyone could hope to overcome—Will jerked his gaze to Julian Dane, one brow lifted. "You approve?"

The Earl of Kettering lifted his hands, and laughing, shook his head. "It was not my decision to make or approve, my lord; I assure you my sister has made that quite clear. But yes, whether she wants it or not, she has our blessing. Her happiness is paramount to any other issue, and I think you can see from her silly grin that she is quite happy."

She rose from the settee, her eyes shining, and glided to where Will sat. "Happy? I think the word does not do justice to my feelings, my lord."

"I know these words. My Sofia, she loves him very much," Honorine said, laughing.

Will's eyes suddenly misted; he looked down at his gnarled hand, and remembered, with painful acuity, the many times he had cried for this son, had wished for him all the happiness he had so surely taken from him with the manner of his birth. It was more than he had ever dared hope for Caleb—to simply be accepted for the man he was. To be loved, to be honored, to be cherished for what was in his soul, and not to be spurned for his lack of name. To fly.

It was, he thought sadly, the perfect antidote to Trevor's betrayal.

He looked up, saw the way his son looked at Lady Sophie, and smiled. He motioned her to him. "Come . . ."

Later that evening, when they sat around the long dining room table, Julian sat admiring his youngest sister. Anyone could see, looking at Sophie now, that she was a changed person. The happiness shining in her big brown eyes made her appear lovelier than he had ever remembered seeing her. She was vibrant, alive—drawing laughter from everyone as she cheerfully regaled them with stories of her travels with Madame Fortier. The stories were, naturally, punctuated with Honorine's disavowal of strange places and even stranger events, much to their collective amusement, and particularly, that of Lord Hamilton. He, too, looked like a new man. And Caleb, well, good God, a man's chest could positively burst with so much pride.

But as Julian sat beside Sophie now, he took her hand in his, leaned toward her, and whispered, "You are the luckiest of us all, you know."

She laughed brightly at that, patted his knee. "Now I know you've had too much wine, Julian."

He shook his head. "I am quite serious, pumpkin. Only you have the luxury to do as you please, you know that? The women in London, they are bound by society's many expectations and rules. When I look at you, I see a woman freed of such earthly bonds, free to be who she pleases, free to love as openly and completely as she desires. For years, you felt imprisoned by your scandal, and I think, buried in your remorse. I so hoped that you would come to see your freedom. I prayed you would find happiness. I suppose I never thought it would be in England, but when I see you sitting here like you are, wearing a smile that could light the night sky, I realize, *you* are the luckiest among us all."

Sophie smiled, glanced at Caleb across from her, the

love shining in her eyes. "I know," she said softly. And when she turned to look at Julian again, her eyes were shining with tears of joy. "All my life, I was never really certain of who I was or where I belonged. But I know now, Julian, I know who I am. I am Sophie."

Epilogue

In the weeks that followed, Sophie and Caleb said farewell to her family, made arrangements through Julian for the house in Regent's Park to be finished and sold—knowing that they would build their home anew—and left a smiling Honorine standing next to Lord Hamilton and Ian at Hamilton House.

Sophie and Caleb had decided that, given their dubious past, they would do better to start fresh in Europe. With his father's help, Caleb had made contact with a group of men in France who were investing in the construction of a railway there. "It's a whole new era of opportunity, Sophie," he told her one evening as they lay in bed.

Sophie smiled, placed a hand on her belly, where a child was in the first stages of development. "A whole new era for us," she reminded him.

It was the discovery of her pregnancy that had prompted Caleb to approach his father about the will that had torn Trevor from his father, and convinced the viscount to leave his holdings to his grandchildren. "I've always made my own way, Father, and I always will. I would that you consider our children before you consider me."

Lord Hamilton had smiled sadly at that, but had agreed. "I r-remember, you know," he had said, his hand on Caleb's shoulder. "I remember how p-proud I am of you. How proud I have always been."

Caleb had smiled, kissed his father's cheek. "I will never betray your pride," he had vowed.

And he never did.

Their destination was France, in the company of a very sullen Fabrice and Roland. As much as the two men adored Honorine—and even Lucie Cowplain—they had determined that they could not abide England, and had therefore agreed to look after Honorine's château. "This will make my Pierre very happy," Honorine had said of her grown son, laughing as she imagined how perturbed the stiff aristocrat would actually be with the arrival of the strange pair.

Lucie Cowplain returned to London. Honorine offered to send her along to France, too, but she refused. "I rather think not, mu'um," she said with a snort. "I hear there are many of the limp-wrists there."

As the years unfurled in France and Belgium, Sophie and Caleb built a new life for themselves and the three children they produced. They began in a set of rooms above a small patisserie, where Sophie quietly built a demand for baked goods, and in particular, fig tartlets. Her business grew so quickly, that she eventually sent a letter to one Lucie Cowplain, requesting her considerable assistance.

She did not hear a word in response until one sultry afternoon a weathered and twisted old woman arrived with two battered portmanteaux, dispensed with all pleasantries, and demanded at once to be shown to the kitchens. In the course of a few years, Sophie and Lucie Cowplain had four patisseries bearing their name. One of them happened to be in a village near Burgundy, near the old Château de Segries, where a pair of very odd and very effeminate men resided as proprietors.

In those years, Sophie corresponded frequently with

Nancy Harvey, keeping her abreast of her life and her children. Nancy, in turn, responded with all the activities of the House on Upper Moreland Street. In one letter, she wrote Sophie that a woman named Charlotte Pritchet Macdonald had come calling. Charlotte's mother, Lady Pritchet, had passed away that spring, and Charlotte, now free of her mother's oppressive control, had taken her inheritance and donated the whole of it to the little house. The happy result, Nancy wrote, was that they had moved to a larger, grander house, along with Charlotte. Moreover, she wrote, they had set up a small shop in the basement of the house where they sold gowns and slippers and reticules and very colorful bonnets. Nancy even boasted that their hats, which they took in donation and enhanced in a variety of colorful ways, were becoming all the rage among women who had donated them to begin with.

Ann visited Château la Claire each summer to see her sisters, always bringing plenty of news from London. One year, she brought Sophie the unsettling news that Sir William Stanwood had been found beaten to death at a seedy port town. That hardly shocked Sophie—she had always imagined he would meet a violent death. But the fact that he was dead was liberating in a strange way. While she had not thought of William Stanwood in several years, the knowledge that he would no longer prey on anyone made her feel she was finally quite free of him.

The other piece of titillating news Ann brought that year was that Miss Melinda Birdwell, the *ton's* most famous old maid, had found herself in the very uncomfortable situation of bearing a child out of wedlock. It had gone undetected, apparently, because Melinda had gained an inordinate amount of weight—no one suspected she was also with child. Even more outrageous, Ann whispered, was that there were a handful of men of questionable character rumored to be the culprit—and not one would own up to it. All in all, Ann assured Eugenie and

Sophie, Melinda Birdwell had created the most vulgar scandal in Mayfair in many, many years. She had been sent, with her bastard child, to Ireland to care for an elderly aunt.

This news, Sophie found rather sad. She harbored no good feeling for Melinda Birdwell, but she would not wish that scandal on even her worst enemy.

Ann would also bring letters from Honorine and Lord Hamilton. Honorine, as usual, spoke in poetic terms, boasting proudly of Ian's accomplishments, now that he was a young man. It was plain for Sophie to see that in Ian, Honorine had found the son that Pierre could never be for her. In Lord Hamilton, she finally had found the man who could make her happy.

Lord Hamilton had, thankfully, regained the use of his limbs and his mind with years of work, although he still walked uncertainly at times. He had lent his experience to the research of maladies, working with a team of doctors who attempted to understand how the mind was so inexplicably seized. Honorine and Will never married, for reasons Sophie and Caleb never understood, but remained entirely devoted to one another and Ian for the rest of their lives.

The missing piece—Trevor—never contacted his father again.

In the years that followed, Sophie, Caleb, and their three children flourished. Caleb's investment in the railroad proved to be quite lucrative for them. They traveled all over Europe in pursuit of the rail business, exposing their children to different cultures and events.

But it was during a visit to his home in Scotland in 1861 that Caleb solved the mystery of Trevor. It happened that an old friend in Edinburgh was hosting him for supper. That evening, Caleb dressed in his best finery, and took a coach to the exclusive address of his friend. After dinner and a little port, the two men decided to visit a gaming hall.

As they walked into the establishment, Caleb happened

to see a group of men—ruffians, it seemed—around a card table. One of them in particular caught his eye—he was disheveled, a whore on his knee, and he looked as if he hadn't slept in days. But Caleb recognized the cut of the man's jaw. It was the same as his own.

He excused himself from his friend and walked over to where the men were playing—they all looked up, instantly suspicious. The whore smiled licentiously. Trevor was slower than the others to notice him, but his recognition of Caleb was instantaneous, and he quickly looked away.

Stunned, Caleb could not move. "Trevor—"

"Leave me!" Trevor snarled without looking up. "We don't want your kind here!" The other men looked up at that and eyed Caleb even closer.

"But how—"

"You've no right," Trevor hissed. "I don't want you here! Leave before I throw you out!"

Caleb stepped away.

Trevor said nothing, but threw a coin onto the table. "Call," he said gruffly, refusing to look at his brother.

Slowly, Caleb backed away, too stunned to think. He desperately wanted to know how Trevor had come to be here, where he had been . . . but he turned on his heel, rejoined his friend, and feigned fatigue, asking that they leave.

He never told anyone about his encounter.

As the years passed, the Hamilton children went on to lead their own lives. The oldest, Will, became a doctor. Honor married a wealthy vintner, and young Geoff followed in his father's footsteps, building a railway across Europe. Those same years took loved ones from them; Lord Hamilton was the first to go, followed soon thereafter by Honorine, who had at last lost her lust for living with his passing. Ann died suddenly of a strange fever, much like Valerie had.

But through all those years, the love between Sophie and Caleb remained strong. It changed, grew with them, anchored them and their children. The home they had created was one of happiness and love, a place where anyone felt welcome and safe.

And as Sophie lay dying with Caleb at her side in the year 1894, he remembered what she had once written to her brother Julian and marveled at how prophetic she had been. They had indeed loved one another desperately until they were ancient and exhausted and it was time to sleep.

And as he watched her slip into that eternal sleep, wrenching his heart from his chest and taking it with her, his eyes misted. The profound loss paralyzed him for several minutes; he sat just gazing at her, seeing the same sweet face that had greeted him these fifty years, and wondering if he just might lay down beside her, relinquish his right to live, and go with her. But a sound from outside called him back, and finally, he stood, crossed to the window, and looked out at the manicured lawns of their home.

His sons were down on the lawn, Geoff pacing anxiously, Will sitting with his hands folded, his head bowed.

Caleb turned away from the window and looked again at his love. With a weary sigh, he walked over to her, laid his hand on hers, now gone cold, and leaned down, kissed her lips for the last time. "Soon, my love," he whispered. "Wait for me by the pond. I'll join you soon."

About the Author

JULIA LONDON was raised on a ranch in West Texas, where she spent her formative years in the middle of vast wheat fields driving a tractor at the reckless speed of 5 mph. Scared to death she might actually have to plow for more than one summer, she studied hard and eventually got herself a real job. She now daydreams in Austin, Texas, where she lives with two enormous Labrador retrievers. You can write to Julia at P.O. Box 49315, Austin, Texas 78765, or visit her website at http://www.julialondon.com.